'5

PENGUIN BOOKS

# LINES IN THE SAND

Anne Deveson was born in Kuala Lumpur and spent her childhood in Malaya, England and Australia. She is a writer, broadcaster and filmmaker whose work has largely focused on human rights issues. Her films on Africa and South-East Asia have won three UN Media Peace Awards, and *Tell Me I'm Here*, her book about her son Jonathan's struggles with schizophrenia, won the 1991 Human Rights Award for non-fiction. In 1993 she was made an Officer of the Order of Australia for services to the media and to mental health. She lives in Sydney.

Also by Anne Deveson

*Australians at Risk*
*Faces of Change*
*Tell Me I'm Here*
*Coming of Age*

# ANNE DEVESON

## lines in the sand

PENGUIN BOOKS

Penguin Notes for Reading Groups are available for this title

Penguin Books Australia Ltd
487 Maroondah Highway, PO Box 257
Ringwood, Victoria 3134, Australia
Penguin Books Ltd
Harmondsworth, Middlesex, England
Penguin Putnam Inc.
375 Hudson Street, New York, New York 10014, USA
Penguin Books Canada Limited
10 Alcorn Avenue, Toronto, Ontario, Canada M4V 3B2
Penguin Books (NZ) Ltd
Cnr Rosedale and Airborne Roads, Albany, Auckland, New Zealand
Penguin Books (South Africa) (Pty) Ltd
5 Watkins Street, Denver Ext 4, 2094, South Africa
Penguin Books India (P) Ltd
11, Community Centre, Panchsheel Park, New Delhi 110 017, India

First published by Penguin Books Australia Ltd 2000
This edition published by Penguin Books Australia Ltd 2000

10 9 8 7 6 5 4 3 2 1

Cover design by Marina Messiha, Penguin Design Studio
Text design by Erika Budiman, Penguin Design Studio
Front cover photograph by Garry Moore
Author photograph by Peter Brew-Bevan
Typeset in 12/17 Bembo by Midland Typesetters, Maryborough,
Made and printed in Australian Print Group, Maryborough, VictoVictoria
ria

National Library of Australia
Cataloguing-in-Publication data:

Deveson, Anne, 1930– .
    Lines in the sand.

    ISBN 0 14 029318 3

    I. Title.
A823.4

www.penguin.com.au

*In memory of my father, Douglas Deveson,*
*a man who rebelled against colonialism and*
*who loved books and writing.*

*You already know enough. So do I. It is not knowledge
we lack. What is missing is the courage to understand what
we know and to draw conclusions.*

SVEN LINDQVIST

*Dream no small dreams.*

ROBERT THEOBALD

# PART I
# 1975

# o n e

Hannah Coady went to Africa at a time of huge and terrible famine. On the plane from Nairobi to Addis Ababa she travelled with two men she barely knew who sat so close on either side of her she could feel the rhythm of their breathing. The intimacy disturbed her. The seats were narrow and uncomfortable, and the man in the aisle seat, who was gently snoring, kept falling against her. His jacket had slipped to the floor and his Panama hat had fallen over his eyes. Hannh plonked it on his lap and stared at him with mounting frustration before delivering a modest pinch. He woke with a start, gave her an amiable smile and closed his eyes once more. She noticed his eyelashes were sandy, like his beard.

The man in the window seat was younger, leaner, and more awake. He chuckled when Hannah pinched Waldo, and adjusted his long woollen scarf. It was purple, black and gold, and twice he had told her it came from the London School of

Economics, first on the flight from Sydney to Johannesburg and then from Johannesburg to Nairobi.

'Why on earth are you wearing that?' Hannah asked him. 'We're in Africa.'

'I didn't think we were in Alaska.'

'It's too hot.'

'Stop bugging me, and don't tell me about Africa.' Ezekiel looked at her proudly. 'I *am* Africa.'

See, she thought, I knew he was conceited. She kicked off her flat brown sandals and placed them on top of her knapsack, which lay between her feet. She had bought the bag at an army disposal store just before she left because it had room for everything she would need or thought she would need: two oranges, a bruised banana, a mouth organ, several maps, some briefing notes on famine, a transistor radio, a Swiss army knife – and a roll of lavatory paper thrust at her by her aunt just as she boarded the plane. She also had a compass and a copy of Virginia Woolf's *A Room of One's Own*, which her father had told her tersely was a rum thing to take on an expedition to a desert.

She could still scarcely believe her luck. Waldo Corrigan had been a guest at a recent Sydney film conference, talking about his forthcoming television series on the politics of famine. She and her friend Bella had sat in the front row, hunched up in their black duffle coats, consuming peanuts and most of Waldo's words.

A year earlier, in their second year of an undergraduate degree in Canberra, Hannah and Bella had wanted to be ethnographic filmmakers, stalking the highlands of New Guinea. But once they'd finished their degrees, they changed their minds. Ethnographic filmmaking was too slow for them. They went to Sydney for the summer break, borrowed friends' cameras, and plunged into films with titles like *Love is Love* and *Seeing Red and Feeling Blue*. Nights were spent editing on ancient flatbeds that clicked and rattled with every turn of the handle, smoking dope and drinking red wine while they debated the ethics of observational cinema and being a fly on the wall, particularly when everyone knew the fly was there. Bella was absorbed. Hannah was restless. She wanted – oh but what did she want? Adventure? Excitement?

'Money,' said Bella acidly.

Hannah knew exactly what she wanted as soon as she heard Waldo that night in Sydney. She wanted to make films that revealed the intimacy of people's lives – to millions on television, not hundreds in art houses. Films that dissected and analysed systems and power structures, that were both political and mainstream.

'Bloody impossible,' said Bella when Hannah told her. Waldo had just finished speaking and they were lingering by the exit. Bella rolled a wisp of paper and a screw of soggy tobacco, lit the cigarette, then looked at Hannah with sloe-black eyes and an obdurate expression.

'Mainstream's never political. Ever seen a chook with teeth?' She flounced off, proclaiming she wouldn't work for any bloke, not even if she were paid.

Hannah remained behind and nabbed Waldo as he ambled out. Somehow she convinced him to take her for coffee, where she plonked herself opposite him, her long legs splayed out either side of the table, hands gesticulating. She told him she was highly experienced, which she wasn't, and highly intelligent, which she thought was possible, although it seemed that her intelligence was not the kind the university desired. She tipped her Scandinavian chair backwards and forwards on its metal legs, declaring she wanted to overcome injustice, to change people's ideas.

Waldo looked mildly impressed. 'Martha Gellhorn started out like that.'

'Who?' Hannah frowned and stirred her coffee, which tasted as if it had been stewed for several hours.

'Martha Gellhorn,' said Waldo cheerfully. 'The great American war correspondent. When she was young, she hoped to be eyes for the conscience of the world.'

Hannah flushed. 'There's nothing wrong with that.'

'I know.'

'And what did she think later in her life?'

He gave a wry smile. 'That the guiding light of journalism was no stronger than a glow-worm.'

'Oh, but that's terrible.'

'It was after she'd witnessed countless wars.'

'Do you think that?'

'Sometimes. Sometimes it feels as if I'm just there for the ringside seat. Other times I'm less cynical. But let's get back to you and what you believe in. Tell me.'

She hesitated. At the end of 1974, hunger and poverty were spreading throughout the world. Starving black babies with swollen stomachs and enormous eyes had yet to become symbols of Third World poverty, the phrase 'compassion fatigue' was unknown, and Mother Teresa had only just begun travelling the world proclaiming, 'God will provide.' Several years of rebellion at a convent school hadn't helped Hannah's relationship with God, but she did believe in the power of love, women's rights, and the need to get herself a good education. She told Waldo as much.

He nodded. After a moment's silence, during which she

sneezed from anxiety and scratched her arm, making it bleed, he remarked, 'You say you want to change people's ideas, but how will you know if your ideas are any better?'

'It doesn't matter,' she said, cupping her thin, angular face in her hands. 'What matters is getting people to think.'

'Do *you* think?'

'Yes, of course I think. My father sees to that.'

'And your mother?'

Her face closed. 'My mother is dead. I was brought up by my aunt.'

And that was how it all began. When she asked Waldo to tell her more about the famine series and he said he was finalising a co-production with Australia and would then be on his way to Ethiopia for research, she had begged him to take her. Production assistant. Unpaid. Do anything, go anywhere Hannah. She even offered to use her savings on the fare. Eventually he relented and suggested she come and see him the following day.

'I don't promise,' he said. But she knew he was hooked.

She ran home to Bella through streets that were dark and shiny with rain, hands in her pockets, hair flying. Exuberant, ecstatic, euphoric, elated – she tossed up every adjective she could think of to describe her joy, shouted out loud, stomped in all the puddles, but when she finally hurled herself on Bella's bed, amongst the books and newspapers, apple cores and the remains of a pizza, Bella was cross at being woken and also deeply suspicious. Hannah was unperturbed.

'But why would this bloke take you on?' Bella said as she heaved herself to a sitting position, her striped flannel pyjamas rumpled up around her neck, her long dark hair like a bird's nest. 'Why?'

7

Hannah stretched her arms, luxuriating in the moment, smiling with satisfaction before she replied, 'He's Pygmalion.'

'Bitch,' said Bella, suddenly envious.

When the plane landed on the single runway of Addis Ababa airport, Hannah shouldered her way to the front. She stood at the top of the steps, all legs and arms and gawky grace, the wind blowing her unruly red hair as she looked out on Ethiopia. A land of deserts and high impregnable mountains, unconquered for over three thousand years, formerly known as Abyssinia and, earlier, to the ancient Greeks as Burnt Face, the farthest away of all the places of mankind. She felt dizzy with excitement. Then she saw the soldiers and was afraid. They milled around the plane, shouting and waving machine-guns.

As soon as she reached the ground, a lanky youth with a missing front tooth and black boots several sizes too large closed in on her, prodding her forward with his gun. The other passengers scurried past, eyes averted, heads down. Two or three Africans in business suits, clutching briefcases; an elegant Ethiopian woman who had been the sole occupant of first class; a large woman in flowing brown robes, shepherding two small children ahead of her.

Waldo caught up with Hannah, clutching his Panama hat and his camera bag, his face flushed. 'They're warning us not to take photographs,' he gasped.

Ezekiel came last, tall and lean like an athlete, strolling as if he had all the time in the world, regarding the soldiers with a look of contempt. His scarf trailed regally behind him in the wind.

An enormous banner was strung across the airport building. Large red lettering in English and Amharic, the official Ethiopian language, proclaimed: LONG LIVE SOCIALISM, WELCOME TO ETHIOPIA. Once inside, all urgency ceased. Chickens ran under foot, music blared from loudspeakers hitched by rusty wires to the iron ceiling struts, and a stooped old woman with a straw broom ceaselessly swept the concrete floor, her shoes tied together with rags.

Their passports and yellow health cards were taken by a man in a crumpled brown suit who yawned, showing a mouthful of gold teeth. A second man began idly going through their cases, probing with tobacco-stained fingers, spilling their contents onto the wooden counter. Hannah saw two pairs of leopard-print underpants which she presumed were Ezekiel's. He saw her looking at them and grinned. The man unzipped Waldo's first-aid kit and pounced on a bottle of white powder which he waved under Waldo's nose. 'Heroin?'

'Salts,' said Waldo, mopping his face with a white cotton handkerchief.

'Not salts.' The man tasted the powder and spat it on the ground. 'Not taste like salt.'

'*Epsom* salts. Medicine.'

'What for?'

Waldo turned pink and shrugged. 'Everything,' he muttered.

The customs man flipped quickly through the other bottles before putting the Epsom salts on a long wooden shelf which ran the length of the wall behind him. A collection of objects had already accumulated and because the shelf had a large dip in the middle, everything had gradually slid towards the centre. Three dusty Bakelite radios, a camera, a collection of gourds, a pair of antlers, two drums, a pile of books, and several large jars containing a mixture of objects – teaspoons, dead spiders, cigarette lighters, beads.

Waldo gazed mournfully at his Epsom salts and consoled himself with a barley sugar. Hannah looked at him with curiosity. Up to this point she had regarded him with youthful admiration. Now she noticed that he was overweight, and he suddenly seemed quite old. At least thirty-five.

An elderly Ethiopian, tall and imperious, had been leaning on a silver-topped cane and staring at them with hard, bright eyes. His nose was beaked and his legs beneath his cream robe were long, like a wading bird's. Now he approached and addressed them in impeccable English.

'I am Solomon Lulu. The government has appointed me to look after you while you are here, to make sure you don't come to any harm.'

Hannah frowned. 'Is that necessary?'

Solomon Lulu gave a thin smile and smoothed his robe. 'Necessary for us all.'

Waldo hadn't asked for anyone to look after them but he wasn't about to argue. Governments in countries with precarious stability often appointed their own media watchdogs. He hastily extended a hand. 'Waldo Corrigan, film and television producer, here to research part of a BBC series about global famine.'

'I know. And I know why you're here.' Solomon Lulu gave a wry smile. 'We have had famine in Ethiopia since biblical times.'

Ezekiel flicked back his scarf, raising dust from the floor. 'Famines are nearly always man-made.'

Waldo intervened. 'Mr Chimeme is a Rwandan authority on the politics of aid and the politics of famine. He works at the London School of Economics and is helping us with initial research. Hannah Coady is my production assistant. But no doubt you're already aware of that, too.'

Solomon Lulu pursed his lips, ignoring Waldo's comments and Hannah's outstretched hand. 'Politics is a dangerous word, Mr Chimeme. We have just had a revolution in Ethiopia.'

Ezekiel ran a long, slim finger along the top of the customs counter. It made an unpleasant squeaking noise. 'Indeed. And one reason you had that revolution was because your emperor, Haile Selassie, kept the famine hidden.'

'His Excellency had to deal with a five-year drought.' Solomon Lulu's voice was silkily polite. 'There was also no infrastructure. A few more roads would have helped. Transport. Health care. Our country is one of the poorest in the world.'

'But His Excellency was rich.'

Waldo shuffled uneasily from one foot to the other. Solomon Lulu was silent, his mouth twitching imperceptibly. Two large rats scurried across the floor, narrowly missing the old woman's broom.

'A system is as good or bad as the people who use it,' Lulu said finally, looking coldly at Ezekiel. 'I have seen them all. Colonialism, post-colonialism, economic colonialism, pre-revolutionary, revolutionary, post-revolutionary – the name means little, it's the intent.'

He turned and disappeared behind one of the flimsy partitions, where they heard him shouting and thumping his cane.

Waldo gazed after him. 'Odd character. Could be a survivor from the old regime. Or could be part of the new guard, in which case we need to be careful what we say and do.'

Outside the airport building one main road led to Addis Ababa, the nation's capital, and to a ring of dark mountains circling the horizon. The air was crisp and sunny. Old men sat on benches, smoking and talking; youths cycled in the square on rusty bicycles; music blared from a handful of houses, which were strung with washing. Young children with lustrous dark eyes and springy black hair squatted in the gutters, playing with toys made of cans and bottle tops.

Two giant advertising hoardings towered above them. In one a fair-haired young man in a black dinner jacket stooped low over the voluptuous cleavage of a Marilyn Monroe blonde. The man was lighting the woman's cigarette. Her red lips pouted, her bosom was draped in voluminous lolly-pink chiffon, her nipple line was branded in heavy black lettering: ROTH-MANS, QUALITY TOBACCO. This had been overstamped by additional lettering: THE TRIUMPH OF SOCIALISM IS INEVITABLE.

On the second hoarding a villainous Uncle Sam clutched a black and yellow hydrogen bomb to his large pot belly. On it shrieked the words: US MAKES WAR.

The propaganda was crude. Once before there had been a similar message. How old had Hannah been? Nine? Sitting in the back row of a history class, scratching a mosquito bite as a school teacher with a ruddy complexion and short back and sides held aloft a poster of Japanese soldiers about to charge. Their teeth were sharpened fangs and their bayonets dripped Australian blood.

Something tugged at her arm and she glanced down to see a stump waving in her face, a hand minus two of its fingers and the thumb. The palm was bent inwards, like a claw.

'The fingers and thumb have been amputated,' said Solomon Lulu in a matter-of-fact voice. 'It's a myth that with leprosy everything crumbles away.'

The owner of the hand was a woman with grey-streaked hair whose nose was also disfigured, cracked and splattered. Other people suddenly appeared. Some hopped round on legs without feet or dragged themselves on bodies without legs.

Bandages made of strips of cloth had been bound around the stumps, forming them into packages which were stained and sometimes seeped a foul-smelling liquid.

Hannah tried not to flinch. Her repulsion made her feel ashamed and, for a moment, angry. She wasn't used to this sort of thing, she hadn't been warned.

Solomon Lulu looked disapprovingly at the lepers. 'The illness is not contagious. But it's unpleasant, because the body dies by sealing itself off from the germs.'

Waldo came to Hannah's rescue by putting a few coins in the woman's palm. Solomon lashed out with his cane and the people skittered, disappearing almost as swiftly as they had arrived.

'Lepers used to be looked after by the missionaries. But now that Marxist rhetoric dictates everything about our lives, Colonel Mengistu has ordered us to fight fascism, imperialism and bureaucratic capitalism. Do you think they understand? All they know is that the government has given them plots of land and told them to be self-sufficient.'

Waldo looked at him quizzically. 'They will dig it with their stumps?'

The old man shook with laughter, his body a vibrating bow, his cane tapping up and down. Tears ran down his cheeks as he plucked at Hannah's arm. 'Your friend has been many places. He knows the ways.'

Solomon Lulu summoned a taxicab, an old red Peugeot which seemed to appear from nowhere, and they drove to Addis Ababa along a potholed road lined with eucalyptus trees. Traffic was sparse. Women carried heavy bundles on their heads or backs, men in long white robes sauntered empty-handed, strings of skinny horses staggered under loads of firewood and charcoal.

Intermittent messages blared from loudspeakers which were strung up at intervals by the side of the road.

Solomon cocked his head to one side and gave one of his amazing laughs – like the caw of an ancient crow. 'They are telling us to behave ourselves, to be good chaps.'

Hannah was about to question him and then hesitated. 'You drive on the left?' she asked instead.

He gave a faintly derisive smile. 'Here, almost everything is on the left.'

Addis Ababa looked as if a heap of rusty corrugated iron had been dropped from a great height. Dilapidated shacks, open drains, meagre shops and markets, a few blocks of workers' flats. A hilly, ramshackle town, and in the middle, unlikely as a unicorn, the shining white marble of the only hotel where foreigners were allowed to stay in the wake of the revolution.

'It's too grand,' protested Hannah, gazing at the fountains and colonnades and thinking of the sprawling poverty that surrounded them.

Waldo shrugged. 'I used to feel like that. But it's not going to save any more lives.'

'Enjoy it,' said Ezekiel, rolling his eyes.


Hannah did not sleep much that first night, knowing they had to be up before dawn to fly to the Ogaden Desert, where famine was claiming hundreds of lives. When her alarm clock rang she was already awake. She fished through her backpack, hesitating. What to wear for a famine? This was not a matter of sartorial correctness, practical considerations were involved. Her aunt had told her to wear one of her hippy numbers.

'Something long, lovey, then no one can see what you're

doing underneath. There are no toilets in the desert and you'll be with all those men.'

But in the dawn silence of the hotel lobby, Waldo raised an eyebrow when he saw her long black and brown striped caftan. 'We're not going to Woodstock,' he said mildly.

Ezekiel grinned. Solomon Lulu looked approving. 'Such garments are good for the desert. They keep away the sun and the flies.'

Back at the airport, everything looked a pale misty grey. The planes, the shamble of buildings, the grass, two jeeps that bounced by carrying soldiers armed with machine-guns – all grey. Their little plane was a wind-up toy in the arc of the runway lights, the kind that teeters halfway across a floor before taking a nosedive into a table leg. Hannah glanced nervously at the mountains ringing the city.

The pilot appeared, a shadowy figure striding out of the hangar, zipping up his leather jacket. His handshake was limp and one eye twitched. He said his name was Max, he came from Montana, and he flew with the Sudan Interior Mission. Max was clearly not a happy man. He bit his fingernails, obsessively smoothed down his fair bushy eyebrows, and spent a long time fiddling with the plane's controls. Eventually, he bowed his head and proclaimed in a deep and lugubrious voice, 'Dear Lord, whatever happens to us this day, Thy will be done.'

Hannah's eyes widened.

'Missionary pilot!' shouted Waldo in her ear. 'Probably suffering from burnout. Usually they say things like, Dear Lord, give us a happy day.' He fumbled in his pocket for his barley sugars and passed them around. Solomon Lulu refused and pulled out of the pocket of his robe a small filigree silver box filled with whitish-grey powder. He took a pinch between his index finger and his thumb, sniffed it, and put the box away.

Their plane shook and bounced its way over a grey, wrinkled landscape that heaved itself into mountains and split open into ravines. Occasionally, Hannah spotted a small beehive-shaped Coptic church clinging precariously to rock. When the mountains ended and they reached the desert, Max brought the plane down lower. Waldo was dozing, Ezekiel reading a book and Hannah keeping her face glued to the window when Max turned round with a look of wild anxiety on his face.

'Shoot! Listen folks, the intercom's not working. We're coming in to land. I'm praying it's on the right side.'

'Right side?' Hannah queried. Below them stretched a vast expanse of desert.

Waldo grinned. 'He hopes we're landing in Ethiopia and not Somalia. So do I. They're at war.'

Small beads of perspiration glistened on Max's forehead. 'Yessir, lost three of our planes already. Shot down.'

'Shit,' said Hannah.

The plane bumped three or four times on the sand before they taxied towards a compound that looked as if it came from a Woody Allen movie about the French Foreign Legion: stone walls, watchtowers, and two ancient cannons peering through holes on either side of massive wooden gates. Jeeps piled high with soldiers and machine-guns hurtled out to meet them. Behind the jeeps came a black Rolls-Royce which delivered up a man so vast he made Waldo look puny. His dark green uniform was emblazoned with medals and ribbons. His beret was black. His skin was black. His eyes were bloodshot.

'Hey, he's a colonel,' said Ezekiel.

Hannah looked at Ezekiel in irritation. Any idiot could see this man was a colonel.

'I am the colonel,' said the man in a voice that rumbled upwards from his brown army boots and issued from his cavernous mouth with such force that Hannah half expected the ground to tremble. When he shook her hand, his grip made her wince.

'The Ministry told us you were coming. We want you to tell the world there is no food, no water. Everything is dying.'

Ezekiel was impatiently kicking at the sand, digging in his toe, circling it round and round. 'Yes, but your war with Somalia has made things worse, especially with Russia and America taking sides. It's war by proxy and the desert people are the victims. How many bombs have you dropped, how many waterholes have been poisoned, how much aid has gone to feed your army instead of those who are starving?'

'The famine would have happened anyway,' said the colonel sulkily.

Hannah looked at Ezekiel with curiosity. His normally languid manner had disappeared, his voice was raised.

'Young man,' said Solomon Lulu, 'you go too far.'


They had been driving for over an hour. The heat was brutal. Sun beat down on Hannah's head and shoulders. Wind stung her eyes. She wiped her parched mouth on the back of her hand before taking a swig from an old army water bottle which hung at her side. Around her, the desert was dotted with bones, flesh picked clean. Skulls and legs and ribcages. The bones gleamed. Vultures hovered.

Waldo shifted in his seat and surreptitiously ate a barley sugar. Hannah wanted one and held out her hand.

'Are they animal bones or human?' Her voice was tentative.

'Mostly animal.' He pointed to a skull. 'Humans don't have horns.'

'I know plenty who have horns,' Ezekiel shouted in her ear. In spite of the heat he was still wearing his ridiculous scarf. His skin shone brown, unlike Waldo's which, in the sun, was becoming decidedly pink.

When the asphalt track petered out, they bucked and slithered over sand dunes which stretched as far as they could see. Hannah stood up, gripping the front rail of the jeep until she lost her balance and fell into Waldo's lap, a tangle of legs and arms and hair. She blushed.

Waldo pointed to a speck on the horizon which slowly grew, first into an ominous-looking black stain and then into the strangest sight she had ever seen. A huge gathering of people, marooned in an ocean of sand.

'Maybe two thousand,' murmured Waldo, gazing through heavy black binoculars which Hannah hoped he would give to her, but he passed them to Ezekiel.

The driver, whose name was Ephraim, brought the jeep to a halt and rubbed his dark brown eyes. 'Nomads. They are walking with their skins and bones.'

'They look like Turags.' Ezekiel was adjusting the binoculars. 'Arab invaders called them Turags,' he explained to Waldo and Hannah. 'It means lost souls.'

'The Turags call themselves Imochagh – the free ones,' Solomon said smoothly.

Hannah gasped as people teetered towards them. Children whose bones protruded like pieces of jagged stone and whose heads seemed grotesquely huge. Women clutching babies to wizened breasts. Men with bowed legs. Her stomach contracted at the grossness of this misery, its random unfairness. The crowd was eerily silent.

Waldo was glancing anxiously at her. 'Okay?'

She bit her lip. 'Okay. But why aren't they speaking?'

'It's called the silence of starvation.'

Oh God, don't cry, don't cry, but tears were already welling as Waldo took her firmly by the arm.

'It's okay feeling like crying, but if you cry you won't be able to work. So, take photographs and stick close to Ezekiel or to me.'

Hannah, nodding gratefully, opened up her camera. She took wide shots then zoomed in close. The child with the copper-coloured hair and swollen belly caused by kwashiorkor, the disease of malnutrition. The army trucks parked neatly side by side in the middle of the desert, as if they were in a city square. Soldiers ladling grain from bags stamped 'A gift from the people of Australia'. Which people? Children scrabbling under the trucks for spills. A naked baby thrusting handfuls of dirt into its mouth. A child licking at the sand on her robe, perhaps thinking it might be powdered milk. Solomon Lulu saying that the trucks had driven a thousand kilometres from the seaport of Djibouti and could only come once a month. The corn would last a family three days.

Ezekiel swearing. 'Small children can't digest this stuff, they need it to be ground, but where's the damned mill?'

Waldo looking gloomy, unwrapping another barley sugar, mopping his face. 'Once, when I was covering the floods in Bangladesh, America sent its first consignment of aid. You know what arrived?'

Hannah shook her head.

'Electric blankets. Double, single and queen.'

She gasped. Should she laugh? Or cry? This was a country where she had neither road maps nor language. Each joke hid a tragedy, and each tragedy was made to sound like a joke.

Nearby, an unknown camera crew sat cross-legged on the ground, patiently waiting. The starving people weren't so patient. Soldiers were trying to beat them into line. Hannah flinched every time they were hit.

Ezekiel waved off the flies. 'Their heads know what to do – get into line – but their bellies say give us food, now, now, now.'

She wanted to shout, 'Do something! Take my wallet, find food, fetch water.' But there was no food. No water. She turned to Ezekiel.

'How can they stand it?'

'They have to stand it. What else can they do?'

She only half heard him. How had these people found the strength to trek such vast distances across the desert, their families and their animals dying on the way? How had they known that food would be given to them on this particular morning and at this particular place, in amongst the soft waves of the sandhills and within such a vast pale ocean of sand?

Ezekiel seemed to read her thoughts. 'They send messages that need no words.'

A large group of people had gathered around a well where a young man was being lowered by ropes so that he could fill buckets of water by hand. Behind the people, camels were waiting, their feet hobbled, their bones like umbrella spokes, their humps collapsed into withered bags of skin. She stared, aghast. How did the camel lose its hump? It had consumed it. But now that the hump was gone, the camel would die.

Ephraim's voice was soft. 'They are waiting for their names

to be called. Some camels wait three days before they are given a drink. Within a month they will all be dead.'

Ezekiel pulled her to come closer, demanding, angry. 'These people love their camels. They know their tracks and the tracks of others; they can tell the tribes which own them, whether a camel is ridden or free, where it has been grazing and when it was last watered.'

Ephraim was shaking his head in disbelief. 'We have never seen camels dying, it is not in our folklore. When the camels go, it is the end of everything. Truly, I tell you we would rather find water than oil.'

But Hannah was looking at something else. Behind the camels stretched a long line of bundles, each one rolled in brown unbleached cloth, like a display of giant cigars.

'Bodies,' said Waldo.

Hannah swallowed hard. She had never seen a dead body. Not even her mother's.

A man stalked past them, so thin he looked like a cardboard cut-out. How did that man lose his buttocks? she wondered. When a man loses his buttocks, will he also die?

Ephraim held out his hands. 'The bodies are buried over two metres down and sideways, so hyenas cannot dig them up and eat them. The hyenas are also hungry.'

Hannah was silent. Sand attacked her face and eyes. The sun felt like a club, beating the back of her neck. Children cried, a thin high sound. Her nostrils were unable to block out the stench of disease and diarrhoea. Her eyes again filled with tears.

Ezekiel picked up her bush hat, which had fallen on the sand, and dropped it on her head. 'Wear it. You'll get sunstroke.'

Her squint turned to a scowl. The hat elastic dangled embarrassingly in front of her nose. Ezekiel gave her a dazzling smile as he touched his blue denim cap.

'Even I wear a hat. Black people can also get sunstroke.'


An overhead noise disturbs her concentration and she looks up to see a helicopter hovering high in the relentless blue of the sky, its struts spread like the talons of an eagle. It swoops down on them so that for a moment she wonders whether she should duck or run. It lands in the sand a little distance away and gusts of air from its blades scatter people like pieces of a jigsaw. Soldiers come running. Out steps a man with a gleaming smile. He wears a blue safari suit, cowboy boots, and a small gold cross pinned to his lapel. Behind him staggers a young man with a long dark wispy moustache and flared jeans, struggling with a large umbrella, a canvas chair and a shoulder bag.

Hannah is transfixed. 'Who is he?' she asks Waldo.

Waldo's mouth twitches. 'The Reverend Dr E. Theodore King, International President of Help Our World, generally known as Help, and never as How. No one ever knows how.'

'Where is he from?'

'He's an old-style American evangelist who put himself through bible college by selling second-hand cars. Gargles daily to preserve his voice. Ignores his indigestion. Keeps photographs of his wife Grace and his sons Bryce and Dean in a maroon wallet embossed with his name and a string of honorary degrees. Anything else?'

'That's enough. And the other man?'

'His name is Eric, I think he's a nephew.'

The Reverend Dr Theodore King moves like someone of

authority, patting children on the head, smiling, clasping the outstretched hands of women, picking his way past human bundles of rags. When he spies Waldo and the others he beams and waves. After a few minutes, he signals Eric to set up the chair and umbrella. As the umbrella snaps open Hannah sees it is stamped in red lettering: 'Coca-Cola'.

Theodore King sits down heavily and peers at himself in a chrome magnifying mirror with a concertina handle. 'I need Panstick Number 2.' He makes a rueful face. 'Number 3 makes me look too dark.'

Eric spreads a cape about King's shoulders. He dabs Panstick on his large and handsome face, tweaks into shape the collar of his jacket, and plucks a few unruly eyebrow hairs. King points imperiously at his nose. Eric takes out a pair of nail scissors and trims King's nostril hair, then he wipes the scissors and puts them away in the makeup bag, which is neatly divided into white plastic compartments. He uses the scarlet and white hair drier last, lifting King's thick white hair, blowing it, curving it, flicking it.

Hannah cranes forward, incredulous. 'Surely not! Does he really have a blue rinse?'

Waldo's face is impassive. 'Sometimes he favours pink.'

And now Theodore King, his makeup complete, is surveying the scene as if he were Charlton Heston playing Moses. He pats his hair before he speaks. His voice is commanding. 'Bring me a dying child.'

Hannah gasps. What did he say? Bring me a dying child? In the middle of the desert, in a mass of starving people, a man in a blue safari suit says bring me a dying child?

'That's right,' says Waldo, seeing the look on her face. 'That's what he said.'

Young men scurry to find the right child. This one is too

big, this one too small, this one not thin enough, this one not sick enough, this one is just right.

'Over here,' shouts a young man from Help, as he carefully lifts a child whose head lolls sideways and whose eyes are almost closed.

The camera crew swings into action. Theodore King cradles the child on his knee. Tenderly he pleads to the cameras not just for this child, but for all the dying children of Africa. Tears roll down his cheeks. Words flow like some enchanted song. He woos, he cajoles, and in such a manner and with such an art that it seems to Hannah money will flutter from the fingers of the rich, and the poor will scrabble in their savings to rescue this child, this dying child who lurches on King's knee like a bundle of kindling wood.

He ends with a flourish. 'Our worst crime is abandoning children. Many of the things we need can wait. This child cannot.'

She watches in silent amazement.

Ezekiel stands with his feet apart, and his voice is angry. 'He's the new look of aid. He can't turn water into wine so he makes dying kids into television shows.'

'But his tears were real,' says Hannah.

Waldo, who has been writing in his notebook, pauses. 'He'll help raise a lot of money.'

Hannah is confused. Had she money right at that moment, had she food, she would have poured it into King's lap. Alas, she has no money and only a few dried-up cheese sandwiches from the hotel, left behind in the plane. And how would cheese sandwiches feed two thousand people? How would one flask of water slake their thirst?

She hears Waldo draw in his breath and she turns to see

King gathering the child's arms and legs together, as if trying to truss him up neatly, but the tiny body flops in all directions. 'The child has died,' Waldo says.

Hannah cannot stop her tears. Waldo hands her a handkerchief. He has a sudden and ghastly vision of his preposterous mother, Enid, peering at the dead child with her button-bright eyes and booming, 'What a shame. But they breed like rabbits, so if they lose a kiddie they don't take it as hard.'

He wanders away, his hands in his pockets, his hat on the back of his head, and squats on the sand staring into the distance. For a long time he does not move.

Ezekiel paces round and round King, glowering.

Hannah feels sick and cannot move.

Later, when the three have regrouped, King ambles up to them, mopping his face with a red and white bandanna. He ignores Ezekiel and Hannah and greets Waldo like a long-lost friend. 'I feel bad about that little guy. All the kids are dying. Cholera, measles, malaria, typhoid – you name it, they've got it. Their resistance is zero.' He puts an arm around Waldo's shoulders. 'That's why we need the help of the Lord.'

Waldo looks away, embarrassed. King beams at Hannah. 'This big guy and I have done the circuits together. Kenya, Zimbabwe, Nigeria, Peru, Ethiopia – and now Ethiopia again. Worst famine in history, that's what we told the folks then. What'll we say this time?'

'Worst famine in history,' says Waldo promptly.

Theodore King clicks his fingers and Eric brings over his shooting-stick. King settles his bulk on the small black leather seat. 'This kind of thing still hurts – even though you and I have been around a long time, brother. Children cannot wait till tomorrow, their need is today.'

'Is that why you're here?' Hannah asks belligerently.

King wriggles to make himself more comfortable. The shooting-stick is beginning to disappear into the ground. 'We're making TV commercials to get the funds flowing. We'll follow up with a medical team and food drops. We might cross into Somalia if we're allowed. Folks are also starving there. If you want to hitch a ride, you're welcome.'

Hannah would like to cross into Somalia, even with King, but Waldo looks dubious. Nearby she sees the parents of the dead boy trying to lay him out on the sand. The father, who looks old but may well be young, gives a high and terrible cry which is followed by the wail of the mother. Hannah wants to say something to register the death of the child. She goes over and kneels down to take the child's hand. 'Sorry, sorry,' she keeps repeating, even though she realises they probably do not understand. She gets up and turns away but is blocked by a group of women. One of them thrusts a small boy into her arms; he is so thin that Hannah is afraid of hurting him. He burns with fever, and every time he coughs his little green shorts slip down his body.

'How old?' she asks, raising first two fingers, then three.

The woman shakes her head and holds up seven fingers. She is gazing at Hannah beseechingly, her dark eyes drawing her down into such pain that Hannah shudders with its intensity and holds out the child. The woman takes him. Then she pulls off one of her bracelets and pushes it insistently over Hannah's wrist.

Later, when Hannah surreptitiously tries to clean her hands in the sand, the woman sees her and Hannah is ashamed.

Women flutter around her like dying moths. Women

pulling at her arms, touching her face, women calling, '*Loshe, loshe.*'

'What does that mean?' she asks Ezekiel, who has come to find her.

'Aching stomach, it means aching stomach,' he shouts angrily.


Throughout the day the desert had kept changing colour, from sweeps of saffron and orange to a startling blood-red. Now, in the late afternoon, pale sand had faded into an indigo sky. The air was surprisingly still.

They had returned to the little plane, which sat jauntily by the desert airstrip, alongside a rusty hangar. Ephraim took his leave to return to army barracks, shaking his head good-naturedly. 'Dear God, I think you all very crazy to be here. No offence.'

Waldo sat cross-legged under one wing of the plane. For such a bulky man he folded up with surprising ease. He had taken off his hat and was trying to adjust its faded band but his fingers were too clumsy. Hannah took the hat from him and returned it with the ribbon in place. He raised a hand in silent thanks.

Hannah kicked off her sandals and lay flat on her back, her head resting on her arms, her mind and body aching with exhaustion. She was relieved when Max approached, offering water and the few cheese sandwiches left from the morning flight. Hannah ate and drank slowly, conscious of every mouthful. Solomon Lulu refused all sustenance and sat cross-legged, his back very straight, taking his snuff. He looked as if at any minute he might blow away in a dark cloud of dust, Hannah thought.

Max's small tight mouth twitched under his sandy moustache. 'Hurry up, you guys, or we'll hit the curfew in Addis. Big trouble if we do.'

Waldo struggled to his feet, dusting off the sand and the sandwich crumbs. He sighed, saying that although the famine was horrific he still found the notion of nomadic life seductive. Nomads could navigate by the sun, the stars and the dunes. It was not man-made systems that gave structure to their lives, but the movement of the universe, the waxing and waning of the moon, the first shout of orange at daybreak, the setting sun at night. 'Wilfred Thesiger, the great British explorer who spent so much of his life in Africa, said the desert was the greatest of equalisers, the mother of selection tests,' Waldo announced.

Hannah grimaced. 'Sounds like *Boys' Own Annual*.'

On the flight back, Hannah pressed her face close to the window and watched the sky change colour still further in the fading light. Indigo gave way to dusky purple, red feathered into black. She was a long way from home and felt oddly pleased.

# t w o

That evening, after they returned from the desert, Hannah's bare feet left trails of sand on the white marble floor of her room. Red stained her face, her hands, and her long Indian robe. She peeled off the garment, catching her hair in its toggles before she dropped it on the bathroom floor and stripped off her underpants. Purple, worn as a concession to having a job. She didn't believe in underwear.

When she was naked, she stared at herself in the gilded mirror and saw a long, slender body, milk-white except for a fine shower of freckles on her chest and her small breasts. Her cheeks were sharply angled and accentuated the hollows under her eyes. Her hair was a wild tangle and when she shook her head it fanned out like a Catherine wheel of amazing brightness. She pinched her thighs, her belly, the tops of her arms. She turned sideways, sucking in her breath.

She had read of Algonquian Indians in a winter famine eating broth made of smoke, snow and buckskin. A rash of pellagra had appeared like tattooed flowers on their emaciated bodies – the 'roses of starvation', according to a French physician's description. It had actually sounded pretty when she read it sitting under the shade of the liquidambar tree in her father's Canberra garden, but sunken eyes and swollen bellies, ribcages protruding like livid scars had not been pretty. Her own ribs fanned in delicate whiteness beneath her skin.

Hannah wondered how one television series could make any difference to such despair. Earlier she had harboured some vague notion – film makes money, money buys food, food ends famine – but now she saw this to be absurd. She turned on the shower and mercilessly scrubbed herself. Water coursed over her head, her face and her body. Water filled her as she drank greedily from a large green Bakelite vacuum flask until her stomach ached. But she did not care and flung herself naked and dripping on the big white bed, arms outstretched. She needed time to let the day seep through her.

One school lunchtime, when the dining room had been filled with the clatter of pubescent girls and a huge crumbling statue of the Virgin Mary stared down at them from dingy yellow walls, they had been confronted by plates of grey stew which smelled and looked like boiled socks. Hannah screwed up her nose in disgust, and in a burst of rebellion upturned hers on the table.

Sister Carmichael, pear-shaped and fierce, had flapped her black wings and descended in wrath. 'Wicked child. That food would feed a family of starving Indians.'

Such a stupid remark, so gross. Hannah scraped the lumps of meat towards her plate, but at the last minute deliberately jerked her fork so that a trajectory of grease flew in the air and settled in shiny globules on Sister Carmichael's starched white wimple.

For starving Indians, substitute starving Africans. And if that stew were put in front of her today, would she eat it? No way. Not unless she was starving, and she wasn't. Hannah felt a rush of gratitude.

Outside, a few small lights twinkled in the blackness. Street cries floated up through her open window, along with spicy smells, strange music. She experienced a familiar longing – I want, but what do I want? – and raised her damp head off the pillow to look around at the large room. Carved ebony furniture and hand-woven rugs of Ethiopian lions – angular, stylised little lions with spiky manes and friendly faces. Over the writing desk hung a picture of the Queen of Sheba, founder with King Solomon of a dynasty which had stretched for three thousand years, until the recent overthrow of Emperor Haile Selassie. Sheba's skin was a dusky blue and her eyes were black and glistening. One eye was slightly larger than the other.

Hannah squinted at the eye for a while. She was too tense and too exhausted to rest. She got up and emptied her knapsack on the floor. Red sand, barley sugar wrappings, her notes, a comb, some suntan cream, two pens and her mouth organ. The compass seemed to have disappeared. She washed out her water bottle and carefully cleaned her camera of any grains of sand. She was determined to be professional. Then she picked up her mouth organ and played 'With A Little Help From My Friends'.

She wondered if Waldo had been pleased with her work.


Ezekiel was playing chess. First he had showered away the desert sand, then set up the ebony and ivory pieces which had been given to him by his father. The set was a miniature, beautifully carved, and before every game he liked to polish each piece with a red silk handkerchief. It had become a ritual, just as the game itself had become a ritual, ever since Ezekiel was a leggy schoolboy of twelve and had begun attending the new high school in Kigali.

Every Sunday, early in the evening, Ezekiel and his father would set up the chess board on the back verandah of their big white house in Kigali. His sisters would be chattering and romping on the verandah, his mother would bring lemonade and his father would ask, 'Have you done your homework, Ezekiel?' Then the game would begin.

Ezekiel liked the feel of the carved pieces and the aesthetics of the board mapped out in black and white. He appreciated being in control of his own moves and found it exhilarating to think strategically and plan ahead. The only thing he didn't enjoy was losing. Once, after his father had captured his black knight, Ezekiel angrily threw the piece on the floor. It rolled on the wooden boards, then settled at his mother's feet. She glanced up from her magazine but said nothing. The youngest of his sisters, Valentine, clapped her hands over her mouth and giggled. His father, normally such a gentle man, looked severe.

'Pick it up, Ezekiel. Throwing it away won't change anything.'

Tonight, Ezekiel was being careless with the pieces, moving them roughly as he brooded over the bizarre appearance of the Reverend Dr Theodore King. He imagined him as a Father Christmas whose beard and whiskers were tinged with an exquisite ice-blue. Instead of reindeer, he flew a helicopter. Instead of a sackful of toys, he hauled a sackful of dying children.

Ezekiel poured himself a glass of water and went to the window, where he stood gazing at the slums which sprawled across the city to the fierce dark mountains beyond. He still had

Waldo's binoculars and swung them round till he focused on the pale pink building in the distance where Haile Selassie had been imprisoned since the revolution – Haile Selassie, Elect of God, Conquering Lion of the Tribe of Judah, King of Zion, King of Kings, Emperor of Ethiopia.

In September of the year before, a shabby old Volkswagen had pulled up outside the imperial palace and soldiers had bundled the frail old emperor into the back seat and driven him away. Ezekiel wondered how he was being treated. Selassie had inherited a kingdom of poverty and isolation. Court ritual had been feudal and elaborate. Visitors to the emperor had to take their leave backwards, bowing all the way; lions were rumoured to roam freely in the palace grounds; Selassie, with his high pointy crown, feasted on banquets of camel stuffed with antelope stuffed with turkey stuffed with fish stuffed with hard-boiled eggs. In the beginning he had tried to introduce reform, but when Mussolini and the fascists invaded in 1935, Selassie was driven into exile and did not return until the end of World War II. Perhaps by then it was too late to reverse an order whose roots stretched back for thousands of years. At a time when only four percent of his people could read and write, he had spent millions on street decorations for a meeting of the Organisation of African Unity. Tattered remnants still hung from some of the lamp posts and festooned the crumbling facade of a government building opposite the hotel.

Down below, on the street, two small boys were selling corn cobs, peanuts and Coca-Cola. Ezekiel felt vaguely hungry and wondered if he should go and explore or wait for Waldo. He liked Waldo.

Such a strange first meeting. Ezekiel had been working on his doctorate at the London School of Economics, writing a few articles and earning a pittance tutoring, when a piece he wrote on the politics of aid was picked up by *Statesman and Nation* and attracted unexpected attention. As a result, the Royal Empire Society asked if he would speak at one of their winter lecture series. The invitation had surprised him; the society was considered by some to be the bastion of conservatism, and he wasn't sure if the sons and daughters of the empire would like what he had to say.

The hall was panelled in dark wood, the lighting low and sombre, the audience – mostly white and elderly – afflicted by a collective cough. The lectern stood in front of a large picture of a smiling Queen Elizabeth and a crabby Prince Phillip. Ezekiel felt momentarily embarrassed when he remembered how he had flung himself into his subject, bouncing up and down on his feet and projecting his voice, the way he had practised in front of a cracked bathroom mirror the night before.

He had taken his audience back to the founding of the United Nations in San Francisco in June 1945, and the origins of post-war aid. Then came the World Bank, the International Monetary Fund, and Harry Truman's Four Point Plan with its appeal for peace, plenty and freedom. Yet, following Truman, one American leader after the other had blatantly proclaimed that aid was good for business. That old scoundrel Nixon even said that the main purpose of aid was not to help other nations but to help the United States. Ezekiel had challenged the whole notion of the Third World, saying it was the creation of foreign aid. 'Without foreign aid there would be no Third World, nor an underdeveloped world, a less developed world, a developing world.'

And then, somewhere on the other side of the hall, he'd heard a loud rustle of paper. A man with a beard was diving into a paper bag, sending clouds of fine white powder into the air. He held up his hand and asked, 'Isn't it naïve to expect the West to give without wanting anything in return?'

Ezekiel nodded. 'Sure. But look how much you've already taken. You exploited our resources, used our labour, denied our culture. In return you gave us social, legal and political systems which were yours, not ours. And when you packed your bags and left, a new breed of colonisers came in your place. Instead of missionaries, we have aid workers. Instead of civil servants, we have economic consultants. Imperial colonialism has given way to economic colonialism.'

'I agree,' said the man amiably, 'but what should the West do when millions starve and we're asked to help?'

'Give help but cut the strings, man, cut the strings. Otherwise it won't be long before Africa's interest repayments exceed Africa's debt.'

A few people applauded limply as he mopped his brow and gathered his papers. The organiser of the evening, a retired colonel, stroked his clipped grey moustache and tried to be jovial.

'Can't say I agree with you, but I suppose you chaps have a different point of view.'

Outside, the streets had been wet and shining. His new trousers, bought especially for the occasion, were already splattered with mud when the man with the paper bag came up and suggested a drink. They had met many times after that, arguing issues as broad-ranging as human rights and the hidden cost of aid to the weekend football and the best pub near Kensington High Street tube. It was a friendship Ezekiel valued and one which might help open doors to a wider international arena.

Meantime, it had been a long day and he felt badly in need

of food. He glanced down at his watch and decided to stir Waldo into action.

Hannah was also hungry. At the lift she found a small boy who looked no more than eight or nine. His richly embroidered Afghan coat reached to the ground, making it difficult for him to move. He smiled sweetly at Hannah. 'You want all fours, lady?'

Downstairs in the marble foyer she found Waldo and Ezekiel surveying a battery of restaurant signs sprouting from a tall pole. Ezekiel wore a red shirt and radiated confidence. Waldo's feet were apart, his hands behind his back. It was late but there were still plenty of people around, well-dressed people. Hannah looked down at her white cheesecloth skirt, bought at a Sydney market, and then shrugged. Too late for anything else.

Starry Starry Night, the nightclub, was up the marble stairs. Desert Sands, the restaurant, was down the stairs. The Milky Way lay east, and Au Rendezvous for a Cock was west.

'We're going to the nightclub,' Ezekiel said.

Hannah eyes widened in disbelief. Waldo intervened. 'It's called preservation. Reminding yourself you're doing okay, that you're not a nomad dying of hunger, or a Bengali woman whose kids have just been drowned in a flood.'

Ezekiel flicked the air with his long fingers. 'It's called living it up, man.'

On the way to the nightclub they passed the coffee shop. A lone figure was perched high on a chrome bar stool, his head buried in the beaker of a milkshake. Theodore King had changed into a maroon tracksuit and running shoes. When he saw them he surfaced long enough to beam and wave a large hand before returning to his milkshake.

Ezekiel loped up and biffed him on the shoulder. 'Held any more dying children?'

Theodore King spluttered before wiping a drop of lime-green milk from his nose. 'No, thank the Lord. That was sad, real sad.' He suddenly looked tired.

In the cavernous nightclub, tables were dimly lit by small red lanterns; electric stars twinkled in a ceiling of midnight blue. Three limp young men, billed as The Blackpool Beach Boys, were playing 'Yellow Submarine'. They wore the latest Beatles haircuts and orange flares. Hannah was disappointed, she wanted African music. She picked up the menu and a buxom Queen of Sheba with perfectly matched eyes stared at her from the parchment cover.

Waldo shook his head. 'Poor soul, she'll never be laid to rest. She's so good for tourism, the Yemeni are now trying to claim her, not to mention Egypt, Iran and the United Arab Emirates.'

The waiter announced in a German accent that they should try Ethiopia's national dish, injera and wot. When it arrived, the injera resembled big flat pancakes. The waiter told them to put spoonfuls of the wot, a spicy stew made of lentils and chillies, into a strip of the injera and wrap it up like a parcel.

Hannah ate a couple of mouthfuls but had lost her appetite. She thrust her plate to one side. Waldo looked at her sympathetically.

'Look, I remember the first time I saw famine. I shrivelled up. I was ashamed, insulted that people should still be dying of hunger when there's enough food to feed everyone in the world. And when someone slapped a large plate of food in front of me, I was appalled. But it didn't last. Not because I was untouched, but because I'd merely observed. I'd never had hunger gnawing at my guts. Never known what it was like to starve.'

Ezekiel didn't appear to be listening. He was digging the tines of his fork into the tablecloth, like a bull rutting the ground. He flicked his head in the direction of the coffee shop.

'He makes me angry. First he takes a kid who's dying and props him up like some doll he wants to show off back home, till the doll's collapsed and so has the kid's life. Then he makes it sound as if . . . as if the whole of Africa's a basket case, as if we're all starving – like beggars, you know, waiting for someone to toss a few bananas in our laps.'

Hannah looked at him. She drew her coffee towards her and began stirring so vigorously that Waldo reached out a hand to stop her from shattering the cup. She put down her spoon.

'But people *are* starving. So what would you do? Walk away and let them die?'

'Rich people never starve. The food's there, you can see it in the markets. It just doesn't get through. And food's a good way of controlling people.'

'It's also one way of saving them.'

Ezekiel stared provocatively at Hannah. 'So who are you saving, Hannah? The hungry Africans?'

Hannah snapped back, 'I've hardly noticed you going hungry.'

Waldo was aware that in their exhaustion they were all teetering on the edge of hysteria. He was searching for something safe to say when Ezekiel suddenly switched mood, jumped to his feet and pulled at Hannah's hand to follow him onto the dance floor. He gave her a dazzling smile. 'Come.'

To her surprise, Hannah went.

Waldo looked on with doleful curiosity. He had never been able to dance.

In the few remaining hours before dawn, Waldo's mind kept returning to Hannah and Ezekiel, seeking some further explanation for the way they'd behaved. Exhaustion certainly, but there had been something more. They reminded him of his first fevered attempts at dating, when he had teased a flat-chested girl called Sybil with clumsy good humour, trying to kiss her and precipitating only the clashing of teeth. Ezekiel wasn't clumsy, nor was Hannah, but they had jousted like adolescents who might end up either having a blazing row or in bed together. Waldo didn't want either of those things to happen. The row would be bad for work. Bed would be – well, what would bed be? He closed his eyes and imagined them making love but found it unbearable, so he hastily wandered out to the terrace where the night air was chill and his feet were cold. He looked for the window where he imagined Hannah had her room. Then he thought, For God's sake, Waldo, she's working for you. You're her boss, she's a baby. No, she's a young woman – oh God, shut up and take your sexual urges to bed.

But when he went inside he was too restless to sleep, so he decided to sort his papers and get ready for the following day. He was a worrier and this project made him worry more than most.

A few months earlier he had attended a World Food Conference in Rome and been irritated by its intensive focus on technology. Little was said about equity. How could he show on film the political and economic forces that helped imprison

*39*

people in poverty and powerlessness? They were such abstract issues, so hard to illustrate. The child who had died that morning – how to link that kind of tragedy with the bigger scene? To show that although natural causes create crop failures, humans usually cause famines. He had been in Biafra in the late sixties, reporting on the fight between the Ibo independence movement and the Nigerian army. The army had deliberately stopped the Red Cross from entering and left four million people to die of hunger. He was also aware that the new government in Ethiopia was frantically trying to convert the country to Marxism and had scant time for famines. The food drop had possibly been laid on just for them, or for Theodore King.

He stretched his left leg. Cramp was snaking its way from his toes to his thigh. He tried rubbing himself vigorously but with little effect.

Earlier in the day he had been envying Hannah's vitality. His seemed to have died some time back. His trousers felt tight, his sandshoes pinched, and although he kept sucking barley sugar he felt faint. He even wished that he was at home in London, with his books and a good malt whisky and soft rain drizzling down the windows of his flat. Except that the rain would probably turn to sleet, his flat would be freezing cold, and his doctor had recently said no more alcohol. Bugger his doctor.

When he was tired, he longed to have the world end in a golden glow – 'Angels from on high shall sing,/Glory be to God our King' – and preferably lots of fluffy white clouds on which he could lie. The trouble was he didn't believe in God, any god, especially not his mother's, which was one of damnation for the infidels and best hats and prayer books for herself on the Sabbath. His father's god was less fussy and more forgiving.

'Sorry, Da,' Waldo used to say apologetically. 'Sorry, Da,' as he tried to explain a philosophy of existentialism to his father, who had been a commercial traveller selling Christmas cards in the north of England until he collided with a garbage truck in Manchester and lost the car and both his legs.

His father had seemed more upset at the loss of the car than the loss of his legs, and Waldo reflected that perhaps his father's car had been like the nomads' camels: a way of earning money and a passport to freedom. He could roam the moors, call in to Sheffield, Chesterfield and York, doss down in commercial travellers' hotels with their musty patterned carpets, their boozy bars, have a pint or two and exchange dirty jokes with his mates. And only return home when he felt ready to face his wife, who wore toque hats, shoes that crippled her bunions, and who, since her husband's accident, had run a boarding house in Scarborough. Guests called her The Foghorn.

Hannah lay in bed gazing at a black sky. No stars, no moon, no wind. Only the sounds of people chattering in a strange language somewhere in the darkness. She curled up small, but she was still haunted by the scenes she had seen earlier that day. When she finally dozed off, she dreamed her mother was sitting in the big blue chair in her bedroom at home, holding a child and singing something sweet and gentle which Hannah had never heard before. It filled her with peace and contentment, and for a blissful moment she thought she was that child. But her mother was cradling the small boy who had died in King's arms in the desert. He was curled up on her lap, his dark skin glowing against the fairness of her own, his limbs no longer thin but rounded.

Hannah held out her arms, eager to join them. Her mother shook her head. 'Don't disturb him.'

'But he's not your child,' Hannah protested.

Her mother looked at her with calm blue eyes. 'No, he is everyone's.'

'And whose child am I?' Hannah cried.

The days were full and passed quickly. Field trips, interviews, visits to government offices, and everything punctuated by interminably long delays which Waldo said were part of the game. Taxis never arrived when they were expected, planes were cancelled, Solomon Lulu altered their schedule with breathtaking regularity.

Hannah learned to do her waiting in the hotel foyer, where she often picked up useful gossip. Disaster experts of every creed and colour danced before her eyes in a saraband of deals and counter-deals, gossip and innuendo.

'The Russians are searching for oil . . . Ethiopia will win the war in the Ogaden because Cuban troops will soon arrive . . . Ethiopia will lose the war because America is giving tanks and planes to Somalia . . . They're asking the nomads to sell off all their cattle and abandon their culture to become farmers, it won't work . . . German transport manufacturers have just outbid the Japanese . . . The Hilton Hotel is offering a Bavarian dinner with special Bavarian sausages and Bavarian potato pancakes . . . The German ambassador will attend with his wife and five red-headed daughters . . . The German ambassador is having an affair with the wife of the Ethiopian Minister for Social Stability . . .'

The hotel reminded her of the opera *Aida*. She kept expecting elephants to appear from between its grand marble colonnades, and Radamès to lead the triumphal march around the magnificent hot-springs swimming pool, which was shaped like a Coptic cross and tended by beautiful young Ethiopian boys who wore black jeans and the latest Italian sunglasses.

Earlier that morning Hannah had piled her hair on top of her head in a desire to look as sophisticated as the Ethiopian women who frequented the hotel. Now it was collapsing and she shook her head, letting it fall free. Her pen hovered over a postcard of a Lalibela mural – three saints wearing crowns and regarding each other askance with enormous eyes. She had decided to send this to her father but she wasn't sure what to write. 'Wish you were here'? She didn't. She scrawled, 'From Hannah with love' in big handwriting.

People drifted in and out, trading stories of failure and success. A young man whose long hair flopped over one eye gave Hannah a limp handshake and told her he had been in Addis Ababa for almost two months, waiting to inspect a World Bank tea and coffee plantation. First his travel permit wasn't ready, then the pilot kept having stomach cramps, and finally, when they were ready to go, he was told that the road to the plantation was temporarily impassable.

'But we weren't going by road, we were going by plane,' he said indignantly. His blue eyes matched the blue and white check of his American shirt.

Hannah impatiently tapped her foot. 'Maybe the project doesn't exist.'

The young man creased up his eyes in surprise. 'Well, I'll be darned. Maybe it doesn't.'

Every morning, the lobby was crammed with safari-suited bureaucrats clutching lunchboxes, waiting for a tour billed as 'a flight to hell and back again'. An elegant Indian woman wearing a pale suede suit and high-heeled crocodile shoes promised that people could fly from the luxury of the hotel to the famine, take their photographs, and return in time for sunbathing round the pool.

'Come and you will know you are truly blessed,' she said, adjusting her mother-of-pearl spectacles, upswept at the sides. 'Guaranteed.' Her laughter tinkled as charmingly as the trinkets around her wrists.

Some people were angry. Like the man in flared jeans, and sideburns that scrabbled down his pockmarked face. He waved a rolled newspaper in the face of his plump young companion, who was about to apply lipstick without the benefit of a mirror.

'See this, honey? The *Ethiopian Herald* – "Long Live Anti-Imperialist Solidarity". So how come we're still helping these jerks?'

The woman didn't answer, but branded herself with a pink gash from ear to ear. She retracted the lipstick, put it carefully into a jewelled purse and announced in an intense whisper, 'There's going to be another public hanging soon. That waiter told me when I ordered a cappuccino. It's Mussolini's influence.'

The man drew out a slightly grubby handkerchief and blew his red-veined nose. 'The hanging or the cappuccino?'

Hannah watched Brother Augustine O'Keefe from Tipperary, observing how his black hair was slicked back from a high and handsome brow. He had little white teeth and little white hands, and was deep in conversation with Patsy Grimbold, the Assistant Field Director of an English aid agency, regaling her with stories of black Jesus and black Mary. Patsy Grimbold shot a nervous look at Hannah. Journalists were not to be trusted, especially young ones. She adjusted her tortoiseshell glasses,

44

which were attached to a silver chain around her neck, and glared.

The day before, Hannah had interviewed them both and Patsy had snapped, 'I hope you're not going to make it look as if we're living in luxury in this hotel.' She'd prefaced her responses to most of Hannah's questions with phrases like, 'One has to take account of the whole situation ... It depends what you mean ... One can't really answer that question in the truest sense.'

'Who is one?' Hannah asked Waldo later.

Waldo looked thoughtful. 'One is an English person's best defence.'


Waldo was enjoying his role as mentor to Hannah. The only piece of information he kept to himself concerned his visit to the men's health club.

There, he had shed his clothes, draped a white towel around his middle and stepped into the sauna, which was large and very hot. In one corner, almost obscured by a cloud of steam, he had seen a naked and generously proportioned Theodore King. Spooned up in front of King was an exquisite young Ethiopian man whose brown hair curled softly down a slender neck and whose legs were cradled inside the sturdy thighs of the preacher. Waldo could see dark lustrous eyes, a gleam of golden skin, buttocks like young walnuts. And from the impressive figure of Theodore King, a pink hand fumbling, a pink cock rising, a large bum heaving. In, out, in, out.


Hannah ventured into the women's health club. Long white slabs of marble veined in softest rose. Mineral baths of deep dark green. She felt pale and unattractive alongside so many languorous brown bodies and such exotic faces. White cosmetic masks ringing dark and shining eyes, delicate nostrils, proud mouths.

How would you manage to gossip behind a mask of myrtle, frankincense and myrrh, or asses' milk and camel dung? thought Hannah as she stared at her face in one of the health club mirrors. She stretched her mouth from side to side, up and down. She peered at her freckles. She did not like freckles, nor did she like her red hair.

She was ten, thin and wan, studying herself in the bathroom mirror of her father's house in Canberra, trying to rub away her freckles and flatten down her hair. She wanted desperately to be like her mother, who'd had silky blonde hair and a creamy skin. If she were like her mother, maybe her father would notice her more. One time, she had tried to turn her red hair fair by sprinkling it with talcum powder. Another time she doused it in peroxide and it emerged the colour of green lemons.

Her aunt had come up behind her and pointed at the freckles on her own nose and on her highly rouged cheeks. 'Look!' as she pulled off her plum-coloured hat. 'Look!' as she bent over, taking pins out of her hair so it fell free. She shook it and strands of copper gleamed through the grey. 'Redheads have fun. Even more than blondes.' When her aunt smiled she had a dimple and a glint of gold in one of her teeth.

When Hannah emerged from the glamour of the health club, she bumped into Ezekiel and Solomon leaning against the registration desk of the hotel, laughing and joking with two women she had seen around the lobby. Grace and Betty-Lou were aid workers, ebony black and buxom. They bubbled with good humour. They were womanly and sexy. She turned abruptly and left.

She had become increasingly conscious of the city's edginess. Every evening she heard volleys of firing followed by silence. In the streets soldiers strutted, carrying guns, and in small dark nightclubs rumours of reprisals were drowned in the defiant beat of music. Two months after Haile Selassie had been so politely and bloodlessly dethroned, the massacres had begun: sixty top officials of the former imperial regime were executed in a drum-roll of bloody paybacks.

One lunchtime, Hannah went alone to the street markets, pushing her way through the crowds, past hobbled donkeys and camels, in amongst the stalls with their goat skins, their bales of hand-woven striped cotton – in blues, pinks and greens – silver jewellery, filigree hairpins, sacks of spices and coffee beans, rhino-hide whips, gourds filled with rancid-smelling goat's butter, rifles, sticks and spears. For her father she bought a paint-ing on wood of a large black Queen of Sheba dwarfing a small brown King Solomon. For her aunt, a packet of frankincense and myrrh.

When she returned she found Waldo reading an old copy of *Newsweek* in the hotel foyer. She waved her painting at him. 'Look, it's an antique. They said it was very old.'

Waldo held out a hand and took the picture. 'About two days old, I'd say.' He put down his magazine. 'You shouldn't go out on your own. It's dangerous. Two German camera-men were lynched a month ago for taking photographs. People are superstitious. They think you're stealing their soul.

47

If you stand in their shadow, they believe you're giving them the evil eye.'

She went out again, confident that if she used her common-sense she would be safe. She turned a corner and confronted a noisy crowd. Music blared from loudspeakers, street vendors sold food and drink – bottles of fizzy drink, chewy sweetmeats, meat and vegetables from big bubbling pots, rounds of rubbery injera.

She wondered if it was a carnival, until she looked up and gasped. Her hand flew to her neck. Towering above her was a huge wooden scaffold, from which dangled three bodies dressed in olive-green military uniforms, twisting round and round like marionettes on strings. Three livid purple faces lolling on three broken necks. Three tongues protruding, swollen and black. Three pairs of feet, vulnerable in their bareness.

As the bodies swayed, the crowd danced and chanted in a frenzy of jubilation. Hannah was drawn into their midst, unable to break away, terrified she might fall. Suddenly she spotted Ezekiel. She cried out and tried to push her way towards him but the crowd kept washing her back into their swell of hatred.

Ezekiel eventually pulled her free, grabbing her by the hand, yanking her after him as she stumbled, head down, out of breath, shocked.

'Waldo sent me to find you,' Ezekiel said as soon as they were away from the crowd. They walked back to the hotel in silence, to find Waldo waiting outside the main entrance. It was the first time Hannah had seen him angry. He took her by the arm.

'Don't ever, *ever* do that sort of thing again. It's dangerous. It's irresponsible. It's unprofessional.'

Hannah apologised, shame-faced, and was promptly sick on the pavement.

She couldn't get the hanging out of her mind. Why were the men killed? Was this the aftermath of the revolution? And what was it like, dying in front of so many jeering spectators? Waldo shrugged and said, 'If I were going to die I'd be shit scared and all I'd worry about is, please God, make it quick and painless.'

Her obsession continued. Why were the feet of the dead men stretched forward, their toes turned upwards as if they were dancing? She asked Ezekiel, who said it was probably contraction of the ligaments.

How did he know this kind of thing? Did they have public hangings in his own country? Was he shocked, or did he take it as a matter of course? 'Tell me about Africa,' she said, meaning, Tell me about yourself.

He spread his hands in exasperation. 'Africa, Africa, I'm sick of people talking about Africa as if it's just one country. How can I tell you about Africa!'

She withdrew, miffed. She was conscious that they had little personal conversation together and she felt jealous of the camaraderie that existed between Ezekiel and Waldo.

Solomon Lulu drove like a man possessed. He squealed round hairpin bends in the ancient Fiat, his foot flat on the accelerator, coaxing the car to stupendous performance heights. An ebony cigarette holder was clenched between his teeth, a magenta silk scarf flung around his neck.

They had been visiting some of the rehabilitation programs

in the north of the country and now were heading for a place to spend the night. Solomon recommended they stay at a mountain village called Serena, which was wedged between two steep and craggy peaks.

As their car edged its way into the village they could see it was eerily deserted. A melancholia surrounded it and Hannah shuddered; a barefoot child scuttled away as soon as he saw them coming.

Hannah was the first to notice a group of soldiers stalking down a dark laneway. When they saw the car, they shouted and ran towards it, guns raised. The soldiers ordered them out and pushed them against the nearest wall, crushing Hannah's face. Hands moved roughly up and down her body, shoving her, feeling her, fingers probing her flesh. She tried to turn but a soldier yelled and slammed her head to the front, grazing her lip. Her senses were exquisitely alive: she could hear the beat of her heart, Waldo's breathing, Ezekiel's shuffling of shoes on the gravel. She smelled her own fear. Saw the dirt on her boots, the frayed edge of her laces. Wondered what had happened to Solomon Lulu, who appeared to have vanished.

Waldo was released first. Brushing the dust off his clothes, he demanded, 'What's all this about?'

A cocky young man in uniform with stars on his epaulettes strolled up and held out a hand. 'Captain Peter, chief of security.' Captain Peter jangled silver chains and silver bracelets. His cheekbones shone, his voice was smooth. 'Three journalists and two aid workers were killed here last week by soldiers of Haile Selassie. My soldiers were making sure you are on our side. Soldiers of the Socialist Republic do not kill journalists and aid workers. We protect them.'

He turned and looked pointedly at Solomon Lulu, who had

miraculously reappeared. Then he beamed at Hannah, whose face was frozen into a scowl. She turned her back.

Waldo made a solemn bow. 'Captain Peter,' he said hastily, 'we are happy to hear this.'

The captain threw a handful of peanuts into his mouth. 'I will take you to your hotel.'

The pink-washed hotel also seemed deserted. Its dark green shutters were closed, as was the front door, but Solomon pushed open a side door which led into an empty dining room. A sign in English was tacked to one of its faded yellow walls: DUE TO REHABILITATION, THE BAND HAS MOVED ELSEWHERE. Scuffed linoleum and old newspapers covered the floor. Fly-papers dangled from doorways. A wooden fan with broken blades spun drunkenly from the ceiling, recycling stale air. On a corner table stood an ancient Gaggia espresso machine, covered in dust.

Solomon found the melancholic owner, who spread a crumpled white cloth on a table and handed Waldo a menu which offered injera and wot, 'cabbidge vinaiger', 'stewed goats' and hamburgers. Hannah ordered stewed goats. Waldo asked for everything. Ezekiel shrugged.

Solomon declined to join them. Later, they could hear him laughing with the proprietor.

'How do we know Solomon's okay?' asked Hannah. 'He could be a royalist, and we could be walking into a trap.'

Waldo speared a piece of goat meat. 'We could. Or government soldiers could kill us, in order to blame the royalists.'

Hannah saw that he was looking at her appreciatively. She hid her bitten fingernails and flicked back her hair in what she hoped was a sophisticated gesture.

Ezekiel was also looking at Hannah but with some degree of irritation. He said they were behaving like people who popped in to see the natives, made a few bad jokes, ate funny food and then went home. Disaster tourists.

Hannah frowned. 'That's wrong. I want to help make things better.'

'Better for whom? And why Africa? Aren't there enough things that need changing in your own part of the world? What's the health of Australian Aboriginals like? What percentage of them are in jails, compared with whites? How young do they die?'

Waldo rubbed his eyes and said he didn't want any arguments. He wanted bed. He pushed back his chair and, just in time, stopped himself from patting Hannah on the head.

'Hannah, try to realise you can't clean up everything in life and you certainly can't do it all at once.'

'I can try.'

Waldo nodded. 'Yes, you can try,' he said wearily, and recited the Lewis Carroll he'd read as a child:

*The Walrus and the Carpenter*
*Were walking close at hand;*
*They wept like anything to see*
*Such quantities of sand:*
*'If this were only cleared away,'*
*They said, 'it would be grand!'*

*'If seven maids with seven mops*
*Swept it for half a year,*
*Do you suppose,' the Walrus said,*
*'That they could get it clear?'*
*'I doubt it,' said the Carpenter,*
*And shed a bitter tear.*

'Our generation's different. Our generation's going to change the world,' said Hannah.

Climbing the uneven stairs to their rooms they heard a volley of gunfire. Hannah glanced at Waldo. His face was impassive.

'Where were those journalists killed?'

'Right here on the stairs.' Ezekiel placed his hand on her back.

'*Not* funny,' she snapped.

He grinned. 'I'm trying to make friends again.'

On the landing she turned to Waldo. 'Aren't you ever scared?'

He shrugged. 'I tremble at the sound of a teaspoon dropping.'

At the top of the stairs a guard sat on his haunches, Sten gun propped between his knees, his head nodding. A small bubble of saliva appeared between his lips. He didn't wake as they went past him.

Hannah's room had a narrow bed with a creaking iron frame, a lumpy mattress with one sheet, one pillow with a yellow and brown floral pillowcase, two brown check cotton blankets, a wooden chair, and a small table that wobbled and was covered in faded red linoleum. She dumped her backpack and went to tap on Waldo's door on the pretext of saying goodnight. He was sitting on the side of his creaking bed, rubbing insect cream into his arms. The room was airless and mosquitoes whined around his head in a cloud. The wire under the thin kapok mattress sagged almost to the floor. Waldo put down the cream when Hannah came in and swatted an insect which was dive-bombing his left hand.

'Are you okay?'

She nodded, shifting from one foot to another.

'Good. Because I forgot to tell you, don't tuck in your blanket. If there's shooting, roll to the floor.'

Hannah laughed uneasily and returned to her room, where she lay on her bed, still fully dressed, gazing out at a big yellow moon which cast angular shadows across the bare floor. For a while she heard the faint sound of music and when it died away the silence became unnerving. She was just falling asleep when she heard floorboards creak. She sat up, startled. Someone was tapping lightly on her door. Waldo? Ezekiel? She went to the door and opened it a crack. For a moment she didn't recognise the man standing there giving her a cocky smile. Red, green and black African shirt, high-heeled black boots, black pistol in a black holster on his belt, a smell of musk. Captain Peter, chief of security, bowing and at her service.

'I came to see if you have wants.'

She looked puzzled. 'No, no, I have no wants.' And then, as an afterthought, 'Thank you.'

She went to shut her door but he swiftly inserted his booted foot. The grin on his broad face grew larger. Her heart was thudding. Should she scream? What should she do?

'Peanuts. I'd like peanuts,' she blurted out, and her fatuous request stopped his pressure on the door for a moment. He put his head to one side. 'You want?'

'Peanuts.'

'No peanuts. You want fuck.'

'No!' Hannah struggled to close the door on his foot but the captain stood firm.

'You not love me because you are a capitalist girl and I am a revolution man.'

Now his knee was inside the door and she felt a surge

of anger. She hadn't marched to reclaim the night for nothing – who the hell did he think he was, this bow-legged, preposterous little man? She shoved him in the chest, hard, and he staggered slightly. She shoved again, shouting, 'Piss off. Go away. Vamoose. Get lost. Scram.' Another shove and he fell heavily.

The guard round the corner woke at the sound of voices and lurched unsteadily to his feet. At the same time, Waldo and Ezekiel hurtled out of their rooms, almost colliding outside Hannah's door where her assailant lay ignominiously on the floor, his face suffused with rage. As if in slow motion she saw him pull his pistol out of its holster and struggle to rise, saw Ezekiel kick the gun away just as the guard lumbered into view waving his Sten gun. Waldo shouted, 'Stop!' Someone else was also shouting. A louder voice than Waldo's and more authoritative.

'That's enough!'

Solomon Lulu towered over them, yelling in English and Amharic, banging his cane imperiously on the floor. The chief of security rose hurriedly to his feet, straightened his shirt, bowed abruptly and left, followed by Solomon.

At the turn of the corridor Solomon looked back at them with an enigmatic smile. 'Always make sure you are on the winning side.' He disappeared.

Hannah's whole body was trembling. Waldo hovered, solicitous. 'Are you all right? Do you want me to come and sit with you?'

Hannah was too dazed to answer. Ezekiel stepped in and swiftly took Hannah by the elbow. 'I'll stay with you.'

Waldo looked nonplussed. 'Well then . . .' His voice trailed away. 'Well, I'll say goodnight then, if you're sure you're okay?'

Hannah nodded uncertainly, went into her room and climbed back into bed.

Ezekiel seated himself on the upright wooden chair, his arms crossed as if in a vigil. A blue and white cloth was wrapped around his body but he was still cold, and tired.

Hannah woke with her face pressed close to the wall. It was still half dark. For a while she was unsure of her whereabouts, but as fragments of memory began to surface, she felt afraid. When she could not see Ezekiel, her fear increased. She peered over the side of the bed and saw him lying on the floor, legs outstretched, feet sticking up in the air. His eyes were wide open.

'Good morning.' He sounded cheerful.

'It's not morning yet.' Hannah's voice was furry. 'Were you down there all night?'

'Yes. Did you rest?'

She nodded.

'I'm glad,' he said. 'You needed it.'

'Did you?'

'Did I what?' He was sitting up now, leaning on one elbow and looking amused. When he smiled she wanted to smile back at him, but then she remembered the way he'd argued with her the night before.

'Sleep.'

'A little.'

She nodded. 'And that man?'

'Gone, I hope.'

Hannah dragged a hand roughly through her hair. 'I'd like to kill him.'

'Sshh.' Ezekiel got up and sat on the bed. He put an arm around her. 'Try to get more sleep.' His voice was calm and when he lay down beside her she allowed him to hold her.

She was drifting back to sleep when she felt his cock move and become rigid, pressing against her. For a few minutes she lay still, wondering how to react, but when his hands began moving up beneath her dress and she heard him murmur, 'Okay?' she drew in her breath, thinking, Is this what I want?


She is softening, realising she wants to be rid of the fear and the desolation. '*Loshe loshe*', called the women. '*Loshe loshe*', as the children died. The sadness has seeped through her and she desperately needs it to be expunged. She turns to him with a sudden movement, pulling off her dress, digging her fingers into his arms.

He comes with a shudder while she hovers somewhere far away on a highwire of expectation.

'Okay?' he asks, looking down at her. His breath is faintly sour and she imagines hers is the same.

'Almost okay.'

'D'you want . . .'

She thinks about it, head on one side. 'No. Let's just lie.'

Her thighs are sticky, she smells of sex and sweat. She folds her fingers around the long limp warmth of his cock, and peers down.

He nudges her ankle with his foot. 'Have you ever made love to a black man before?'

She shakes her head.

'What about the black people in Australia?'

'What about them?'

There had been one Aboriginal student in her first year at university and she barely knew him. She raises herself on one elbow, scratching at a patch of dried skin on her pale freckled arm. 'It's a myth about black people being better lovers than white.'

He looks hurt. 'You wouldn't let me.'

'Next time.'

'You will?'

'I will.'

'You'd go crazy.'

'No doubt.'

He grins. 'I'd please you.'

'Good.' She nuzzles up close.

Daybreak at last, and the first rays of sun filter through the tattered brown blind. Hannah clambers across Ezekiel to the window, jerks the piece of string attached to the blind, and squints at the sudden flood of light. The window looks over a stretch of dirt where hens are picking their way amongst rusted metal machinery and the broken carcasses of cars. A cock crows and then several more. She turns round. Ezekiel lifts two fingers and lazily waves them.

When she flops on the bed again, she touches the dark stubble on his chin. He wraps his hand round her fingers.

'Tell me about home. And your family.'

'Well, my mother died when I was four and I was brought up by my aunt. She wears purple hats, reads the tarot and gets stuck into the gin.'

He laughs. 'And your father?'

'He's a bit weird too, but in a different way. He's a scientist, more at home in the world of quarks and black holes than the world of humans.'

'Go on.'

She shoots him a quick glance to make sure he isn't just being polite, but he still appears attentive so she talks about the Brindabella Ranges near her home in Canberra. Skies that seem to stretch forever, bush with its pungent smell of eucalypts, trees whose trunks are darkly knotted or festooned with banners of peeling bark – vermilion, orange and grey. She describes rocks so ancient they make her feel as if they might lead her to the centre of the earth. And then she is silent, taken aback by her own intensity.

'I went to a convent school,' she says at last.

'You are Catholic?'

She hesitates. 'Sort of.'

'I am Catholic. Lapsed, I think.'

She smiles. 'My mother was very lapsed! But then she died, and a bit later my father sent me to this convent so I'd learn to behave. My aunt was angry. She said she could look after me perfectly well.'

'How did your mother die?'

All the old rumpled memories return. She pulls her hair over her eyes.

'She drowned. In the lake. We think she fell in. My father still blames himself.' She swallows. 'Sometimes I think he resents me because I don't look like her.'

'What did she look like?'

'Blonde and beautiful.'

'And you? Aren't you beautiful? I think you are.'

She blushes. 'I wish I were.'

'You are like a rocket that goes flying into the sky and gives out a beautiful red light.'

'And then falls? I don't want to fall.'

'No. It stays in the air forever.'

'Promise?' she laughs.

'I promise.'

'And I'm like a beautiful red rocket? Really?' She preens.

'Yes, your nose is peeling,' and he laughs as she jumps on him, shouting, 'Bastard, bloody bastard!' She is a wanton woman and proud of it. He holds her chin in his hand and says her eyes are tiger's eyes. She likes this. He says her hair is bright as the flame trees in his mother's garden. She likes this too. She explains that she is a feminist and a revolutionary.

He interrupts her and asks how many people she has killed.

'I kill them all the time.'

He burrows his head in her belly, making her crease up with laughter.

'I eat white revolutionaries, unless they are on my side.'

'I am,' she giggles, 'I am.'

'I am angry about injustice,' he says, pulling a little apart from her.

'So I have noticed.' For a moment she looks at him critically. She doesn't want him to look different or be different. A thread is spinning between them and she is afraid it might break.

'It's not a joke,' he says sternly. 'One day we shall see the end of white minority rule in Africa. It's happening. Mozambique has just won independence after centuries of Portuguese rule. When the Portuguese left, the illiteracy rate was over ninety percent.'

Hannah pulls up the sheet so that it covers the bottom half of her body. 'There was a lot of fighting, though, wasn't there?'

'Of course. For eleven years. My father always hopes for peaceful transitions from white to black. He's an idealist. He says revolutionaries have to be dreamers as well as men of fire.'

She kicks him. 'Women are revolutionaries too.'

He ignores her.

'Why are you called Ezekiel?'

He laughs. 'From the Bible. Remember?'

She shakes her head vehemently. In spite of her schooling, she has little knowledge of the Bible.

'God sent Ezekiel to the children of Israel to tell them to behave. He used heavy language, telling them they'd be punished by their fathers eating sons and sons eating fathers. Stoning and burning. Fire and famine. Baldness.' He grins as he pats the top of his thick dark hair. 'God also said to beware of foolish prophets who lie and seduce with false hope, who say there is peace when there isn't, who have seen nothing because they have not gone up into the gaps.'

She looks puzzled. 'The gaps?'

'The high places and the hard places, the spaces in between, where nothing is sure. When I was growing up, my father used to say we have to take risks if we want to make life worthwhile. There are no formulas.'

She was silent for a moment while she considered this. 'Is your father a minister?'

He laughs. 'Heavens no, he says the Church is corrupt. He's a poet and a professor. Joseph Emmanuel Chimeme. There's another bit in Ezekiel about a man who is clothed in linen and has a writer's inkhorn. That's my father.'

'Does he see you as a prophet?'

'I hope not. I am an academic. An academic with an eye to politics.'

'And your mother?'

'She is called Ruth and she has five children. Four of them are girls. My mother is a good-looking woman, generous and smart. She thinks I am the finest son in the whole world. Which of course I am. And that I can do no wrong. About which she is also right.' He gives her a broad grin.

'Is she also Rwandan?'

'She is.'

'Then why did they send you to study in England?'

'They wanted me to have the best education, the best of everything. They sent me to school in England for my last two years, and then to university.'

'So that's why your accent's so good. Better than mine. And you don't often swear.'

He laughs. 'My mother would be shocked. She's an Anglophile. I don't know what she'd make of you, Australian girl.'

Hannah does not care, at this moment, what his mother might make of her. She pulls him down, wrapping herself around him, but he loosens her hold and kisses her on the forehead, her cheeks and on her nose, as if he were kissing a small child.

'Time to get up.' He rolls off the bed and picks up his blue and white cloth from the floor. Then he waves and is gone.

For a while she does not move. Her mind drifts lazily back to the past few astonishing days. She has no desire to analyse them, rather she wants to let the experiences float through her. She wriggles her feet. They are dirty. She enjoys this.

Only two days remained before they had to go home. Days in which Hannah wanted to make love again, but Ezekiel did not come to her, and she was too proud to go to him. Days in which they finalised their research, leaving Waldo with material for an outline from which to develop a fuller script. Days in which there was a sense of endings and beginnings, of one bubble of experience dissolving and another one taking its place. Theodore King breezed into Addis Ababa from Somalia, invited them to milkshakes but not to Turkish baths; the young man who had been trying to inspect his World Bank tea and coffee plantation finally secured a flight, but the plane crashed and he was killed; Patsy Grimbold's distrust of Hannah intensified, which Hannah reflected was probably wise; and Beverley, the young woman with the pink lipstick and a penchant for hangings and cappuccinos, confided in Waldo that she had decided to become a journalist, and could he give her a job? He declined. Solomon Lulu took a pinch of snuff, sneezed, and said Beverley reminded him of a rhinoceros in full charge.

And Hannah? Hannah did not want endings. Did not want to say goodbye to Ezekiel, nor to stop working with Waldo, nor to relinquish her life of intrigue.

'Can I come with you on the actual shoot?' she asked Waldo. It was a question she had asked several times before, and Waldo had several times told her it mightn't be possible. In all probability he would have to use a BBC crew.

She burned with indignation. It's not fair, she thought. I'll show them. I'll have them begging to take me on.

On Friday morning they gathered in the hotel lobby to farewell Ezekiel, who was leaving a day earlier than Hannah and Waldo. He was flying to Rwanda to see his mother, his father and his four sisters, but had hoped to be available for Waldo when he returned to London. Waldo was jovial, patting everyone, including Solomon Lulu, on the back, making jokes, passing round his depleted store of barley sugars. All Hannah wanted was Ezekiel to say he would see her again.

At the last minute he drew her aside, kissed her on both

cheeks and handed her a small blue enamel box. Inside, wrapped in blue tissue paper, lay a silver Coptic cross and chain.

'You like it?' he asked.

'I love it!'

'You will remember me from it?'

'Of course.'

'It's a souvenir.'

A souvenir? What did he mean, a souvenir? It sounded like a pay-off.

'I do not need a souvenir.' She considered hurling the box at his feet, but instead stuffed it in the pocket of her jeans and strode off, waving dismissively at the three men. She passed between two marble columns, spied a doorway on her left, entered, slamming the door behind her, and found herself gazing at a large mop. She stood in the broom cupboard until she decided it was safe to reappear. When she ventured out, the hotel manager was staring at her over his rimless spectacles, a puzzled look on his face.

She went to the market and bought her own kind of souvenir. A love potion – a crumpled cone of thin brown paper, no bigger than a teabag, and inside a pinch of coagulated powder that smelled like camel dung. It came with a written testimonial: 'Make your lover pant with desire. Guaranteed by the Queen of Sheba'.

# *three*

Six weeks later, Hannah sat drinking coffee outside a tall thin hotel in Paris. The hotel, which was strung with washing, was called La Puce – the flea. It was built above a café which had small round tables on the pavement, and larger tables with dark red leather banquettes inside. Cut-glass mirrors advertised Dubonnet, Cinzano and Pernod. Mounds of croissants were imprisoned under high glass domes. The coffee smelt strong and welcoming.

Although it was cold, she had elected to sit outside, where she had been waiting for almost two hours, feeling groggy from the flight. She had been surrounded on the plane by the family from hell, who ate and drank and belched for twenty-four hours. Her backpack, propped against the table leg, kept tripping people as they passed by. Her clothes weren't warm enough, and she was wondering if she had been wise to come.

After Ethiopia, life in Australia had seemed drab and un-eventful. She felt caught in a limbo between that first tantalising glimpse of work and, now, nothing. Her father barely noticed that she had been away, let alone come home. Aunt D, who had never married and was still living with her brother, beamed with delight at Hannah's return, but Hannah found drinking cups of tea in the kitchen inglenook scant compensation for the excitement she had just left. She shivered and complained that it was cold, even when it wasn't. She played endless tapes of African music and mooched around the big dark house, picking up books and putting them down again. She had never liked this house, never liked its grave silences, its heavy velvet curtains, moquette chairs and sofas, stained-glass lamps. Now she found them repulsive. She went to bed early and rose late. Each morning she hung about the front door to see if the postman was coming.

She received the odd postcard. One from Ezekiel with a picture of an airport hotel in Johannesburg, signed 'Love, Ezekiel'. One from Waldo featuring the head and shoulders of the Queen of Sheba, signed 'Love, Waldo'.

One night she rang Waldo, noting that it would be five-thirty in the morning in London. With a bit of luck she might wake him. She did. But when he stirred himself out of his sleep, he sounded delighted.

'Hannah, we've just heard that the series will go ahead. I'll be responsible for Ethiopia and maybe one of the other sections. Good job they made up their minds. They were taking so long I was thinking of going to the commercials.'

'Would they have been interested?'

'Only with lots more starving black babies.'

'Don't be cynical.'

'Just realistic.'

'If I come over, will you give me work?'

'Difficult.'

She tweaked the ear of the cat, asleep on her lap. 'I am difficult.'

'I know.'

'But you'd try?'

'Maybe.' His voice softened. 'It was only supposed to be work experience, Hannah. And yes, you were good, so if anything further does come up, of course I'll keep you in mind.'

'Blah, blah, blah.'

'Don't be like that. I mean it.'

'Maybe.' She hesitated. 'How's Ezekiel?'

A silence. 'He's in Paris. Finishing his doctorate.' Was she imagining it or did Waldo's voice tighten?

'Do you have his address?'

'I do.'

'Can I have it?'

'You may.'

She took down the address in her large, still childish hand and stowed it away in one of her Indian patchwork bags. It made her feel worse, not better.

Most of her friends were still away on vacation, but she finally arranged to meet Bella. It was raining and Hannah drove too quickly, squealing round corners, slamming on the brakes. The bar smelled of damp socks, cigarette smoke and beer. Umbrellas had dripped on the floor. Bella was wearing new boots under a long purple skirt and had tied her hair back in a ponytail. She held Hannah at arm's length.

'About time. Thought we'd lost you to Africa.'

Hannah took a swig of beer. 'I had jet lag.'

'Jet lag, my foot, something's happened to you. You haven't fallen for anyone, have you?'

She made it sound as if Hannah had contracted the plague. Blokes were currently out, lesbians in.

Hannah tipped her seat backwards and contrived to look weary. 'Maybe.'

They lit cigarettes, drawing deeply.

'African bloke?' asked Bella, scrutinising her friend.

Hannah looked poe-faced and then decided to laugh.

Bella wiped her hand on the back of her mouth. 'Well, you know what Gertrude Stein said. A bloke is a bloke is a bloke is a bloke.' She shook with laughter at her own joke.

Hannah gave a wan smile. For once she found it difficult to talk to Bella and she was reluctant to tell her about Ezekiel, it all seemed so unreal. She left the bar after only one drink.

As Hannah's ennui deepened, her aunt showed increasing concern. She pinned her down one morning in the kitchen when Hannah was toying with a cup of black coffee and Aunt D was loading a large plate of porridge with brown sugar and butter.

'It's only a knob,' she said as she put the butter away in the fridge. 'Well, out with it, who are you missing?'

Hannah shrugged.

'The English bloke, Waldo?'

Hannah was silent.

'The African bloke, then?'

Hannah pulled her hair over her eyes. 'How d'you know it's any bloke?'

Aunt D leaned across the table and patted her niece's hand. A smile crumpled in her kind face. 'I don't. I'm guessing.'

Hannah wriggled. It was late February and hot. The white painted wood of the kitchen chair was sticking to her bare legs. She scratched at a mosquito bite on her arm.

'Where is he?'

'Paris. He's moved to Paris.'

'Why?'

'To study.'

Aunt D sighed. 'Hannah, you know what happened to the girl who did nothing?'

Hannah shook her head.

'Nothing. I've got some money stashed away. Take it, and go.'

Ever since Hannah could remember, her aunt had been her good companion, rather than her substitute mother. Hannah had shortened her name from Doreen to D when she was learning to read. 'D,' she had said firmly, pointing to her alphabet book and then her aunt. 'D.' Aunt D had loved her, protected her, and led her down the pathways of magic and fantasy. If Hannah was ever bullied at school, which wasn't often, Aunt D would plot the most heinous forms of revenge.

'Fix 'em,' she'd say, 'fix 'em with the evil eye. Oh never mind, you don't have an evil eye, just squint. Or make them drink witch's brew. Toad spit and frog spit and the hairs of a goat, mixed up like a milkshake, and a pinch of gravel at the very end.'

Sometimes Aunt D would not let Hannah walk on the pavement lines. Other times, they must touch every ninth paling in a picket fence, or look out for white horses or men with three ears. When Hannah was sixteen and about to leave for Sydney on a school excursion, Aunt D took out one of her many large bags and shook a cascade of silver medallions onto the kitchen table – St Christopher medallions to protect Hannah from harm. They were a job lot that Aunt D had won at the races when one of her tipster friends had been unable to honour his debts.

'Choose!' she said dramatically, as the medallions glittered and Hannah peered in bewilderment at identical faces of a smirking St Christopher.

'But they're all the same.'

'No, lovey, one of them's got your mark on it.'


Hannah fingered her St Christopher medallion as she waited in an unknown Paris street outside this unknown hotel. She had written a postcard to her aunt saying, 'Wish me luck,' a postcard to Bella saying, 'Fuck all men,' and a postcard to her father in which she said she was about to visit the Orangerie and the Louvre.

When Ezekiel at last came strolling out of the glass doors of La Puce wearing a black duffle coat, his hands thrust in his pockets, for one moment she didn't recognise him. This man's hair was Afro. Then she saw his familiar long scarf dangling round his neck and hurled herself at him, almost knocking over a large and grumpy waiter.

Ezekiel looked bewildered.

Oh God, thought Hannah, disentangling herself, he's appalled to see me.

But then he held out his hands. 'Hannah! What are you doing here? I thought you were in Australia.'

Hannah stammered her reply. 'I'm hoping to work for Waldo.'

He sat down next to her. 'But Waldo isn't in Paris!'

'No, no, he's in London – that is, I *am* hoping to work for Waldo ...' Her voice trailed away. 'He says the famine series will go ahead,' she said, looking anxiously at Ezekiel.

He ordered two coffees and sat down, leaning back in his

chair, studying her as she prattled out an account of her journey.

'Where are you staying?' he interrupted.

She ignored his question. 'Is your doctorate going well?'

'Okay.' His eyes narrowed. 'Hannah, where are you staying?'

She took a deep breath. 'Can I stay with you?'

He didn't answer. The pause was so long, she wondered if she should get up and leave. She was bracing herself when he gave a wide smile. 'It will be my pleasure.'

Her heart stopped feeling as if it might drop to the pavement. She no longer noticed the cold, or that it might rain, or that a dog had just pissed on the leg of her chair and her boot. She unwrapped a sugar and dipped it in her coffee, then she reached back and untied her hair, letting it fall over her shoulders. She couldn't keep the smile off her face.


Ezekiel's room was at the very top of the hotel. In the tiny lift she could feel his cold breath on her face, and the closeness of his body. She panicked, but it was too late to turn back and when Ezekiel unlocked his door she followed him inside.

The room was small and wedge-shaped, with grimy windows, a narrow balcony, torn lace curtains, and an iron double bed, neatly made. A brown cardboard suitcase sat on top of a rickety wardrobe, books were piled up on a desk, alongside a cheap, shiny souvenir of the Eiffel Tower. Hannah accidentally kicked a waste-paper basket, which lurched sideways, spilling out discarded scraps of paper, cigarette butts, orange peel, half a croissant, the brown and rotting cores of apples. The air smelled stale.

'It's not very big but it could be worse.' He sounded apologetic.

Hannah didn't think it was very big either, the bed seemed to dominate the room. She began questioning what she had done and, more to the point, what she was going to do. For the first few minutes she talked nonstop while she put her pack on the bed, took it off again, moved restlessly round the room, asked inconsequential questions.

Ezekiel took hold of her. 'You're making me giddy,' he said, and kissed her gently on the mouth, but by now her apprehension was so great that she flung herself backward on the bed, pulling him down on top of her.

Better get it over with, she thought as she chucked the pillows on the floor. She kissed Ezekiel with an intensity she wasn't feeling but hoped would materialise. And then she suddenly stopped, fearful. What if he didn't really want her here but was just being polite? What if he got up and left her like the time before? She pushed him away and went to stash her backpack on top of the wardrobe, even though it clearly wouldn't fit.

Ezekiel watched her with amusement. 'Hey, you haven't even unpacked, so what's this business putting your bag away?'

'Let's go out,' said Hannah. 'You can show me Paris.'

Outside, the rain had arrived, lashing the streets, filling the gutters, causing people to scuttle from one awning to another, umbrellas tangling as they ran. For the rest of the day Hannah and Ezekiel walked aimlessly, getting soaked to the skin, coming home to dry off, then out again to the banks of the Seine where most of the little stalls were closed because it was Monday. Her feet were sore, her teeth chattering with cold, her hair hung down her back like seaweed. They held hands, but their hands froze against each other. They tried to talk, in sporadic, disconnected sentences, but mostly they walked in awkward silence.

The majority of bistros and restaurants were also closed – how could Hannah have known that Monday was not a good day to arrive? At nine o'clock that night, when she was dropping from fatigue, they found an Algerian café open. The seats were close together, the noise excruciating, and when Ezekiel ordered couscous she didn't know what it was. She downed two glasses of red wine in quick succession.

He sat opposite, telling her he was glad he'd chosen to switch his doctorate from London to Paris.

'Why?' Her head was swimming.

'I have many more African friends here. The city is more dynamic intellectually. It's more tolerant. Black is in if you're an African.' He paused. 'It's out if you're Arab.'

He wiped his mouth on a paper napkin and grinned. 'It's the jazz. They love jazz, black heart of Africa beating in the Bronx and now Paris, all that sort of thing. Existentialism, structuralism, deconstructionism – it's all here. More interesting to talk about than the weather.'

'Okay, okay,' she said, lost for words. 'But couldn't you find that in England?'

He looked bored. 'I've never liked life with the English. They're condescending.'

Hannah screwed up her mouth. 'Waldo isn't.'

'Waldo's an exception. The rest of them are surprised that you're even educated. They say, "Oh gosh, you went to Oxford, or the LSE, jolly good," but deep down they still think of you as a shoeshine boy.'

'You exaggerate.'

He ignored her, drumming his fingers on the table. 'I've met an American woman, Susan George, who lives in Paris and who's working on a book called *How the Other Half Dies*. She was involved in the last World Food Conference about the causes of global hunger and says only the poor go hungry.' As he spoke Ezekiel stabbed the white paper tablecloth with his fork, bending the tines, just as he had done in Ethiopia.

'They don't need population control or the green revolution. They need justice. Democratic government. With that they could resolve most of their problems themselves. Do you understand? No, you don't understand.'

'Yes, I do understand. But don't be so angry.' Her eyes filled with tears.

Ezekiel lit a cigarette and drew deeply. 'No, you don't understand or you'd be excited, not miserable.'

'I want to understand.' His tobacco smoke was making her retch, her eyes were smarting, her head spun from jet lag. She needed to escape but she did not know how or where to. 'Let's go somewhere else for coffee,' she suggested.

They walked to a bar round the corner. The pavements shone with rain and it was too wet to be outside, too cold. They sat side by side on a banquette and she tensed the muscles of her thighs, trying to keep from touching his. Behind the bar, a record played on an old-fashioned radiogram; a woman was singing about *l'aigle noir* – the black eagle.

'It's Barbara,' Ezekiel told her. 'She's all the rage in Paris. She's singing about me. I'm the black eagle.'

Back at the hotel she heard him pissing loudly in the toilet on the landing outside the bedroom and the intimacy of the sound repelled her. She pulled off her clothes as quickly as possible, leaving on a singlet, and climbed under the layers of blankets. She faced the wall, bedclothes pulled to her chin. When he climbed in beside her the bedsprings squeaked and the mattress dipped. He put his hands on her back and she stiffened.

74

'I'm tired,' she mumbled.

He was breathing into her neck, her shoulders, stubble grazing her skin, hands running down her back towards her legs, between her legs. She jerked away.

'I'm tired,' she repeated, feeling his cock stiff and hard against her, angry at its insistence, angry at the mess in which she found herself. 'Stop. Leave me alone.'

He grabbed her protesting hand.

'Leave me.' Her voice was loud, she was pushing him away.

'Okay, okay.' He heaved over on his side and they lay back to back.

Twice in the night when he tried to come close to her she made grunting noises and moved herself to the edge of the mattress. The wire bedframe sagged and she kept rolling back to the middle, back to the warmth of his strange, threatening body. Eventually she was reduced to holding the edge of the bedframe as if it were a crevice and she a mountain climber.

She slept fitfully. Once she woke with her head pounding, frightened she was going to be sick. She longed for a glass of water but was fearful of getting up in case she disturbed him and he wanted her again. He appeared to sleep well.

When she woke at daylight she hastily pulled the bedclothes over her head.

'Hey woman,' said Ezekiel, gently pulling the covers down and nudging her shoulder. He was perched on one elbow, gazing down at her. She took in his smooth, chiselled features, the high cheekbones, the light brown sheen of his body. But his eyes were darkly opaque and she had no idea what he thought or felt.

'Hey woman,' he repeated.

She adjusted the sheet and started counting the reasons why

she should immediately leave. His arrogance; the fact that he called her hey woman; his assumption that she would have sex with him (why could he not see she had changed her mind about that?); his souvenir of the Eiffel Tower, tasteless and cheap. She turned to tell him she would leave unless things got much better, unless he were more considerate, unless they could just be friends, then spied an ant crawling over the bed covers, a black speck moving slowly between small pink daisies and deep pink leaves. The ant was an omen. If Ezekiel harmed the ant in any way she would leave. This was how she would make up her mind. This was what she had learned from Aunt D. When in doubt, ask the gods.

She watched the ant as it zigzagged erratically towards Ezekiel's hand, ran over his outstretched palm and started moving to the top of his index finger.

Ezekiel held up his finger, brought it close to his face and inspected the ant. 'Little ant,' he said solemnly, 'the lady is unhappy. What shall I do?' He put the ant carefully on the side table and said gently to Hannah, 'Hey woman, I am glad you came. That was really brave.' He touched her hair and said he loved its dark red wildness. He murmured soft crooning sounds in her ear, he stroked her neck and her shoulders, saying, 'Let me be loving, I want to be loving,' and her body began humming with such pleasure that she forgot about the ant and didn't mind being called hey woman any more.


Hannah stayed on with Ezekiel in Paris. She had some French from school and university, enough to hold down a job with the American–French journal *Réalités*, where she helped an Hungarian economist with articles on world population written in English. She typed for him and did his basic research. Most of the time she worked at his apartment in the old Jewish quarter of the Marais, and on her way home enjoyed its bookshops and galleries, and places that sold exquisite handmade paper and writing books with beautiful leather covers. All she could afford were two Florentine pencils. Their wood was a soft pink and they were covered in paper marbled in aqua, rose and palest yellow.

In the mornings, whenever the economist and his elegant wife left the apartment, she would raid their fridge for hothouse grapes, fat salamis, crumbly white goat's cheese, Belgian chocolates. She would make up a plate and eat in their handsome sitting room, pretending she was rich. The fact that she might get caught added to the zest of her feast.

She also took French lessons at the Alliance Française.

'*Allez, tu veux un petit* after eight, *là*?' she asked Ezekiel one night, a mischievous glint in her eyes.

He looked puzzled, particularly when she unzipped his jeans and began teasing his cock, first with her hands and then with her mouth.

'After eight,' she grinned, stopping for a moment and looking up. 'English dinner mints – latest Franglais or slang for blow-job.'

'How do *you* know?' he asked, sucking in his breath as she took the whole of him into her mouth.

Next morning, when they were leaving the hotel together, he tapped her briskly on the shoulder.

'Who told you after eight means a blow-job?'

'My professor at the Alliance, he often talks about after-dinner treats,' she said demurely.

Their relationship quickly became a fucking game, in bed

and out. Sometimes they were tender and gentle with each other, at others they pounded as if they wanted to achieve oblivion, so that she was left beached and exhausted before she stumbled back for more. But this was not a victim game, they were in it together.

They built up a domestic intimacy that Hannah at first found threatening, then reassuring. They shared the *Herald Tribune* over breakfast in the café below, dined in the evenings at cheap restaurants and drank even cheaper Algerian wine, went to jazz dives, cinemas, book stalls and galleries. On Sundays they explored the markets, or took a train into the country. When Saigon fell at the end of April and Vietnamese tanks knocked down the gates of the presidential palace they watched it on the television set in the bar of the café. They joined in rallies protesting the treatment of workers from Algieria. In early June they met up with Waldo when he came to Paris to meet with a French production company which was helping with footage in the Sahel. He said stuffily that the series was going quite well, thank you, and what a pity they weren't there for any of the actual shoot. When he left, Hannah felt a moment of panic that her career had also gone out the door.

One warm afternoon later that month, Hannah lay on the small strip of floor beside the casement window, her head resting on her arms, pondering her situation in Paris. Her only friends were a young white South African woman who had changed her name from Dorothy to Dusty and lived with an Angolan revolutionary, and Josephine, an English au pair from Bournemouth who was homesick and spent most of her evenings weeping unless Hannah cheered her up by playing Beatles tunes on her mouth organ.

Ezekiel's friends were mostly African. They flitted in and

out of the hotel at all hours. Ezekiel said that their meetings were political and that it was safer if Hannah stayed away. Violence from political opponents was always a possibility and he didn't want her endangered. He also said that as she wasn't African she wouldn't understand. She found this insulting but he was obdurate.

Now she kicked the leg of his chair and said, 'I need more friends.'

He looked down from his writing and smiled at her. 'I'm your friend.'

When she berated him for not talking to her he touched her and said simply, 'But I love you.'

He asked her one night what it felt like to make love with a black man.

'That sort of conversation is boring,' she said sharply.

He stroked her hair absent-mindedly. 'Let me tell you what it's like for me to make love with a white woman.'

She turned her head. She wasn't sure she wanted to hear this. He kicked off the bedclothes, his voice intent.

'There's this book by a guy from Martinique, Frantz Fanon, he's a black guy, a psychiatrist, and the book's called *Black Skin, White Masks*. It's about what it's like to be black in a world where whites hold the power. Where we wear the livery that white men sew for us. And where to get acceptance we find ourselves trying to be more and more white. We go to white schools and white universities –'

'But –'

'It's a wound. It won't heal.'

'But!' shouted Hannah, kneeling on the bed, her face flushed. 'Okay, so it's not fair, but in the long run how you feel is up to you.'

He appeared to ignore her. 'And what's the best way of proving you're worthy of white love, eh? Find a white woman, someone who'll love you like a white man.'

Her eyes sharpened in anger – tiger's eyes, he'd once told her. 'So I give you the white seal of approval, is that what you're trying to tell me?'

She moved to get out of bed but he pulled her back, his hand easily encompassing the slenderness of her wrist as she tried to wrestle free. She said, 'If that's why you love me, it's horrible.'

He released her and she rubbed her wrist.

'That's not why I love you, but it's sometimes how I feel,' he said.

They glowered at each other in silence for a few minutes before he shifted to his side of the bed and lit a cigarette, ignoring the greying white ash that fell on the greying white sheets.

Hannah flicked the ash away. 'Being a victim isn't going to help.'

'I am *not* a victim!' He got up and thrust his legs into his jeans, pulled on a shirt and left, slamming the door. She remembered how she had slammed the broom cupboard in Ethiopia.

She dressed slowly and went downstairs to the café. There was no sign of Ezekiel. She ordered a citron pressé and sat with her forehead creased in a frown.

Ezekiel came in half an hour later. He pulled up a chair, scraping the legs and setting her teeth on edge. He said, 'You know, you really don't understand.'

'You always say that, but I do understand.'

'No, you don't, how could you?'

'But it's important to try,' she insisted. 'I want to try.'

It was a Saturday morning in October, with white clouds scudding across a greying sky. Ezekiel stood by the window of their little room reading a letter. Down below, a boy in a red jumper was jumping into puddles of rain. Hannah had just returned from the markets where she had bought flowers and fruit, and was arranging anemones in a glass jam jar. The flowers hung limply, hiding their brilliant beauty – their petals of red, purple and blue, their dark furry stamens. A recalcitrant purple anemone kept falling out of the jar and she turned to Ezekiel, waving it under his nose.

'Is that a letter from home?'

He didn't answer.

'Is it?'

'Uh-huh.'

'You look worried. What's it about?'

'It's too hard to explain.'

'Tell me. Tell me everything.' Her voice had a wailing sound which she did not like.

'It's from one of my sisters. She says my cousin has just lost his job at the university. They say staff cuts, but it's because he's a Tutsi. My father says it's okay but my mother is scared.'

'Why?'

'Because the Hutus want to get rid of us.'

She raised her eyebrows.

He began pacing the room. 'Rwanda is made up of Tutsi and Hutu people, I've told you that, and until colonisation – from the end of last century – we always lived peacefully together. We shared the same land, the same language. We were mostly Christian, and we intermarried.

'The Tutsis were hereditary rulers – we had an ancient monarchy – and as we traditionally raised livestock, we were

*81*

generally better off. But we were the minority, less than ten percent. When the white colonisers came, they singled us out for special favours.'

'Why?'

'Because in darkest Africa, hah hah, the more we could look and behave like Europeans, the better for us. So we Tutsis did rather well. Missionaries thought of us as Hamitic Semites, or African Jews, even though we were Christian. Never mind. We were tall and thin, with narrow noses and light skin. Almost acceptable. Whereas the poor old Hutus were short and squat with flat noses and dark skin – Negroid. Our Belgian masters separated us out, made us carry identity cards. Divide and rule. No wonder the Hutus began hating us. We became the scape-goat for all the frustrations caused by foreign rule. Then, in the late fifties, a Hutu rovolt killed many Tutsis and sent thousands into exile. So now it was the turn of the Hutus. Less than two years after independence in 1962, over half the Tutsi population of Rwanda was in exile and the issue of our return has plagued Rwandan politics ever since. There was a new wave of perse-cution against the Tutsis only two years ago, so the threat of exile hangs over us all the time.'

She felt a moment of panic and held him tight, tracked her finger across his chest. 'Ezekiel, when you leave Paris we will stay together, won't we?' She could not imagine being without him. She studied his face, memorising his features. She touched him, memorising his feel.

And then, a month later, in mid-November, as she was pulling on a pair of long woollen stockings, she heard a cry from the room next door where Ezekiel had gone to take a phone call. She rushed in to find him collapsed in a chair, a shocked expression on his face.

'My father,' he whispered. 'They've murdered my father.'

A jolt ran through her. 'What?'

Tears ran down his cheeks. 'Why did they do that? He was a gentle man, a kind man.' His eyes were filled with horror. 'They beat him to death. With clubs. When he was coming out of the university. Before he had time to call for help.' His nose was running, he reached blindly for a handkerchief. She held him close and felt herself fill with tenderness. It flowed with an abundance that surprised and pleased her, but her calmness was short-lived.

After a while he took a shuddering breath. 'I will have to go home. I will have to leave you and Paris.'


On their last night together she took his head in her hands and shook it so violently that he had to jerk it free. Afterwards she cried like a child.

'*Loshe, loshe,*' the women had called. Hunger, hunger.

'Hannah, I love you. But I am needed at home.'

Words singing in the darkness. She reached out to catch them but they slipped through her fingers.

She said goodbye at Orly airport, a crumpled handkerchief in her hand, her nose red from the cold, hair flying about her shoulders. In the shout and clatter of the airport bar, people pushed against her, smelling of cigarettes and damp wool. Ezekiel ordered coffee and cognac.

'To keep out the cold,' he said.

'You won't be cold in Africa.'

'No, no.'

The inane, staccato conversation of parting. In this public exposure of their private sorrow, the world contracted until there was only her knowledge that Ezekiel was leaving.

He rose and pulled her to her feet. 'I'll come back, Hannah. But now we need to say goodbye.'

She cried out, protesting that his plane hadn't yet been called, but he was already walking away. After a few paces, he turned and waved.

She tried to smile but she could not.


In their empty room she picked up objects and put them down again, finding a sock of Ezekiel's, throwing away a pile of cigarette butts. She would write immediately. She sat at the green painted table by the window and pushed the jam jar of dead flowers to one side. The water was beginning to smell.

Later she went for a long walk by the riverbank, wondering how she could have become so dependent on another human being. Weeks passed and she did not hear from him. She rang constantly but could not get through. She bit her fingernails, she did not sleep at night. When she telephoned home, her father answered.

'Paris must be costing you a pretty penny.'

She bridled. 'I'm earning. Where's Aunt D?'

'In Sydney, staying with a friend. Try next week.'

Her father's voice was distant. She had written very little since she'd been in Paris and she guessed he was hurt. She wanted to say, I'm lonely, but the words wouldn't come.

She tried Waldo.

'Waldo, Ezekiel's gone home. His father has been killed.'

'Oh God, poor sod, he lived with that possibility and dreaded it.'

'I know. I'm worried about him and I'm miserable. I wondered if I could come over to London?'

'It's Christmas,' Waldo said, after a pause.

'That'll be good, I like Christmas.'

'I hate it.'

'I'll cheer you up. Will you be there?'

'Yes. I'll be here.'

She waited for him to say it would be all right to come.

'Well?' she said at last.

'If you want, you can come and stay.'

After she hung up she sat by the window and tried to play the Barbara song about *l'aigle noir.*

'Hello, Australia' said Waldo at the airport, giving her an awkward hug. 'It's jolly good to see you again.'

Waldo didn't sound as if it was jolly good and Hannah guessed he had cold feet about her visit. He bustled her into his car. London was revving up. Plastic reindeer hurtled along the length of Regent Street, Father Christmases heaved with merriment inside department stores. At night carol singers would huddle on street corners, and all serious news would be swallowed up in the frenzy of Christmas.

Waldo lived in a comfortable top-floor flat in a Regency house in Kensington. 'You can stay here as long as you like,' he said when they arrived. 'But there's one condition. Whenever I am working I am not to be disturbed. Under no circumstances. I'll be rude and horrid and you'll wish you'd never come. Apart from that, make yourself at home.'

Books and papers spilled from shelves and tables, leaned like termite nests from darkly polished floors. There were two typewriters in the flat. Cans of film in racks. Pictures lining the walls. A portrait of a woman with a long sad face that Waldo said proudly was an early Lucian Freud; two abstracts with brilliantly coloured shapes by someone called Heron, she thought he said; and African tribal art. At least she recognised that. Wine was stacked in the hall. The kitchen was well stocked with tins of marrons and jars of peaches in brandy; spices like saffron, turmeric, mace and juniper; lemons pickled in salt, and arborio rice, coffee beans and several kinds of tea. Her aunt's kitchen was more likely to have peanut butter and Marmite, jelly crystals and tins of fruit salad, Nescafé and billy tea.

Hannah watched Waldo grind some coffee. 'Are you rich?' she asked.

Waldo stopped turning the brass handle of the grinder for a moment. It was made of poplar wood and he had bought it in a market near Assisi. He chuckled. 'Not rich, but sometimes I make good money, and when I do I spend it.'

'And when you're poor?' She picked up a coffee bean and crunched it.

'I also spend it. My parents are poor. I won a scholarship to university.'

He jerked the brass handle and turned it, hard and fast, so that the noise drowned out any chance of further conversation.


On her first night in London he took her to a restaurant called The Ark in Notting Hill Gate and said, 'Let's celebrate.'

She wasn't sure what they were celebrating, and sat restlessly while Waldo beamed at her approvingly. His mood had eased during the day and he was back to his usual cheerful self. He ordered snails and tucked his napkin into his shirt front, enjoying each garlicky morsel with delight.

'Last time I ate snails was with Theodore King,' he said somewhat apologetically.

'That bring-me-a-dying-child man? Oh Waldo, how could you?'

'Easily. We were at a Feast and Famine Conference in Paris. On the first day we all ate bowls of white rice, on the second day it was brown rice, and on the third and final day we had escargot, lobsters and pheasant. The old boy was worried about his ulcers, his wife's arthritis, and his son Dean's elopement with a Bunny Girl. I almost became fond of him.'

On the second night, Waldo offered to cook Hannah injera and wot. He produced a huge flat tray, apologising for having to make square injera, not round. Hannah watched the pale dough bubble and rapidly cook. The wot was simmering away in a cast-iron dish on top of the stove, filling the kitchen with an exquisite aroma.

Waldo poured cold beer. 'Haile Selassie died in August – did you pick that up in Paris?'

Hannah shook her head. How had she missed hearing that? Ezekiel hadn't mentioned it either.

'You should keep in touch,' Waldo said mildly. 'It's important if you're going to be a journalist that you know what's going on in the world. Or were you too busy with other things?'

She blushed.

'Will you see Ezekiel again?'

Hannah could feel her eyes brimming with tears. 'Yes, oh yes. I hope so.'


Hannah's room at the back of the flat was small, with dark green curtains and a window overlooking a garden square. The trees were bare, and people hurried through the darkening square because of the cold. A narrow divan rested on top of a mound of boxes and cartons, hastily shoved out of sight. The boxes were making the bed sit unevenly on the floor, and as Hannah tried to restack them she found old books and files, and boxes of Waldo's comfort food. Tins of Danish biscuits, Mars Bars, barley sugar and other assorted sweets.

Waldo had just put on a recording of the *Missa Luba* and ambled in to ask if she wanted any dinner. When she teased him about her find, he looked embarrassed.

'Some people drink, some eat jelly-babies.'

'Jelly-babies are probably safer. My mother drank. And drowned.'

'What a rotten thing to happen. You told me she died but you didn't say how.'

'No one ever talked about it. I always blamed my father. He was older and not very loving. Didn't know how to be, I guess. But once, when I was still quite young, I found him crying and holding a picture of her he kept on his bedside table. He was wearing those baggy white underpants and his legs were thin and bony, like a plucked chook's. I laughed at him. I didn't mean to be cruel.' She wiped her eyes with the back of her hands.

'He probably understood.'

Waldo sat on the bed beside her, stroking her hair because he didn't know what else to do. He was wondering if Hannah would laugh at his own underpants, which could certainly be described as baggy.

'He had his microscopes for comfort. I bit my fingernails,' said Hannah after a moment's silence. 'I haven't changed, except now I bite only one and try to save the rest.'

Waldo felt a surge of tenderness. Hannah felt it, too. She took away her hand and got to her feet. Light from a standard lamp shone on her hair so that for a moment it looked as if it were on fire.

She brushed down her brief skirt. 'That's probably why I keep looking for other fathers.'

'If you mean me, thanks.'

She sighed. 'I don't know what I mean. Once when I was seven and tried to climb on my father's knee he pushed me off and said I was too old for that sort of thing. Yet I think he tried. He used to make a slide of my blood every year and keep it, just like other parents make marks on doors. "Hannah, age six." That's what he'd write. The first time he did it, I saw my blood on the slide, watched him seal it and then was furious. I wanted it back again.'

Waldo had been absent-mindedly eating his way through a pack of orange and yellow jelly-babies. 'Is he better now you're older?'

'Not much. Once he told one of his friends that he'd heard I was clever but he couldn't see any signs. I think he just doesn't know how to be a father.'

'I wouldn't have thought Ezekiel was a father figure,' said Waldo crisply.

She laughed. 'No, although he does cut off from me sometimes so I find it hard to know what's really going on.'

'You're not sure of him, are you?'

'Yes I am,' she said. 'He's coming back. He said so.'

'Have you heard from him?'

'His father's just died. Of course I haven't heard from him.'

Hannah was four years old again, sitting up in bed, staring into the darkness. Strange noises had wakened her. The sound of a siren, her father's voice, shouting, the cry of her aunt, footsteps running across the gravel, thumping sounds. She was frightened. Too frightened to get up and open her door. Eventually she curled up in a ball and put a pillow over her head but still she could not sleep.

The following morning her father came into her room with its blue and white wallpaper and said those strange words. 'Your mother is dead.'

Was dead the lamb that she ate for Sunday lunch? Would her mother be eaten? Was dead the kitten who was run over by a car and squashed? Had her mother been squashed? Was dead for this morning only, and would her mother come back that afternoon, swinging into the kitchen with her long fair hair and her eyes as blue as the sea? Her mother sometimes stayed in her room for several days. Was that what her father meant?

Night after night, Hannah had kept a torch under her pillow so that it might light the way in case her mother came home. Night after night, her small thin body hid under the blankets, and her pillow was wet with crying.

That night in London she couldn't sleep, and went into Waldo's room to ask if she could get into bed with him. He was propped up with pillows, his papers neatly laid out on the bedclothes. More papers were stacked up on the bedside table and on the floor. His spectacles were lost somewhere in the folds of his dark blue eiderdown. He was trying to revise the post-production schedule for the famine series, which had already given him countless worries. He had panicked about the shoots. Worried that the film stock would be faulty, the exposures wrong, that the production manager would have forgotten to procure any releases. And there was still that last and final dread, that there would be a hair in the gate of the camera.

When he had produced his first royal television address, several million viewers were treated to the spectacle of one of Waldo's hairs tenderly clinging to the lips of the Queen as she proclaimed, 'My husband and I . . .'

Waldo was therefore not immediately enthralled by Hannah's suggestion. He wanted to work. He wanted to worry. He didn't want to be a mere comfort stop. But Hannah was already climbing in, putting the papers on one side and gratefully burrowing into his warm and comfortable bulk.

They lay for a while in silence, watching the lights of Kensington flicker against the white cotton blinds. Warmth wakened their bodies, which began to send small quiet messages to each other, lazy seductive messages. They rolled into a sleepy kind of lovemaking, so soft Hannah was barely conscious of how it began and when it ended.

When Hannah returned to Paris, the weather was bitter. There was a strange metal heating contraption in the hotel which made alarming noises and seldom worked. On two or three nights she was so cold she lit a fire in the bidet, and then hid the black streaks with a pile of newspapers. Her job had come to an end and so had her money.

Every morning she woke to a narrow square of dismal grey. The windows were grimed, the sheets had that peculiar clamminess of extreme cold. Waves of nausea engulfed her. She tried to imagine the warmth of an Australian summer, the small amber lizards that basked on her walls, the lemon-scented gum tree whose fragrance wafted into her each morning when she woke. She remembered the garden and the hills beyond, her bare feet on the grass. She remembered Jaffas at the movies –

chocolate on the inside, hard and firm, orange on the outside. At the thought of chocolate she was sick into the bidet, and almost too late. Ezekiel had not reappeared. It was time to go home.

She began to pack and found her mouth organ lying under a pile of clothes. She pulled it out and played by the open window 'Mademoiselle From Armentières'.

# PART II

# 1992–1994

# four

December of 1992 and Waldo is sitting on a yellow plastic milk crate at Mogadishu harbour, waiting for the arrival of three thousand United States marines. Their arrival is supposed to be secret – so secret that Waldo is surrounded by large crowds of Somalis.

President Bush had said the marines could save Somalia over Christmas and be home by the end of January. The new world order, Bush had said, in between jogging and playing golf.

'The new world order? Oh yeah, tell that to the marines after they've been there for a few years,' Hannah had quipped when Waldo rang her in Sarajevo to tell her he was going to cover the Somalia story, both for a documentary and for TV news. She was working for a national television program in Sydney and had been going in and out of Bosnia for several months. The line had crackled so badly that her voice sounded like someone talking with a mouthful of nails.

'The new world order,' Waldo mutters again as he swats a

plague of flies swarming on his nose. The heat is intense, he is sweating profusely, and in the scrum he has lost his television crew but found the milk crate. Anxiety pumps through his veins. Everyone else will get the breaks. He will be left with a piece on how the marines taught Somali street kids to sing 'Rudolph The Red-Nosed Reindeer'.

According to official media releases, Operation Restore Hope is the world's first collective commitment to genuine humanitarian intervention. Somalia is starving. The reasons are many and complex. Wars, internal and external; scorched-earth campaigns; debt from high-interest loans; a widespread break-down in law and order. President Barre was overthrown nearly two years earlier, fleeing Mogadishu in women's clothing and leaving competing warlords and clan leaders to carve up the country, killing and looting. Now the UN has decided to take action: under US leadership, the marines are to oversee the safe delivery of aid. Force has been sanctioned where it is necessary.

Waldo is uneasy about the whole operation. George Bush is nearing the end of his presidential term: how much of this mission is due to his desire to go down in history as the man who saved the starving Africans? And how can his advisers possibly think that it will be such a pushover? Never mind the fact that no one is addressing any underlying causes of the famine.

Waldo gets up from his milk crate and rubs his backside. The harbour front stretches in a long and graceful crescent bordered by palm trees, buildings with painted wooden shutters, mosques with minarets. Many have been devastated by the fighting.

'Hey, what we waiting for?' says a pop-eyed Somali man wearing amazing 1970s purple flares. He is chewing miraa, bitter leaves which bring an instant high.

Waldo clears his throat. 'Operation Restore Hope,' he says pompously. 'President Bush says it's God's work and therefore will not fail.'

The Somali man wipes his brow with a handkerchief and adjusts his large sunglasses. 'Okay, but what we waitin' for?'

'The marines.' Waldo is apologetic.

'You mad or what? How come the marines?'

Waldo considers launching into an explanation, then changes his mind. His throat is dry and maybe they are all mad, waiting in this stinking heat for the United States marines. And who thinks of those dinky titles? Operation Restore Democracy for Haiti, Operation Desert Storm for the Gulf War, and now Operation Restore Hope for Somalia. Do they have a marketing man attached to the Pentagon, and what would they call a gun? he wonders. Operation Restore Peace? What was that war poem he had learned at school?

> *To-day we have naming of parts. Yesterday*
> *We had daily cleaning. And tomorrow morning,*
> *We shall have what to do after firing. But to-day,*
> *To-day we have naming of parts.*

A loud cheer erupts from the mass of people in front who are slowly being pushed into the dirty waters of the harbour.

'What's gonna happen now?' asks the man plaintively. 'What's this Operation Restore Hope? Whose hope?'

'Yours, old boy. Thirty thousand troops will be landing to give aid to the starving and to keep the peace.'

The man takes a deep suck on a bottle of purple drink. 'No starving here,' he says in surprise. 'Starving far away, long distance. Why the marines come here?'

'President Bush thought it would be a good idea. Makes better television pictures than many miles away.' Waldo finds himself enacting some inane charade meant to represent an old-fashioned movie cameraman.

The man likes this. 'Then why we wait?'

'President Bush said to hold the secret landing till dawn – prime-time viewing in America.'

'Make war movies?'

'Sure. Just point the camera and shoot.'

The man grins, shakes hands with Waldo and disappears into the crowds. Suddenly he is back, still clutching his purple drink. ''Scuse me. Who is this Bush?'


Midnight. Waldo has cramp. He has found his crew and they have moved to the beach, where the wet sand is freezing his feet.

Dawn. Waldo still has cramp. His whole body is chilled and he is convinced he will catch pneumonia. The light is misty grey and needles of sun prick his eyes; the beach seems full of vague, insubstantial shapes. He is about to pack it in when he hears a series of muffled sounds. His eyes swing back to the dark of the sea where he can make out the silhouettes of half a dozen landing craft. Figures are being lowered into the water. They splash, they swim, and near the shore they rise out of the sea like prehistoric monsters of the deep.

Behind him, Waldo hears the voice of CNN correspondent Barney Cole: 'Marines going ashore in the grey dawn of another African day in Somalia,' he intones as arc lights suddenly flood the entire waterfront and flares shoot into the sky like orange stars. Camera crews are wading into the water to meet the marines wading out. Barney Cole's feet are getting wet and Waldo can hear him swear. Somebody else is swearing. A familiar voice.

'Sweet fucking Jesus, it's the Black and White Minstrel Show.'

Waldo turns to see Daniel Keneally, Magnum photographer from New York, one of the last of the great photojournalists, a man with flowing silver hair and a theatrical red bandanna round his forehead. Waldo waves a hand and returns his gaze to the harbour, screwing up his eyes in disbelief. All soldiers with white faces have had them blackened and the black has streaked.

Waldo groans. On his way back to his billet, he passes a group of twitchy young journalists who are chewing miraa and wearing new white T-shirts branded 'Doing the Mog'. Three thousand media people are already in Mogadishu competing for scarce resources. Several thousand more people are administering aid. And now thousands of marines have arrived to oversee delivery of that aid.

Two weeks later, Waldo emerges from the back door of the large house where he is billeted and sits on a cane chair in a small courtyard filled with banana trees and bougainvillea. The bananas were once lushly green, and the bougainvillea magenta, orange and purple, but now all vegetation is uniformly grey with dust from the bombings.

Until recently, the house belonged to a wealthy Somali merchant, who fled when the fighting began. Every stick of the merchant's furniture was looted and Waldo has ferreted in the markets for a few small items to help make his stay more tolerable. A lumpy but clean mattress, the cane chair, a card table, a wind-up gramophone, and a mixture of scratched and dusty 78s, mostly from the period of Italian administration – Neapolitan love songs, selections from Verdi operas, and the Italian national anthem.

At dusk, when it is cooler, he takes the gramophone into the courtyard and does a crossword. He figures that at this time of the day there is a fair chance that the snipers will have packed it in. He gets stuck on the clue 'Grog and hiccups are always too much for this exemplary Hindu', and writes a letter to Hannah instead. He knows it may take a while before she receives his mail.

*Dearest Hannah,*

*It's hard to realise it's Christmas, even though our driver insists that the fairy lights near the port say 'Hello, Happy Christmas, Americans'. In fact, they don't. They say 'Happy Birthday, Americans', which is perhaps more appropriate for a largely Moslem community.*

*We went to a feeding centre in the south where people were dying at the rate of three hundred a day – starvation, typhoid and dysentery, war wounds. No water. Everything had to be filtered from the river. Thousands of Americans arriving by road and air, with helicopter gunships shooting down low over the houses. Almost every day convoys being looted, people driving around in technical cars with machine-guns, like a bad gangster film.*

*I miss you and keep thinking of when we were both here in 1980 for The Biggest Refugee Crisis in the World, and you made one of your smartarse jokes about Australia having The Biggest Banana in the World. Alice was four and you hated leaving her and kept sending postcards of giraffes and zebras. So far I have seen neither giraffes nor zebras, only dead dogs and cats. Postcards are of Elvis Presley.*

*I am full of foreboding about this mission for pretty obvious reasons. Already it seems to be the most terrible cock-up. I remember once telling you that I enjoyed having a grandstand seat while history was in the making, but it's no use being in the grandstand if it keeps collapsing. You say you're worried about Alice's last year of school, but she'll cope. She's obviously very bright and if she wants to get into medicine I've no doubt she'll make it, even if she is very young. Some time soon I'll go ferreting for presents for her and Aunt D. Your father's such a funny old stick it's difficult to know what to send.*

> *Take care.*
> *All my love,*
> *Waldo*

*P.S. What makes a Lincoln assassin stall – five letters?*

Waldo stabs his biro on his writing pad several times because it isn't working, then swaps it for a pencil. The card table wobbles. Mosquitoes plague him – he is sure they are malaria-ridden – and although the sun has gone down it is still excessively humid. When sweat drips from his nose onto Hannah's letter he smiles with grim amusement. He can think of more romantic ways of leaving his personal imprint.

Later, he goes for a walk along the harbour front, but has to duck into a doorway when a bullet goes whistling over his head. At least one sniper is still at work. He finds himself examining the doorway, which has some faint familiarity even though the building has been shelled and the windows broken. He runs his finger up and down the solid stone portico, unusually grand for a shop, the outer door of delicately curved iron, the inner door heavy and handsomely carved. The portico stands unsupported on one side. The wall has been shelled and lies in a mass of rubble spilling into the street.

When he hears a creaking sound overhead he looks up, and to his amazement and delight sees a barber's sign. This is the very place where he had a shave twelve years earlier. He strokes his chin. He could do with another, but where is the barber? Poor devil, he hopes he hasn't copped it.

The barber had been a big man, dressed in an immaculate short white jacket, tied behind. The surprise came when he turned round and revealed a large bare brown back and a voluminous pair of bright red and white spotted underpants. When Waldo admired them, the barber's pockmarked face beamed and he grabbed Waldo's arm, directing it towards his backside.

'Feel. Very good quality. The best. From Marks and Spencer, London. You know Marks and Spencer, London?'

When they finally got down to the business of a shave, the barber had used an old-fashioned cut-throat razor. The blade gleamed, the leather strap was stiff and dark with age, the liquid soap came in a white enamel mug. Foam covered Waldo's face as the barber advanced for the first cut, and Hannah had stood behind, apprehensive, eyes wide open, hand covering her mouth.

What a strange time it had been, and, considering what was happening today, how ironic. Somalia had lost the war with Ethiopia – the very one they had witnessed when they had gone into Ethiopia in 1975 – but that old scoundrel Barre had turned a military loss into an economic victory by encouraging an exodus of nomadic peoples into the northern regions of Somalia. The more that came, the more aid he received.

There seemed to be these cycles – America supports Ethiopia, Ethiopia turns communist, America switches to Somalia, Somalia loses war with Ethiopia, US aid props up Somalia, debt from that aid causes President's downfall, US 'invades' Somalia and confronts warlords. The next thing might well be Somalia ejects US, US turns to Ethiopia. What was that song he learned at school? 'Big fleas have little fleas upon their backs to bite 'em, little fleas have lesser fleas, and so ad infinitum.'

The Somali refugee camps at that time had been a living hell. Every skerrick of vegetation ripped from the sandy soil; a vast sprawl of fragile shelters covered in heavy black plastic; clouds of choking, blinding dust; burning heat; sick and dying people. But were there really two million refugees, as had been claimed? Or even one million? Instead of moving from one watering hole to another, the nomads had roamed the aid camps, sometimes going from one country to another, and were probably counted several times over.

Back then German aid teams had flown in portable surgeries equipped to perform the latest open-heart operations when the most desperate medical need was saline drips. Two young French women had refused to stay with the rest of the aid teams in the town of Hargeisa, and had instead camped in the desert; they were rumoured to be nuns who rolled naked in the sand dunes on moonlit nights. A large Englishman in a brown woolly waistcoat stirred huge pots of gruel as he proclaimed, 'Women and children first. Queue here please.' And a young Chinese doctor who was dealing with a death rate of two or three hundred a day had looked up at Waldo through steel-rimmed glasses over the body of a dead child and said, 'I have no drugs. I've never felt so helpless in my life.'

Waldo feels momentarily helpless himself. Twelve years later and here he is again, like one of those bouncy toys in fairgrounds that keep bobbing up, no matter how often you push them down. He gazes at the swinging sign and misses Hannah. He feels suddenly guilty. It was here, in Somalia, that he had acted in a way he would rather forget.

He had been at the US Information Centre in Mogadishu when he heard that an M. Ezekiel Chimeme, UNHCR special representative, would be arriving in Hargeisa in two days' time. Waldo was surprised that Ezekiel had gone to work with the United Nations. He had always vowed he would stay outside bureaucracies, especially one as entrenched as the UN, but Waldo supposed that, with over fifty million refugees in the world and the numbers growing, people of Ezekiel's calibre would be sorely needed. Not that he felt particularly benign towards Ezekiel, the man who had disappeared from Hannah's life the day he left her in Paris. Left her heartbroken, in fact. Waldo had wondered what he should do. Warn Hannah? Give her a gun so she could shoot him dead while she sang 'Miss Otis Regrets'? Or an axe, so she could be like Lizzy Borden and give him forty whacks? Yet he had once liked Ezekiel and had never been able to understand why he had behaved like that.

Curiosity had driven Waldo to the airport at Hargeisa. It was raining softly, puddles had collected on the ground. Palm trees were dripping, the water coursing down their smooth ribbed trunks. Waldo stood outside with his shoulders hunched and his shirt collar turned up, trying to spot Ezekiel amongst the aid workers and journalists who straggled off the plane. As soon as he saw him, he barged through the crowds and tapped him on the shoulder.

'It's Waldo, remember?'

He had forgotten Ezekiel's height and felt unfavourably

short. Ezekiel had filled out just a little and his face had acquired the look of those bureaucrats who learn to reveal nothing while sounding as if they are telling all.

Ezekiel beamed with surprise and pleasure. He clapped Waldo on the arms, embraced him, and then was suddenly whisked away by several high-ranking military personnel and a group of journalists. Ezekiel waved helplessly, flashed his charming smile and shouted, 'I'll try and catch you later on tonight. At the hotel.'

Waldo remembered that smile. Ezekiel relied on it, used it when his seriousness made him almost a bore. Waldo had waited that night for Ezekiel at the hotel, where hunting scenes adorned the walls and animal tusks hovered over doorways. There were stuffed fish in glass cases and two vast tapestries incongruously embroidered with hollyhocks and marigolds. Once, it had been the drinking ground of European expatriates. Now it was full of journalists and aid workers. But no UN officials. No Ezekiel. Waldo drank his way through several whiskies and stumbled off to Hannah's billet, still undecided whether to tell her.

Hannah was staying in a large house surrounded by barbed wire. Waldo hesitated outside the gates. A sprinkling of stars in a velvety sky, palm trees like paper cut-outs in the darkness – no one would guess that somewhere way out in the distance, thousands of refugees were sick and dying. A single streetlight outside the house had turned his hands a sickly yellow.

Hannah slept in a room with two other women journalists. Waldo knocked on their door. When there was no reply, he opened it gingerly.

Two strange women sat bolt upright in alarm. One wore a bright pink pyjama top, the second was bare-shouldered and clutched a sheet to her neck.

No, said the woman in pink pyjamas, she had no idea of Hannah's whereabouts, and as she had to be up at dawn, get the fuck out.

Waldo hastily retreated. Wrong room. He tiptoed to the next door along, which he was pretty sure was the right one, but to avoid risking further wrath, he scrawled a hasty note about Ezekiel. And then changed his mind. He stuffed the scrap of paper in his pocket, along with two jelly-babies, an old movie ticket, and three macadamia nuts covered in sand.

Now Waldo absent-mindedly pats his pockets and wonders if by some miracle the note is still there. He fishes deep and pulls out a crumpled scrap of paper. Outside the barber's shop, he holds it up to the light and reads his own handwriting: 'Try Dettol for mouth ulcers'.

So why hadn't he told Hannah about Ezekiel? He hunches his shoulders, forcing himself to remember. Ezekiel's disappearance had devastated Hannah. He, Waldo, had helped repair the damage. Yet Ezekiel remained as a very real presence, a shadow which came between them – and any other men in Hannah's life, come to that.

Waldo turns and walks briskly back along the promenade, his feet echoing on the uneven stone.


*December, Sarajevo*
*Dear Waldo,*

> *This is a hell-hole of the highest order. Yesterday a market was shelled. Shattered glass, blood running in the street, people with limbs blown off, an old woman with a gaping hole in her stomach. You've seen it all and so have I, but it doesn't*

make it any easier. At least we can leave, whereas these poor devils have to stay.

I feel frightened a lot of the time, which is just as well. I even wear my flak jacket – see how I've improved! A respectable reporter's kit in this neck of the woods now consists of a flak jacket with heavy metal plates, front and back; a hard helmet; and, preferably, an armour-plated vehicle.

Aunt D disapproves of my being here. She says if I am killed, what would become of Alice? I tell her you'd be there for her. Anyway, I will be home well before Christmas Eve, which is Aunt D's birthday. She will be 80 and is talking about walking Cradle Mountain in Tasmania with a walking stick in one hand and a bottle of gin in the other. I think she's decided to outlast both of us.

Take care.

Love,

Hannah

January, Mogadishu

Dearest Hannah,

I'm writing this from Harry's Bar. The place is a godsend. The UN cafeteria serves greasy French fries, the American cafeteria greasy hamburgers, and the Sahafi Hotel in downtown Mogadishu swarms with newly arrived boy journalists showing off their green fatigues and boasting of their conquests.

Harry's is a small dark slit of a joint, with a neon sign that never works because it's used for target practice. Its walls are plastered with girlie pinups, postcards, messages, graffiti, the odd condom. Children use condoms for balloons.

*Harry is Australian, tall and thin, with a stringy yellow ponytail. He generally wears a grubby singlet, bathers and disintegrating blue thongs. He says that he's married to a Somali woman who owns the store, but no one has ever seen her. Harry sells everything from chewing gum to liquor. He displays his foodstuffs on a narrow ledge running round the room: tinned plum pudding, bottles of Louisiana hot sauce, jars of peanut butter, Boston beans. I presume his grog is black market. If not, he has to find a darned good reason for his outrageously high prices.*

*The other day he told us that he used to work for an Australian catering firm which had the UN contract, but when the UN never paid their bills and the catering company therefore couldn't pay theirs, they ran into big trouble. Somalis don't send reminder notices. They use AK47s. Four staff were murdered, twenty wounded and ten taken hostage. Harry quit. Which is a bit like I'm feeling at the moment.*

*Two days ago we made a quick field trip into the interior and flew with a pilot who was very pukka — Bostonian accent, well-polished boots, blue linen shirt, talked lots about books and reading before telling us his wife is a school teacher in New York, his mistress runs an opium farm in Northern Thailand, and he flies for God every three years to expiate his guilt. He explained himself in such a calm, rational way.*

*I send my love,*

*Waldo*

*January, Sarajevo*

*Dearest Waldo,*

*It's cold here, so cold I can see my breath in puffs of white and I wear my long red scarf, the one you gave me. We run everywhere because of the snipers, particularly when we have to cross open spaces. Last night I went to meet Charlie Drake – the American, remember? – in a restaurant, but when we arrived all that remained were the walls. A few people were huddled around a brazier drinking slivovitz, and at the invitation of the owner we all carved our initials on a piece of sculpture he'd made out of spent artillery shells.*

*We've had the international brigade in town, including a clutch of generals and politicians. Most of them claim they can't do anything to help the Bosnians because it would make things worse, not better. When we showed them footage of a bombed-out orphanage, I asked how much worse could it get for all the dead and wounded children. They weren't amused.*

*I only had a short break at home. Alice was fine. Christmas was good, but we missed you.*

*Love,*

*Hannah*

Waldo looks disconsolately at Hannah's latest letter and wonders yet again why she has decided to stay in Sarajevo rather than come to Somalia. Even when he'd teased her on the phone about missing The Biggest Humanitarian Mission in the World, she had said no. When he said he'd heard on the grapevine she was having an affair with a Hungarian tree lopper called Adam, she corrected him sharply.

'Tree surgeon.'

'Specialising in roots?'

He shoves the letter in his pocket. He is late for a UN press conference, but arrives just in time to hear a harassed official admitting that the last crop of famine figures were 'crap'.

The man is a short, nuggety New Yorker with the biggest ears and the largest gold wristwatch Waldo has ever seen. For one moment it looks as if he is weeping, but it is only sweat. Not many people are at this press conference – mainly a few bored journalists who are there as much for the air-conditioning as the briefing.

Oh gawd, thinks Waldo. He doesn't want to be cynical, doesn't want this mission to end in a mess, but it is now obvious that the scale of the famine and the problem of looting has been exaggerated to justify US intervention.

He does a stand-up to camera, framed by the most desolate backdrop he can find: shattered buildings, barbed wire, burned and looted trucks and cars. His camera operator, Hamish, a thin wiry young Scot with a sharp humour, reminds Waldo that only the day before, his London producer had sent a message that the folks back home were sick of starving babies. They wanted kids with smiles.

Waldo says sourly, 'When the kids are smiling it's because they've just robbed you.'

He is squinting in the sun as he runs through his lines. 'The Somalis now protest that they were never adequately consulted, and there is growing Somali resistance to the UN presence, particularly the marines. Even aid programs are not always welcomed. Local farmers claim the famine had been naturally abating anyway, and that cheap food from the West which now floods the market makes their prices uncompetitive and is forcing them out of business. Aid agencies are having to hire armed guards, which doesn't sit easily with the notion of dispensing humanitarian relief. Without the guards, there'd be less aid and more corpses.

'All aid has to be transported in specially imported armoured Toyotas, known as technicals. The UN program is known amongst the locals as Shoot to Feed. This is no longer a humanitarian mission. It has become a war in which children are the main victims. Half the under-five-year-olds who are alive in January will be dead by December.

'This is Waldo Corrigan from Mogadishu, Somalia.'

He wipes his brow. 'Another one in the can,' he grunts to Hamish and to his sound operator, Maggie, whose ankle socks and hair in a ponytail make her seem more like a schoolgirl than a sound recordist, except that her chin still bears the scars of shrapnel wounds collected in Sarajevo.

Waldo helps pack up the gear, at the same time keeping a sharp eye on the swarms of kids who are even more persistent than the flies in maintaining their attacks. Just in time, he catches a small boy with a hand inside his bag. He picks him up and twirls him round and round, the kid screaming with delight as his feet leave the ground, the other children clamouring for a turn. Waldo is gasping for breath as he puts the child down.

'Time to go home, wherever that may be.'

Maggie sighs. 'I wish! When I get to London I'm going to buy me the biggest bunch of flowers I can find. Daffs and roses, and bugger the season.'

Hamish grins. 'I'll grow them for you, sweetheart.'

Waldo makes his way back to his billet, where a blast of acid rock from an upstairs window makes him blanch. The house is now packed to the rafters and he has to share his room with two young journalists who heave shiny silver weights at ungodly hours in the morning and wear sneakers that look like aircraft carriers. He can't even take refuge in the courtyard, since a sniper sprayed the wall with bullets just where he used to sit.

At six o'clock, when the air is cooler, he wanders over to Harry's Bar. Tonight's drinking companions include the red-headed Barney Cole from CNN, an old hand at the game who is credited with knowing everything but revealing nothing, except when he has a microphone in his hand. Daniel Keneally from Magnum is still wearing his red bandanna and beads. There's a woman journalist from *Somalia Free Press* called Habiba. He doesn't know her second name. A heavy-eyed Italian war surgeon whose expertise lies in amputation. And a buxom woman called Beverley Prettyfoot from AAP, whom he first met with Hannah in Ethiopia when she had a ghoulish interest in public hangings and wanted him to give her a job. She flashes Waldo a smile, tucks her broderie anglaise blouse into her khaki shorts, and says she is in trouble because her producer in LA has just bawled her out for not wearing makeup.

' "You're looking like a dyke." That's what he said. "Go and buy yourself a lipstick for godssake."

' "Oh yeah, honey, from the nearest department store?" I asked, deeply sarcastic, you know.

' "Honey, I don't care what damned place you buy it from, just stop looking as if you're in a goddamn morgue." '

Waldo laughs as Beverley shakes her long hair, and then notices Theodore King, a bottle of Coke in his hand, nodding his head in sympathetic disbelief. A Samsonite case rests by the side of his well-polished black leather boots. His hair is now silver, cropped very short. A small gold cross is pinned to the lapel of his khaki shirt.

Waldo has a flash of King in the men's health club in Ethiopia all those years earlier. The young man's buttocks like walnuts, or was it olives? Waldo still wants to ask King what the hell he was up to in such a public place, but he is sitting some distance away and Waldo can hardly shout, 'Been to the sauna lately?'

Daniel Keneally is signalling him, waving a beer bottle. His voice is slurred. 'Waldo, Waldo my friend!'

Waldo waves his own bottle in a cheery greeting.

Keneally's dark eyebrows knit together. 'You wanna film a dead baby, a girl with a beer bottle up her arse, a kid with his head cut off? Think it's gonna change the world? You're wrong, doesn't change a fucking thing. Jesus could fall off the fucking cross and make prime-time news, wouldn't fucking well matter, we don't change a fucking thing unless the big guys decide they'll get a pay-off if they intervene.'

'Like the oil in Kuwait?' The voice was Habiba's.

'Like the fucking oil in Kuwait,' said Keneally, knocking over several bottles lined up at his feet and sending them skittering across the floor.

Habiba smoothes her skirt. 'Economic imperialism determines most power moves made by the West.'

Waldo finds Habiba an attractive woman. She's thirty-something, alert and cool, self-contained. How does she see us, he wonders?

'Everyone's jostling for power, not just the West,' he says, conscious that he sounds somewhat lame.

Theodore King has come over to them. His voice is like maple syrup. 'And everyone's important. Everyone counts. You, me, Barney there, even old Daniel the cynic.'

'And me, I hope.' Indignation makes Beverley's voice rise. 'Don't I rate a mention?'

Theodore King takes her hand. 'Honey, you surely do.'

Beverley continues, her voice shrill and penetrating. 'But what about the shots of those poor dead American soldiers being dragged through the streets of Mogadishu? That led to questions.'

'Our guys have the right to kill, not the right to die,' says Barney Cole quietly. 'People don't ask how and why it happened. How come people are turning on their rescuers? What's gone wrong with this operation? Every damn thing's sanitised to make it look like a teddy bears' picnic. Even the burial of those kids who were dragged through the street. Full military honours. Lose your life for Uncle Sam, but save the world. Bullshit.'

Keneally rises unsteadily and claps his hand on his heart. ' "My confidence in you is total, our cause is just. Now, go be the thunder and lightning of a desert storm." ' He belches and sits down with a thud. 'President Bush. Kuwait.'

Waldo has his eyes closed because of the cigarette smoke but he opens them to see Habiba leaning back, showing the polished smoothness of her slender throat. Her eyes are large and lustrous. Her voice is cool. 'The problem is that all we get is a very Western view. We never learn that in many famines only a small amount of the aid comes from outside. Most of it is supplied from within, but that doesn't make good media, doesn't make the West feel good . . .'

She lights a cigarette. 'So we rarely see stuff about people helping themselves. And they do. The UN concentrates on shop-window stuff, short-term cures, instead of healing slowly and patiently. They have barely touched the underlying reasons for our problems in Somalia.'

Waldo picks up his tumbler of whisky, squinting at it through the dirty glass to see how much is left. He has been present in such discussions more times than he cares to remember. When he speaks, his voice is morose. 'We exaggerate the extent to which humanity is in control of its own affairs.'

He wanders outside, leaving the others arguing. The moon is thin, yellow and nasty. It lies on its back, as if defeated. One streetlamp gives an eerie glow, the rest have been blown to smithereens. He takes a deep breath of warm soupy air before he spies a small boy doubled up in the gutter, groaning, apparently ill or injured. Waldo walks over and bends down. The boy looks up with dark soulful eyes and gives him an angelic smile.

'Mister, I kill you.'

'Not today,' says Waldo, as a sniper's bullet whistles over his head. Back in the bar, he finds the boy has pinched his wallet.

Waldo stays on, talking with Habiba. When she asks if he wants to stay the night with her, he is surprised and grateful. They have only just reached her room when they hear the harsh clattering of helicopters. They run to the window and look up to see five or six gunships firing missiles into buildings on the other side of the street. Soldiers dangling from ropes that hang like umbilical cords from helicopter bellies. Soldiers hurling themselves into windows, smashing them with their boots and batons, firing machine-guns, throwing grenades.

Waldo looks questioningly at Habiba. She shrugs. 'Tell them they're not invited here and come to bed!' She turns down the pale green sheets.

Waldo hesitates. She slips off her sandals and draws him to her. 'Don't go. I'll find out for you in the morning.'

He has just slipped into bed when the helicopter noise gets louder, so loud he cannot hear himself breathing, and out of the corner of his eye he sees a large black boot and a chunky man in uniform come crashing through Habiba's window, followed by five more men, all of them marines, brandishing guns.

'On the floor, move move move, drop all weapons, hands behind your backs. *Move, you sonofabitch, move!*'

Waldo rolls to the floor with a thump, remembering his counsel to Hannah all those years ago in Ethiopia, wishing his bum didn't feel so pink and exposed, trying to see Habiba. He can't.

'What have you done with her?' he shouts, enraged, just as a boot kicks him in the gut and a hand tugs at his hair, yanking his head backwards. He stares into the yellowing eyes of a youth with pockmarked skin who is trying to look ferocious. The other soldiers appear to have left the room. Waldo can hear yelps, shouts and gunshots in the corridor.

'Up up up!' shouts the youth.

Waldo staggers to his feet. 'You've just told me to drop,' he says, brushing himself down until he realises he is caressing his naked skin. He draws himself up to his full height, which is still way shorter than the beanpole youth, and says, 'I'm an English journalist, minding my own business. Who the fuck are you?'

He still cannot see Habiba, but he thought he caught a flash of her long legs leaving the room just after the first marine crashed through the window.

'Papers, grandpa,' demands the youth, chewing gum with his mouth wide open and poking Waldo in the stomach with his gun.

'Oh put that ridiculous gun away. I don't keep my papers up my arse, so I'll have to get them, okay?'

Waldo takes his papers out of his shirt pocket. The soldier reads them, very slowly, and hands them back.

'Okay, grandpa, you can go.'

'You still haven't told me what the fuck you're doing here, grandson.'

'Routine check,' replies the youth, waving his gun. His boots scrunch on the broken glass from two large windows as he leaves the room.

Waldo gets back into bed, pulls up the sheet and puts a pillow over his face. He is still fuming when he hears Habiba enter the room. She has her finger to her lips as she climbs in beside him. 'I have ways of hiding,' she whispers in his ear.

He turns to her, filled with relief.

Later, as they lie in each other's arms watching the dawn light filter through the shattered windows, Waldo traces the outline of Habiba's features, her delicate nose and cheekbones, the hollows in her neck. He asks her why she wanted him.

She smiles. 'You are a kind and thoughtful man.'

'Oh,' he says. 'Oh,' trying not to sound disappointed. He would rather she'd said, 'You are a passionate man and I lusted for you.'

She giggles, an unexpected and delightful sound. 'Also I like you.'

'Ah,' he sighs, and takes her in his arms again, feeling the warm silkiness of her body.

When Waldo eventually rises, Habiba has already left. He goes hurriedly to the US Information Centre, which is surrounded by journalists, waves his pass, pushes and shoves his way in closer, spots his camera crew, and then sees Habiba driving a Toyota truck at high speed towards him. She pulls up alongside him and he sees that in the back seat crouches an elderly man dressed in striped pyjamas. He has cuts on his fore-head and arms and a deep wound on his head. His wrinkled face peers out of his pyjama top, his thinning dark hair stands on end. Habiba appears calm and self-possessed. She tells Waldo that last night's raid was supposed to capture the most powerful of all the warlords, General Mohammed Farah Aidid.

'Forty special forces and about seventy-five marines raided the house, took hostages and murdered the wounded. They used the bodies of dead Somalis as barricades, and invaded or fired anti-tank missiles at surrounding houses and buildings. The Americans also had gunships circling the port, firing into houses, apparently at random. The official Somali death toll is two hundred but medical people are saying it's more likely to be a thousand.'

'And Aidid?' asks Waldo.

'He wasn't there. Never had been.'

'So who used the first building they raided?'

'French aid workers, sleeping peacefully in their beds.'

When Waldo sends his story to London he is pleased with it and expects a pat on the back. Instead, the young BBC producer who receives his piece has a tantrum. He complains that he can't hear any guns, grenades or choppers.

'Listen, Corrigan, I don't want information, I want bang-bang.'


Waldo spends his last night in Mogadishu in a restaurant by the harbour. His companion is a portly English gossip columnist, Cecil Hardacre. Waldo asks why on earth he is in Somalia and Cecil says loudly and fruitily that he intends telling it to the marines.

Waldo wonders if Cecil is a spy; perhaps he is hoping for some frisson of excitement to end his tour. He looks around him at the cavernous dining room whose ceilings and walls are disintegrating from constant shelling. The place has candelabra bolted to the walls but no running water in the lavatories. Tables but only three chairs. A thin, tired-looking waiter spends half an hour finding a grubby menu, which Cecil studies then pushes away. Waldo hastily picks it up.

'Bring me your wine list,' demands Cecil imperiously.

The waiter disappears and returns some time later carrying a dusty bottle of wine which he swings by the neck.

'No wine list,' he says. 'Last bottle of wine.'

Cecil waves for the bottle to be opened, wipes his glass gingerly on the tablecloth, swirls the wine and tastes it. His face puckers in disgust as he indignantly waves the wine away. 'It's corked.'

Before he leaves Somalia, Waldo does one last stand-up to camera. He delivers it outside the US military compound:

'The UN operation in Somalia, conceived with the best of intentions, has become one of the biggest failures of the Western world. What began as a peace mission has turned into an army of occupation. Millions of dollars have been spent, thousands have died, but no underlying political or economic problems have been solved. Intervention has not relieved the famine, nor made progress towards economic rehabilitation. It has not dis-armed the factions or the bandits. It has not achieved peace or democracy. The country has been delivered back into the hands of precisely the same people who presided over its destruction. This is Waldo Corrigan, signing off from Mogadishu, Somalia.'

*five*

By the time he returns to London, Waldo aches. He peers at himself in his bathroom mirror to see how much of his beard has turned grey, buys six bottles of Berocca – orange-flavoured – and writes to Hannah:

*I've had enough. I quit. I feel as if all my working life I've been playing some weird game of musical chairs. In each disaster, the same kinds of people, sometimes the very same. Every aspect of human behaviour paraded before me, every act of love and selflessness, every cruelty and venality. I've never wanted to save the world, like you – although you sounded pretty jaundiced last time you wrote – but I think at least I expected results. Beginnings and endings. Victories and defeats. Goalposts that don't keep moving. I don't want to live like this any more. I want to barrack from the sidelines. In comfort.*

He is not quite sure what has triggered his decision. Perhaps it was that idiot young producer asking for more bang-bang. Perhaps it was the impact of his second Somalia trip, showing that, for the Somalis, life was not better but worse. Perhaps it was the child in the gutter who pinched his wallet while he nearly got him killed. Trouble is, he can't see himself retiring to some thatched-roof village in England, where the hedgerows will probably be more interesting than the people.

He thinks of Habiba and wonders if he will see her again. But she would be another Hannah. Impossible to pin down. Not like Crum, his first girlfriend, who had terrified him because all she wanted was to be pinned down. She had worked in the library at Balliol when he was up at Oxford, was flat-chested, short-sighted, good-natured, and serviced his every whim. For Waldo this mostly meant books. Poor old Crum. He doesn't think he was very kind to her – perhaps that's been the trouble, he has really felt better keeping women at a distance. But now that he feels his roving days are over, he is having a change of heart.

He sits at his desk with the sun warming the back of his neck and rings Hannah. She sounds alarmed.

'Have you gone mad? What on earth would you do? Some boring old desk job, or retire and take up fly fishing? You'd hate it.'

He reaches out for a Mintie and tries to unwrap it with one hand. It's time he changed his phone and bought one of those cordless jobs. 'Why don't you quit too?' He tries to sound confident.

'What for?'

'So we can quit together.'

'And?'

'Get married.'

The silence is palpable. Then, 'Don't be bloody ridiculous.'

'Or we could just live together.'

'That's also ridiculous. I'd hate you, and you'd hate me.'

'Yes, but I know your nasties and you know mine. That's a good start.'

Another silence.

'No, Waldo, no. You're just feeling knocked around after Somalia.' Her voice softens. 'You're my dear, good friend. Let's leave it like that.'

When Waldo hears himself making such a proposal, he is stunned at his recklessness. Whatever could have possessed him? The delights of the night with Habiba reawakening old desires? The fantasy of domestic bliss? Or is it just that he loves Hannah? Simple. He makes himself a coffee and finds a packet of wizened dried apricots which look as if they have been in his flat for several months, if not years. They bring him little comfort. He plays Schubert's *Death and the Maiden* as he ponders his friendship with Hannah. Why would he even contemplate the risk of change when he has so much? What should he do? Go back to another hell-hole like Somalia? His gut says no. But Hannah is right, he would hate a desk job.

Over the next few days he finds himself escaping into the kind of fantasies he had as a child when he read in bed by the pinpoint glow of a torch, the room freezing, but no matter because he would be Beau Geste riding the desert sands, or the Scarlet Pimpernel plucking French aristocrats from the cruel blade of the guillotine – Waldo would feel his own neck in horror, reading until he dropped asleep.

Other colleagues have switched from the world of fact to the world of fiction and are making splendid amounts of money writing film scripts in Hollywood. Why shouldn't he? His mind, which for too long has been straitjacketed into two-minute grabs of dangerous reality, could then roam freely in a never-ending delight of shoot-outs, car chases, kidnaps, passionate encounters with beautiful women. And because even the most violent of Hollywood movies usually ends in a mushy glow, he could also vanquish from his life wars, famines, pestilence and disease.

Waldo buys himself a new dark red spotted silk dressing-gown, drinks the best Scotch whisky, basks in hot baths up to his chin, sings Italian opera and Victorian hymns, sleeps exhausted but safe in his capacious bed at night, writes down his ideas and selects the best, which he takes to a producer friend in Hollywood. To his everlasting surprise, he is given a hand-some contract to sublimate his fantasies in a celluloid world. He can't believe his luck.

Before he leaves for America, Waldo decides to spend time in Australia with Hannah and Alice. On his first night he and Hannah go out to eat alone as Alice is away for the weekend with friends. The Vietnamese restaurant has red and gold dec-orations, white tablecloths, graceful people serving their meal. They have started with ricepaper rolls, exquisitely wrapped and filled with mint and prawn, but whereas Waldo is licking his fingers, enjoying himself hugely and glad to be with Hannah again, she is uncharacteristically despondent. She has had a new haircut, short and severe, her face is strained and she seems jumpy.

'Aunt D used to sit at my mother's piano and bellow out an old song about things getting better, better, better every day – that's what she'd sing, and I used to believe her, but it seems to me they're getting worse. There's so much violence, so many wars, so many millions suffering.'

Waldo is more concerned with diving into the next round of food which has appeared, an aromatic broth of mysterious pieces of glistening meat and slippery rice noodles. 'Don't think too much, it's bad for you.'

Hannah plunges her chopsticks into his bowl. 'Don't eat too much, it's bad for you.'

He protests. He came here to be with Hannah, not to be plunged back into the distressing world he has just left behind.

'Okay, then tell me about your latest script,' she says reluctantly.

He leans forward, eager to share his ideas. 'The heroine, Hannah, is lashed to an iceberg by an environmental terrorist who rips open her pale pink parka and leaves her there to die.'

'And does she?'

'She's rescued. In the nick of time. But not before she develops frostbite on both her breasts.'

Hannah gives an acid smile. 'Can the frostbitten breasts and give the guy a frostbitten penis. Preferably one that snaps off in the hand.' She drops a noodle in her mouth and bites it in two.

He smiles uneasily.


A friend from Western Australia lends him an old pearling master's house in Broome and he invites Hannah and Alice. Hannah is in the middle of a documentary on homelessness and says she can't make it. Alice has holidays and accepts with alacrity. She is sixteen and a half, tall and lithe like her father, with thick dark hair. Her eyes are calm and widely set.

Waldo and Alice travel well together, respecting each other's need for space. They sleep on the open verandah, with mosquito nets and coils. Inside, the house is kept cool by an enormous upright fan. They fish from the long timber jetty where the pearling vessels used to call, hire an old bomb of a car to drive to Riddell Beach and Cable Beach, where Alice swims and Waldo huddles under an umbrella to keep from getting burnt. At night they eat Chinese food in restaurants with red paper lanterns and red plastic chopsticks.

The season is only just starting – even at the end of March it is still very hot – so they confine most of their activities to the end or the beginning of the day. He takes her camel riding on the beach at sunset and she falls about laughing as he climbs gingerly onto the animal. He sits behind her and is mildly offended by her mirth. I'm not that funny, surely, he thinks as they sway along the beach and a huge sun hovers above the horizon long enough to light up the entire sky with sprays of orange and red, softening into purple as the day ends. The camels smell surprisingly clean and he thinks of telling Alice that they are shampooed every evening for the gathering tourist trade, but then decides against it. Alice would give him a withering look for treating her as a child.

He persuades her to come with him to a lecture given by James, a tall, charming young man from the English auctioneer house Sotheby's who has brought along a small collection of slides and talks to them about the identification and valuation of precious objects. Alice sits in the front row, surrounded by middle-aged women who wear loose garments of creased white linen and carry large straw hats. When the slide carousel breaks down, James doesn't say 'bloody' or 'bugger' or even 'shit', he says, 'Oh dear, oh dear,' in a voice that has a delicious drawl. Alice flips her hair over her shoulders and opens her eyes wide.

But later, when Waldo suggests they might meet James for a drink, Alice is unimpressed. 'Don't be silly, I'm too young and he's too old.' She is more pragmatic than her mother, and at times formidable in her ability to express the essence of an issue.

One evening they are lying back on long wooden planter's chairs on the jarrah verandah of their house, with mosquito coils burning at their feet and the air heavy with that sweet rotten smell of the tropics, when Alice says, 'Do you love my mother?'

Waldo balks. He is not used to people asking him direct questions. Friends know that he always beats an immediate retreat. He tries to do this with Alice, telling her that he loves a lot of people, especially her mother.

Alice is not satisfied. 'Why don't you marry her?'

'I once asked her.' Waldo surprises himself with the honesty of his answer.

'And she said no?' Alice looks disapproving. 'She's very foolish sometimes.'

The following night, as they are peeling prawns and dropping the shells around their feet, giggling at the smell and the mess, Alice launches a second attack. 'Did you know my father?'

'Yes.'

'What was he like?'

Waldo snaps the head off a prawn. He does so with some satisfaction. He would like to say, 'Arrogant shit,' but fears it might be a mistake. He phrases his answer carefully. 'He was good-looking, clever, very sure of himself, and he could be a lot of fun. He also believed very strongly in his country and in trying to achieve peace.'

'And now?'

'I don't know him now.' Waldo is cautious. He doesn't

know what Hannah has told her daughter about Ezekiel.

Alice takes another prawn. 'Did he love my mother?'

He thinks for a moment. 'I'm not sure. They didn't know each other for long. But probably he did, yes.'

'Then what went wrong?'

Waldo becomes uncomfortable. 'Haven't you asked Hannah all this?'

Alice shakes her head. 'She's too proud.'

Waldo collects the debris of the prawns, wraps it in newspaper and stands holding the bundle. He wants to be fair. He adjusts his blue-checked sarong and looks down at his bare feet. The thought occurs to him that if he tried to touch them he mightn't succeed. He waves the wrapped-up prawns. 'I'll tell you when I'm back.'

When he returns from the rubbish bin, Alice is sitting on the verandah steps, scratching in the dirt with a frond from a coconut palm. He sits beside her, wincing slightly as he lowers himself down.

'Ezekiel's father was assassinated while Ezekiel and Hannah were living in Paris. There were troubles between the Tutsis and the Hutus and he went back to Rwanda but he never returned. Hannah wrote, he didn't reply.'

Alice looks troubled. 'That's what Hannah said, but I don't understand. Why would he do that?'

'I don't know and I don't think your mother does either.'

'She wanted to be with him. Quite sad, really. I know she used to write him letters she never sent. I've done the same. Told him he's a deadshit, also told him I love him.'

'But you don't know him.' Waldo is curious.

'Listen, he's my father. And he loved my mother. Okay?'

Waldo stares at the geckoes feeding on the end of the

verandah. 'Perhaps he felt your mother would find it difficult living in Africa. Different culture, all that stuff.'

'Perhaps he never got her letters.'

'Perhaps.'

'Mind you, she'd be hard to live with. She's always on the move.'

'Do you mind that?'

She hesitates. 'I guess not. It's all I've ever known. And Aunt D is always there, and Grandpa, two doors up. But when I'm grown up I'm not going to be like Hannah, no way.'

Waldo shoots her a quick glance. 'Do you worry about her?'

' 'Course I do. Especially when she's in Sarajevo. And I worried about you in Somalia. Remember when that photographer was killed by a mob of Somalis after America shelled the harbour? That made me feel sick. I thought if he could cop it when he was only young, what chance would you have?'

'Thanks,' says Waldo dryly.


Waldo has read that Broome is famous for its spectacular bird life and he takes a somewhat unwilling Alice to the bird observatory at Roebuck Bay. A minibus bumps them over a dirt road to a rocky headland dotted with grey-green scrub and small wattle trees and banksia, twisted by the wind. The sea is a startling turquoise, Alice gasps at the intensity of its colour. As Waldo is setting up one of the observatory telescopes, six pelicans fly past in formation and touch down on the water, ruffling their wings after they have landed, tucking in their giant bills. Dozens of birds are clustered on the red sandy beach and on the rocks – sooty and pied oystercatchers, ruddy turnstones, whimbrels, bar-tailed godwits, black-tailed godwits, curlews, sandpipers. The birds blend in with the mudflats. They are mostly greys and browns, with an occasional bird standing out on its own – an exquisite white egret with elegant long black legs and a yellow beak.

Their young guide, Colin, is lean and fit. His arms are covered in scratches from trekking through the bush, he wears a red, orange and black peaked cap and his voice sings with enthusiasm as he tells them how each August and September two million shorebirds arrive in Australia from the tundras of Siberia, half of these landing on the west coast between Port Hedland and Broome.

'Why do they come all this way?' asks Alice, scratching her ankle. She wears very brief white shorts and her legs are long and brown.

Colin grins appreciatively. 'Because the feeding grounds here are as big as Sydney Harbour.'

Alice peers through his telescope, ignoring the one that Waldo has prepared. 'What do they eat?'

'Worms, crabs and shellfish.'

Waldo chuckles. 'Sounds pretty good, except for the worms.'

The rest of the party has gathered round. They mostly wear comfortable baggy clothes and well-worn hiking boots. Their faces are tanned, their bodies robust, their hats well secured. Colin goes from one telescope to another, helping people find interesting groups of birds. When Waldo looks through the telescope that Alice and Colin have just used, he finds to his chagrin that he has to adjust the eyepiece. Damn it, there was once a time when his eyesight was perfect.

Colin waves a hand at the vast expanse of sea and sand. 'In March and April the birds leave here and fly back to the Arctic to breed. They've already got themselves ready by changing their plumage so that it will blend in with the lichen in the Arctic forests – the godwit males turn from a greyish brown to a rich brown with bright red chests. It also helps attract the females.'

An elderly man adjusts his khaki bush hat. 'I once had a red sweater. Never did much for me.'

Colin smiles patiently. He has heard these jokes before. 'They increase their body weight by up to eighty percent, which they lose in two or three days' flying. Their hearts get larger and their stomachs smaller. So they're a pretty lean, mean flying machine by the time they're ready, and that's just as well because they're in one helluva hurry. They've got to make a journey of 12 000 kilometres in less than a week, with only one stopover, in China. If they're not ready – perhaps they've not gained sufficient weight, or they've been sick – well, they stay behind.

'The males arrive first and fight for their territories. The females arrive and hustle for a mate. As soon as they've laid their eggs, the females leave. The males stay to brood the eggs and protect the newborn chicks.'

Waldo shuffles uneasily. The sun is hot and as he looks down at the smooth turquoise sea, he longs for a swim.

Colin stands with his feet apart on the rock face, spreading his arms. Alice notices small patches of damp. Her damp is spreading down her back, and her thin white cotton shirt is sticking to her skin. Colin winks at her.

'The male birds spread their wings wide apart, like this, and the chicks shelter under them, numerous tiny dangling legs. The little birds have a bald patch on their necks which matches a bald patch on the underwing of the adult males.'

'Like Velcro,' says Alice, kicking the ground. 'And do the dads fly back with the baby chicks?'

'Nope. The male birds take off two weeks after the chicks have hatched, and about three weeks later it's the chicks' turn. All on their own. That incredible distance with no one to show them the way. But they make it, over ninety percent of 'em.'

A large man dressed in white, who looks as if he should be on a bowling green, wants to know if 'those birds that turn over stones to find their food' are also migratory. He means to say ruddy turnstones but calls them ruddy rock lifters. Everyone laughs.

Alice doesn't even smile. She leans against a small wattle tree, even though she knows the blossom will soon make her sneeze. She wants to see the yellow against the blue of the sky.

'So in one lifetime, how far does a godwit fly?'

'From the earth to the moon and back again.'

Alice's eyes shine. 'Cool!'

Colin looks pleased. 'They leave in late afternoon and fly in V formation, taking it in turns to lead. They take their directions from the setting sun and angle in on the stars.'

Alice stares dreamily out to sea at the ceaseless movement of small rolling waves, at gulls soaring and falling on currents of air.

Waldo wipes a large splatter of bird dropping off his arm.


On their last day in Broome, late in the afternoon, Waldo and Alice drive back to the observatory and stand on the headland, waiting to see if any birds decide to leave. The air is still. The sea is no longer turquoise but a dark, intense blue. Shadows of fading light dapple the surface of the water. The sand shimmers. Suddenly a flock of godwits rises before their eyes, followed by more and more, until they fill the sky in one splendid, huge formation which circles the foreshore once with a great whirring of wings before it disappears into the orange and purple of the setting sun.

They drive back to Broome in silence. At their favourite Chinese restaurant the waiter spreads a clean sheet of white paper and Waldo tries to resume their conversation about the wader birds and their spectacular flights. Alice is more interested in the menu. She has also spotted Colin the bird watcher and is trying to make eyes at him. A little unsurely, observes Waldo, but give her time.

He spears a golden fried battered prawn, observing with disappointment that it is more batter than prawn.

'Perhaps we're like the birds,' he says. 'We make this amazing journey. Except that birds have the sense to fly together; they know that on their own they wouldn't make it.'

Alice grins mischievously. 'And humans might just decide to stay at home.'

Waldo calls for another bottle of beer. 'I guess in the long run, it's not where we go that's important, it's how –'

She rolls her eyes, interrupting him. 'Blah-de-blah-de-blah. We've done all that stuff at school. Pretty boring.'

She is wearing a sleeveless white top and her shoulders gleam honey-brown. She looks more adult than child, but Waldo presses on.

'I'm not much good at advice, but remember that it's your journey in life, not anyone else's.' He picks up another prawn, this time in his fingers. 'Your mother's been an adventurer all her life. Challenges herself. I'm a coward.'

Alice pats his hand. 'You can't help it,' she says in a comforting voice.

That night, Alice has gone to bed and Waldo is packing up the last of his bits and pieces in his usual meticulous way. He is about to turn off the light when he pauses outside Alice's open door. She is lying with her arms flung back like a baby, her eyes wide open.

'Can't sleep?' he asks softly.

She doesn't answer.

'Goodnight, then.'

Waldo is some distance away when he hears her voice, so quiet that he can barely make out the words.

'Do you think my father would like me?'

# *six*

Outside the yellow and pink Café Sol in Marina del Ray, row upon row of pleasure yachts and launches bob gently up and down under a smog-grey sky. Some of the boats look more like gross white wedding cakes. Waldo is sitting behind a palm tree eating a pistachio gelato. He has been enjoying the warm sun and the indulgence of his surroundings until he is rudely disturbed by one of his many producers, Irwin, whose head is shaven and who wears the latest ridiculous sunglasses – mean black slits rimmed in chrome.

More than a year has passed since Broome and his present major assignment is to write a film script about a struggling aid worker in darkest Africa, which will hopefully star someone 'bankable' like Harrison Ford (Waldo's choice) or Tom Cruise (Irwin's). Scripts are written with stars' names tagging them. Waldo has to fight Irwin about notions of darkest Africa: Africa, Heart of Darkness; Africa, the Darkest Continent.

'How dark is Bosnia?' Waldo asks Irwin.

'Don't gimme that political crap. Gimme a story that sells,' said Irwin, impatiently drumming the table top with a plastic spoon.

Waldo blanches. A group of kids on rollerblades zoom in front of him and, lulled by the pattern of their movements, he is tempted to order another gelato and shut up. But Irwin irritates him.

'What's the difference between hacking someone to death with machetes and setting them alight with napalm?'

Irwin chokes on his Diet Coke. 'Is that some kind of riddle?'

Waldo gives him a sour smile. 'When Africans kill with machetes, it's called savagery. When the West kills with missiles, it's collateral damage.'

Irwin jabs him with the index finger of his right hand. 'Crap. The first is barbaric. The second is strategic.'

Waldo runs his fingers over the palm tree and feels a sharp sting. He looks down and sees a thin line of blood. He had thought the palm was plastic.

Two months later, Waldo is prowling round his newly leased penthouse apartment in Santa Monica, trying to reclaim his territory after the departure of his mother, Enid, earlier that day. He is also trying to deal with the aftermath of his feelings. Dislike, disdain, a sliver of admiration, possibly love. The hardest thing is that he recognises parts of her in him. Virtues are Janus-faced. Her capacity for gratuitous nosiness translates into his inquiring mind. Her pretentiousness is his aesthetic sensitivity. Oh yes, she had loved, adored the designer decorations in his vulgar apartment – the spa bath shaped like a whale, the cocktail cabinet moulded in banana yellow, the way the cream leather sofa blended with the cream and apricot walls. She had revelled in flinging herself into the plumpness of the sofa, her little legs, swollen by oedema, raised in the air as she hooted with coy delight.

'Well,' she said. 'Well, who would have thought you'd do this well? Your brother Tom's head of the London office now, did you know that?'

Waldo had gesticulated in irritation, accidentally spearing himself on an orange-flowered cactus plant which, like everything else, came with the apartment. He tried to move the cactus and speared himself again.

'Bloody hell!'

'Pardon?' His mother's teeth clattered as she opened her mouth in protest.

'I said bloody hell. Yes, I know Tom's done well. Good luck to him. Who'd want to be an accountant?'

'Tom. And now he's worth a lot of money. Home of his own. Lovely wife. Children. Did he tell you they're having another?'

Waldo was silent. He liked his brother's children.

One night, after his mother had kept complaining that she knew nothing of his work, he tried to tell her about Africa, but she interrupted incessantly and then fell asleep. He looked at her lying on the sofa, her head tipped back as she snored, her dentures rising and falling with each breath. At that moment, he hated her. He marched into the kitchen, grabbed a string bag and went to the nearest supermarket. There he bought okra and fresh chillies, ginger and aniseed, eggplants, tomatoes and onions.

'African food, Mother,' he said firmly as he plonked a big yellow dish of steaming vegetables on the table. He ladled her a generous helping and stood over her as she dipped her spoon dubiously into her bowl, wrinkling her nose in suspicion. She took one mouthful. And choked. The chilli burned her throat and her nose, made her chest heave, her eyes stream, so that tears ran down her face and the gruel dribbled down her chin. Aniseed seeds stuck in her dentures.

'Okra,' he shouted at her. 'Everyone in Africa eats okra, you can bloody well eat it too. Botanical name *Abelmoschus esculentus*, its seeds smuggled in the ears of slaves when they were first carted off to America. Their comfort food. Eat it.' For one delirious moment he thought he might tip the whole bowl down his mother's throat, drowning her in okra.

His revenge was brief. He atoned for the rest of her visit. But oh, it had been worth it. A curious thing then happened. Having expended his rage, he grudgingly appreciated his remaining time with her. He even found himself admiring her guts – seventy-eight and still going strong. Unlike his father, Evan, who had died from lung cancer, so that not only had the poor old coot lost the bottom half of his body, his top half had also let him down.

Waldo had been with his father the week before he died. The weather was foul. Cold bleak winds blowing off the sea, rattling the casement window panes. The grey and cream wallpaper showing blotches of damp. The room filled with his father's wheelchair, his heavy Edwardian bed, a leather armchair losing its stuffing, and the smell of urine competing with the smell of boiled vegetables coming from the kitchen end of the house.

He had topped up his father's tooth glass with whisky, which he had smuggled in, read him Dylan Thomas (Waldo's choice) and the *News of the World* (his father's). Told him about his impending move to Hollywood, with his mother hovering in the doorway, her sharp nose twitching, her hands fumbling at her pink mohair cardigan with its spangled embroidery.

His father had gasped for air, turned puce in the face, choked, and finally managed to say, 'Good lad, glad you're doing so well. Your mother will be proud of you.'

Hadn't fucking well said that he was proud of him. Never did. Great on riddles and jokes, but not much chop at anything else.

Well, I am doing well, aren't I? Waldo thinks. In spite of such unlikely beginnings. He has several scripts on the boil, including the one that might snare Harrison Ford. Money in the bank. A red sports car with an open hood, excellent food at the best of restaurants, pistachio gelato instead of jelly-babies. And yet he feels unsettled. He sits carefully on the sofa, trying not to let it make the sighing noise that his mother's boister-ousness produced – it always sounded as if some animal were being rapidly suffocated. His shoes are tight so he wriggles out of them, kicking them to one side, and chews a piece of his mother's homemade gingerbread, packed in a tartan cake tin all the way from Scarborough. The gingerbread is inedible, but durable. He decides to settle down with a video of *A Night at the Circus*, has a shower, changes into an old white towelling bathrobe, and has just poured himself a Scotch, without ice, when the telephone rings. It is Hannah, in an imperious mood.

'I'm going to Rwanda. Joining a film crew in Kigali. Leaving almost immediately. Coming?'

'No.' He is trying to open a packet of salted almonds. He shouldn't be eating salted things. He rips a hole and digs in.

'It'll help your research.'

'I've done my research.'

'Not on Rwanda.'

'You're only going because of Ezekiel.'

'Give me a break. Ezekiel's been out of my life for almost twenty years. I wouldn't know him if I saw him. I have to go. I can't stand it any longer. Up to a million people have been killed in the past three months. How can you *not* be there?'

'Hannah, I'm no longer a journalist. I'm a screenwriter.'

'Then write a film script about Rwanda and call it *Evil Triumphs When Good Men Do Nothing*. Cast Harrison Ford as an aid worker.'

'Maybe.' Waldo is surreptitiously trying to fish out an almond from the crack between the leather cushions.

'There'd be a terrific part for Susan Sarandon. She could be a nun toting a syringe full of saline mixture instead of a gun, tap-dancing her way through landmines.'

'How come she's tap-dancing?'

'She learned it so she could teach other nuns how to find the inner rhythms of life. Interested?'

'No.'

'Well, try this one. Clint Eastwood is the UN big cheese who insists that this isn't genocide, no sir, it's some kind of tribal war and it'll all be over soon.'

'Not enough drama.'

'What, with a million dead! Okay, so Clint Eastwood's son is married to a Rwandan girl played by Oprah Winfrey. Coming?'

'No.'

'Oh come on, Waldo. You must be there.'

Waldo pulls his wrap firmly about his middle. 'Why?'

'Because that's what you're really on about. You're not a flipping screenwriter. You're still a journalist at heart. And a good one.'

'Not this time, honey child.'

'Look, I need you.'

Waldo wriggles amongst the cushions.

'Desperately.'

'Maybe.'

'Darlink, you give but do not much receive,' he had been told at a healing centre in Notting Hill Gate a few years earlier, when he had wandered in seeking a massage.

'My neck hurts,' he had mumbled to a woman with orange hair who told him to lie in a foetal position on a massage table which she could raise and lower with her foot. For a moment he wondered which end of his body she was going to assault, his mouth or his bum. Magda wore purple pantaloons and some kind of gauzy, semi-transparent top which revealed a weathered bosom. She smelt heavily of a musky perfume.

'Lovely, darlink,' she had said, turning on a tape which she announced was to soothe his psyche. 'Sounds of rainforest from my country. Very special place, very spiritual place, hear the water falling and let it heal your soul.'

Waldo straightened up and lay rigidly on his back. The music sounded like someone peeing.

Magda approached him carrying fistfuls of crystals which she waved over him with her jewelled hands. It gave him pleasure to see that they had liver blotches and veins, unlike his hands which were unmarked, slim and well shaped. He was less pleased by the price tags on the crystals. He had craned his neck to see, making it hurt even more.

Magda made him roll over on his stomach, wagging a finger at him in arch disapproval. 'Darlink, I can tell you have deeply suspicious soul. No funny business here.'

She shoved his head downwards into a leopard-spotted nylon pillow so he was unable to reply. Then she balanced the rock crystals on his buttocks and his back.

'Not to move, darlink. Good boy. Now I give you Reike. Not to look.'

'No worries,' muttered Waldo grimly into the leopard spots.

He lay there for about fifteen minutes and nothing much seemed to be happening, except that the rainforest had given way to tubular bells.

'Fuck it,' he decided, struggling to his feet and sending the crystals tumbling to the floor. The room was empty. There was no sign of Magda. He found her in a back parlour with her feet up – she had kicked off her black platform sandals and was watching television, eating a salad sandwich.

'You were in karmic sleep.' She smiled, showing a piece of beetroot clinging to one tooth like a bloody fang. 'How is your neck?'

Waldo rubbed his neck. 'Not sure,' he said, remembering that he had been brought up to be polite and kind by his impolite and unkind mother.

'Darlink, settle your businesses of the heart and all will be better. You don't believe me, but I tell you. Your neck is hurting because your soul is hurting. Twenty pound, please.'

'My neck hurts because I've been at the damn computer for six hours,' Waldo muttered.

When he got home he found he wanted to cry. Perhaps his soul was hurting. Perhaps he had been too long on his own. Perhaps he had been surrounded by too many horrors in his life.

Now he finds that Hannah's phone call has upset him. He switches on the television and feels even more alarmed when he is confronted by the latest CNN news of the massacres in Rwanda. Stick-thin children with swollen bellies parade across his screen. Shots of helicopters, troops, guns, bodies lying on the sides of roads, truckloads of bodies tipped into pits, bodies clogging rivers and lakes. Live by satellite and broadcast in real time.

'The genocide that nobody stopped,' says the commentator. 'There was no mercy here and no deliverance from evil.'

Media hype, and yet he might well have used the same words himself. At least they haven't talked about collateral damage and friendly fire. Pentagon copywriters have learned to sanitise cruise missiles and cluster bombs but haven't had to apply their skills to machetes. The tender cut? Stop it, Waldo, he orders himself, and stares again at the television, rubbing his eyes.

'After the Holocaust the world said, Never again. So why have we once more failed? Who will bear witness?'

This time, the face and the voice are African. Probably Rwandan. Waldo shifts uncomfortably and drags his chair nearer the television set for one more look.

He knows he won't get much sleep as he heaves himself into his king-sized bed, which both fascinates and repels him. It has an oyster satin headrest, ruched and braided; bedside tables that swing over at the touch of a button; iced water in flasks recessed into the wall. The curtains – he refuses to call them drapes – are also oyster satin; the walls are painted oyster and cream, and the carpet is apricot to tone with the room next door. A hideous blandness seems to wash over everything, including himself, so that there are times when he thinks he might disappear. Or reappear as an oyster satin bolster, buttoned, braided and ruched. He burrows into the many pillows on his bed and drags a navy blue singlet over his face. This is his comforter and he sleeps with it every night, using it to block out the world.

Tonight, Waldo is unable to block out the world. He has fitful dreams of haunted faces and dead and dying children, so that eventually he turns on a light, blinks, and fumbles for his ancient and battered copy of Thesiger which he always has by the side of his bed. On sleepless nights he can project himself into the desert and feel space and calm. Even the thought of danger has its own capacity to soothe. He turns to one of Thesiger's journeys into the deserts of Assah and the Red Sea, fifty degrees centigrade in the shade, lorry tyres melting on the track. Thesiger is to meet the Sultan of Aussa, who had been responsible for the killing of three previous European expeditions. The explorers had been left to the hyenas, their genitals cut off as hunting trophies.

Waldo wriggles in the plumpness of his bed, adjusts his spectacles and reads:

*I knew that this moonlight meeting in unknown Africa with a savage potentate was the realisation of my boyhood dreams. I had come here in search of adventure: the mapping, the collecting of animals and birds were all incidental. The knowledge that three previous expeditions had been terminated, that we were beyond hope of assistance was something I found wholly satisfying.*

Waldo understands, oh he understands. He feels his muscles tense, senses he is about to walk the tightrope yet again. He sits upright, chucks his pillows on the floor, wiggles his toes. He could escape, get back to that life of magic intensity, an intensity which colours everything, including his relationship with Hannah.

The churning in his stomach is familiar. Once, when he confided in a friend that he didn't understand why this happened whenever he was about to see Hannah, the friend, a writer, had looked at him in amazement.

'Don't you know?'

Waldo had swirled his whisky. 'No,' he said eventually.

'You're still in love with her, man. L-o-v-e. "Love is a madness most discreet/A choking gall, and a preserving sweet."'

'Hmph.'

'*Romeo and Juliet*.'

Waldo retaliated. '"Love does much, but money does more." Old proverb.'

'Unfair on Hannah.'

'S'pose so,' said Waldo morosely.

But tonight he is not morose. Tonight he has made a decision. He pulls down his travel bags and starts sorting out his gear. This could be the very trip when he will cop a bullet, catch malaria, or need a blood transfusion and be infected with HIV. He has a sense of heroic excitement as he folds his clothes in an old leather portmanteau he bought for an outrageous amount of money in Egypt. He is hopeless at bartering. His packing is meticulous, as usual. Cotton pants and T-shirts, a navy sweater, a jacket, cotton socks, one pair of decent shoes, and one pair of white sandshoes – comfortable but dirty. In a second bag he has his computer, spare batteries, paper, his sponge bag, and the flat oilskin package from which he is never parted. It contains a thermometer, dressings, bandages, antiseptic creams, scissors, antibiotics, analgesics, various drugs for malaria and diarrhoea.

Waldo does not like to admit he makes such detailed preparations because he is afraid people will laugh at him. But they add to his sense of security, which rapidly disappears as soon as he steps on a plane. Any plane.

# seven

The flight attendant, a tall woman with a face like a Pekinese dog and a bright pink mouth, offers peanuts and drinks from the bar. Hannah declines. She tries to settle back and rest but her mind keeps returning to that awful last night with Alice, which has left her with a headache and a sick feeling in the pit of her stomach.

She had been in her kitchen, doing last-minute packing and helping Alice prepare their evening meal. The room was in chaos, which always irritated Alice – books and videos piled high on every available shelf and ledge, strings of garlic hanging by the blue painted windows, an overturned tin of cat food, some half eaten Turkish bread, a jug of marigolds, her case on the floor, a shoe on the table. Various things for Rwanda were strewn around the room – two black T-shirts, a yellow cotton scarf, old khaki pants, her camera, and her mouth organ wrapped in a purple Indian scarf.

Alice had been methodically chopping an onion for some

kind of pasta sauce. She cut in small, fine lines, first one way then the other – unlike Hannah's usual onion surgery, which was criss-cross and led to wounded fingers and weeping eyes.

'I am going to Rwanda,' Alice had suddenly announced. As calmly as if she were saying, 'I am going to Melbourne.'

*I am going to Rwanda, I am going to Rwanda, I am going to Rwanda . . .*

They were words Hannah hadn't expected, even though she had known one day Alice might want to go – but not now, not in the middle of such horror. She had thought Alice had more sense.

Hannah's father had had the same reaction when he dropped by a little later. 'Ridiculous nonsense,' he said, followed by, 'Not like you to be so foolish, Alice.'

Her father had demonstrated confidence in Alice's intellect from the time she was only a few hours old. 'Mewling and puking,' he said as he gazed down at her as if she were a specimen beneath one of his microscopes. 'Why call her Alice?'

'I like it.'

'Doesn't look much like Alice in Wonderland.'

'She's not supposed to.'

'Ah.' Tentatively he'd held out a hand towards the tiny fingers. 'She's like me.'

Hannah had raised a bemused eyebrow as she glanced from her baby's brown skin and dark hair to her father's pale skin and white hair.

'Intelligent eyes,' he explained as he pulled awkwardly at the hand-woven russet tie his sister had bought him for his birthday.

Intelligence be damned, thought Hannah as she remembered how she'd shouted at Alice when she delivered her news. Hannah had forbidden her to go, threatened to burn her passport, told her she wouldn't be able to cope, and all the while the pan of onions and tomatoes was burning on the stove. Alice had grabbed a tea towel and put the pan outside.

'Your nose is running,' she said when she returned, calmly handing her mother a box of tissues.

Hannah shoved the box to one side. She wiped her nose on the back of her sleeve. 'I suppose you think you'll find your father? Great timing, Alice. If he hasn't bothered to see you all these years, why would he want to see you now?'

Alice flushed. 'I'm not going because of him.'

'Okay, so give me another reason.'

'You're going. Why shouldn't I?'

'It's my job.'

'It's going to be mine.'

Hannah plonked a packet of spaghetti on the table. 'Alice, you've no training!'

'I'm to be an aid. With Help. They'll take me on because I'm a medical student. And it's okay, I won't become like you.'

'What's that supposed to mean?'

'A disaster junkie.'

Hannah slapped her daughter's face. When she saw the red mark on Alice's cheek, she was ashamed.

Alice's eyes filled with tears and so did Hannah's. It was a familiar kind of exchange. Alice rubbed her cheek. 'You shouldn't have done that.'

'You shouldn't have said that.'

'I want to find my father.'

'Yes. But what if he's not there, or dead, or doesn't want to be found?'

Alice picked up the cord of Hannah's dressing-gown, which was trailing on the ground. 'He'll be there, and I'll find him.'

They had eaten their meal in silence, the marigolds separating them as Hannah glared at Alice and Alice sat with her eyes fixed on her plate. Tinned tuna and garlic instead of the abandoned pasta sauce, with Hannah picking up crumbs of bread from the table and rolling them in her fingers. Once, and only once, she tried switching to pathos, holding out a red and swollen arm.

'Look. It hurts.'

'Your fault, you shouldn't have let your injections expire. Here.' Alice put two Disprin on the table in front of Hannah and a long glass of warm water with a slice of lemon.

Now Hannah crunches the lemon pips in her Bloody Mary, restlessly moving her legs, wondering whether all mother–daughter relationships were so fraught. Hers and Alice's had been tense from the very beginning.

'I'm pregnant, and I don't know who dunnit,' she had told her aunt after she returned from Paris. Aunt D had been in the garden wearing an old linen hat tied under her chin and cutting dead heads off blowzy pink and white roses, their petals softly falling.

Aunt D had paused, secateurs in one hand. 'Don't know who dunnit? That's a bit careless, lovey.'

In fact, Hannah had been pretty sure who dunnit. She decided to ring Waldo, no matter that it would be three o'clock in the morning, London time. Her news was more important than Waldo's sleep.

'Waldo, do you miss me?'

'Of course.' His voice was furry.

'Are you well?'

'Most certainly, until you woke me up.'

'Sorry.'

'Hannah, are you in trouble?'

'I'm having a baby.'

'Good grief.'

'It might be yours.'

Silence.

'But I don't think it is.'

'Hannah, you're incorrigible. I don't know what to say.'

'Tell me you love me.'

'I love you. In a manner of speaking.'

Another silence.

'Hannah, whose baby is this?'

'I told you, I don't know.'

Ezekiel's baby or Waldo's? Waldo was a friend and comfort stop who produced cups of tea and red and yellow jelly-babies. Ezekiel was her love.

Such a long, awful wait. Anxiety every time the postman dropped letters through the letterbox. Disappointment afterwards. Concern that Ezekiel might have been hurt – she dare not think of the possibility of him being killed. And all those abortive attempts to reach him. Phone calls with the operator saying there was no one there. Letters that never received a reply. Plaintive letters:

*I am missing you and need you to write. I am missing the feel of you as we lay together, the scratching of our feet as if they were talking to each other, your lovely wide smile, your tenderness, your humour. I imagine I can feel the baby inside me, such small fumblings of life, and I wonder whether it will be a boy or a girl, and who it will look like, me or you? Perhaps it will have my red hair and your dark skin? Now that would be a strange and wondrous sight. Why haven't you written?*

Finally, when her aunt had said, 'May he fry in hell and may the worms wriggle their way through his bones, amen,' she had written, 'Dear Ezekiel, I hope you fry in hell.' This letter had been returned.

At what point had she considered an abortion? Was it when her aunt warned that babies were around for the rest of their lives? Hannah had stopped beneath the stand of eucalypts at the end of the garden, watching a flock of noisy galahs jostle for space on the telegraph wires, counting their pink heads bobbing up and down.

I cannot deal with this, she had thought. I want this baby but I do not want it without Ezekiel. I want an abortion but I do not want one. If I can count an even number of birds on the wire, I will have the baby. If it is an uneven number, I will have an abortion. Inside me, I am growing a cluster of cells. Soon they will start to differentiate themselves, take shape, become a foetus with a heartbeat, become a child. But at the moment they are cells, cells, cells, they are not yet a child. Definitely not a child.

Her ambivalence had been huge. Maybe Alice had picked this up in the womb? Knock, knock, my mother doesn't want me. Nonsense, lots of women consider having abortions and then produce bonny, accommodating babies who grow up to be bonny, accommodating adults. And anyway, she had only considered an abortion in those very early weeks. Once she'd decided against it – the same day she tried to count the galahs – her resolve hadn't wavered. She had been returning from the garden when she looked up and saw an eagle hovering over-head. A black eagle. *L'aigle noir.*

She had taken a deep breath and made her way back to the house.

'I'm going to have the baby,' she told Aunt D. 'I've decided.'

'And the father?'

'Who needs fathers?'

'Babies,' said Aunt D, wiping down the cream laminex bench top with vigorous sweeps.

'Did you ever have an abortion?' It was an impulsive ques-tion and Hannah wished she could withdraw it when she saw her aunt's face tighten.

'I did.'

Hannah was silent for a moment. 'But I didn't think you could get abortions in those days.'

'You couldn't. Not unless you said you were going to jump out of the window and go mad, or the doctors said you would die, or you paid some back-street operator a hundred pounds for the privilege of a knitting-needle job.'

Hannah shuddered, and decided against asking which option her aunt had chosen. 'Did you know the father?'

'I didn't go to bed with a paper bag over my head.'

'Who was he?'

'Hannah, I am not in the witness box.'

Hannah had pressed on, even though she knew it was unfair. 'Why didn't you marry?'

Aunt D shrugged. 'I didn't love him, that's why.'

'But why didn't you keep the child?'

'Oh no, not in those days! Unmarried mothers went to church homes, where they knitted baby clothes for the babies they weren't allowed to keep and sang 'What A Friend We Have In Jesus' while they purled their way through matinée jackets, bonnets and bootees. Pink and blue.'

'Do you regret it now?'

Her aunt ferreted in the kitchen dresser for her bottle of gin. 'Mother's ruin!' she exclaimed, pouring herself a tot neat, which she downed. 'No, I don't regret it. I have you. And if you're going to keep that baby, my girl, I'll have one more. I can't see you staying at home all day.'

'Would you like to marry now?'

Her aunt pushed her velour hat to the back of her head. A strand of hair floated loose and hung over her shoulders. 'What?' she snorted. 'And have some old man with long toenails snoring beside me? No thanks.'

She shook powdered Vim onto a cloth and then onto the bench. Hannah dreamily wiped it up.

'Sometimes I think that what's happening to me is a miracle.'

Aunt D turned to roll herself a joint. She had taken to smoking marijuana for her arthritis and had two big pots of cannabis in the bathroom. She talked to the plants every day in order to help them grow.

'It'd be more of a miracle if that bloke, what's-his-name, showed his face.'

Later, she searched for her pack of tarot cards. She found them wedged between a Country Women's Association cook book – good for pumpkin scones, Aunt D claimed – and a King James version of the Bible. She made Hannah shuffle and cut, once, twice, thrice. Then she peered closely at the cards, screwing up her eyes. 'It'll be a long journey, my love.'

Aunt D was right. For Hannah the journey had been long,

and not always easy. In the plane, she pulls out a red pocket album and starts thumbing through photographs. The first is Alice, newly born. Wrapped in some kind of swaddling cloth which had slipped, so that only her nose and eyes are visible, and a crest of dark curly hair. In spite of this truncated presentation, Alice is not a blobby baby. She stares into the camera with a strong and definite presence, just as she had made her presence felt in the months before she was born.

Alice aged three, just before Hannah left for Kenya. Photography is a language which lends itself to reading between the lines. Alice wears a yellow sundress and carries a teddy bear. She smiles. She also looks wary, as if she has been caught in the moment just before something significant occurs. In this case, Hannah was saying goodbye at the airport and had handed Alice to her aunt so she could take the snap. But when she clicked the shutter and held out her arms for the return of her child, Alice burrowed her face into Aunt D's ample bosom. The creamy brown curve of her neck made Hannah ache with sudden longing.

Alice often hid her face when Hannah left, and ignored her when she returned.

'Has Alice been good?' Hannah had self-consciously asked when she came back from Nairobi ten days later.

Alice had looked equally self-conscious and sucked her thumb. She was wearing a pale pink jumper which didn't suit her.

Aunt D had beamed, stroking Alice's rebellious dark hair. 'Very good.'

'Why shouldn't she be good?' Hannah's father had asked, surprised. He had been ill with pneumonia and Hannah was worried about his health. His eyes had faded, he coughed frequently. He was sitting at the kitchen table wearing a tweed jacket, even though it was summer.

Hannah had been unpacking presents – she always brought back gifts. A tape of music of the Masai for Aunt D, an African version of a bushman's hat for her father, and for Alice a doll. Alice had taken the doll, examined it, and dropped it on the floor. She didn't want black dolls, she wanted white ones.

Alice is six in this picture, hair in plaits, a look of determination in her eyes. A child who will not be easily diverted. On the Sunday morning the snapshot was taken she had confronted Hannah in the garden, demanding, 'I want my father.'

'You've got me.'

'I want my father,' Alice had said firmly. Her dark plaits stuck out from the side of her head, her socks were pristine white, her arms were crossed.

'Your father's in Africa,' said Hannah crisply.

'I wanna go to Africa.'

'One day.'

'Now.'

Hannah thought of enlisting Waldo's help, but at the time he was rarely in Australia. Instead, she bought Alice her first puppy. She wanted to call it Boris, but Alice called it Spot. It was black all over.

Hannah reaches for a tissue. The pictures are sticking together and she has just put an imprint of tomato juice on a photograph of Alice aged ten with her hair in pigtails. Her bag was, as always, neatly packed and ready for school. Her lunch, which she made herself, was Marmite sandwiches and a fresh green apple. Her homework was consistently ready and usually correct. This was about the time that Alice became a joiner, of Sea Scouts, of Guides, of book clubs and Sunday school drama classes, of anything that would help her feel accepted. Hannah did not understand this. Hannah was a loner.

Ah, this one, this is a picture of Alice, Hannah and Waldo, taken by Bella just after Hannah had bought her first house, a dilapidated terrace in Paddington, a suburb where dilapidation was no longer welcome. Hannah had moved to Sydney some five years earlier for work reasons, and she and Alice had rented until Hannah had scraped together enough money for a deposit.

When Bella first saw the peeling cream paint of 'Mon Repos', and the frangipani tree leaning drunkenly over rusty iron railings, she had snorted something about 'Mon junk heap.' Bella was now married and living in a Mexican-tiled apartment with Italian marble bathrooms, French provincial furniture, and an American Indian sweatbox for Fuller, her American lawyer husband who was given to double-breasted suits and pale grey shoes and socks. They had all gathered in the courtyard at the back of Hannah's house. The estate agent had described it as generous but there was barely room for a round slatted wooden table and four uncomfortable benches. Fuller had beat a hasty retreat, Bella had stayed to take photographs, particularly of Alice, who was celebrating her fourteenth birthday and was on a fulcrum, tipping from the gaucheness of adolescence to the carriage of a tall graceful young woman.

Alice had made iced coffee for Waldo, who was perched on one of the benches, using two straws to try to drag the ice-cream out of his glass.

'Are you dieting?' asked Alice, dismayed.

'Good God no, I want to eat it.'

'Could've fooled me,' said Bella, pressing the shutter just as Waldo spilled a large dollop down his shirt.

He had been telling Alice there was no such thing as ordinary. 'Once I interviewed an old man who kept telling me how ordinary his life had been. Turned out he had kept an elephant in his back garden till the neighbours complained.'

Alice looked unimpressed. 'He could still have been ordinary. Once he got rid of the elephant.'

'Rejoice that you're not ordinary,' said Waldo. 'You look magnificent, you are magnificent, your mother and your aunt and grandfather love you, and so does Bella, and so do I.'

Alice's mouth had turned up at the corners into a wide smile. 'I wish you were my father.'

Hannah turns to her last and most recent picture of Alice, taken when she had just been offered a place at Sydney University's medical school. She is standing at the entrance to her immaculately tidy room, leaning against the door jam, light from her window illuminating her face and the high wide cheekbones, the young smoothness of her skin.

When Hannah first saw this photograph she found herself longing, quite absurdly, to find Ezekiel and send it to him, to let him know that he had this child, this beautiful daughter called Alice.

Scumbag, she thinks, suddenly enraged.

She must stop thinking about Alice, she has to pay attention to the job ahead. She dives into a leather briefcase which she has pushed under the seat in front of her and pulls out her briefing notes which she has barely had time to glance at:

*Rwanda: a small, landlocked country in central Africa, bordered on the north by Uganda, on the east by Tanzania, on the south by Burundi, and on the west by Zaire. Its population of some 8.2 million makes it the most densely populated country on the African continent,*

*and one of the world's poorest. Over ninety percent of the labour*
*force works in agriculture. Chief crops are coffee and tea . . .*

She scans a newspaper editorial which describes what has
happened as one of the largest and most brutal massacres of
modern times. Perhaps one million Tutsis have been slaughtered
in a span of less than three months – the most efficient killing
since Hiroshima and Nagasaki. Most were killed by machete,
but the organisation of the genocide was sophisticated and well
planned. When she comes to the horror stories, she begins grim-
acing. Bloated bodies floating down the river, mutilated limbs,
decapitated heads, a woman killed with her baby still strapped
to her back.

God, Alice is about to land in the middle of this terror,
in search of a father who may well be dead.

Hannah tries to divert her mind from disaster scenarios by
playing her favourite aeroplane game. Spot the aid worker, spot
the arms dealer, spot the priest. She has already spotted the Reverend Dr Theodore King at the front of the plane and wishes
she hadn't. Once, when she was very green, she had asked
Waldo how she could tell the spies, and he said with a straight
face, 'MI5 talk into their wrists, CIA use their fountain-pens.'

She stretches her legs as much as she is able and wonders
idly if she is suffering from burnout. Is she playing some weird
game of musical chairs with the same players, like Waldo had
once said? With every aspect of human behaviour flashing past
her as she spins through cycles of disaster and achievement. Para-
chute drops of chocolate and cheese for refugees who are too
sick for chocolate and cheese and who don't eat them anyway;
dam construction guaranteed to provide jobs for two hundred
yet make twenty thousand homeless; villagers lining up for adult

literacy classes, sitting cross-legged in the sun, sharing scraps of paper and pencils. Programs for street children that are left unprotected by governments and are dependent on drug-running groups for survival.

It's all too much, she says to herself, horrified by the fact that she sounds like Aunt D. She pulls her hair, which is long again now, back from her face with a couple of combs, searches for tell-tale signs of grey in her handbag mirror and is relieved she can't find any. But God, her eyes are baggy. She rings the flight attendant's bell and peremptorily orders another Bloody Mary.

The man sitting next to her shoots her a sidelong glance. The air-conditioning jets are lifting the few strands of brown hair which he has carefully trained across his balding head.

One of Hannah's shoes rolls under the seat and for a while she occupies herself playing footsy with the woman who sits in front. Eventually, the woman reaches backwards and hands Hannah the offending shoe, holding it gingerly between finger and thumb. Her fingernails are long and pink, she smells of expensive French perfume.

Hannah suddenly wishes that she had such pale, well-manicured hands; she wants a diamond ring or two, a house with a swimming pool, ten servants and a rich husband – even if she also has to have ten Rottweilers in the house, what the hell.

She fidgets. If she can't have a husband, then it's time for another lover. Sometimes it amuses her to consider what life would be like had she paired herself with this one or that. The black American journalist from the *New York Times* whom she met in Kuwait; he made love as if he had a metronome in his hand. The English expert on soil erosion who took her on walks and told her the botanical names of plants, whether she wanted to learn or not. The Peruvian diplomat who taught her to tango and gave her an emerald as big as an egg. Well, almost as big as an egg. Maybe she should have settled for a company lawyer and made sure he gave her a Porsche.

She smiles grimly at the man next to her, who looks alarmed and adjusts his blue and gold tie which rises and falls gently on his rounded paunch. His blazer is maroon, with gold buttons to match the buckles on his shoes. For some time now he has been making a series of small snorting noises, which in Hannah's state of tension are almost more than she can bear.

The man snorts again and looks apologetically at Hannah. 'Sinusitis. Can't help it,' he says in a nasal voice. 'Made worse every time I fly.'

He holds out a pink and brown mottled hand. 'Name's John Pearce, founding president of Feed the Needy.' His voice crackles with sincerity. 'I'm going to Rwanda. God bid me go. My first confrontation with God was on the twenty-fourth floor of the Hilton Hotel in Manila some years back. I was selling sanitary fittings when a voice came out of my belly and said, John, go forth and feed the needy.'

When his meal arrives he tucks his white napkin under his chin and begins devouring his boeuf bourguignon. 'See this?' he says, tapping at a gold enamel badge on the lapel of his blazer. 'It symbolises a dish of food, blessed by the Lord.'

Hannah is about to say that it looks more like a glass of champagne than a dish of food, but thinks better of it.

The house in Paddington always seems quiet after Hannah leaves. Alice goes through each room, methodically tidying up the debris her mother has left behind. She accepts that she is neat and Hannah is chaotic. As she stacks up the books and papers, the exercise calms her. Breathe in and out, she tells herself, meditate on the breathing, have faith in the universe.

She is still upset after the confrontation with Hannah, although she thought something like this might happen. It will not deter her. This journey is becoming a pilgrimage, an imperative to discover a country whose culture must surely be imprinted within her – a country to which she belongs but does not yet know. She deliberately avoids words like 'birthright' and 'heritage'.

'Black, white, white's right.' That's what the children had yelled in the playground when she first went to school. 'Black, white, white's right!'

One evening, as she was climbing into bed in her red and white striped pyjamas, she had said to Hannah, 'The other children won't play with me, they say I'm too dark. I'm getting lighter, aren't I?'

The principal of the school told her mother the other children thought she was Aboriginal. There were not many Aboriginal children in Canberra schools.

Hannah had done her best, trying to awaken her daughter's pride in being Rwandan, but Alice had made it quite clear to her mother that she had no intention of banging African drums or eating peanuts in her stew. She wanted to be ordinary, like everyone else. White bread sandwiches cut in triangles, with peanut butter or Marmite.

But in this past year or so she has been changing. She is interested in her background, wants to know more.

She goes up to her bedroom, puts on a tape of Angelique

Kidjo, and crosses to the big oak desk underneath her window. Above the desk is a poster of Nelson Mandela. She opens a drawer, pulls out a large tin box which she unlocks, and begins thumbing through a bundle of letters until she nears the bottom of the pile.

*Dear daddy,*

*This is a picture of me. I am six. I have a dog spot and mummy says he hunts lions only their aren't any lions at home. When are you cumin to see me.*

*Love Alice*

*Dear daddy,*

*Why don't you rite. I am seven. Its my birthday. I had a chocolate cake and grandpop read me a book. Come soon.*

*Love Alice*

*PS I love you.*

She'd stopped writing the letters soon after that. By her eighth birthday she had given up hoping for a father she could no longer imagine, given up drawing pictures of tall black men striding through the jungle, even though Hannah had told her many times that her father was more likely to be striding through the city streets.

Alice closes the box and carefully puts away the key in another smaller box – a painted round box Hannah had bought her in India. Then she opens her old-fashioned oak wardrobe, which has twin oval mirrors, and looks at her clothes, a worried expression on her face.

She will have training before she leaves Australia and hopes that it will be enough. The man who interviewed her had been dubious about taking her because of her age, but had relented in view of her medical studies and her Rwandan parentage. Already she needs to plan the things she will take away. She hasn't any idea what she might require and wishes she had asked her mother before she left. Jeans and her Swiss army knife, walking boots, her camera, her first-aid gear, some T-shirts. As little as possible. She is determined to look professional and be professional. How had Hannah felt the first time she went to Africa, when she was only two years older than Alice is now? Twenty when she'd met Alice's father, twenty when she fell in love. Alice has no romantic fantasies of her own, but she does permit a fantasy about her father. He will be at the airport in Rwanda, waiting to greet her. She will know him from the small photograph Hannah gave her, taken in Paris. He will hold out his arms and say, 'Alice!'

Stop, she tells herself, stop this. He won't be at the airport, he may not even be in Rwanda, and the possibility that he is dead is a realistic one. Hannah is the one who has fantasies. Not her.

She feels depressed, closes the wardrobe doors and walks round to the house her great-aunt and her grandfather share, two doors up the street. They had moved to Sydney a few years earlier when her grandfather retired. He had said jokingly that he needed to keep an eye on his only granddaughter. Aunt D said she needed to watch over them all.

Alice loves her great-aunt. An unquestioning love that accepts her eccentricities, the wrinkles in her sagging plum-coloured woollen stockings, the hats that get more and more bizarre with every year, the tarot cards which are now grey and dog-eared with age. Aunt D doesn't project waves of anxiety and guilt like her mother, making Alice shut her emotions away in a refrigerator of calm. She is less sure about her grandfather, his presence is wraithlike but he peers at her with distant affection and occasionally makes a wry joke.

Aunt D is at home in her kitchen, which looks more like an herbarium. Bunches of herbs hang from hooks in the ceiling and from string looped across the walls; herbs are laid out on newspaper on top of the kitchen table, the window sills and the stove. Herbs of all kinds are drying or growing – mint and parsley on the window sill, rosemary in bunches overhead, seedlings of balsam, plaits of garlic, shiny black juniper berries. More herbs grow just outside the back door in beds lined with brick and protected by straw. Aniseed for flatulence and sleeplessness, caraway for digestion, fennel for coughs. Hyssop for asthma, catarrh, muscular rheumatism, bruises and discoloured contusions. Marijuana for her arthritis.

'Now, is marijuana a herb?' asks Aunt D.

Alice doesn't know. She is into healthy living – spring water, tofu (which Aunt D says tastes like old mattresses), organic vegetables, miso soup, dandelion tea.

'Marijuana helps my arthritis,' persists Aunt D for the umpteenth time. 'And the doctor says I should lay off the booze. Do you think I should lay off the booze?'

'It's not good for you, but you know that already.'

'Just a little nip every now and then.' She makes a small face. 'My ears are hurting lately, that's why I'm going into woolly caps for winter.'

She looks wistfully at her collection of splendid hats hanging from pegs on the kitchen wall, the famous rosy hats, assorted sunhats, and black and ruby red velvet hats for best. 'The wool should do the trick, shouldn't it? Now, let's talk about you and Rwanda. Are you sure, certain, definite that you want to go?'

Alice crosses to the tap and gets herself a glass of water. 'Sure.'

'You could change your mind.'

'That's not what you told my mother when she went to Paris.'

'Rwanda's more dangerous than Paris.'

'Oh, I dunno, Paris was pretty momentous for Mum. Changed her life, I reckon.'

Aunt D pats Alice's arm. Her hands are veined and blotched with brown spots, the hands of an old woman. Alice feels momentarily worried about leaving her, and then even more worried about the mission that lies ahead.

She looks directly at Aunt D. 'D'you think I'll find him? My father?'

'If it's right to find him, you'll find him.'

Alice is impatient with any suggestions of determinism. 'If he's dead I won't find him.'

Aunt D scratches her head. 'I think you'll find him. I feel it. Don't ask me why.' She turns to the shelf behind her and pulls down her pack of tarot cards, dog-eared and old. Alice leans forward. She doesn't believe in the tarot, but all the same she loves to see the different pictures on the cards. The major Arcana and the minor. Cups, Swords, Rods and Pentacles. The Lovers – face to face and intense, his moustache is a bit clipped for Alice's liking. Two of Swords, the blindfolded woman with the flowing red hair and the swords dark against the whiteness of her shoulders. And the Knight of Pentacles, the plume on his helmet a fiery red, his visor just pushed up enough to show the gleam in his eye.

'Well,' said Aunt D, 'there he is, Alice, there's your father. Look how he's smiling, it's because he wants to see you. But it won't be easy for him, mind; he'll have a choice, a difficult choice.'

'And will we meet?'

Aunt D looks troubled. 'Maybe, it's not very clear.'

Alice stares critically at the Knight of Pentacles. 'Why didn't he ever try to find me?' She has asked this question many times.

Aunt D packs up the cards and puts them to one side. 'I don't know, but his reasons had better be good.'

# eight

At Johannesburg airport Waldo comes towards Hannah, arms outstretched, beaming with delight. He has lost weight and he is better dressed than when he lived in England. His black cotton pants are trendily baggy, he wears a white T-shirt, a black linen jacket, and his grey hair is cropped very short. He is also oozing with expense-account money. His producer Irwin has sent him off with a brief to develop a script about a high-powered American with the UN whose aid worker daughter falls in love with an arms dealer. Waldo is trying valiantly to keep an open mind.

'God, this is an arsehole!' he says cheerfully, glancing at his Mickey Mouse watch with its orange plastic wristband. 'We've three hours before the plane to Kampala. Let's see if we can rustle up some coffee.'

The terminal is a horror of moulded beige plastic chairs lined up two deep against a mosaic of trumpeting elephants and knock-kneed yellow peacocks. Hannah and Waldo stare dubiously at some red jam tarts and a few soggy-looking canapés wrapped in cellophane. Waldo eats the jam tarts; Hannah unwraps the canapés, smells them, and chucks them in a bin. They seem to be the only passengers in the lounge. Before they board the plane to Uganda, Hannah sends a card to Aunt D of a Masai witch-doctor and one to her father of a flamingo. She writes a brief note to Alice in which she tells her to take care, crosses it out, says she misses her, leaves that bit in, and describes Waldo's Mickey Mouse watch. An inadequate note but it's the best she can do. Then she tells Waldo about Alice's plan to come to Rwanda.

He is aghast. 'She can't. She's too young. Stop her.'

'I tried.'

'It's dangerous.'

'I know, and she knows.'

'It's especially dangerous because she's Rwandan.'

'At least she'll look the part.'

'Hannah!'

'Short of chaining her to the bedpost I've done everything I can think of. I give in.'

Waldo looks amazed. 'That's the first time I've heard you say that. Maybe you've met your match.'

Later, as the plane circles to land, Hannah peers out of the window and sees the grey charred corpse of another plane, like some monstrous bird that has been pinioned to the ground and incinerated. Needles of rain bounce off the tarmac of Entebbe airport and partially obscure her vision. Without thinking, she rubs the glass.

Fifteen years ago she was in Uganda, a few days after the overthrow of Idi Amin. It had been raining then, but heavier. Mud on the runway. Bombed-out planes. Piles of abandoned military equipment. No power, no transport, no telephones. A few people wandering through the streets of Kampala looking dazed and apprehensive. Amin's troops still fighting a rearguard action in some parts of the city and in the surrounding hills. Up to a million people killed or missing, family set against family, a nation anaesthetised by fear.

On her second day she had been followed by an elderly man carrying a rusty umbrella who walked up to her sideways, like a crab, clutched her by the arm and whispered, 'Do not look, do not talk, avoid the company of others. If you are captured, refuse to give your name.'

She had watched two women greet each other with incredulity, generously built, competent women – the kind who cooked large meals, wiped children's noses, lived through the ordinary dramas of life with stoicism and good humour. But in these first days of liberation, their eyes were wide with wonder as they hugged each other, laughing and crying at the same time.

'Greetings, cousin, greetings, you still exist!'

'Pinch me, cousin, pinch me to know I still am here!'

As Hannah turned away from the women, a loud male voice came from a slowly travelling orange van: 'Are you still being harassed? The authorities will help free you from terror. Liberators are on their way, so keep your spirits up and save life where you can. If your area is not yet liberated, don't give up, continue praying and hoping.'

Only one hotel was operating, and on her first night she had wandered into the large dining room, attracted by the light of hundreds of small white candles. People huddled at long tables, some played with the candles, dripping wax onto the tablecloths. A few aid workers and journalists were exchanging

Idi Amin stories: 'Amin's telegram to Nixon: "Get well soon from Watergate." Amin's telegram to Tanzanian President Julius Nyerere: "I want to assure you that I love you very much, and if you had been a woman I would have considered marrying you although your hair is full of grey hairs, but as you are a man, the possibility does not arise." '

A grey concrete wasteland lay outside the curved windows of the dining room. Snipers probably lurked there, hoping for one last kill before being killed themselves. Hannah chose one of the inside tables, well away from the glass. She recognised a few faces, waved to friends and colleagues, and picked up the menu. To her surprise, it was handwritten in beautiful copperplate French:

> Le Dîner
> Bananes
> Les biscuits militaires
> Le cacao – Cadbury's Bourneville

After she had consumed two army biscuits, a banana and a cup of cocoa, she went round the back to a darkened kitchen and asked who had written such beautiful copperplate. Large tins of army biscuits were stacked on the floor, strings of bananas hung from the rafters. Two timid young girls, their hair tied back with shoelaces, were washing up.

The chef emerged, wearing black and white check trousers tied round his waist with string, and a chef's cap which kept tumbling to one side. Livid scars ran diagonally across his left cheek and across his neck. He said that bananas, biscuits and cocoa were the only provisions he could find. The alternative was dead dog or cat.

He urged her to visit the State Research Bureau, head-quarters of Amin's three thousand secret police, the place where he had been imprisoned and tortured. 'Go, I beg you, take your camera and go.'

She had driven there one balmy day with a young Ugandan bishop called Jerome, who had also been imprisoned and, like the chef, was one of the few who survived. His clothes hung about him like a scarecrow's, his eyes were red-rimmed, he coughed continuously. His crime had been to park too close to Idi Amin's car at a state reception. He had been tortured, charged with wanting to assassinate the president, and sentenced to death. His wife and three children had fled. He had no idea where.

The drive took them through a parkland of flowering shrubs and trees until they reached a pale pink building which looked like a modest suburban motel. Two iron gates opened into a large courtyard with a profusion of beautiful white roses clam-bering over the walls, but instead of roses, they smelled rotting flesh. Decomposing bodies lay inside the courtyard, including the bodies of two young girls. A sign by the entrance read: 'Secret! When you come here, what you see here, what you hear here, when you leave here, leave them here, secret!'

In the dark of the dungeons, the smell of putrefaction was overwhelming and Hannah was forced to bury her head in her arms so that she could breathe in the freshness of her living skin.

Jerome's voice echoed in the emptiness. 'The guards had a death list. Every day, you wondered if your name would be called. The killings began at nightfall and Amin would sit and watch, drinking and joking. Each man had to kill the man in front by bashing his brains out with a sledgehammer, on and on down the line. Death was simple. Bang-bang and then no more. Women had their throats cut. Children were strangled. Amin kept some of the heads in his refrigerator at home.'

'And you?'

Jerome closed his eyes. 'They would make me walk the line, and at the last minute pull me away. I used to wish I was dead so I had no more to hear the screams. I am in shame, Hannah, shame that I lived and others died. Shame that humanity could be so evil. Every night I pray for a heart that does not want revenge.'

His torch lit up the remnants of people's lives: papers, passports, clothing, toys, a pink Manila folder labelled: 'Secret, an alleged plot to kill the president'.

Hannah stooped to pick up an identity card which lay at her feet. She opened it to see the face of a seventeen-year-old boy, a smiling face, large sticking-out ears, more the picture of a child than a young man. His name was Nsubuga Joshua Luzinda, admission No. 418 in the Department of Electrical Engineering, Uganda Technical College. His identity card was issued on 11 May 1977. Hannah did not know when he died.

Around her, the floor and the walls were smeared with blood that had darkened as it dried. Blood on clothing, blood on a baby's pink shoe. High up on one of the walls someone had scratched the word GOD in large wobbly letters.

She could hear Jerome's breathing and the sound of water dripping down the dank stone walls. In the darkness, she said to him, 'You must write this down.'

She could not see his face, but she heard his voice, low and quiet. 'How will they ever believe me?'

In Kampala, all these years later, Hannah bends and picks up a handful of soil from the hotel garden. She sifts it through her fingers, thinking that even the worst of man's bestialities do not survive for long. Worms eat bodies, ashes are blown away, horror turns into dust. The thought troubles her. She does not want to live in a world where evil is so swiftly absolved. She has an obligation to record the pain in any way she knows how, to honour those who have suffered and died, even though she knows testimonies will be lost or transformed and each will have its own subjective truth. But with a sinking heart she knows that testimony alone is not enough and neither is memory. For how is it that the world could still allow Rwanda? The Holocaust didn't come about because of the immense and terrible sins of one man but because of the complicity of many.

'Disasters are good for business,' the smiling young clerk tells Hannah and Waldo as he tries to sort out the fact that the hotel has apparently given away their rooms. The city is overflowing with aid workers, soldiers and journalists, all hot-footing it across the border to Rwanda. A group of young American servicemen joust with each other like friendly puppies. They wear the blue berets of the United Nations and their battle dress is a camouflage of orange, yellow and pink.

Hannah nudges Waldo's arm. 'That camouflage was computer designed for Kuwait. Not Rwanda.'

Waldo hopes that Hannah won't become argumentative. 'The UN can't keep producing new gear every time there's a war. It'd go broke.'

Hannah says tartly, 'It's broke already. America hasn't paid its debts.'

Waldo is irritated. 'Stop bashing the US.'

He strolls off, leaving Hannah with a surprised look on her

face. The hotel clerk tells her with a nervous smile that he has found not two rooms but one with two beds, and she says okay, okay.

By now it is afternoon, the weather has improved, and they stroll through amiable crowds of colourfully dressed people. Shops are filled with goods – groceries, electrical gadgets, bales of brightly coloured cloth, silver filigree jewellery, bead necklaces, shoes and clothes. Hannah has studied data about Uganda's economic and democratic recovery but she also feels a sense of freedom blowing through the air. Waldo grunts and says tell that to the people who are still being terrorised in the north. He wants to go to a Woody Allen film as his last bit of light relief before he enters Rwanda. He thinks it is the one where Mia Farrow – or could it be Diane Keaton? – finally has an orgasm but her psychiatrist tells her it's the wrong kind. Hannah says any kind would do.

Next day on a street corner, a man with a red toupee, a red velvet jacket and a red carnation is trying to assemble some kind of revivalist meeting. 'Jesus loves you,' he booms, waving his hands.

Hannah wants to linger, but Waldo says Jesus will wait, they have a long drive ahead. They are on their way to collect a four-wheel drive vehicle, plus driver who will take them to Rwanda and stay for as long as they require.

George is a stocky middle-aged man who wears a black leather jacket with a white daisy in his buttonhole. He gives a flower to Hannah and another to Waldo before he sprays the car with something called Heather Mist, which smells more like a funeral parlour than the Scottish moors. Once they are on their way, he asks if can play one of his cassettes and blasts them with 'Onward Christian Soldiers' as they hurtle through lush green countryside and plantations of mango, pineapple and tea. Women in brilliantly coloured kangas carry large woven baskets and pots of food and oil on their heads, swaying as they walk. Boys on bicycles laden with bananas weave in and out like shoals of minnows. Creamy-coloured cattle with great pointed horns graze along the roadside. People squat behind beautifully stacked pyramids of tomatoes, oranges and sweet potatoes. Children play in the dust with toys made from tin cans, string, wire, bits of wood, old rags.

They have just driven through fields of white flowers when they reach a giant white arch, signposted UGANDA EQUATOR, S AND N. They take it in turns to stand at the equator and be photographed. George asks to be snapped first on his own, then with Waldo, then with Hannah. He starts cutting up slices of fresh sweet pineapple and says he will give the pictures to his wife, who is a nurse.

Hannah looks at George, with his leather jacket slung over his shoulders, pictures of his wife and four children in his wallet, and wonders how this decent man has survived. When she asks him, he considers her question carefully.

'After Amin came Yusuf Lulu, and then Obote and all of that was bad. But now, for eight years, we have President Museveni. Good leader, good government, good economy.'

Hannah wipes the juice from her face. 'But what about the hatred, the cruelty, the way people were made to turn against each other, to kill and betray?'

George looks down at his hands. 'We wanted to live more than we wanted to die. We had to stop revengeful thinking. It was the only way.'

'And forgive?'

George frowns. 'My father was killed. My mother was

killed. I cannot forgive. But I try to understand so that it will not happen again.'

An hour later their jeep pulls in to a small lodging house, the Antler Hotel, in the Ugandan market town of Kabale. Their rooms are little airless boxes with grimy windows facing a back yard full of rubbish and rusty cars. Each room has a bathroom and each bathroom has an enormous seven-foot long bath.

'Oh frabjous joy,' chortles Waldo as the huge tap disgorges a torrent of hot brown water. 'Baths are a legacy of the British,' he says, beaming with pleasure as he lowers himself gently into the tub.

'Pity they don't use them more,' yells Hannah from the adjoining room. 'Present company excepted.'

Waldo doesn't hear. He is soaping his hair, his face, his whole body, scrubbing himself with a small wooden brush. When he has finished he holds his nose and dives beneath the water, wallowing this way and that in an orgy of delight. Baths are the only place where he feels his body looks appropriate, unlike the beach where he is generally depressed at the sight of young men and women, thin and bendable as wire. He knows he shouldn't care, but he does.

He is trying to turn on more hot water with his toe when Hannah appears at the connecting doorway, brushing her hair. She looks at him with affection, aware that she hasn't always been an easy friend. She is glad he has come with her; the thought of the trip is making her increasingly uneasy.

They eat that night in a dining room with bare floor, bare-topped tables, bare electric lightbulbs. George has elected to visit some cousins.

Three large blackboard menus offer 'billygoat stew'. Waldo opens a bottle of Sprite. 'There must be a plague of wild goats.'

But Billy Goat Stew is off, and so is Boiled Captain's Beef, and Boiled Spaghetti with Tomato Sauce. Spaghetti on its own, okay. The spaghetti is dry so they fetch grated cheese from a table where three exhausted aid workers from Rwanda are about to leave. They are on their way to Kampala for two days' R&R.

'Bad, eh?' says Waldo.

'Think of the worst and you won't be within cooee,' says the oldest man, blowing his nose. He tells them he comes from Brisbane and his colleagues are Danish, from Copenhagen.

After they have eaten, Hannah picks up a faded cardboard table mat which is stencilled in red and black ink: 'The Warm and Wonderful. The Best Drinks Sold Hot or Cold since 1967. Milkshake, cherry tea, coffee.'

'I'd like a cherry tea,' says Waldo hopefully.

'No cherry tea,' says the waiter.

Waldo's face falls. He looks like a child denied a treat.

'Don't worry,' says Hannah, 'one day I'll buy you cherry tea.'

She looks to the table where the aid workers sat and sees they have left behind an old copy of the *New York Times*. Waldo fetches it and they divvy it up between them. On the front page, running alongside a story about hundreds more bodies found in Rwanda, is a blurry picture of a good-looking man staring stern-faced to camera.

*'We urge everyone to return to their homes,' says M. Ezekiel Chimeme, prominent leader of the Rwandan Patriotic Front. M. Chimeme is expected to be one of the key players in the newly formed Rwandan Government.*

Hannah grabs the paper and peers closely at the picture, her hair falling over her eyes. She feels a confusion of emotions: panic, joy, disbelief, anger. She stares again, even more closely, stabbing at the picture with her finger as Waldo looks over her shoulder and says, 'Well, at least he's alive.'

Hannah turns on him. 'Don't be so churlish.'

Waldo looks bemused. 'I thought you were supposed to be angry with him. If you're not, that's great. Twenty years is a long time, Hannah.'

She rocks her chair backwards and forwards, and Waldo has a sudden memory of the time he first met her in Sydney, rocking backwards and forwards as she convinced him he should take her to Africa.

'I don't know what I feel. I thought it might be nothing – that would have been easy, but it's not like that.' Hannah smiles. Her smiles are not usually tentative, but this one is.

Waldo holds the newspaper to the light. 'Either he's grown a beard or developed multiple chins.'

'D'you think he looks like Alice?'

He puts his head on one side. 'Hard to say. Alice doesn't have a beard.'

Hannah has never told Waldo that she saw Ezekiel at a UN conference in Paris five years earlier. He did not see her. She had just finished briefing her film crew when he walked right by her, so close she could have touched his arm, but by the time she had registered his appearance he had gone. She looked him up in the list of delegates, scrolling through hundreds of names in the press room, and discovered that he was staying in the Georges Cinq – which meant either he had much more money than she, or was a senior delegate at the conference, or possibly both. She decided to put a call through to his room at the end of the day.

She had spent the next few hours thinking about Ezekiel, what she would say, what might happen, what she wanted to happen. Meantime, she recorded an interview with an Indian woman lawyer who had developed a radical street program for homeless women in Bengal, and another with an Ethiopian woman who was campaigning the length and breadth of Africa against clitoridectomy. In both interviews she felt as if she were operating on automatic pilot. When she'd finished, she went to her hotel – much smaller and more modest than the Georges Cinq – and rang Ezekiel. Her stomach was churning as she rehearsed some of the things she might say. Hello, guess who this is? Hello, Ezekiel, this is Hannah. Hello, Ezekiel, you bastard, you creep, you coward.

She jumped when she heard a click in her ear. Someone had lifted the telephone receiver off its cradle.

'Allô, allô, qui parle?'

The voice was female, low and confident. Hannah put down the telephone.

She thought about hanging around outside the Georges Cinq, hidden from view, so that she could see the woman who'd answered Ezekiel's phone. Madame Chimeme? A mistress? She could deal with mistresses. Wives were harder. No, she wouldn't demean herself that way.

Later, much later, the thought crossed her mind that maybe the woman on the phone had been the hotel maid.


She wills herself to dream of Ezekiel but nothing happens, other than she wakes with a sore throat and a fuzzy head. It is already 6.30, and she is to meet Waldo and George in the dining room in a quarter of an hour. She lifts her bag onto the bed and finds herself wondering what to wear – as if Ezekiel might be standing at the border post, graciously waving them to enter:

Welcome, my darling Hannah, I have been waiting for you all these years.

Too late, Ezekiel, I don't need your help.

For good measure, she shouts, 'Fuck off, Ezekiel,' out of the hotel window, and then hurries to breakfast feeling considerably better.

After they have eaten an omelette and fresh fruit, they go shopping with George at the small open-fronted shops and huts which line the main road. They buy three grey blankets, red and yellow plastic jerry cans for water, three wooden spoons, three sets of pale green enamel bowls and mugs, a tin opener, lavatory paper, soap and two 'best British' sultana cakes, plus rice and several tins of soup. From the noisy food markets they collect a large pineapple, avocados, onions, garlic, green peppers, passionfruit and limes.

For the first two or three hours of the drive Hannah curls up in the corner of the jeep, her head banging against the window with each rut in the road, worrying about Alice and occasionally thinking about Ezekiel. Two hours later, she has begun to feel more cheerful. She is singing with George and Waldo, and eating peanuts they have bought from a roadside stall. But by the time they reach the Rwandan border, her mood has changed to apprehension.


The last thing Ezekiel is thinking about at this moment is Hannah. As the newly appointed Minister for Communications he is trying to set up an office in the bombed-out buildings of

Parliament House. He has found himself a small room overlooking a courtyard and is directing two soldiers and a young woman secretary to carry up his few boxes of papers. Almost everything has been stripped by the fleeing army. He and his secretary grab two upright chairs from a passageway and the soldiers retrieve a reasonably solid table. Their shoes slap on the bare wooden floor. Ezekiel goes to one of the windows and stares outside at piles of corpses waiting to be buried. Tears fill his eyes as he tries to deal with the scale of the tragedy and its brutality. If only he had known.

He had left New York nine months earlier, worried about events in Rwanda, fed up with the bureaucratic inertia of the UN, feeling it was time to join the second generation of Rwandan exiles under the banner of the Rwandan Patriotic Front, the RPF, who had been fighting since 1987 for the right of return for Tutsi refugees, and for a more progressive government within Rwanda. Civil war, punctuated by talks in the presence of international observers, had waxed and waned for several years, with France training and equipping the Rwandan army under President General Juvenal Habyarimana. The president's supporters embarked on a campaign of racial hatred, calling for a common Hutu front against the exiles – the *injenzi*, cockroaches. Radiotelevision Libre des Mille Collines, the country's only private radio station, funded and staffed by extremists close to Habyarimana, poured out unending streams of hatred directed at the Tutsis, leaders of human rights associations, journalists, and other Tutsi supporters. All the ingredients were there for genocide, but when it happened it had taken Ezekiel by surprise. He was so disgusted by the UN's inertia that he knew he would never be able to work with the organisation again.

On the evening of 6 April the presidential plane was shot down as it was about to land in Kigali, killing Habyarimana and his Burundian counterpart, Cyprien Ntaryamira. Within an hour, army blockades had gone up around Kigali, where the killing started the following morning. All the evidence pointed to an organised genocide: death lists in circulation the day after the crash; the systematic and widespread nature of the massacres; the organised groups to which the killers belonged; the role of Radio des Mille Collines, which called on its listeners to kill 'even the children' and to fill the common graves.

When Ezekiel drove into Kigali with the liberating army and saw the burned-out buildings and the bodies in the streets, he made his way home as quickly as he was able, dreading the turn in the road, feeling sick at the broken gates, the smashed windows and doors.

He had discovered the body of his wife Bertha flung across the big bed they shared whenever he was home. She had been shot in the heart. Blood from her wounds had saturated the sheets and her clothes. Her skirt had been pulled up, showing her bare legs. Her underclothes were ripped. Her hands and arms looked as if they had been pinioned backwards. Almost certainly she had been raped.

Ezekiel stood in silence for several minutes, his hand over his mouth, unable to take in the full horror of everything, then he had smoothed down her skirt, tried to cleanse the blood with his handkerchief, but it was dry and there was no running water. Her hands and arms were too rigid to cross over her chest, so he had kissed her poor stiff fingers, and kissed her forehead, blanching at the smell of decay which came from her body, gagging after he had left the room. He could not bear to think of the dear smell he knew, Bertha's smell, becoming so terrible.

He knew the whereabouts of his sons, François and Jean-Paul, long before he actually saw them. A swarm of flies buzzed around the rubbish heap. Both boys had been beheaded.

In a daze of anguish, Ezekiel arranged a burial service, put flowers from the trampled garden on their graves, and finally locked and bolted the house and gates. He did not know if or when he would return.

He felt himself tormented by screams, repulsed by the horror, yet needing to drench himself in its pain, over and over again, until he moved into a state of emotional catatonia where he could abandon his feelings and become flinty as rock. He remembered a poem by Pablo Neruda, 'The Enemies', in which Neruda scorned forgiveness and forgetting. He wanted judgement. Punishment. Right now.

*nine*

The rain is heavy and the windscreen wipers are not doing a particularly good job. Hannah leans out, trying to read a mud-splattered sign by the side of the road. Rain beats against her face and soaks her hair. She yells, 'Stop!' to George and clambers out to have a closer look. The sign is incongruous: '*Bienvenu en Republique de Rwanda*'.

The place has an air of seedy desolation common to frontier posts around the world. Buildings with iron-barred windows, sheds and outhouses, searchlights, soldiers with rifles, cigarette butts at their feet, a cacophony of music from several large radios. Armed guards wearing blue UN berets motion them to stop. More UN soldiers are gathered on the verandah of a large wooden shed playing cards and drinking Coca-Cola.

Up the road, in a second shed, a captain from Botswana and a major from Pakistan warm themselves in front of a brazier. The major wears a blue scarf knotted around his neck, and he and Waldo talk incongruously about a Pinter play they each recently saw in London. The rain is now heavier, drumming on the iron roof like bullets. The major apologetically asks them to sign the security records, a large school exercise book with a red cover on which is printed 'God is love'.

Hannah rummages in the back of the jeep and hands out bananas and slices of the best British sultana cake. They eat in silence. Waldo gathers up the banana skins and puts them in a plastic bag. George starts up the engine.

Hannah tries to dry her hair on a small green towel they bought in the market. She rubs vigorously.

'If I'd been a UN soldier in Rwanda, I'd have vomited in my blue beret. Two thousand of them having to stand by and watch the bloodbath because they didn't have the authority to intervene.'

Waldo looks up from examining one of George's maps. 'People expect too much of the UN. It can only do those things its member nations permit and support.'

'Then it needs to change, if we want to prevent these kind of tragedies from happening in the future.'

Waldo shrugs. He has had these conversations before with Hannah.

The rain is easing and they can see more clearly that the vegetation on either side of the road has been burned to the ground. Fertile land which once grew bananas, coffee, tea and avocados is choked with weeds. The stumps of farm buildings look like blackened teeth protruding from a face of devastation. Buzzards beat their wings over muddy ponds. Steady trickles of refugees carrying food and bedding on their heads shuffle along the road, heading back to the city.

'I am told that people paid money to their killers, begging them to use bullets instead of knives.' George's voice is sombre.

Closer to Kigali the road is littered with the twisted carcasses of lorries and cars. A few market stalls offer pumpkin and sweet potatoes, boys repair bicycles, a very old man squats by the side of the road trying to sell a scraggy goat. Three girls in bright yellow wave at their jeep.

The city opens up into avenues of sweet-scented frangipani and pink oleander. Buildings are without windows, without doors, pitted with holes. The Cabinet Medical de Consultations has had all its windows blown out and a crazy pattern of bullet holes covers its faded pink facade. In another, more modern building, the plate-glass window has splintered into exquisite patterns like icicles. Underneath a road sign which reads '*Bienvenu a Kigali*' two piles of corpses are neatly stacked, like a newly made garden wall.

'Stop!' says Hannah, clambering out of the jeep to take photographs. When she returns, she has a splash of mud running across her forehead. Waldo would like to wipe it but he knows better than to try. He holds a handkerchief over his mouth and nose. 'I'm out of practice, I'm not sure I can stand this.'

George turns the key in the ignition and accelerates quickly, skidding in the mud.

A boy soldier, wearing huge shiny black boots, stops their jeep and politely says in French they are driving the wrong way down the road. There is so little traffic they haven't noticed.

The capital has an eerie emptiness. People move silently and quickly down the roads. Snipers hide in parks and empty buildings. If there are no civilians handy they take pot-shots at dogs and cats. The stench of decaying corpses permeates the air they breathe and everything they touch. Vultures and other birds of prey wheel, hover and dive. George has taken off his leather jacket and stopped playing religious music. He drives in silence.

Avenue de la Paix leads into Place de la Paix, where the ground is strewn with grenades, frangipani flowers and unexploded landmines. It is not safe to walk in the Place of Peace.

A policeman directs them to a hotel where most of the journalists are based, a gracious colonial building set in gardens which once were beautiful but now are trampled and dying. People are bedded down anywhere they can find a space; they move from room to room carrying kitbags, mobile telephones, laptops, camera gear, editing equipment, beer and toilet paper. Cigarette smoke curls through broken windows. Cigarette butts and polystyrene cups litter the floors. A place of loose camaraderie and sharp deals. At night, mosquitoes whine in the darkness.

A communal kitchen operates, and occasionally the hotel throws on some food and drink. It's catch as catch can. There is no running water, and bush latrines have been dug in an area cleared of mines. Hannah wonders how long it will be before she begins to pong. She finds a satellite phone, and for the third time rings her house in Sydney to hear Alice's recorded voice: 'You've rung Hannah and Alice. We are both in Rwanda. Aunt D is minding the house. Please leave a message if you must.'

There is no sign of her film crew so she assumes they are already out working. Hannah wanders outside to find Waldo sitting on the wide entrance steps, enjoying the sun after so much heavy rain. He says he is also appreciating the weeds. Dandelions with fluffy heads, pink mallow, and daisies grow rampant on the uncut lawns. Little blue birds flit through the trees. Waldo picks up a new-washed pebble from the driveway and jiggles it in his hand. For some time now Hannah's jumpy behaviour has been troubling him – her surreptitious fumblings with a mirror and comb, the way she keeps smoothing down her clothes with uncharacteristic concern, the anxious look on her face.

Waldo gets up. 'Time to go in. Feeling okay?'

In the shabby gold and white ballroom of the hotel, Ezekiel Chimeme is about to address the media as the Minister for Communications in the new government of the Rwandan Patriotic Front.

Hannah pushes her hair back from her face for the ump-teenth time. 'Fine. Except I wish I could see Jack and his new sound guy. I presume they'll turn up on time.' She looks search-ingly at Waldo. 'How much have we changed?'

'I've got fatter, you've got thinner. I've lost my hair, you've kept yours.' He chuckles and pulls down the peak of his red and yellow cap from Venice Beach.

Since going to live in Los Angeles, Waldo has been indulg-ing in flashes of childlike exuberance – the watch and now the cap. Hannah thinks that perhaps she could do with a bit of that herself.

They have been in the ballroom for five minutes when she hears a slight commotion at the back of the room. A tall man in jungle greens enters, flanked by armed soldiers. His beard is slightly grizzled, his face is heavier than she remembers, his shoulders are slightly stooped. He emanates wariness, a man who is unlikely to be taken off guard. Hannah draws in her breath. She has insisted on a position where it is unlikely they can be recognised; she wants any meeting with Ezekiel to be on her terms.

The audience is restless as Ezekiel takes the podium, hands clasping the lectern, eyes moving round the room. He stays silent for at least two minutes. Gradually, people become quiet.

'Welcome!' His greeting is sudden and comes with a wide and compelling smile. A smile Hannah remembers.

Another silence. Is he deliberately stage-managing this, or is she seeing a man who is exhausted and needs to take his time? When he finally begins talking, she finds herself seduced by the power of his words and his presence.

'In the space of less than three months, up to one million people in my country have been murdered. The people who died – men, women and children – were victims of a systematic campaign to exterminate the Tutsi people. The West initially tried to pass it off as civil war, then tribal war. It was neither. It was genocide. Genocide unparalleled since the defeat of Nazism, when the world said never again. If only we had known, the world said, this would never have happened. Well, the world did know about the genocide in Rwanda. It watched it live on television. And did nothing.

'In December 1993, when the international community sent forces to Rwanda to keep the peace, we were filled with trust and expectation. But as the violence kept brewing, senior UN officials in Rwanda began sending warnings that danger was imminent. They asked for reinforcements. What happened?

'After ten Belgian soldiers were killed, you might have expected the UN to increase its peacekeeping forces. But no. It withdrew them, abandoned its own Rwandan staff, and left us unprotected even though we begged.

'Had we oil, would this have happened? No. You would have come with your tanks and your Scud missiles, as you did in Kuwait. Had we strategic ports, would you have done nothing? No. You would have launched an armada, as you did in Somalia. Were we a Western country, would you have ignored us? No, you would have sent in forces, as you did in Eastern Europe.

'Our skins are dark. But our blood is the same colour. Yet who mourns for us now?'

A man sitting near the front asks if Ezekiel regards the killings as tribal.

Ezekiel leans forward, grasping the lectern. The anger in his voice reminds Hannah of his anger when he used to talk about race in Paris.

'As I have already said, no. Whenever we use that word tribal, it makes it easy for us to dismiss what has gone on in Rwanda as something specifically African: dark, savage, primordial. Yet we are all capable of crossing that threshold into savagery. Yugoslavia, Northern Ireland, Cambodia, Vietnam, Germany, a chain of brutality links us from this century to earliest times.'

Someone else stands to say, 'You've said you wouldn't seek retribution, but how's that possible after all you've suffered?'

Ezekiel nods and shifts his body. He quotes Martin Luther King. ' "Morality cannot be legislated, but behaviour can be regulated; judicial decrees may not change the heart, but they restrain the heartless." Which means that we will try to enforce civilised behaviour. We may not always succeed, but we will do our best.'

He folds his papers. 'In the long run, Rwanda must not become a country accustomed to living off handouts. Meanwhile, we welcome your support.' He gives his papers to a young woman aide and leaves by a side entrance, followed by a few journalists.

Hannah spots Jack shouldering his camera in the crowd and

attempts to reach him but fails. She won't try for an interview at this stage, it's too soon and she needs to get her bearings first.

An English journalist winks at Hannah. He does a line in Irish accents which she finds tedious. 'Jaysus, a clever one is it then? A man of uncommon charm. There's no denyin' that.'

'Tedjus,' she says to Waldo, dragging him after her and making her way to the peeling yellow balustrade that encircles the entrance.

Waldo picks up a stone and skims it along the driveway. 'So, how do you feel?'

Hannah gazes out through a white flowering magnolia, wondering how she feels. 'Impressed,' she says finally. She looks at Waldo impatiently. 'Oh God, Waldo, take off that nanny look, will you? He didn't even recognise me.'

'Okay, but take care.'

'What of?'

'Yourself. I know you'll try to see him and it might be the last thing he wants.'

Hannah smiles wryly. 'And what about Alice?'

'He mightn't want to see Alice either.'


Ezekiel feels as if there are two Ezekiels. One lies dead with his family; the other is walking, talking, making decisions, issuing orders as if everything in his life were under control. He does not eat, unless his secretary reminds him to. He does not sleep, but he is used to that. His time is consumed by his work. Setting up communication channels with the foreign media, ensuring they are given as much co-operation as possible, speaking on behalf of his government whenever he is required to. The only time he is thrown off balance is when an American journalist asks what he would like to do with the people who murdered his wife and sons.

'I would want to kill them,' he says slowly. 'But I hope I would not. It is important that the murderers are punished, but by the courts of law, not by individuals.'

'What did they do to your boys?' the journalist persists.

He turns away for a moment, afraid he is about to be sick. 'I do not want to tell you what was done to my sons,' he says. 'We are not talking about individual retaliation.'

'But surely –' she starts, waving a microphone in his face.

Ezekiel interrupts. 'My father, who was also murdered, once told me to remember a saying of Gandhi's: "If you follow the old code of justice – an eye for an eye and a tooth for a tooth – you end up with a blind and toothless world." '

But after the woman has gone and the door has closed behind her, he bangs his fists so hard on the desk that they bleed. He feels he should weep, weep for the people he loved who were killed so brutally, weep for Bertha and his sons, weep for himself. But he cannot. All he wants is revenge.

For Hannah, the intensity of the horror takes over. The churches where men, women and children were burned alive, or cut down with machetes, even as they ran. The rivers swollen with corpses where babies were tossed while they still drew breath. The bodies eaten by dogs and the bones scattered on the blood-stained grass. The women and girls raped and tortured and thrown into sewage pits to choke and die. The building of Centre Christus where eight nuns, thirteen Jesuit priests, and an unknown number of gardeners, cleaners and watchmen were murdered, chairs overthrown, tables smashed, windows broken. In the nuns' quarters the bolt on the metal door was bent inwards and the door smashed in. The women's bodies were huddled behind the door. The pity, the terrible pity.

Sometimes, the brutality is almost more than she can bear. She marvels at the resilience of people in being able to carry on, to walk placing one foot after another, to eat, to talk, even to smile. And to say thank you. Especially to say thank you.

Hannah is picking her way through rubble and broken glass in Kigali hospital, a low-lying building high on a hill. Windows are smashed, rooms look as if they have been flattened by a bulldozer, sterilisers have been upturned, equipment trolleys crushed, filing cabinets emptied of their contents. In the upstairs corridors, a line of empty baby cots has been tipped upside down. Blood has dried on baby mattresses and baby clothes, on bed linen and towels, on walls and floors.

A woman in a green and white spotted dress walks towards her, tears streaking her face. She says she was a nursing sister at the hospital when the soldiers came and has returned to see if anyone is left alive and needing care.

Hannah asks if she will be interviewed and the woman says in a whisper, 'Yes, if it will help.'

Jack takes a light-reading and the new sound man, Cambodian-born Kim who has only just graduated from the film school, fixes their microphones. He looks very young but his movements are swift and professional.

Hannah and the woman sit on a bench outside the hospital. The woman's hands keep turning in her lap and her voice is so low that Hannah has to ask her to speak louder.

'They carried lists of Tutsis to be killed and I was one of them. But the soldiers ordered all the patients out first, pulling them out of their beds, beating them, throwing them into the courtyards. I heard machete blades chopping into flesh. I could hear their screams but do nothing. I knew that my turn was coming because one of the soldiers said, "We will be back for you." So I hid under the bed of a Hutu priest and stayed there all night. The following morning I had just crawled out and was rubbing my aching legs when they came again, that soldier down the corridor with his lists like the Auschwitz lists of death.

'He said, "I have come for you."

'My eyes and my body were filled with terror.

'He said, "I am not a murderer, I do not want to kill you, so put on robes and go into the operating theatre. I will say I have not found you."

'The running footsteps and the guns and the steel knives passed me by. But I could not stay. So I ran up the hill to where the Red Cross was working and I tried to hide there, but I could see the soldiers pointing to me, so again I ran, ran, ran, till my side ached and my head felt as if it would burst. I saw a building with the United Nations sign, and ran inside before anyone could stop me, up the stairs, into a bedroom, and hid once more under a bed. And there I stayed for several days till the killing was over.

'When I went home, there was no home. It had been burned to the ground. My family was all dead. Mother, father, brothers, sisters. All dead.'

Tears run down the nurse's cheeks but she makes no sound. She raises her head, looks at the sun dancing through trees.

'I remember that beautiful life before the killings. Somebody took it away.'

At the village of Nymata, not far from Kigali, hundreds of corpses are strewn about the church. As people tried to flee they were slain with machetes or blown up by hand grenades. The bodies are dissolving in the rain, the stench is overwhelming.

'God almighty,' says Jack. 'How could they do it?' His normally good-natured, craggy face has hardened. He is a veteran, wearing an old Digger's hat as his talisman from Vietnam. After that war he embarked on a crusade to save the world through his photos, but when the world ignored them he returned to mainstream television. Jack is like the old-fashioned stereotype of an Australian, laid-back, cussed, kind.

Hannah looks at Jack, her face stricken. 'This is the worst I've seen.'

A man whose head wounds are being carefully bound by an elderly and frail nun tells them that people fled to the churches for safety. When they realised nowhere was safe, they joined hands and prayed and lost their fear. 'They say the spirits of those who had already been killed were with them, telling them it was all right to die.'

Kim shudders. 'But not in such a terrible way.'

A young man wearing a blue UN beret on the back of his head and carrying a long-handled shovel stumbles in a dazed way outside the charred ruins of the church. He is about nineteen, big feet, big hands, raw innocence. His freckled face is streaked with dirt. Hannah asks if she can interview him, and when he nods yes Jack rolls the camera and Kim moves in close with his microphone, squatting on his haunches. The young soldier says that his task is to help bury the corpses. He studies the dried blood on his hands, then gazes at Hannah with a look of disbelief.

'We saw it happening, we saw it fucking happening. There

was this kid, about ten with big brown eyes, and first they killed her mother and her sister and then they raped her, in front of us, and then they h–h–'

He stumbles, and dribble runs down his face. 'They hacked her to death while I just stood by and let it happen, those were my orders.'

He puts his head in his hands, and his shoulders heave. When he looks up, his face is ashen.

'Sweet Jesus, I obeyed them.'

His voice drops to a whisper. 'I *let* it happen. She screamed and screamed but I let it happen.'

After the boy has gone, Hannah says to Waldo, 'They *all* let it happen, that's the terrible thing. No one disobeyed.'

Waldo looks across the graveyard of corpses to where a second nun, her white robes flapping, drags a dead woman and her child. His reply is bitter. 'We face only what we want to face. And that's why nothing ever changes.'

Away from the churchyard, in warm, bright sunlight under a sky of Botticelli blue, they look out across a football oval where people had once run and jumped and shouted and laughed and hugged each other with the excitement of the game. But it was here that players from Rwanda's international prize-winning football team were confronted by Hutu militia and forced to embark on one of the most gruesome games possible to devise. Hannah knows it; she has recorded an interview, taken pictures, felt sick with horror, just as she feels sick now when she repeats it to Waldo.

'The militia chopped off the head of the team's football coach because he was a Tutsi. Then they ordered his team to play a match using his head for a ball. They said that if anyone refused, they'd hack off his leg.'

Waldo says he wishes he hadn't heard the story; he wants to block it out, to bring some kind of sense back into this most beautiful of sunny days, where insects are humming in the grass at his feet and a blue and yellow butterfly flits gracefully between the trees and the flowers.

The ingenuity of the atrocity appalls Hannah. She calls it evil.

Waldo is uncomfortable about moving into the realms of the supernatural. 'Evil suggests some kind of demonic forces.'

'Well, fuck you too,' snaps Hannah, pulling fiercely at the branch of a tree which bears enormous cream flowers with dark brown stamens. 'What would you call it? Strategic retaliation against forces hostile to the enemy?'

'No,' says Waldo, 'but what's happened here is more than a frantic bloodlust, it was a long-term plan to destroy an entire people. It was intended to get out of hand. You said so yourself.'

Hannah squints at him. 'Yes, but I bet if you wrote about this in one of your film scripts, you'd use the word evil.' She repeats the word, spitting it out, 'Evil.'

Waldo holds his ground. 'And when soldiers are trained to kill, to be untroubled by scruple, what would you call that?'

'Evil.'

'Oh tosh,' says Waldo, suddenly annoyed. 'Once you're able to dehumanise the enemy then anything is possible.'

'But in Rwanda these were people who lived side by side, as friends and neighbours, sometimes from the same family.'

'And the Jews? Didn't they live side by side with Aryan lovers and friends and neighbours? Humans are capable of being the most bloody destructive creatures on God's earth, and have been from earliest times. Look at the cruelty in our literature, the myths of our ancient gods. Even the most civilised cultures raped, tortured and killed.'

Waldo watches a child totter across the football field on his own. A UN soldier appears, running, sweeps up the child under one arm and carries him off the field, disappearing from sight.

Hannah's face is white. She longs for a cigarette but she gave up smoking years ago. Instead, she takes a swig from a bottle of water. She wonders what it would be like to live under a totalitarian government hell-bent on enforcing total obedience to power. At what point might she be seduced or frightened into betrayal? Would complicity be frenetic and unbridled but fed from an underbelly of intent? Or would it be slow and imperceptible, so that people could draw their blinds and say politely, 'No, we did not know, we did not know at all.'

'No one becomes depraved all at once,' says Waldo suddenly.

Hannah makes a face. 'I guess none of us knows how we'd behave.'

Her sentence lingers. Waldo pulls at a piece of grass. 'I'd be a coward. You'd be the flaming martyr.'

'I'd escape,' says Hannah simply.

'Jung used to say we should be grateful to our enemies, for their darkness allows us to escape our own.'

'And where are your dark shadows?'

'I hide mine. Why else do you think I put on so much weight?' Waldo's face is sombre. When he was thirteen, he had killed a cat. Violently and without pity. He had been wrestling with his homework when a cat began to yawl in the darkness outside his bedroom window. The noise became excruciating and he thudded downstairs to find his father sitting in his chair, wrapped in a rug, reading the sports pages of the *Daily Mirror*. His mother was shelling peas into a metal colander, her face flushed from the heat of an ancient Aga stove. His brother Tom was making a model aeroplane and trying to avoid spilling glue on the kitchen table. No one seemed in the least bothered by the cat. Waldo grabbed one of his mother's heavy black frying pans, opened the kitchen door and hurled the pan in the direction of the cat. He heard a loud and terrible screech.

'Bull's-eye' said his father, who refused to wear any prosthesis and so looked slightly sinister, a large upper body but nothing beneath.

Waldo found the cat lying under some bushes with its back arched and its claws outstretched, saliva frothing round its mouth, howling piteously. It looked as if its back were broken. Without thinking, he picked up the frying pan and hammered the animal ferociously and relentlessly, wanting to stop its noise, wanting to obliterate it, and he did not stop until some time after the animal was dead.

When he came inside, white-faced and shaking, his mother said good riddance to the cat, it sprayed her tomatoes and should've been put down years ago, a proper tom.

His father said, 'Poor Tom,' winking at his youngest son Tom.

Tom said Waldo was weird and Waldo remembered he'd eaten his mother's tomatoes the day before.

Late that night, when he was in bed staring into the darkness, he had to confront an appalling awareness. Once he'd started to batter the cat, he wanted to continue, to bash and bash until the animal was dead. And all the while he had felt a growing and intoxicating sense of power.

When Waldo tells Hannah his memory, she laughs. Not unsympathetically, but nevertheless she laughs.

'I didn't have to kill a cat to know I could be cruel.'

Waldo frowns. 'It frightened me.'

They stand in silence for a while, gazing at the brilliance of scarlet and purple bougainvillea growing over nearby rooftops. Small grey lizards flick through the dirt, a dove is cooing in the trees, and a child plays with a toy car made of bent wire and bottle tops. Hannah holds out a hand to let a small bird with a bright red breast hop onto her finger.

'They're very tame.'

Waldo cuts two small pieces from an apple. 'They're hungry.' He wipes the blade of his French fishing knife, which he likes because it folds neatly in two.

'Show me.' Hannah reaches out a hand.

'Picked it up in Dieppe ten years ago.'

'It looks like a cut-throat razor. When we were in Paris Ezekiel had one like that.'

She is starting to incorporate Ezekiel into her conversation. Reclaiming him as part of her past.

# *t e n*

The nuns at Hannah's school had worn severe black robes and white wimples. The nun who is presently bearing down on Hannah on the terrace of the hotel is decked in a brightly coloured floral sarong wrapped around her ample middle. On top she wears a purple tunic. Her shoes are brown lace-ups.

'My walking shoes,' she booms in the voice of an English gentlewoman.

Sister Helene has a strong handshake and a formidable jaw. She announces she is looking for women journalists. Women aid workers. Women. She wants to invite them to the Feast of the Assumption. In her wake come four small Rwandan nuns dressed in brown.

Hannah looks up, shielding her eyes from the sun which glares in her face. She has lost her sunglasses and Kigali in its present state certainly doesn't stock sunglasses.

'Feast of the Assumption?' she asks, curious.

'The feast day of our order,' says Sister Helene, who came from Kenya to see if any nuns had survived the killings and found the four Sisters of the Assumption hiding in the roof of a Kigali house. She had taken them under her wing, she told Hannah. 'Some of the things we saw were so terrible. I think Christ knew all this when He took our suffering to Him on the cross.'

Hannah wanted to say it was all very well for Christ to have suffered, but why everyone else?

Sister Helene is beaming enthusiastically. 'Do come,' she says in a voice that sounds as if she's issuing an invitation to tea with the headmistress. 'That would be grand.' In spite of her apparent vigour, her eyes are tired. 'Tomorrow evening, seven o'clock, archbishop's residence. Women only, but be jolly careful walking through the garden. Landmines.'

Hannah tucks this invitation in the back of her mind. She is on her way to meet up with Alice at the Rwandan head-quarters of Help. The government has commandeered numbers of public buildings for use by international agencies, and Help has been installed in St Joseph's High School, a cluster of modern buildings surrounded by a high wire fence.

A couple of large lorries are parked at a loading bay to one side of the main entrance, and a man is supervising the unload-ing of a consignment of powdered milk. Hannah recognises Joe Schwartz, Help's Director of Operations in Rwanda, a man she already knows from New York and Cambodia. He waves a hand in her direction and beckons her inside. Schwartz was a senior finance bureaucrat in Bush's administration until he found God, quit government employment, and climbed up the cor-porate aid ladder with impressive speed. Now he is a star in the Help firmament. He has swapped his thick horn-rimmed glasses for steel-rimmed spectacles, become a vegetarian, and he applies his management principles with meticulous accuracy to aid workers and refugees alike. Hannah remembers an exasperated aid worker asking him if quality control meant the difference between a live refugee and a dead one. She had forgotten how neatly dressed and well ordered he always appears. and wishes she looked tidier. Her black T-shirt is okay but her khaki pants are decidely the worse for wear.

Joe Schwartz is still quite young but he is thin and bent, like a wire coathanger that someone has twisted slightly out of shape. He greets Hannah cordially and tells her Alice arrived with a group of Help volunteers the day before; she is already at work.

Hannah wants to ask, 'How's she doing?' Instead she says, 'How's it going?'

'Difficult,' Joe says over his shoulder as he makes her a cup of tea, shaking out a teabag from a large plastic canister. 'There's a two-way traffic of refugees. Many of the Hutu are still pouring over the border into Zaire because they're afraid of reprisals from the RPF. Others are returning, and that's what we're encouraging.'

He pours a mug of hot water for himself and takes a sip. 'I cut out stimulants two years ago. You're a buzzard's breakfast if you're unfit in this kind of job. Besides, you've got to keep your eye on the goal.'

'And what is the goal?' Hannah is polite.

'Clean up the camps, especially in Zaire.' He wipes his spectacles. 'I've never seen such bad conditions. Severe malnutrition, cholera, typhoid. No water. No latrines. Health hazards are enormous. We daren't even begin to think about AIDS. And the militia who committed the killings are mixed up with the refugees. We can see them retraining, and they've terrorised the camps so they control most of the food and steal it from the women and children. But we can't sort them out, so what can we do?'

'You could stop feeding them.'

'The French have done this, and it's logical of course. But if we all followed suit, everyone would starve.' His face creases in pain. 'I pray for answers, Hannah, I pray every night, it's a moral dilemma, but . . .'

'But what? If the humanitarian organisations are silent, it's almost as if they approve.'

He shrugs. 'You know we don't – but *you* try and make that kind of decision. It's not easy.'

She makes a face. 'But you're providing a facade for brutality to continue.'

He stiffens his back as if he were a child at Sunday school. 'We're also saving lives. It's a big task, and Zaire is where we're sending most of our people. That's where Alice will go.'

She tries not to interfere. She wants to remain neutral. But she can't lose her acute awareness that Alice is her child. 'You can't do that. She hasn't had enough training.'

Joe isn't going to be shifted. 'She's good. A little headstrong. Thinks she's in control, but then it takes time to know that none of us is ever in control. We're breaking her in with the food runs, looking after the refugee traffic on the roads. They're all in poor shape. And then of course there're the people here in Rwanda where the suffering has been beyond belief.'

He collects her cup and waves his hand in a gesture of hospitality. 'Make yourself at home. We still don't have running water or electricity so if you want water it's there.' He points to three large plastic containers – red, yellow, blue, labelled 'drinking', 'washing', 'toilet'.

'Latrines are out the back. But don't stray off the garden path. The land's still mined. El Supremo nearly got himself blown up two days ago.'

'El Supremo?'

'Theodore King. You'd think he'd know better after all these years, but he never listens to anything anyone says.'

'Except God.'

Joe stares up to the heavens. 'He's even been known to take on God!'

After he has gone, Hannah has another look at the flagpole just outside the building with its big blue and red flag, emblazoned 'Help'. Blue and red Help pennants fly from the two supply trucks. Help stickers brand the windscreens. Help logos on the literature, Help lettering on T-shirts and hats. Everything market-researched, tested, manufactured, quality-controlled and distributed to Help centres throughout the world. One hundred and fourteen aid agencies registered with the UN in Kigali alone, some of them on disaster merry-go-rounds, two weeks in and out.

'Help, help, help!' she shouts, hoping Joe will hear. She thinks of telethons at Christmas and Easter, cheques in charity envelopes, money boxes in the shape of loaves of bread, global rock concerts, Walk Against Want, go without food, sponsor a child an orphan a family a village a water well. Compassion is good for you, better than therapy. University students' immune systems improve when they watch footage of Mother Teresa. No wonder when Bob Geldorf was knighted he told the media, 'Fuck off, I'm not Mother Teresa.'

Before she left Australia, her producer had asked her to file a story called 'Does the Aid Get There?' She had shaken her head. 'That's one problem, but it's not the agencies' fault. Most of them are pretty professional, it's just that aid can get siphoned off by corrupt governments, or used to feed troops in cases of war. It's the long-term consequences of aid that becomes so tricky. Somalia, for example, had some of the best national anti-famine programs in the world. Today, after huge infusions of international aid, everyone's chronically hungry and dependent on foreign food. Charity may even help to prolong famine. Yet agencies are such mammoth business concerns, they're hard to turn around. Look how they go on using pictures of starving kids to help raise money.'

She pulls a face as she remembers she has promised to do some fund-raising appeals using Rwandan children. Different perhaps, as the appeals are about children of the genocide, but it's a fine line. It always is.

Hannah pours herself another mug of tea and wanders around. So much is familiar – the makeshift quarters, rows of bunks with family snapshots pinned to the walls, long trestle tables end to end, hurricane lamps and clusters of non-drip tropical candles. Food stores. Drugs and medications. Rat traps. Ordered chaos, held together by a bunch of people who spent much of their lives moving from one disaster to another. Long, harsh hours, discomfort, exhaustion, a strong camaraderie. There is even a particular smell – disinfectant, damp washing and the pungency of fatigue.

A piece of paper flutters off one of the cupboard doors. She picks it up and reads a list of contents of hygiene parcels for refugees.

> 200 pieces of tissue
> 4 rolls toilet paper
> 3 soap

1 lice shampoo
2 boxes panty liners
4 toothbrushes
2 toothpaste
1 razor and 5 blades
3 kg washing powder
1 soap for manual clothes washing

Such a strange existence, thinks Hannah as she sticks the list back on the cupboard door, wondering why it is so hard to accept that this is now her daughter's world. Pinned on the wall is a chart of camp movements, and there, with a line of her own, is the name Alice Chimeme. Hannah suddenly feels proud.

The light is beginning to fade and she is still waiting for Alice. Mosquitoes whine around her head with malevolent intent. They bite at her ankles and her arms and she is just anointing herself with insect repellent when the first aid workers start returning from their long day, dumping bags, grabbing a drink.

'I'm starving.'

'Well, I'm not starving, I'm hungry.'

'Hah, hah, smartypants!'

Faces and places merge then separate in the pleasure of recognition. Judy Morrison, last met in Cambodia, and before that Mozambique and Ethiopia. Stocky, competent and irreverent. Hair cut in a cockatoo's crest. Says she works for God, and to buy herself a bright red sports car by way of compensation when she's at home. Her husband is also an aid worker, presently in Cambodia.

Andy, in charge of all transport, first encountered in Uganda, wears body-clinging nylon shirts even in the heat, and once sat up all night telling Hannah about breeding camels in the Sudan.

Stewart, a relative newcomer, a young man with jug ears and pimples who worked on a Melbourne suburban weekly before coming to Rwanda, and who has had to switch from reporting weddings to telling the folks back home how their money will help save a starving child. His face has a tic and his hands twitch. Hannah's expert eye tells her he is probably in need of counselling, poor boy, and no wonder, with all the horrors he must have observed – although come to think of it, she's never had counselling, this is a new approach. *Seen the slaughter of two hundred children? It's okay, Stewart, it's quite appropriate to feel distress, you're doing fine, just fine.*

In the middle of the greetings Alice walks in, canvas bag over one shoulder, her face streaked with dust. Hannah notices she is wearing the boots which last took her bushwalking in the Blue Mountains. Hannah's impulse is to rush and hug her but when she sees the self-conscious smile on Alice's face she tries to be restrained. Her restraint doesn't last long.

'Hey,' says Alice, smiling. 'Don't eat me.'

But when Joe Schwartz invites Hannah to stay for dinner and Alice's dark brows lower, Hannah tactfully says she has to leave.

Outside, night is rapidly falling and an unexpected smell of eucalypts fills the air.

'Makes me homesick,' confesses Alice, walking her mother to the gates and wrinkling up her nose.

Hannah puts her arm around her daughter. 'Me too.'

Alice kicks the ground with her foot, digging in her toe, circling it round and round just as Ezekiel once did.

'Have you found Ezekiel?' she asks eventually. 'I wanted to ask you earlier but not with other people around.'

Hannah feels a chill of responsibility. She should have immediately tried to contact Ezekiel, for Alice's sake, rather than hold back because of her own fears. Fears of what? Of being reminded of past pain? Of her anger? Of recognising what she has lost? Or is it also because she is being protective of Alice?

She realises Alice is looking at her expectantly and that her silence cuts the air. 'I did. I saw him at a press conference when we first arrived, but he didn't see me. He's a minister now, in the new government. And he was in the Rwandan Patriotic Front – the liberating army.'

'Was he!' Alice's voice is ecstatic. 'Then are we going to see him? Please, *please*.'


The following evening Hannah collects Alice and two other women who want to take up Sister Helene's invitation to the Feast of the Assumption. One is Judy Morrison. The other is the journalist Beverley Prettyfoot, whom Hannah last saw in Uganda as part of a group of journalists interviewing the daughter of the former chief justice, whose murder had been ordered by Idi Amin. The interview had taken place in the judge's old office, which still had bullet holes in the glass-topped door, overturned furniture, papers and files strewn on the dusty floor. Beverley, true to form, had worn a frilly white blouse with a broderie anglaise sailor's collar. She had a habit of moving in close to anyone she was interviewing and would stand with poised pencil and a large notebook. The judge's daughter was recounting the circumstances of her father's death.

'They killed him by dismemberment. They cut off his ears,

his nose, his hands. They cut off his penis and stuffed it in his mouth.'

Beverley's jaw dropped slack and she licked her pencil. 'My,' she said, 'and then what did they do?'

On the way to the archbishop's residence the four women link hands in the blackness of night, only one torch between them. Trees loom in strange tasselled shapes, frogs croak in the bushes, and the only light comes from a yellow rind of moon lying spent on its back. The building has been badly shelled. In the sea of dark they inch their way along the damaged walls, trying to find an opening. Broken doors and windows are barricaded with heavy pieces of wood.

'Cooee!' calls Alice. Her voice is loud and clear. The light of Hannah's torch illuminates her daughter's face from below and she feels a rush of protectiveness.

'Cooee,' echoes the unmistakable gravelly voice of Sister Helene, beckoning them down long dark corridors. Still holding hands for fear of stumbling, they follow the direction of her voice, their footsteps ringing in the emptiness. A murmuring of voices in the distance, darkness growing into light as they turn a corner and are confronted by the strangest of sights. An enormous, lavishly painted banqueting hall lit by a myriad tiny candles which throw pinpoints of white on walls and beamed ceilings. A hall filled with nuns. Nuns of all nationalities and ages. Nuns in robes of every colour.

'A numinousness of nuns,' whispers Hannah to Alice.

Alice wrinkles her nose. 'A nattering of nuns.'

Sister Helene welcomes them into the hall, her arms flung wide. 'Women were never allowed in here. This was men only, the archbishop and his chaps. Probably he's turning in his grave. Whoops! He hasn't got a grave and serves him jolly well right!'

The nuns break into girlish laughter, hands clasped in front of their mouths. Sister Helene is whispering loudly in Hannah's ear. 'The old archbish was a bit of a baddy. Went with the other side. Got himself shot. Good riddance and may God save his soul.'

'A hard task,' observes the dry voice of Sister Asteria, one of the four Rwandan nuns.

A long table in the middle of the hall bears the feast. Hannah's eyes fill with tears. Such a modest spread of food. Two plates of dry cracker biscuits, each topped with a small sliver of tomato, a bowl of rice, some bananas, six small bottles of brightly coloured fizzy drink, three jugs of water. And, in the centre of the table, a glass bowl full of bright yellow custard lovingly decorated with crumbled biscuits and slices of banana which carefully spell the words, '*Bonne fête*'.

'Sister Helene found the packet of custard powder,' whispers a young Dutch nun sitting next to Hannah. 'She's very clever.'

Beverley jangles her gold bracelets as she peers closely at the table. 'I can't eat packet custard,' she says, flashing a bright smile around the table.

The nuns sing grace and the banquet begins. Sister Helene dives under the table and brings out an enormous unlabelled bottle. She uncorks it and pours out the first glass of ruby-coloured liquid. Such richness, such sweetness, such exquisite red wine.

'My,' says Beverley, 'where did that come from?'

'Don't ask, it won't turn into blood but we don't have any bread either,' roars Sister Helene as the nuns flutter and giggle, their voices floating upwards to the gilded rafters of the archbishop's banqueting hall.

After they have eaten, Sister Asteria is bidden to tell the

story of the Rwandan nuns. She speaks in French while Sister Helene translates, and the other three Rwandan nuns lean forward on the edge of their chairs. At each pause they say urgently, '*Et puis?*', sometimes making the candlelight flicker, so strong is their need to hear this story over and over again, as if each time might relieve one more shade of agony.

Sister Asteria is also leaning forward. Her glasses accentuate her eyes, making her seem like some huge owl. 'The churches became the killing fields. We were there when they came, these men with guns and grenades and machetes, and because thirty of our order were killed in the first massacres, we knew it would be our turn soon.

'Two Spanish nuns who were fleeing the country suggested we hide in their house. For two months we hid, with no lights and the curtains drawn. A neighbour told us what was happening in the village and dealt with suspicious questions from the villagers or the police. Smell of cooking? That's from those Spanish nuns who had all that funny foreign food. Water running? Must be mice.

'One day the neighbour told us that soldiers had been ordered to search the house. She and her husband helped hoist us into the roof, and there we sat on one of the beams, four little birds in a line. We pinched each other to keep awake. For days we perched on the beam. We had only just climbed down, thinking the danger was past, when we heard three loud knocks on the front door. Imagine how our hearts beat. The door was forced open and there stood a major from the army and six soldiers. We joined hands, expecting to die. But he was a good Hutu. Some of them were, and even risked their lives to save us. He said a priest who was fearful for our safety had asked him to rescue us. He thought we would be safer in the church where everyone had gathered for sanctuary. He was wrong. People flocked to the churches, thinking they would be safe, but it was the contrary. The churches were the places where the soldiers did most of their killing. They used grenades, or set fire to the buildings. Then, when people were forced outside, the would be hacked down with machetes. They were very brave. They prepared themselves to die. They sang as if they were in a trance and they kept on singing while, one by one, they were being killed.'

The face of Sister Asteria is now stern and drawn. 'We are people who nourish ourselves on the word of God, and we are told to forgive. We have the desire but it will be hard. Yet without forgiveness, we cannot reconcile.'

On the walk home, when they are holding hands, Alice says softly, 'They *were* brave, so very brave.'

When they reach the Help compound, Hannah wants to hug Alice. She is prepared to be rejected but Alice doesn't hang back and teases, 'It's okay, we're not mother and daughter, we're workmates.'

Moonlight is breaking over Alice's face and Hannah catches her breath at her daughter's beauty. She wants to avoid an emotional answer. 'Drink plenty of boiled water, wash your hands, change your knickers every day, and don't talk to any strange men.'

Alice giggles. 'And, as Aunt D would say, beware of men with three ears.'

In bed that night, in a room she shares with Beverley and two French photographers, Hannah lies staring into the darkness. The nuns' story reinforces all she has seen and heard. The people who committed such atrocities are still at liberty. Alice is bound to encounter them, particularly if she is sent to the aid camps outside Rwanda. What can Hannah do? Nothing. She has to let go, know that her daughter's life is now her own, and Hannah's feelings must not interfere. She grimaces. She used to be good at detaching herself from the horrors surrounding her, but since Kevin died, it's been different.

Kevin was only thirty-three when he photographed a little girl in the Sudan. She was alone, squatting in the desert, too weak to go any further. Behind her lurked a large black vulture. Waiting.

After he had taken the photograph, he chased away the vulture and saw to it that the child was safe. It was an extra-ordinary photograph – in one shot he had captured Africa's despair. When Hannah read that he had won a Pulitzer and been on the front cover of *Time* magazine, she rang him with her congratulations.

He told her he'd received thousands of letters. The one that touched him most came from a young Japanese schoolgirl who wrote, 'You have true heart.'

A few weeks later, Hannah woke up to read that Kevin was dead. He'd climbed into his pick-up truck and gassed himself in a Johannesburg suburb.

His father told the newspapers, 'Kevin always carried around the horror of his work.'

Hannah used to deal with her own horror by imagining that she had a shelf inside her, located somewhere around her navel. Above the shelf were all her experiences. Below it were her feelings, tucked out of harm's way. But now the shelf has become thin, and with Alice in the picture she isn't sure how it will hold.

'What if I don't hear from Ezekiel?' Hannah asks Aunt D, phoning by satellite. 'What if he ignores me? If I can't tell him about Alice?'

'Well, he's no friend and he's never been a father to her, so if he doesn't answer, good riddance.' Her aunt pauses. 'That's not what you want to hear, is it?'

Hannah is silent.

'How's Alice?' asks Aunt D.

Hannah smiles. 'Terrific. She's going really well, she's off to Zaire. I hope she'll cope.'

'She'll cope. She's your daughter.'

Hannah has a sudden need to know what her aunt is doing, a link to small domestic happenings, however mundane. Her aunt chortles.

'I've got arthritis so I'm sitting with my feet in a bucket of hot water and Epsom salts. I'm wearing my yellow knitted hat, the one your father says looks like an egg cosy.'

Without warning, Hannah is overwhelmed by the contrast between her aunt's world — comfortable, safe, and relatively predictable — and the one that now surrounds her. Here is a world where violence spills into people's daily lives, where trust is splintered, and where fear drives out love.

## eleven

T he air should be sweetly perfumed from flowering shrubs, but as they approach the border it is no longer possible to keep their windows open. The smell of putrefaction invades the jeep, blows through their hair, touches their skin. Pathetic bundles of bloodied rags lie strewn along the side of the road. A woman's body floats face downward in the reeds, a child still strapped to her back. The lake has a hard metallic glitter, broken by drifting mounds of swollen corpses which have overflowed from the waterways in Rwanda and are polluting the water system.

Around the corner is the frontier between Rwanda and Zaire. Concrete huts, rusted iron roofs, drunken soldiers, piles of ammunition strewn everywhere, rotting rubbish. People shove to get into an airless little office made of corrugated iron, where a man is stamping passports and collecting money. Rumours fly:

'They won't give you a visa at the border. Stopped doing

it yesterday.' 'Two days ago.' 'Three.' 'They will give you a visa but it will cost you fifty dollars, one hundred, two hundred.' 'They won't give you a visa and if they don't like the look of you they will arrest and maybe kill you.'

Thump, thump, go the official stamps. A man in a dark blue suit with a dark face and a dark moustache looks at them unsmilingly and says, 'Go!' He has a revolver hitched to his belt.

As George noses the jeep forward, Hannah sees that the countryside is no longer green and hilly but flat and treeless. Roads are full of potholes, buildings ramshackle, the atmosphere restless and seedy. Waldo sticks his head out of the window and sniffs the foul air.

'Welcome to Zaire,' says a white painted sign, peppered with bullet holes.

'Fiefdom of President Mobutu Sese Seko,' says Waldo. 'We're also supposed to say, All-powerful warrior whose endurance and inflexible will to win sweeps him from conquest to conquest, leaving fire in his wake.'

'What's worse than being attacked by the Hutus?' asks George, swerving to avoid one of the many potholes in the road.

'Give in,' says Hannah.

Waldo shakes his head. 'Don't know.'

'Being defended by the Zairean army.' George grins with delight at his own joke. 'Rob, rape and run away.'

Exhausted refugees shuffle towards the refugee camps. Some are blindly fleeing, fearing reprisals for the massacres; others move in the opposite direction, returning home to Rwanda. Twin streams of treacle oozing their way along the road. People whose lives and livelihoods are bundled on their backs. Sometimes only their eyes are visible above cloth that covers their mouths and noses in the hope of warding off disease. Random objects seized in terror – bags of grain and blankets, pots and pans, books and radios, crockery and matting, mattresses and bags. Belongings from times when morning breakfasts steamed on fires and stoves, children in their clean white shirts and shining knees pranced their way to school, and men and women went about their working lives. When there was order and sweet reason.

Rwanda's defeated Hutu soldiers do not walk. They commandeer trucks and buses. Drunken soldiers lob mortars indiscriminately into the hills or hunt down women and children. Mobs of young men parade through the villages waving machetes, metal bars and wooden stakes. They believe they are invincible, magically shielded by the twigs and leaves sprouting from their pockets and headbands. Small children run alongside, giving the war dance a sense of carnival. Boy soldiers, scared and scary, spit at their jeep with a precision that Waldo admires. They carry rifles as big as themselves.

George swings the jeep off the road and comes to an abrupt halt. Ahead lies an Hieronymus Bosch scene of deplorable horror. One million people gathered on a mean patch of black volcanic rock, still active, still shooting flames into the air. A place festering with violence. In amongst the refugees are those who took part in the killings. It is impossible to separate the two.

There are no trees, no grass, no water. Small fragile shelters are stacked so close together they would blaze in minutes. Thousands of tents covered in blue and white plastic sheeting with barely room to walk between. Huge trucks bringing water, food and medical supplies. Earth-moving equipment. Lorries laden with corpses. Wagons from all the aid agencies in the world criss-crossing the ground in no apparent order, pennants like crusader flags waving white in the acrid air. A great hellish bubbling of trucks, cars, people and machinery, and all the while the volcano smoulders, spewing forth its blackened ash. In this lunar landscape there are no roads, no tracks, just this seething mass of people. People sick and dying, people dead; people sleeping, defecating, pushing and shoving for food, hitting one another with machetes, sticks and rifle butts. People in every conceivable state of distress.

Hannah taps Waldo's arm and points to the right where hundreds of journalists have pitched their tents, set up generators, edit suites, satellite discs and telephone uplinks. This part of the rock has the highest vantage point, and from here an ever-changing chorus line of television commentators emote stories of indescribable massacres, unutterable horrors and incomprehensible grief. A few metres away, camera operators are filming these declamations, squatting, standing, moving, their cameras zooming in and out. Running amongst them are the stills photographers, their clicking cameras sounding like a plague of locusts.

Waldo tips back his hat. 'It's called smother cover. In three weeks, they'll have packed their gear and decamped to the next disaster. Come on, let's go and see who we know.'

He signals as he spots Daniel Keneally striding over the rock. He thought he'd see him here, black cap pushed to the back of his head, black jacket bristling with pockets, red bandanna this time tied around his neck. He works silently and swiftly, ducks, weaves, focuses, refocuses, his gold signet ring with its giant diamond winking as his hands move deftly. He bounds over the black rock, swooping and squatting, moving in on groups of children, picking them out in singles, barely talking to them but his energy somehow making them move or stay still, whatever he wants. Ah, now what is he doing? Smearing ash under the eyes of a group of kids.

'Poor little buggers,' says Keneally. 'Got to make 'em look as bad as possible.'

Hannah stares at the children's black smudged eyes. 'That's cheating.'

He rounds on her. 'Listen, all I'm doing with my pictures is saying this is shit and we gotta see it's shit. I know it. I feel it. You know it, you feel it. But everyone else out there? We gotta make sure they know it and feel it.'

Hannah shrugs.

Keneally glares at her. 'Don't be so holy-moly, I bet you've pulled some swifties.'

'Well, I can condense a massacre into two minutes and a genocide into four, I guess that's a start.'

Keneally grins as he changes film. 'In the American Civil War, one guy telegraphed the whole genealogy of Jesus Christ to stop his rivals from using the wire. Other guys wrote brilliant eyewitness accounts of battles they'd never seen.'

'Nobody could imagine anything as bad as this,' says Hannah.


Meantime, in another part of this camp, some distance away, Alice is trying to cope with an epidemic of cholera which confirms her worst fears. People are fighting for their lives in grass shanties scattered across a barren lava plain four hours' walk from the nearest source of water. Those too weak to make the journey depend on water drawn from three tanks set up by the United Nations High Commission for Refugees. The water shortage sets up daily scenes of desperation. Alice is detailed to move down the long queues of people, identifying those who are dropping from illness.

The crowds are shouting, 'We want water, we want water!' They wave yellow plastic cans in her face and at first she shrinks from their anger and misery, until she learns to help them understand that if they are patient, eventually they will reach the water they so urgently need.

The bearded Irishman who is working by her side is swearing softly.

'It's a complete and utter disaster. The UN asked for eighty water tankers from foreign donors. Only twelve have arrived. People are quick to offer us food, but slow to give us water purification tankers or latrines. It's sexier to feed people than help them shit in a safe place.'

When she has finished helping in the water queue, Alice returns to the cholera station. She works alongside four Rwandan nurses, helping to carry patients into the courtyard, mop the makeshift clinic clean of faeces and vomit, and spray it with disinfectant. She carries a young boy of about ten and places him naked and unattended on a straw mat. She thinks he is dying and wants to stay and hold his hand but there is no time.

In another tent, four young men have died during the night. Masked workers zip the corpses into white body-bags. Further up the hill, the body-bags have run out and they are using sacking. A Hutu government functionary holds the clammy hand of his young wife, who hasn't improved despite two days on an intravenous saline drip. He wants to pull the drip out, but Alice restrains him. She crouches by the woman, stroking her hair back from her face. As the man speaks urgently to his wife, she closes her eyes and dies. Alice looks at the stricken face of this man and wonders if he was a member of the killing squads. What a mess, what a terrible useless mess, she thinks as she stands up and straightens her aching back.

The Irishman massages her neck and shoulders. 'It *is* a mess,' he says as if reading her mind. 'We mess it. But life goes on.' He points to a small brown bird patiently building a nest in one of the branches of a shelter, then hands her a green army flask of water. 'Here, have this with you at all times,' he says. 'And make sure you keep your hands away from your mouth.'

Alice doesn't know that Hannah and Waldo are in the same camp, and they are equally unaware of her presence. Hannah is pointing out their next destination to George, a small cluster of tents bearing the blue and red flags of Help and located high on a distant hill. When she looks at the confusion of people and machinery that stretches between them and the hilltop she wonders how they will ever reach their goal.

A gaunt, exhausted woman comes stumbling down the hill towards them, carrying a child in her arms, not realising that she is being filmed. Later, her image will appear on television, an aid worker overwhelmed by the enormity of misery, calling out to no one yet everyone, 'This is the end of the world.'

A little further up the hill, their jeep lurches to a halt by a pile of corpses. A young French army lieutenant looks at them in despair. 'We've lost the body count. We're a transport regiment, not morticians.'

The UN has formed a burial squad drawn from the refugees. They wear masks and yellow rubber gloves, and are paid two dollars a day.

'Softly, be compassionate,' says the young French officer as the workers toss a dead pregnant woman onto the heap of corpses. Hours later, a French bulldozer fails to penetrate the rocky volcanic earth and the grave-digging plan is aborted. One thousand bodies are left to rot while aid agencies debate how best to dispose of them.

Hannah and Waldo's destination is one of several camps specially allocated to children whose parents were killed during the fighting, or who have become separated from their families. Sometimes, women bring their children to the camp, begging that they be taken in. Fourteen hundred babies and children are crowded into it. No one knows the real figures yet, but up to half a million children in Rwanda are thought to be orphaned, or separated from their families.

Jack and Kim are already there and have begun shooting background footage. Hannah mops the sweat from her face as she sits on a flat section of the rock with small children crowding around her. She has agreed to make a fundraising appeal for Help, well aware of the irony that she is doing exactly the same thing as Theodore King.

When Waldo raises an eyebrow, she says, 'Oh go take a jump, if this camp weren't here, these kids would die.'

She pulls her khaki hat low over her eyes to protect them from the glare and begins trying to learn her lines: 'Of all the victims of Rwanda's horror, it's the children who are suffering most. Become a Help Orphan Sponsor. Call two five six, sixty-five.'

Help's assistant marketing director hovers nearby, fanning herself with a clipboard and looking distressed. Hannah snaps, 'They're not all orphans.'

The marketing director sighs and hopes that Hannah isn't going to be difficult. ' "Orphans" is emotive,' she pleads. 'It'll bring in the money.'

'But it's untrue.'

'What do you want to say?'

'What the national government says – unaccompanied children.'

'Mmm.' The marketing director sounds doubtful as she fingers the heart-shaped locket around her neck and smoothes out her khaki shirt and khaki safari pants. Help is one of the top fundraising agencies and she does not want to be beaten by her rivals.

Hannah swats the ants which crawl up her legs. Small brown feet keep inching towards her own feet and she reaches forward to tickle two little girls, who double up with laughter. Her audience of children has grown.

Jack lifts onto her lap a small boy who is swamped by a giant T-shirt that says 'Kentucky Fried' in red lettering. His garment doesn't disguise the fact that his head lolls because he hasn't the strength to hold it upright. His legs and arms stick out in strange directions.

The child was brought in by a soldier who found him wandering on his own down the road. His name and village are unknown so he has been called Vendredi, after the day on which he arrived. As Hannah stares down at his dark unblinking eyes she has an urgent desire to shake him out of his sickness, just as she had once wanted to shake Alice out of her crying.

Soon Vendredi's details will be coded and sent to Berne, where the Swiss have established a database for lost children of the world. Children who have seen and heard too much. Rwandan children rocking backwards and forwards, their fingers in their ears to blot out God knows what sounds of horror. Children with machete wounds on their bodies and their heads. Babies too weak to suckle, found abandoned by the side of the road. But these children are now being cared for by adults who have come to help from all over the world. Babies wriggle like little fishes, shrieking with delight as young Rwandan girls, themselves probably orphans, soap and oil them, pat them dry. The children call them mamas.

A grey-haired German paediatrician, who gave up his successful practice in Frankfurt to help in Rwanda, smiles when he sees Hannah holding Vendredi. 'These children have been so damaged they need to be held, need to know that not all adults do them harm.'

Jack takes a light reading, and wipes Vendredi's nose with a faded yellow and black scarf he bought in a Thai market. Hannah says to hurry, Vendredi is squirming and feels as if he has a fever.

Jack looks up from his viewfinder, sweat running down his face. 'I know, poor little bugger, but it's got to be done.'

Jack is ready to begin, waving his hand. Kim adjusts the microphone. Hannah clears her throat and away she goes. What a rich, vibrant voice, what feeling, she thinks wryly as she blinks back her tears, remembering Theodore King.

The child's body burns and his thin, weak cry is barely heard above the din of jackhammers drilling into the rock to make latrines, the rumble of huge trucks containing water, food and medical supplies, and the constant roar of planes landing and taking off.

'Every two minutes,' says Jack. 'Worse than Sydney airport. Come to bloody Rwanda, metropolis of the world. Let's go for one more take.'

This will be their sixth. Others have been spoilt by noise or by Hannah forgetting her lines or by the child hiding his head. What was it her aunt once said? You can't fart against thunder.

Waiting for Jack, Hannah forgets her frustration as she spots her daughter further down the hill, moving with her own particular grace, so tall that she stands out above the crowd. Hannah is elated and waves furiously. At first Alice does not see her; when she does she gives only a small wave in return. Hannah makes a grimace. She would probably disapprove of her mother parading dying babies to the television audiences of the world. Hannah moves her gaze away from Alice and searches for Waldo, who is clutching a small video camera and looking like Pooh bear trying to climb a mountain. He appears oblivious to the fact that a large French water truck is about to run him down, or that a woman is dragging a corpse past his sandalled feet. A dead hand bumps over his toes.

Waldo has seen the hand but feels it would be unkind to withdraw his feet. He is wondering if the rock is cutting the dead man's knuckles, and do dead men bleed? The thought is too distressing so he turns back to his camera. His idea for a film story is fast fading. The heat is relentless; he has no energy, damn it. He regrets eating so many apple Danish in the middle of the night before he left home. The back of his cream shirt is sticking to his skin. He cheers up when he spots a young aid worker Hannah and he have nicknamed Bath Shop Bruce.

Bruce smells of lime and coconut aftershave. He has been sent to Africa as part of a corporate community service scheme, and behaves as if he has been press-ganged into someone else's script, one he does not much enjoy. Bruce has confided to Hannah and Waldo that he takes vitamin B complex and ginseng for energy, vitamin C for disease resistance, echinacea for his immune system, and Bach Flower Rescue Remedy for emergencies, which, for Bruce, occur all the time. He works in a shop in Canberra with pretty window displays, its shelves full of pink and orange and angelica-green soaps, coconut oil creams and male toiletries, all packaged in scarlet and white.

Hannah sighs and returns to her script. This time she will get it right, but she is immediately disturbed by an angry Joe Schwartz, striding between her and the camera, pushing his cap to the back of his head.

'Move,' he says, waving his arms. 'You're in the way. Both of you.'

Two monster trucks are trying to nose their way into the camp, jolting over large boulders, skidding in ditches.

Jack leans on his tripod and camera, arms crossed. 'Wouldn't hurt him to be polite. Seems to forget we're helping him keep the show on the road.'

The heat is formidable. Hannah is nursing her fourth child, a little girl with dark ringlets who wears a pale pink dress covered in yellow roses. Her father and mother have both been killed, her mother's unborn baby cut out in front of the girl's eyes. Hannah is feeling sick with the horror of everything when she sees a young boy lying on his back with his fingers stuck in his ears. His legs are stretched out stiffly in front of him. His mouth opens and closes in silent screams. An aid worker comes to him and he grabs her wrist so hard that he hurts her, and when she tries gently to free her hand he clings harder. The woman strokes his forehead and his tight curly hair, but he stares ahead with a fixed expression. When eventually she frees herself his fingers again fly up to his ears. He rocks back and forth. He will not speak, he does not eat his food.

Hannah remembers reading somewhere that traumatic memories are stored in a different part of the brain to ordinary events, and they will be retained not as stories or words, but as sensations. Years later, some smell or other sensation can trigger the return of a trauma, like a sensory flashback.

Jack moves in for a close-up. 'God, what did we do to you?'

At the end of the day, when they have finally finished shooting and Jack and Kim have returned to Kigali to send the footage back to Sydney, a jeep bounces over the rock towards them, brakes, and Joe Schwartz and Waldo clamber out. Joe is shouting above the noise of the camp, 'We've lost Alice.'

For a moment her world empties, except for this single piece of information.

'We've lost Alice,' she hears again.

This is the terror she has slept with, the terror she has tried to deny. 'Lost her? How do you mean, lost her?'

Waldo hitches up his pants, his face distressed. 'We can't find her. Everyone else is ready to leave but there's no sign of Alice.'

'Don't be ridiculous, she can't just disappear.' Hannah's hands are clammy, she has difficulty breathing.

Joe gazes towards the horizon as if he expects Alice will suddenly appear. 'She'll be okay,' he mutters. 'She's probably helping out with one of the others, or maybe she's holed up with a sick child.'

By dusk, Alice has not returned. All the way down the hill, in the acrid streaky light, Hannah scans the crowds. But no one has seen her. No one knows where she might be.

'Shoot,' says Joe, for the first time sounding worried.

Hannah scowls. It's not the time for euphemisms. 'If she's been held up helping someone, is it okay to stay out on the hill? All night?'

Joe inadvertently takes his foot off the clutch and the jeep lurches forward. 'Are you kidding? With this mob? No, sir, but almost certainly she'll be back at base. Hitched a lift with someone else.'

But Alice wasn't at the house in Goma which Help used as its base for all the nearby camps. George was there. And Bruce. But no Alice. Joe rings other aid agencies and local police. 'Maybe she got lost and just couldn't get a lift. It often happens,' he says unconvincingly.

Outside the night is dark and without stars. Waldo, who has been quietly drinking from a hip flask, offers it to Hannah. She takes a swig. They hear shooting over the hills.

# twelve

Hannah lies in her sleeping bag under a few straggly eucalypt trees, trying to keep her eyes closed, half conscious
that something terrible awaits her but not yet ready to be confronted. She smells of sweat, and dirt at the bottom of her bag
scratches her feet. She reaches out blindly for her drinking bottle
but she has knocked it over some time in the early hours of the
morning and it lies on the ground, empty. She struggles to a
sitting position and looks around. The sky is still dark, with a
few streaks of pale lemon. Dawn is breaking. Birds make a few
tentative chirps in the blindness of the new day. Soon they will
burst into a fanfare of song. A dull ache flickers somewhere in
her middle. Then she remembers.

She jumps to her feet, notices that Waldo's sleeping bag is
already empty, flings on some clothes, and bursts into the nearby
house. Waldo and Joe are standing in the mysterious light of
early morning, deep in talk. Waldo is dunking a teabag, Joe has
his habitual mug of hot water.

Immediately Hannah sees their faces, she knows there is no point in asking for news – but she asks anyway.

'Anything? Have you heard anything?'

Joe shakes his head.

The sun, which first appeared as a strident orange gash over the black rock, has quickly blurred into a smoky haze as the camp stirs into life. From every flimsy shelter comes the rustle of tiny movements, a baby cries somewhere on the hillside, small children wipe the sleep from their eyes, women struggle to coax a fire from meagre bundles of twigs. A jeep belonging to an Irish aid agency is already bouncing over the rock face, its green and white flag waving jauntily, its driver shouting good morning to Joe as they pass. Now come the big battalions, the earth-moving equipment, the lorries, the water tanks, revving up their power, churning into action. A plane roars overhead, circles twice and lands.

Joe thumps the gears into four-wheel drive, and the jeep strains and buckets up the hillside towards the hospital with its cluster of white tents. By now, the din of the camp is so great that they have to shout to the young French nurse who comes to greet them. She takes them round to the back of the compound, where rows of sacking shrouds lie neatly stacked, waiting to be collected and burned. They look at the feet, they look at the hands, sometimes they pull down flaps of sacking, they hope, oh they hope that this part of their quest will fail. Hannah sees the face of a young Rwandan woman, probably about the same age as Alice, but thin and ravaged by illness before she died. Hannah looks at her with infinite tenderness and infinite relief.

Bruce, the young corporate volunteer, lags behind. After they have checked the shrouds he ventures a question. 'How can you be sure it's not Alice unless you unwrap every one?'

230

Hannah glances at his pudgy unformed face and for a moment feels sorry for him. He is probably terrified, wondering if his turn will be next, an amoeba adrift on a landscape full of strange and terrible peril.

All day they criss-cross the rock, by jeep and by foot. Hannah covers each area with meticulous precision, pushing her way past flimsy shelters made of twigs and straw, through plastic tents so close together it is hard to walk between them, past old men who are too weak to move, past women with babies at their withered breasts. Her feet ache, her arms and legs are scratched.

'Alice, Alice!' Hannah calls, standing on the rock in the purple dusk, howling like some wild animal. Behind her, the volcano spews its poisonous ash. Alice has now been missing for over twenty-four hours.

The roads at night are even harder to navigate than during the day. Soldiers with machine-guns and boys with machetes swagger insolently in front of the convoy, banging on the sides of the aid wagons. Hannah sits beside Joe, who is chewing gum and saying nothing. She stares ahead, her eyes no longer focusing properly. It is as if they are gazing into some distant landscape where she is not required to look or feel.

'Alice is pretty smart, y'know,' says Joe after they have cleared the camps and are down on the flat again. 'She could still turn up okay.'

Late that night, Hannah and Waldo are sitting on the veran-dah of the Goma house. Everything is in darkness, except for the fireflies which waft around the brass lamp on the rickety green card table. Inside, the other occupants are quietly pre-paring their evening meal. A stir-fry, a watermelon somebody bought from the side of the road, mugs of tea. A few are writing letters. They are leaving Hannah alone. Either they are embarrassed and do not know what to do, or they are reminded of their own vulnerability and this is not pleasant.

Waldo is trying to divert Hannah with a game of cards when she says in a determined voice, 'I'm going to demand an interview with Ezekiel.'

'You can't demand an interview.'

'Why not? She's his daughter.'

'He doesn't know that.'

'He soon will,' says Hannah grimly.

'But her disappearance has nothing to do with him. It happened in Zaire, not Rwanda.'

'Oh for God's sake, Waldo, he's got more power than either of us. He must be able to help.'

Waldo pulls a face. He is doubtful that Ezekiel Chimeme will have much time for helping.

In Kigali Hannah finds herself in the midst of a round of interviews – with the media, with United Nations personnel, Rwandan government officials, camp officials, the police. Her colleagues are the hardest to deal with.

'When did you first miss Alice?'

'Why are you here?'

'Why was your daughter here?'

'*Is* here,' insists Hannah.

'Any idea what might have happened?'

'What's the aid agency doing?'

'What's the government doing?'

'What kind of a girl was Alice?'

'*Is* Alice,' shouts Hannah.

She is being judged. The woman who puts her career first,

232

is always away. Imagine allowing her daughter to come to Rwanda, no wonder this happened. Who's the father and why isn't he around?

No, it's not like that, she wants to shout, but pride inhibits her. Some reporters try deals for exclusives. She is affronted yet remembers when she did the same. She is angry about the invasion of her privacy but she knows that media coverage might bring information. She does not tell them that Alice has a Rwandan father. When someone asks her about Alice's dad, she says shortly that she has no communication with him. At one stage she thinks of revealing Ezekiel's paternity, but Waldo warns her against it.

She makes lists of people to see, people to ring, media colleagues who might be able to help rather than just use her for a story. Two days after Alice's disappearance, she is sitting cross-legged on her bed, forcing her pen to move across the paper. She is trying to write to Bella, but she is tired, so tired. Anger with Ezekiel licks through her, just as it had in the plane, and she is dismayed. God, after all these years you'd think it would have lost its heat. Perhaps this is what therapists mean when they bandy around words like 'closure'. Maybe she had never wanted closure. Bella had been more direct. All those years ago, when she first came to the hospital after Alice was born, she had whisked Alice out of her bassinet and said firmly, 'Stuff the guy, Hannah, put him in a box and slam the lid.'

Then she had made cooing noises into the baby's ear and walked round the room for a while, jiggling Alice up and down. When she returned the baby to her bassinet she flopped down beside Hannah.

'Cheer up, Han, she'll be much more fun to have around,'

and she had waved her black-stockinged leg vaguely in the direction of Alice.

Hannah's face had crumpled like a child's. 'But I want Ezekiel to see her, Bella, I want him here.'

After Bella had gone, Hannah continued to embroider Ezekiel's memory in the darkness and rage against it in the light of day. She is doing this now, she realises, the more so since he hasn't responded to her request to meet.

She collects Waldo and they set off in search of Gerry Phillips, an Australian who is working for the UN in Rwanda and who is acting as an informal link with the Australian embassy in Nairobi. Phillips receives Hannah and Waldo in his office, which is temporarily located within one of the university buildings. A small Australian desk flag sits alongside a blue UN flag.

Phillips says good morning in a voice that matches the beige of his linen suit. He runs a hand through his thinning hair, apologises for not having any diplomatic status, expresses appropriate concern and promises to do all he can.

Hannah sums him up as a career diplomat, one of the old school still tied to the apron strings of Mother England. Still, he is kind enough and expresses appropriate concern at Alice's disappearance. She hands over a photograph of Alice. 'My daughter,' she says proudly.

Phillips looks at it with curiosity. 'Pretty girl.'

Does Hannah imagine it, or does he linger over the photograph before glancing up at Hannah and then down to the photograph again?

'All right, I'll do my best for you.' He extends a hand. 'Keep in touch.'

Hannah speaks with Aunt D, whose voice is, as always, robust and cheerful.

'I did the *I Ching* and it could've said abyss upon abyss but it didn't, it said it furthers one to cross the great waters.'

Hannah says that Rwanda is landlocked, and her aunt tells her kindly that she is being too literal.

'What about that man who's supposed to be her father, Bluebeard?'

'What about him?'

'Well, where is he?'

When Hannah's father comes on the line, he tells her in a dry crackly voice he has managed to see the Australian Minister for Foreign Affairs.

'Hopeless. Mouthed all the usual platitudes but didn't come up with anything positive, just said they were leaving it to the RPF because that was the best course of action, and when I said that the RPF were leaving it to the Australian government, he said, 'Well, now.''

Hannah winces. The words have a familiar ring.

'Look, darling, don't give up, we'll get her out, somehow.'

This is the first time her father has ever called her darling. She thinks of all those years when he was lost in his own grief, a shadowy figure who flickered through her life. When she first told him she was having a baby, he had chewed on his evening meal in silence – roast lamb and roast vegetables – no emotion registering on his thin lined face, no response. Finally, he wiped his mouth on his napkin and carefully laid down his knife and fork.

'I presume there's a father?'

Hannah's mouth tightened. 'It's not an immaculate conception.'

'Do I know him, this father?'

'No, you don't know him. He's the African friend I lived with in Paris.'

'The one with the funny name,' her aunt had said, trying to help.

Ernest Coady polished his spectacles. 'So he's not here?'

'Not yet.' Aunt D's voice was conciliatory.

'And not ever likely to be, judging by the way you two women are tiptoeing around. Well, my dear, if you're old enough to vote, you're old enough to have a baby. Let your aunt look after you. She always has.'

He rose and wandered out of the room, leaving Hannah with a familiar hollowness.


On the third day Hannah succeeds in getting an appointment with Ezekiel and now she is driving through the old part of Kigali where shopkeepers are opening shutters in a brave attempt to return to work. A large, chauffeur-driven car pulls up in front of a French patisserie and an elegant Rwandan woman strolls inside, followed by a soldier. She wears a tight black skirt, a leopard-print silk shirt and gold jewellery. Her legs are long and her walk is sassy. Many members of the new government are women, and Hannah assumes the woman is probably a minister in her own right, or a minister's wife. Perhaps she is Ezekiel's wife. Hannah honks her horn imperiously, making the chauffeur move, and looks at herself in the mirror of the jeep.

'Bloody hell,' she says, trying to push her hair into some semblance of order and wondering if she looks reasonably presentable. She is wearing a dark green shirt and black silk pants which she shoved into her bag at the last minute. Or rather, Alice had shoved them in, saying that if she did ever track down Ezekiel, she must at least try to look decent. She is at that stage where the reality of Alice's disappearance occasionally fades. She forgets. She breathes again. And then remembers.

She remembers as she approaches Parliament House, a yellow building so full of shell holes that it is like a monstrous block of Gruyère cheese. Boy soldiers with machine-guns escort her up a circular stairway into a large room, which Hannah thinks is empty until she realises that Ezekiel is seated behind a desk, writing, with his back to the light and his face in shadow. A pile of books lies at his feet and a chess board has been pushed to one side. The pieces are not to be seen.

He doesn't look up. She examines him and sees the pain in his face. She wonders if hers shows similar pain. She would like to see this meeting as a time of reunion, however tense, but her worry about Alice dominates everything else she might have to say.

'Ezekiel –' she begins, but he interrupts, rising to his feet and holding out his hands. 'Hannah, how great to see you.'

She feels a surge of warmth, followed by irritation when he says, 'I'd have known you anywhere.'

She does not want flattery, which she suspects this is, and yet she would have known *him* anywhere, especially now he is no longer in military uniform but wears a dark suit and open-necked blue shirt.

A young soldier, who looks no more than thirteen or fourteen, drags across a chair and stands behind her, holding his gun. Ezekiel dismisses him.

Hannah is about to mention Alice when he gets in first. 'Is it your work that's brought you here?' The question is almost formal.

She brushes his question aside. 'Ezekiel, my daughter Alice, who's working for Help, has been kidnapped in Zaire.' She has said 'my daughter' deliberately. Not 'our daughter'.

He interrupts her. 'I knew a young aid worker had disappeared but I'd no idea she was your daughter. That's terrible.'

Hannah looks at him coolly for a minute, then makes a decision.

'Ezekiel, she's not just my daughter, she is also yours. I wrote and wrote, you never replied. Why? What happened? Why did you disappear?'

He looks shocked and tells her to stop. Stop and repeat what she has just said. When she does, he raises his hands in amazement, then begins to pace the room.

'Hannah, I fled to Burundi. We all fled. Our mail was stopped. I tried to ring you in Paris but you weren't there. I'd lost your Australian address ... I ...' He lifts his hands in a gesture of despair and helplessness. 'God, what a mess!' He sits down heavily. 'She is mine, you're sure she's mine?'

'Ours,' she says tersely. 'Yes, I'm sure.'

'Does she look ...? Is she ...?'

'She hasn't got red hair, if that's what you mean,' says Hannah dryly. 'Yes, she could be Rwandan. Could be Tutsi. Could be your daughter. *Is* your daughter.'

The words hang in the air.

'Then why didn't you tell me?'

'I told you, I tried.'

'And she's the one who is missing?'

'She's all I have. Her name is Alice and we have to find her.' Hannah pulls out the photograph of Alice taken when she was accepted into medical school and Ezekiel studies it carefully.

'She is beautiful,' he says finally. 'Just like her mother. She's got my eyes, eh?' He grins and pats his head. 'And my hair. I'd have recognised her anywhere.'

'You'd have walked straight by her.'

He frowns. 'What I don't understand is why you let her come here. You must have known it was dangerous?'

Hannah is disbelieving. 'Hasn't it occurred to you that she might have wanted to find you?' To her chagrin, she feels tears in her eyes. She wipes them away on the back of her hand. 'She's exceedingly stubborn. Just like you. She was determined to come, I couldn't stop her.'

He offers her a cigarette, which she refuses, and lights one himself. 'Tell me more about her disappearance. How can I help?'

'Find her.'

'I'll do everything I can, but she disappeared in Zaire. It's hostile to our new government.'

He walks over to the window. She joins him, and hesitantly puts a hand on his arm. He appears oblivious to her touch and she sees he is gazing down at a courtyard where the cobblestones are stained with blood.

When he swings round to face her, his voice is unexpectedly harsh. 'You must understand the scale of the killings. Everyone has lost someone. But your media makes almost more fuss about the disappearance of one young white woman than the murder of one million blacks.'

His remark fills her with sharp anger. 'She's not some young white woman. She's your daughter!'

Ezekiel reaches out an arm. 'I'm sorry, I apologise.'

She is picking up her bag, reaching out for the photograph, but he stops her with his hand. 'Hannah, I've said that I am sorry.'

'Okay, okay,' she says, refusing to look at him for the simple reason that she might hit him. Almost over her shoulder, she says, 'And you? You're married? Children?'

He hesitates and then says in a flat, emotionless voice, 'My wife and my two sons were murdered.'

'Oh God! How terrible!' She reaches out a hand in sudden remorse.

His face is closed. 'A lot of things have been terrible.'


After Hannah has left the room, Ezekiel sits at his desk in silence for a while. He is trying to absorb the impact of Hannah's news and how he feels about having a daughter. He can scarcely bear to acknowledge she has disappeared. His grief leaves no room for other feelings and he is still too tired, too shell-shocked to deal with this. He wants to stay in his public role, wearing his official face, the role that protects him from his agony. But the bat-light of gloom in which he has been living is now blazing with every feeling he has ever possessed, exposing all his wounds, shocking him with their pain.

Since the death of his father and his own exile in Burundi, Ezekiel's life has been carefully disciplined to honour his father's, by working for peace. Not as a political activist, but as someone who played out a career role in the most powerful and yet paradoxically one of the weakest bureaucracies in the world. He had thought this was the way to go. To achieve change through influence, to move the pieces slowly across the board, to check but never checkmate. He had closed down on all other options, all other lives.

This is what I am doing, Father, he would say to himself as he polished the chess pieces and set them carefully on the board.

Now he draws the chess board towards him, polishes the pieces and sets them up.

I thought it would work, Father, I tried. No more violence, I didn't want any more violence. Just move the pieces, pawn to white knight, but who would have thought that black knight would smash black pawn off the face of the earth? Why didn't I see it coming and get Bertha and the boys to leave?

He buries his head in his hands. This is something he can neither forget nor forgive. And there is something more. Something that keeps flickering in his gut. Why did he never really try to see Hannah again? At one level he had, and his explanations to Hannah were correct, but at another level he knows he could have found her had he wished, instead of shutting down on his earlier life and trying to make a new one.

In the name of the father and the son. But now it's in the name of the father and the daughter.

He begins to weep.


Hannah is bitterly disappointed by her meeting with Ezekiel. She isn't sure what she expected – more of the old Ezekiel perhaps, his buoyancy and his energy – but now that she can see the extent of his suffering she realises his help will probably be limited. Strangely, now that she has heard the reason for his disappearance, it doesn't seem to matter any more. The past is irrelevant compared with the present.

She goes with Waldo to confront Joe Schwartz in his office at Help headquarters. He is wearing his long white Indian shirt, which makes Waldo raise an eyebrow and say, 'Mahatma Gandhi, I presume.' Joe looks somewhat pleased.

Night is falling, and they talk against a loud chorus of frogs.

Joe says that the situation in all the refugee camps is becoming increasingly dangerous. Hutu militia are tyrannising the refugees and he feels almost certain that they or the army in exile are responsible for Alice's disappearance.

'So what do we do?'

Joe polishes his spectacles. He doesn't answer immediately. 'My guess is we'll hear pretty soon.'

'How soon, how soon?'

He looks unhappy. 'Be patient, Hannah. I know it's hard.'

Be patient, he says. She has never been patient.


Early evening, and Hannah sits cross-legged on a dusty tarpaulin inside a huge army tent whose canvas ceiling, flaps and ropes enfold her in this strangest of gatherings, somewhere in Rwanda. God knows where, she is losing her sense of place. She is one of thirty or so guests at a dinner given by a bishop whose name she can't remember but whose residence is out of town so they must stay the night. All she knows is that he was a good guy during the massacres – unlike many other church leaders, who failed to condemn the violence and even went out of their way to support the leaders of the genocide, or aided and abetted the killers. Vast numbers of people died in churches and on church property, including hundreds of nuns and priests who were stripped of their cassocks and robes, hacked down as they tried to save the frightened people huddled in their churches seeking sanctuary, but who instead met bullets and machete blades.

'Good Bish' is how Sister Helene has described their host, who has brought outsiders to this dinner so they can join together in common purpose and prayer. Good Bish and his wife and children narrowly escaped with their lives. Good Bish saw his church and his residence in flames, heard the screams of his people, and torments himself that perhaps he should have stayed instead of allowing his rescuers to bundle them away.

'No, no, no,' urges Hannah when she talks to him, this frail man with the sad face and black shadows under his eyes. 'The church needs leaders now more than ever before.'

She feels despair at these relentless accounts of savagery. Somewhere in this jigsaw of violence is Alice. She chokes, acid bile filling her mouth as she looks desperately for Waldo, who is separated by several large white tablecloths spread on the floor of the tent. He smiles, such a dear comforting smile.

Waldo is no longer able to fold up as neatly as he did in the Ogaden. His legs are thrust out in front so that people keep tripping over him and he can't reach the food. It took him a long time to get down and he can't face the immediate task of getting up, not even for Hannah.

The bishop is now pattering around the tent, peering at everyone over half-moon glasses, trying to smile. His wife adjusts her pink cardigan, which keeps falling off her ample shoulders, and whispers to staff who have been given the charge of preparing a banquet of sweet potatoes cooked seventeen different ways. This is the only food that is readily available.

Waldo is wondering how the seventeen varieties will be cooked. Mornay? With chocolate sauce? Hollandaise? With lemon grass, ginger and chilli? He is hungry and looks hopefully at Theodore King, who would surely be wanting his dinner too.

Theodore King is not looking quite as robust as on previous meetings and Waldo feels worried. He has become fond of Theo over the years, recognising that beneath his plastic exterior is a man with a real concern for human suffering. King has deteriorated since Somalia. His face is flushed and puffy, his neck shrunk so that his collar seems too big. He looks like a man in retreat. He says grace with an urgency in his voice, as if he hopes to impress both God and his fellow guests. God bless the hungry, the sick, the suffering, the dead, the dying. His words boom out across this small gathering of people as if he were addressing two thousand. He wants to be the messenger of Christ, the receptacle of God, the prophet from on high, even if he is seated very low; he thrills at the sound of his voice, feels his tongue touching the roof of his mouth, exalts in the ringing in his ears. It's his last desperate throw, his path of redemption. With rising panic he feels that God is deserting him and he has only himself to blame.

The bishop sighs and says a few modest words of his own. He is troubled by the burning, troubled by the violence which surrounds the people he knows and loves, troubled that the mercy of Jesus does not enter the hearts of all. The candles cast long silhouettes on the walls of the tent.

That night Hannah reluctantly shares sleeping quarters with Beverley Prettyfoot. They have one small army tent, two bedding rolls, a stool and two white candles, already alight and flickering. Beverley clutches at the front of her blue floral dress as the bishop's wife gives them a kerosene tin with the top sawn off. She says it is for their 'night-time convenience'.

'Please do not go outside because of landmines. Please.'

Once the bishop's wife has left, Beverley giggles and starts unpacking her zippered bag, processed to look like English tweed. She gets out something pink and shiny and dives under her bedclothes, pulls the sheet up to her chin and wriggles. Gives a small squeak of triumph. Wriggles again. A large white bra falls to the floor, followed by a pair of knickers. Beverley emerges like an aging Venus, wearing an oyster-pink satin night-dress, pink negligée, and pink satin mules trimmed with swans-down. She blushes when she notices Hannah staring at her.

'I guess you'll think I'm crazy but my mom always said, Beverley – she always called me Beverley, never Bev – Beverley, behave like a lady and you'll be treated like a lady.'

Hannah is speechless.

Beverley jiggles from one foot to another, a plump unhappy child. 'I've tried to do that ever since.'

Hannah looks down at the oversize man's shirt she uses for sleeping and wonders how she would rate with Beverley's mum. When she looks up, Beverley is stepping out into the dark and dangerous night, pink swansdown slippers ruffling in the breeze.

'Stop!' shouts Hannah. 'Pee in the kero tin. You'll have us all blown up.'

But it is too late. The tent flap closes, Beverley has gone.

Hannah flops back in her bed, wondering if a piss is enough to trigger a landmine. She wonders if a trickle is ... enough ... to ... Hannah is asleep.

She wakes up to the sound of Beverley snoring on her back, arms outstretched, small bubbles of air gently popping through her open mouth. Hannah wants to dump the kerosene tin over Beverley's head.


Waldo is typing notes, oblivious to Hannah's struggles with the night. Two old camping lanterns swing from low branches of a tree, their light casting long shadows on the blackened grass. Waldo has just accepted a large mug of rosehip tea made by Bruce, using his own portable stainless-steel, single-ring burner.

He has already assured Waldo that it is caffeine-free and he frowns as Waldo swamps it with sugar.

Waldo works at a rickety trestle table, which is just outside the opening of the tent. He has decided that, if there were any mines, someone else would have already set them off. His canvas chair sags and wobbles as he writes:

'Is Africa becoming the symbol of worldwide breakdown as war, famine and oppression force millions of people into exodus? Is there any end to deserts encroaching, drought persisting, internal wars and brutality . . .?'

Tap, tap, tap goes Waldo, what the hell is he writing? It's supposed to be research for his film script, but it sounds more like a newspaper piece. Film stories are about people, about men and women, about young women who get lost, maybe forever. Alice. If he allows himself to think too much about Alice he will worry all night, so he returns to his keyboard. His head is nodding and he knows he makes little sense: 'These are the journalists who write the stories that bring in the cash that goes to the aid workers who help the governments that cause the famines that kill the people. These are the questions that have no answer, the sighs in the night, the screams in the dark.'

Sometimes Waldo has a vision of the world as a triple-decker sandwich, with governments and the UN on top, aid workers and the media in the middle, and Dante's inferno filled with the sick and the dying at the bottom.

Bruce is now stretched out in his silk inner sleeping bag and is gently snoring, wearing a black velvet eye mask and looking like Pierrot. Waldo's sleeping bag is unzipped, revealing a horrible collection of biscuit crumbs, wrappings from sweets, bits of paper, squashed insects, dirt.

Waldo raises his head and regards the moonlit profile of a

large mass grave. He thinks how ridiculous it is for him to be here, marooned in this tent in the aftermath of a massacre, when he could be in London, Paris, New York. Or even Santa Monica.

Suddenly, Bruce cries out. Waldo thinks of giving him a fatherly pat but decides against it. It's too hard to rise from his chair.

'Wotcher doing this for?' says Bruce, nodding towards Waldo's work. Bruce is sitting bolt upright, his hair standing on end, his mask dangling over one ear and a startled look in his soft brown eyes.

Waldo pretends he hasn't heard.

'Wotcher doing this for?' repeats Bruce.

Waldo doesn't look round. After a pause he says mildly, 'I'm addicted.'

Two days later, at the Kigali hospital, Waldo encounters someone else who is addicted. An Italian doctor, Mario Fabiani, has just performed his two-thousandth amputation and wonders if this is cause for celebration or suicide. Fabiani has the looks and build of an Italian opera star. He chain-smokes and wears his surgical cap rakishly over one eye.

'Wherever there are wars you will find me. I have operated in Afghanistan, Kuwait, Iran, Angola, Mozambique, Cambodia.' He lights up a cigarette and has an immediate coughing bout which makes him bend almost double. 'Now I help these nice Australians.'

He waves generously at a group of army nurses who are also having a smoke and who are part of Australia's UN contingent in Rwanda. Fabiani introduces a young freckle-faced doctor from Queensland, Michelle Roberts. She runs her fingers through her tow-coloured hair and tells Waldo she volunteered to come to Rwanda because she thought it would be an interesting experience. Waldo has a strong feeling she wants to go home, particularly when she says nervously she is about to perform her first amputation. Waldo has always associated the word 'perform' with concerts of heavenly chamber music, not the cutting of flesh and bone.

Fabiani regards Dr Michelle from beneath heavy-lidded eyes. 'You'll be terrific. I will be there.'

The operating theatre is devoid of air-conditioning. The generator, which supplies the only light, periodically fails. There is no running water and they must scrub up using bottles of antiseptic. The patient is a young man whose leg has been shattered by a landmine. He has been given an anaesthetic by a Swedish doctor, who strokes his brow and from time to time holds his hand.

'Cut a little bit more stronger,' Fabiani says over Michelle's shoulder as she saws away at the young man's leg. 'It is not a chicken bone.'

The noise makes Waldo sick and he goes outside. Every young person takes his mind back to Alice, Alice in Broome, Alice at school, Alice when she was little with her hair in bunches, and Alice new-born. He had just returned to Australia to work on a co-production about Gallipoli, and Hannah had rung him at his hotel in Sydney. She said the birth was grisly, the baby was beautiful, and he must come. 'Immediately.'

'She's all right, is she?' he said anxiously.

'Of course.'

'Black or white?' He was still harbouring a grain of hope.

'Piebald.'

He hired a car so he could drive from Sydney to Canberra and have time to reflect on this baby, and to romanticise about being with Hannah and the child in a kaleidoscope of exotic and beautiful places. In Kashmir, gliding across flower-filled lakes in a shikara; in a vineyard in the north of Italy, ambling between rows of luscious grapes; in the Antarctic, marvelling at the penguins. He would tell her stories about the witch of Wookey Hole and the wombat who lived in a wheelie-bin. She would be a charming little girl, with white-blonde hair and the bluest of eyes. His fantasies were so engrossing that he was startled to find himself already driving into Canberra.

The Coady house was set in a garden with flower beds and gravel paths, but the lawn was no longer a lawn, it was over-grown with dandelions and daisies. Hannah came out to meet him in some kind of orange velvet skirt and a red and orange striped jumper that drooped in all the wrong places. She greeted him with exuberant hugs, crushing the armful of yellow roses he had brought her, and pulling him inside to a room which was newly painted yellow and white. Small, snuffly noises came from a corner of the room where he could see a wicker basket and an overhanging mobile of blue and red clowns.

Waldo wanted desperately to see inside that basket, to know if the baby was his, but Hannah was blocking the way, grasping his hands and talking nonstop.

'She's very beautiful, her name is Alice, but you know all that anyway, and the birth was a bit gruesome, but it was worth it, wasn't it?'

She was looking at him for some kind of response but he didn't know what to say. Did she want to be told that having a baby was 'worth it'? But whose baby?

He went to the basket, pulled down a corner of pink and white blanket and saw a crest of brownish-black hair. He ran

249

his hand self-consciously through his own sandy hair and grinned foolishly, trying to hide his disappointment.

'Here!' Hannah thrust the bundle into his arms. Huge dark eyes stared at him unblinkingly, small fists jerked sideways, he smelled mice. He jiggled the baby awkwardly from side to side.

Hannah laughed. 'Like this, silly!'

She flung herself into the old blue chair which used to be in her bedroom. Her voice was pleading. 'What have I done, Waldo? I don't feel ready to have a baby.'

Waldo passed the baby back, wiped his damp hands on his jacket, and said somewhat ponderously, 'Babies grow up, so one day you'll be able to get back to work. Probably sooner than you think.'

'And I could work with you?' asked Hannah as she returned Alice to her basket. Her voice was muffled and Waldo could not see her face.

'Yes,' he mumbled. 'If it's possible.'

'Why wouldn't it be?'

'Well, maybe, yes, oh you know, of course.' He cleared his throat. 'Is Ezekiel coming over – I presume he's the father?'

'Don't be spiteful.'

He had apologised. Yes, he had felt spiteful.


Hannah drifts into the Tivoli, the only bar in Kigali which has reopened for business. She goes there regularly, always hopeful of picking up some useful piece of information which might lead her to Alice. It is needle-in-a-haystack stuff, but the city is buzzing with gossip.

At the bar, a young man dressed in tight black jeans with a silver studded belt and a black T-shirt pushes back his sunglasses so he can take a closer look, tells her his name is Hugo, and buys her a beer. She tells him about Alice. She tells everyone about Alice.

'But that's terrible,' he says in the consciously well-modulated voice of an out-of-work actor. 'Look, I know a few people around town, leave it to me. We'll find her for you. Use the old network.' He puts his forefinger to the side of his nose, suggesting he has secret assignations he will pursue.

When Hannah asks him what he is doing in Kigali, he explains that normally he lives on his yacht off the coast of Madagascar. He only leaves it when the old dosh is running low and he comes to work for the UN in Africa, any old place in Africa, just so that he can earn enough to spend six months each year back on his boat. The international community pays well – never mind if it turns local economies upside down.

'I suppose you'll think that's terrible,' he says with a charming smile. 'But I'm damn good at my job, worth every penny, and there are already enough people starving in Africa without adding me to the list.'

Hannah downs her beer. 'So what job are you so good at?'

'Communications. Communications. Communications.'

'Quite,' says Hannah.

He ignores her. 'Have you heard about the film guy who's just arrived in town and is taking people on for a movie about Rwanda? With luck I'll get a reasonable part.'

Hannah raises an eyebrow.

'His name's Waldo,' continues Hugo. 'Supposed to be hot stuff. If you're interested, I could probably arrange an introduction.' He slides off his seat and lifts a languid hand as he wanders away into the crowd. 'Ciao.'

On her way back to the hotel Hannah is stopped by Joe

Schwartz, who is driving a large white Toyota bearing the insignia of Help. When he motions her to climb in, she scowls but accepts his offer.

'You're angry because you think it's my fault Alice disappeared.' His voice is calm.

'Alice wasn't ready for field work,' says Hannah.

Joe flicks his nicotine gum out of the window. He hasn't yet shaved. Looking less pristine suits him. 'Alice was quite ready. She was already doing excellent work. Any one of us could disappear at any time, you know that. It's a new kind of war and aid workers make good bargaining chips. No one is safe.'

His face is still controlled but his voice carries a harsh edge she hasn't heard before. 'Yesterday, we came across the burned bodies of about fifty children. Killed and burned.'

She puts her head in her hands. When she looks up, her face is stark. The memory of other disasters returns. The betrayal of East Timor. Somalia. Bosnia. That time in 1991 when she and Waldo flew to a remote part of Mozambique with two aid agency VIPs, a UN official, the Australian ambassador and his wife, and a handful of journalists. The country was still embroiled in a savage guerilla war with Renamo, a movement mostly financed by wealthy Zimbabwean and South African dissidents who were trying to overthrow the country's democratically elected government by a campaign of terror.

Their plane was about to land on a tussocky runway. As the wheels hit the ground, an explosion sent them tumbling in all directions. They had hit a landmine. When they clambered out, shaken but unhurt, some of them began frantically taking photographs of the gaping hole in the undercarriage. Suddenly, it dawned on everyone that if there was one landmine in the field, there might well be others. They tiptoed off, as if tiptoeing might make all the difference, saying with exaggerated politeness, 'After you. No, after you.'

At the end of the runway was an ancient armoured car, covered in garlands of flowers. Hannah was stuffed down the gun turret together with the Australian ambassador's wife, who was huge with child. The ambassador, Waldo and the others clung like barnacles to the outside of the car, fingers digging into any available ledge or crevice they could find. As they proceeded slowly and impressively along a red dirt road, they were cheered and welcomed by large crowds. Women and children were dancing, clapping their hands and blowing whistles, lovely shiny metal whistles whose sounds shrieked defiantly through the trees. Yet Hannah had been uneasy. Renamo terrorists were hiding in the jungle even as they feasted at the house of the administrator, a vigorous young man who was proud of the way the region had prospered, proud of the plantations of bananas, limes, coconuts and papaya.

Aid agency officials, the ambassador, the UN representative all gave praise to the work of rehabilitation, to the support of the World Bank, the involvement of aid agencies from around the world. Three weeks later, Renamo terrorists descended on the village, killing, raping and burning. They decapitated the village leaders and stuck their heads on jam jars for public display.

Hannah reminds Joe about all this. Joe had been there. Joe had seen it all. Joe *knows*.

Joe shakes his head impatiently. 'Okay, okay, so what are you trying to say? Do nothing? If you passed a child who was bleeding from machete wounds, or blown up by a landmine – which had been manufactured in the West, incidentally – what would you say? Sorry, kid, got to fix up the politics first. See you later – if you're still alive.'

Hannah shrugs and stares out of the window to hide the tears that are coursing down her cheeks. She sits in silence until, just out of town, Joe takes a sharp corner and she is thrown against him. Two small boys scuttle into the bushes and bounce back with their hands outstretched. Joe stops the jeep and the boys approach, wide grins on their faces. Joe gives them two biscuits – high protein, he explains, and is about to detail their composition when she stops him. The children devour the biscuits, licking their fingers and the crumbs around their mouths. One child wipes his hands on his bright red shirt then giggles and licks that.

Joe sighs. 'We have to do the best we can.'

Hannah isn't sure why she climbed in with Joe when he stopped the Toyota. She has been doing a lot of random wandering in the last few days, unable to concentrate on her work, unsure of what to do next, drifting between various UN departments, the press room at the hotel, and sometimes turning up at the Help headquarters in case, by some miracle, they have unexpected news.

She follows Joe into his office. On a large trestle table lie all the latest agency and government releases. One of them is signed by Ezekiel:

'The government of the Rwandan Patriotic Front welcomes the presence of international aid agencies and the media. The government pledges its support and gives assurances that every effort will be made to ensure security and safe passage for overseas personnel.'

Outside, she is nastily wondering if Ezekiel has issued this release as a sop to his conscience when she bumps into Sister

Helene and, in her wake, like little brown ducklings, the four Sisters of the Assumption, all on their way to offer help with food runs and medical clinics. Judy Morrison is hurrying by with an armful of papers, on her way to interview Rwandan citizens who are lined up for job interviews. She calls out a list of names: 'Donatella, Silas, Ephraim, Glorieuse, Jean-Claude, Marguerite, Emailia, Samuel, Casimir, Alfonse, John the Baptist.'

One by one, the people come forward, desperate to impress because they are desperate to earn. An upright man with a neatly trimmed moustache, well-pressed khaki clothes and well-polished shoes was a high-school principal before the war. He has come for work as a driver and settles for a job as janitor.

'Madame, I am grateful for anything.'

Hannah is troubled by the fact that, at this moment, she feels anything but grateful.

# *t h i r t e e n*

George turns the steering wheel of the jeep and Hannah and Waldo find themselves driving up a sweeping red gravel driveway, bordered by palm trees and bougainvillea. Three armed guards are performing drill. Up and down the driveway they march, their rifles dipping at odd angles over their shoulders. Hannah opens the window and closes it again quickly. The heat is intense. Soldiers in jungle greens lounge against the rotting colonnades of a splendid colonial building, once white but now a leprous yellow. At one time the home of some Belgian colonial administrator, it now houses the considerable bulk of Colonel Frederic Dondo, Zairean governor of the province in which the biggest refugee camps are sited, and where Alice disappeared. Joe Schwartz has helped them get an appointment.

George says he will wait in the jeep and is already selecting a stack of hymns to lull him to sleep. He would never admit this is what happens, but they have caught him out on several occasions.

A guard lazily reaches out a gun and uses it to bar Hannah and Waldo's entrance while another guard demands their documents. When they are finally allowed to pass, they enter through huge mirrored doors which open into a cavernous hall, tiled in black and white. Two absurdly small gilt chairs are placed discreetly in one corner. A few potted palms droop in corners. From somewhere far off Hannah hears music. She ignores the chairs and flops down on the floor because it looks cool, leaning back against a wall. It crumbles, sending down a shower of small mouldy pieces which are immediately attacked by ants.

Waldo, obediently perched on his uncomfortable chair, looks at her with astute and affectionate concern: the shadows under her eyes like purple bruises; the high sharp cheekbones, so thin, too thin; her wrists like a child's; her feet somehow absurdly vulnerable. What is it about feet? thinks Waldo, remembering the bare feet of two Australians who were convicted of drug running in Malaysia. Their feet sticking out of body-bags after they had been hanged. He wonders how their mothers felt when they saw those feet. His thoughts stray to Alice and her slim brown feet, but the connection with the hanged men is too painful. He tries to look at his own feet. Hasn't seen them properly in years.

Hell, he thinks, feeling powerless about Alice, powerless about Hannah and deeply depressed. Occasionally a servant dressed in white appears and disappears, bare feet slapping on the marble floor.

By the time they are shown into the sanctum of Colonel Dondo, Waldo is ready for sleep but Hannah is ready to fight. Two enormous teak doors, elaborately carved, open electronically and Bach organ music overwhelms them.

'You like it?' shouts a deep voice from a large armchair

draped in leopard skin. Hannah takes in the dark wood-panelled room, the recessed lights shining on rich rugs and marble floors, huge crystal vases of flowers, bound copies of Reader's Digest condensed books, an enormous television set, the latest Bosch speakers. In the far corner is a model railway with a small red engine careering wildly round and round. It has no carriages, no trucks.

Colonel Dondo struggles to rise from his chair and then decides against it. He is a vast man, bursting out of some kind of military jacket with red and gold epaulettes. A servant adjusts the volume on the stereo, another brings tea on a silver tray laden with Victorian rose-patterned china and a chocolate cake.

Colonel Dondo smiles congenially. 'I have a sweet tooth,' he says, stirring five spoons of sugar into his tea before passing the bowl to Hannah, who refuses.

Dondo handles his tiny cup with dexterity, cocking his little finger. He takes a sip, making a noise like a vacuum cleaner, wipes his moustache, helps himself to a large piece of cake and says in between mouthfuls, 'Have you stayed at the Ritz Hotel in London? An excellent hotel. You know it?'

'Yes,' says Waldo, 'No,' says Hannah, their voices over-lapping.

'And Simpson's, for English roast beef?'

'No,' says Hannah again, with irritation. She leans forward in her chair, determined to make herself heard. 'Colonel, I have come to see you about my daughter, Alice Chimeme, who disappeared from one of the refugee camps and has been missing for five days.'

'Such excellent roast beef,' muses the colonel, stretching out his feet, which are clad in Nike running shoes with purple laces.

'Do you know where she is?' insists Hannah.

'Wait, wait!' He belches again, wiping some chocolate from his cavernous mouth. 'The English have mad cow disease, but now that I have eaten their beef, I am a mad bull.'

His laughter penetrates every corner of the room, jangling in Hannah's ears, making her head spin, silencing her speech.

The colonel sips his tea and says softly, 'I cannot help you with your daughter.'

'Why not?'

'I do not want to.'

He takes off his heavy tortoiseshell glasses, polishes them with a silk handkerchief and leans back in his chair. The interview is over.

As they leave, Waldo glances back. The little red engine has overturned. It lies on its back, wheels churning, going nowhere.


Dondo's comment right at the end of their meeting seemed to indicate that he knows the whereabouts of Alice; on the other hand, he might deliberately be playing with them for his amusement. Hannah feels desperate. When she returns to Kigali she asks, on an impulse, if she can move to the headquarters of Help. There is no reason why the agency should receive news any sooner than the media, probably the reverse, but Hannah feels a need to be linked more closely with Alice. She is no longer able to work, she cannot concentrate, but at least she can give a hand with routine tasks around the agency. Waldo is less than enthusiastic.

The afternoon Hannah moves, the heat has not yet left the day even though it is almost dark. She takes out a comb, pulls it impatiently through the tangles, finds some sandals and makes her way back to the dining room, nearly bumping into a tall lanky woman with grey hair who is wandering amongst mounds of washing, one blue sock clutched in her hand.

'Heavens to Betsy, it's all those single socks, the Lord knows where they go.'

'Waiting in the great bright beyond, to shower down on us come Armageddon,' retorts Hannah.

'Whoa, dear,' says the woman, putting her hands on Hannah's shoulders. 'Take it easy.'

Hannah pushes the hands away. 'I can't take it easy.'

The woman folds her in her arms. She is wearing a pink T-shirt embroidered with bush parrots. 'Hush, dear, hush, your girl will be safe, we'll find her.'

Dinner is almost ready but Hannah isn't hungry. She watches as one of the English aid workers, Nicola, arranges a line of candles down the centre of three long tables. The Rwandan cook, who was a chemist before the massacres, hovers behind her, a thin wispy man who holds a wooden spoon as if it were a test-tube.

Nicola turns to him with a pained expression on her face. She speaks in the kind of voice commonly used for idiots, old people and foreigners. 'No spoons on the outside. On the inside.'

The man nods and goes back to his large black cooking pots full of rice and vegetables for the evening meal.

Hannah pushes her food around her plate. Already she is beginning to regret coming here. She knows she is being capricious but she is a stranger to these people, no matter how kind they are. She doesn't want any questions or solicitous concern. She is too tired to respond. She wants bed.

In the dormitory she makes her way to her bed through rows of bunks with sagging mattresses and loops of mosquito nets. The beds have iron bars dividing their length, so that her choice is sleeping in half the bed or lying with an iron bar thrusting into her middle. Nobody sleeps on the floor because of rats. Small white candles give the only light. Those damnable small white candles – once she used to enjoy them, now she wants floodlights to scour every corner of darkness and find Alice.

People have pinned photographs of their families and their pets to the dormitory walls. Hannah hopes that Alice has pinned up a photograph of her. She hasn't. She finds her bunk and climbs in, immediately hitting the bar.

She lies in bed, looking at the rows that stretch ahead and on either side of the dormitory, just as they had when she was ten years old and away from home for the very first time, her eyes wide open, legs stick-straight, staring at the mosquito nets that repeated the shape of the nuns' black hoods. They had been told to go to the bathroom before they said their prayers. The nuns had not said lavatory, nor did they say toilet, but their meaning was clear. Any little girl who had to get up in the middle of the night would be a naughty little girl. Hannah had tried to pee but nothing had happened. Slowly, to her mounting distress, she found herself crossing and uncrossing her legs. She clambered fearfully out of bed, ran barefoot down the dormitory, terrified of bumping into nuns with shaven heads – one of the older girls had told her nuns shaved their heads. She couldn't find the bathroom door, seized a metal wastepaper basket, lifted her nightie, missed the basket and knocked it over with a loud clatter. On went the lights. Out came the nuns. Children sat bolt upright in their beds. A large puddle of urine shone on the floor by Hannah's feet.

'Hannah Coady, you *disgusting* little girl!'

Now, on her first night in the Help dormitory, she has to

get out of bed in the dark and find the latrines with their dank walls and horrible smell. At the last minute she heads for the garden. She has just hitched up her sarong when she is transfixed by a strong yellow light and a guard's voice yelling, 'Stop!'

But Hannah Coady cannot stop. She is ten years old and she does not care.

Back in bed, she tosses and turns, trying to calm the horrors in her mind. A week has passed without word, and surely if Alice had been kidnapped they would have received a ransom note by now? Joe says any one of a number of groups could be holding her prisoner – mercenaries, Hutu soldiers, even RPF guerillas. A cruel and wild thought niggles. And niggles again. Could the RPF be holding her because it pays them to capture a few aid workers, so that the agencies are forced to withdraw? By now it is obvious that the new regime feels the aid agencies in the camps outside Rwanda are helping the very people who caused the bloodshed. The thought stays: is Ezekiel a part of this plot? Surely not, he wouldn't kidnap his own daughter. But then he hadn't known Alice was his daughter until after she had disappeared.

The thought is too macabre and she shifts to another. Perhaps Alice has simply met some kind of accidental death? Been run over? Become ill? Involved unwittingly in a camp brawl and been hurt and died? There were enough corpses in the camps for her death to be absorbed unnoticed.

Hannah wakes in the morning with a dry mouth and a thudding headache, made worse by the penetrating voice of Nicola ordering everyone around. Nicola, who sounds as if she is trying to make her world safe and predictable, like the life she left behind. In England she had grown up in a neat brick house with door chimes that played 'Home Sweet Home'. Her father was a suburban bank manager, her mother cooked a nice Sunday roast. Pretty Nicola, who sang in the church choir, escaped by running away with a car mechanic. After a miserable two years with a man who drank, swore and wanted to hump her most nights, whereas she thought once on Saturday was quite enough, she had left him and expiated her sins by working for an aid agency. Which is why she is in this place of horrid uncertainty where the staff ignore most of her precision demands.

'We do not have soup for breakfast,' she is saying slowly. 'There will be no soup.' She frowns as she surveys the trestle tables, already set with peanut butter and purple jelly. 'We do not put the breakfast plates in a pile, we place them in front of each person, in a line.'

'God give me dominion over all I rule,' murmurs Waldo who has come to collect Hannah to take her to the UN headquarters.

Nicola flushes and pushes back her long hair. For the next two days she is on her hands and knees each morning, scrubbing out the latrines, her small mouth twisted in determination, her face pink with exertion.

'Somebody's got to do it, or we'll all get sick,' she says. 'It's quite therapeutic, actually.'

Hannah pulls a face. 'I can think of kinder penances.'


Help comes to life every dawn when people begin crawling out of their beds, washing in a handful of water while the cook lays out breakfast – slabs of bread, cereal, powdered milk, peanut butter, purple jelly jam. This morning Nicola is adjusting her pink and white sarong, prior to ordering everyone around. She looks at Hannah carefully.

'You look terrible.'

Hannah moves along to make room for Joe Schwartz, who bangs his cup with a spoon to announce that a delegation of agronomists and health economists is arriving from the US looking for land suitable for an agricultural research centre. He wants to take them on a reconnaissance mission and needs to commandeer two of the four-wheel drive vehicles.

Judy Morrison says emphatically that the research centre can wait. She slaps two pieces of bread and peanut butter on the table. 'We're already short of vehicles for the food runs.'

A large French-Canadian woman who worked as a nurse in Alaska before coming to Africa folds her massive arms and says in a matter-of-fact voice, 'Everyone is short of everything. This woman turned up this morning, clutched at my sleeve and said she had twenty orphans in a large house and nothing to feed them on. She wanted food and blankets.'

'Give them to her,' says Joe.

'I already have.' She smiles and the gold in her teeth glints in the early morning light.

Joe frowns and returns to his initial statement. 'I'm taking the vehicles.' His voice is dry and precise as he cuts his bread into small neat squares.

Hannah places her bet on Schwartz getting his way – until Theodore King wanders in clutching a glass of bicarbonate of soda for his ulcer. 'Joe, people are still dying out there. They're going to need that food.'

'There'll be even more of them dead if we don't get good land management.'

Theodore King gives in. He settles himself on one of the benches and drinks his bicarb in one loud gulp. When Hannah asks him about Alice, he gives a hiccup and says, 'Honey, I'll see what I can do.'

Everyone Hannah speaks with says, 'I'll see what I can do.'

# *fourteen*

Alice is in some kind of timber hut, blindfolded and chained to a wooden post. She has checked out her environment by running her hands over everything she is able to reach, including the wooden bench on which she can just manage to sit. She is frightened.

She had been working in amongst the fragile twig shelters of the camp, bending over a tiny baby with dysentery, wondering if he had any chance of survival, when she felt her arms pinned to her sides. Rough hands propelled her out of the hut, and when she tried to cry out above the din of jackhammers, a man's voice said in her ear, 'No noise or I shoot.'

So many soldiers in this mass of refugees, so many guns, so much violence – who was going to worry about a young woman being bundled down the hill and into a truck? Alice had tried to make a run for it but collected a savage blow to her head. Whack! The shock was almost worse than the pain. She must have lost consciousness because the next thing she knew she was lying on the floor of a truck, blindfolded, her hands tied in front of her. Dirt blew into her mouth and nostrils, and with each bump of the truck she rolled from side to side. She had no idea in which direction she was travelling.

She tried to work out why she had been captured. To tend to someone who was sick and at a distance from the camps? Aid workers had been kidnapped before for this reason, she'd heard. Aid workers had also been kidnapped for political reasons.

After about two hours, the truck came to an abrupt halt. Alice was hauled out and dragged up a rocky path into some kind of building. The blindfold was beginning to slip; someone's hands pulled it tight again, tweaking her hair and hurting her scalp. The same person fastened chains around her legs. She sensed that two or three people were in the hut, talking in low voices which she thought were Rwandan, but she couldn't be sure.

The people left, locking the door after them. Outside, she could hear children's voices and the clucking of hens. She needed to urinate. She called out but no one came. In the end, she was obliged to pee where she was, standing up, and then to scuff the dirt floor of the hut with her foot. The blindfold was suffocating and her face was running with sweat.

She estimated she had been there for about three hours when two men returned, removed her blindfold and marched her out of the hut. They were squat young men with muscular bodies, dressed in military uniform. Her eyes found it hard adjusting to the daylight. She blinked, anxious to observe everything she could. The hut seemed to be part of some kind of military compound, judging by the number of soldiers, all of them armed. Behind the compound was a village, presumably a village somewhere in Zaire. A few mud houses, flower beds, women with babies, children, pigs and chickens. Older children were playing under the shade of an enormous baobab tree and they scampered into scrubby bushes as Alice was pushed along a narrow track towards a much larger hut.

Inside, she found herself staring into the thin mournful face of a man with a crooked nose. He wore a khaki uniform with epaulettes on his shirt, and he was flanked by armed guards. As soon as Alice appeared he became agitated, thumping the table and loudly questioning the soldiers in the same language the men had used earlier. When eventually he turned to her, his voice was calmer and he spoke in English with a heavy French accent.

'Where are you from?'

'Australia.'

'Not America?'

'My mother is Australian and I have an Australian passport.' She paused, her voice faltering. 'I want to see the Australian ambassador.' Even as she said these words she knew they sounded ridiculous. 'If that's possible,' she added hopefully.

The man gave a wry smile. He had a wide gap between his yellowing front teeth. 'We don't have the Australian ambassador here. I don't think he would like it very much.'

'I don't like it.'

'But I hope you are being well looked after?'

Alice could feel the thud of her heart. 'No. I am not. I am being badly looked after.'

The man observed her for a while. His gaze was not unfriendly and Alice tried not to fidget or look alarmed. He pulled out a packet of Gaulloise from his breast pocket, offered her one, and lit his own when she refused. His hands were long and slim and the nails well shaped.

'My name is Raymonde Mgumbo,' he told her. 'I am a general of the Rwandan army in exile.'

'What do you want with me?'

'A hostage exchange. Twenty of our high-ranking soldiers are being held prisoner by the RPF. We want them back.'

'And will the RPF agree?'

Mgumbo shrugged. 'I hope so, for your sake.'

Alice blinked. 'What's that supposed to mean?'

'You would die.' Mgumbo said this smoothly. Almost politely.

Alice felt faint, but tried desperately to remain calm. 'It won't get you anywhere. It would be much better to negotiate.'

'We are. And you are the tool.'

'But why me?'

General Mgumbo took a deep draw on his cigarette. 'A mistake. I wanted an American aid worker. Australia is not as powerful as the United States and is likely to make less fuss. But,' he frowned and removed a piece of tobacco from his lip with his little finger, 'but as we have you, we have to make the best of it.'

Alice was indignant. 'Australia will make a fuss.'

The general's mouth twitched. 'No doubt.' He pushed a pad of lined paper towards her and a pen. 'Write a letter saying that no harm will come to you if the exchange takes place. We also want supplies. From your aid agency. Medicine, food, transport.'

'And if I won't write the letter?'

'We will make you.' His voice seemed to carry regret.

Alice stood there, gazing down at the pen. This was weird, so weird she wondered if it was really happening. She was beginning to feel cold and recognised it was probably shock.

'Write!' said General Mgumbo, sneezing and wiping his nose with a cerise handkerchief.

Alice picked up the pen, and hesitated. 'Could I have a drink of water first?'

Mgumbo drummed his fingers on the table. 'Write!'

She scrawled a note in capital letters, trying not to show that her hand was trembling.

'Sign!'

She signed 'Alice' and her hand hovered. Hannah had warned her not to use Ezekiel's name but Hannah wasn't always right. Alice wrote 'Chimeme', and immediately realised she had made a bad mistake.

Mgumbo pounced. 'Chimeme? Why Chimeme?'

She thought of trying to pretend that her father was an Australian Chimeme, but she did not want to deny Ezekiel was her father. She was proud of it.

'Ezekiel Chimeme is my father.' Her voice rang loudly in the hut.

The general leaned forward. His eyes seemed no longer kindly but hard. 'Ezekiel Chimeme is your father? The man who calls himself Minister for Communications?'

Alice nodded, apprehensive. 'Yes.'

Mgumbo poured her a glass of water. His voice was smooth and cold. 'An interesting piece of information, Mademoiselle.'

When Alice was returned to her hut she leaned back against the wall, rerunning her conversation with Mgumbo. What else had she said that was foolish? She was caught between accepting the reality of her danger and a sense that none of this was happening, that it was all some dream from which she would awake. Or else she had strayed into one of her mother's film shoots, and soon Hannah would march in, waving her arms, ordering everyone around and dismissing Alice from the scene. Even coming to Rwanda had been unreal. She had made the decision without really thinking it through in her customary way. Suddenly it had just seemed necessary to be there, to find her father before it was too late. But perhaps it was already too late.

Alice sat upright, her back very straight. Being morbid would only drag her down and she needed her wits about her if she was to get out of this alive. She looked around her, glad that the soldiers hadn't replaced her blindfold. The floor of the hut was hard packed dirt, the walls were rammed earth, the roof consisted of random pieces of corrugated iron and palm fronds, thrown carelessly on top of one another. The place stank of urine – hers, she presumed – and a general smell of decay. Apart from the narrow bench, there was nothing else in the hut. Nothing. She was one person, chained up in a strange country, with a price upon her head.

Ezekiel is agitated. He stands by his office window, holding Alice's note. It is early in the morning and down below, on the cobblestones which had been washed in blood, two women are watering some pink geraniums in tins. He would like to encourage them, but instead he keeps returning to the note.

Alice has signed her surname as Chimeme. Doesn't she realise this is dangerous? Didn't Hannah warn her? He wonders how she is being treated and closes his eyes.

A second piece of paper demands the release of twenty named high-ranking prisoners held by the government of the RPF, with instructions on where to set them free. There is also a list of aid requirements, to be directed to Help.

Help might agree to deliver the aid, but Ezekiel knows there is no chance of releasing any prisoners.

A mosquito settles on his forehead and he swipes at it, missing. His capacity to cope with anything that touches his feelings is perilously fragile. Horror images of this unknown daughter are now imprinted over images of his two dead sons. This is not the kind of situation he can discuss with his colleagues, even though some are his friends. Bigger issues fill their minds. Hannah is out of the question, there is too much anger between them. And then he thinks of Waldo. If only he could talk with him, Waldo would understand.

He arranges to meet him at a friend's house in the country, half an hour's drive from Kigali. On his way there, he passes a small patch of land which seems to have escaped the fighting. Ears of yellow corn wave bravely in the breeze. Ezekiel wants to ask the driver to pull up the car so he can clamber over the fence and pluck two or three ears – ignore the possibility that the land might be mined. He needs to taste the sweetness, eat the fresh cobs by the side of the road while the sun warms his body; for a long time now, he has been cold. But of course he can do no such thing.

As the car turns into the driveway he sees Waldo waiting on the terrace and Ezekiel shouts out spontaneously, waving his hand. A few scraggy hens peck at Waldo's feet and a brilliant orange creeper covers the windows behind. He is leaning back in an old cane chair, feet outstretched, arms behind his head. Ezekiel feels a surge of excitement. A friend has miraculously returned at a time of desperate need. Waldo with his civilised kindness, Waldo who will surely listen and help, Waldo with his Panama hat lying on the ground beside his feet. Good grief, it can't be the same one that he wore all those years ago?

The two men embrace and Ezekiel gestures to the hat, smiling broadly. 'That's how I remember you. The hat!'

Waldo laughs. He says he has kept a whole Panamanian family in a lifetime's grog with his hats. Ezekiel holds the hat aloft admiringly, then puts it on Waldo's head.

'Bravo, it still suits you.' He grips Waldo with both arms. 'And how are you, my friend?'

'Older, and at the moment, grimmer.'

Ezekiel sobers up. 'You mean Alice?'

Waldo nods and sits down. 'Alice, and everything else that has happened. The scale of the killings is still hard to grasp.' He twirls his hat in his hand. 'Hannah told me about your wife and sons. I'm sorry. That sounds inadequate, but sometimes when something so monumentally awful occurs it strips everything, including language.'

Ezekiel pulls up a chair and lights a cigarette. 'It feels as if I am in the middle of an ocean of grief. I swim and swim and every now and then I raise a hand and wave it to show I still breathe, I live, but no one comes to rescue me. We are all drowning and I am tired.'

'You poor old sod.'

Ezekiel crinkles his eyes against the glare of the sun. 'When my father died and I went home, I was angry at the manner of his death and furious that we had to flee. I was also sad, I loved my father and we were close. But then it was different. I had been the anointed son, the one who would take up the flag and wave it high, follow the cause of justice, fight for universal peace. Ha ha, I didn't see the paradox in those days, I didn't want to. Rhetoric has its own balm. It hides reality. This time, there is nowhere to hide.'

Waldo is finding this painful. He fingers the barley sugar in his pocket, then reaches out for one of Ezekiel's cigarettes. Ezekiel lights it for him.

'I am like Prometheus, but my torture continues by night as well as day. The eagle never stops. The black eagle.' He smiles ruefully. 'Did Hannah ever tell you that when I was young and we were living in Paris, I used to call myself the black eagle, *l'aigle noir*?'

'I don't remember,' says Waldo. 'It's too long ago.'

'Hannah remembers. Everything.'

Waldo swallows. He had always found it hard to cope with the thought of Hannah living in Paris with Ezekiel and he is surprised that it still pains him. He changes the subject. 'Alice. We need to talk about Alice. What's the problem with arranging a prisoner exchange?'

Ezekiel throws his half-smoked cigarette on the ground and lights another. 'You make it sound as if we're exchanging hats. These people are murderers. They committed terrible atrocities. They should be brought to justice and punished.'

'Alice isn't a murderer,' says Waldo sharply. 'She's your daughter.'

Ezekiel pulls a face, deepening the lines on either side of his mouth. 'I haven't been a father to her. And I regret that. Deeply. I regret it. But I can't do anything because it's not just my decision. It's the government's. This is supposed to be a democracy. Remember?'

'Try in every way you can,' urges Waldo, leaning forward in his chair, for one moment tempted to take Ezekiel's hand. 'You don't know Alice so you'll have to take my word for it, she's ... she's an extraordinary young woman, strong and loving. It's unthinkable to let her die.'

He sits back, waiting for Ezekiel's response. When it comes, it is slow and deliberate. 'Of course I will try. I will do everything I humanly can. But –'

'If there are buts, she will die. Don't do that to her, Ezekiel. Don't do it to Hannah.'

Waldo reaches down for his briefcase and pulls out a bottle of red wine, a corkscrew and two glasses. 'South African. Probably the last remaining bottle in Kigali. Let's drink to setting Alice free.'

For a moment, Ezekiel holds back. It will take more than a goodwill toast to save Alice.


Hannah has already gained admittance to Ezekiel's office and is prowling up and down when he arrives exhausted. He takes off his jacket and rolls up his shirt sleeves, indicating she should sit down. When he tries to explain that it is unlikely his colleagues in government will agree to anything, particularly a prisoner exchange, she shouts at him.

'She's your daughter, Ezekiel. If you've done nothing else for her, you can at least save her life!'

He blanches, stubbing out his cigarette in a cheap yellow ashtray piled high with butts. 'It was her choice to come here, it's a risk she's taken and now she's paying the price.'

'She came here to help.'

'In today's wars, aid workers can no longer claim to be neutral. Every bit of help they give benefits one side or the other. Sometimes both.' His voice is tired and he pulls towards him a photograph of his two sons. They wear school uniforms and are smiling. 'My boys,' he says. 'This is François and the little one is Jean-Paul.'

Hannah takes the photograph but doesn't know what to say.

'It's strange how I find myself using the present tense,' Ezekiel continues, 'even after they're all dead. I wonder how long that happens? Do you think it passes?'

She shakes her head and feels a choking in her throat. 'And your wife, do you have a photograph of your wife?'

He pulls a snapshot from his wallet. 'Here, it's not very good, it was taken in our garden last year.'

The photograph is blurred and Hannah can see little except that the woman is possibly younger than she, a handsome woman in a summer dress. Hannah hands the photo back to Ezekiel and he stares at both photographs, side by side, his sons' and his wife's. There are tears in his eyes. For a brief moment Hannah feels envious of this woman who had the closeness she was denied. Then she remembers what happened to her and the savagery of the killings.

'What do you think will happen to Alice?' Her voice is almost a whisper.

He doesn't answer her question. 'You must get in touch with your government again, and with Help.'

'And your government, what will they do?'

He grimaces. 'Very little, I'm afraid. I'd like to be more optimistic and I'll try all I can, but –'

'That's not good enough,' she says coldly, rising to her feet. 'What you are doing is wrong. Morally wrong.'

He raises his voice. 'Don't preach to me about morality, Hannah. Yes, for me there are moral absolutes. A few. But in the end we have only ourselves for answers. And each time will be different.'

She leaves him without saying goodbye and without shaking his outstretched hand. The two young guards outside his door look at her with curiosity as she runs down the stairs, her face frozen in anger, or is it grief? She does not know. She has been raised with the concept of moral absolutes. Do not kill or harm children. Do not kill or harm anyone, come to that. Do not steal. Do not covet thy neighbour's wife, nor his oxen nor his ass – nor his arse. That's one for old Theo King. Would she have traded the life of Ezekiel's two sons for the life of Alice? And then that more sinister thought. Could Ezekiel have been an innocent part of an RPF plot without realising the kind of fish he'd caught in the net? Alice fish.

She draws breath and forces herself outside, where she is met by a fierce wind battering at her face, picking up twigs and branches of trees as if they were specks of dust, blowing them in all directions.

Ezekiel has forced himself to return home, to push open the heavy gates, to walk up the driveway and into the house, into the bedroom where he found the body of Bertha. He sits on the bed feeling a vast emptiness. He cannot even recall his wife's face. He picks up a photograph of her which lies amongst broken glass on the floor and feels he is looking at a stranger. He has buried all his memories, buried them deep where they can no longer hurt.

He had wanted Bertha to leave with the two boys when he was still with the UN and there were rumours that violence might occur. Bertha had said, 'The boys are at school. The UN will protect us.'

A few weeks later he had quit the UN and joined up with the Rwandan Patriotic Front in Uganda, where he was quickly welcomed as one of the leaders. Once the killings started and it was obvious the UN was holding back, it was too late to do anything. All he could do was hope.

He traces his finger over the photograph of his wife, lingering on her eyes and her mouth. Whatever he wanted, Bertha gave. This he remembers. He loved her. He respected her. But he had never experienced the kind of intimacy with her that part of him craved. Their marriage had been arranged, he had accepted his role as husband and, later, father. But he had a journey to make and Bertha had carried his bags. Not uncommon in his country.

He picks up a yellow dress of hers which lies trampled on the floor, buries his face in it, hoping to recapture her smell. He does not succeed.

Outside, in the back garden, lies the rubbish tip on which he found the bodies of his two young sons. He can't see his sons' faces either, but he can hear their voices, their shouts and their laughter. Outside is not to be borne.

A tremendous accumulation of tiredness overcomes him as his mind roams again over the capture of Alice, the child he has never known, and now, his only child. What would have happened had Hannah come back with him to Africa? Would she have ended up being killed in the bedroom of their house? He realises all this is ridiculous and destructive speculation, but he pushes it as far as he is able. He is like a man who sticks pins into his paralysed body, hoping to feel pain.


Out in the streets of Kigali, Hannah knows that no one will listen to her. There has been so much devastation, so many deaths, that one more is neither here nor there. Never has life seemed so terrifying; never so desirable. The warm sun on her shoulders, the scarlet and yellow hibiscus, the stretch of her body as she moves one leg after the other, her hands when she reaches out and studies their lines and freckles, the ants under her feet, the small yellow bird wheeling in the air, the children who run ahead of her in the street, chattering and laughing. Alive. But somewhere, in a place that she cannot even imagine, Alice's life is under threat.

She finds herself longing to ring home, to speak to Aunt D, even her father, who has always seemed closer to Alice than to her. Perhaps that's unfair. There was that time when she was pregnant and had burned all her unsent letters to Ezekiel in a fit of pique. She set fire to them inside a tin wastepaper bin, but instead of smouldering, flames leaped high in the air. She panicked and chucked on the dregs of a cup of coffee. Her father had appeared from his study, sniffing the smoke, looking at her tear-streaked face and at the ashes flying through the air.

'Anything wrong?' he asked.

'No,' she said. 'Everything's fine.'

He patted her awkwardly on the arm. 'Look here, if it's the baby, we'll manage.'

At the door, he turned back, a tall gaunt figure dressed in corduroys and tweed jacket, his face already beginning to mottle with age, his eyes growing pale. A musty-smelling man whose inner loneliness was beginning to surface like a worm that had been buried away for most of a lifetime and could no longer be hidden.

'Well now, Hannah,' he had said. 'Well, now,' his voice trailing away as he returned to his study and his micro-scopes.

For a moment she had nearly run after him. Instead, she

held back, just as she holds back today. When she does ring, she talks about facts, not feelings.

Gerry Phillips greets Hannah cautiously. He sends for coffee, fiddles around with small talk until the tray arrives, then reveals that the Australian embassy in Nairobi and the UN have also received news of the ransom demand.

'And?' asks Hannah, teaspoon suspended in the air.

He coughs, a polite nervous cough. 'I believe that both organisations will wish to leave matters in the capable hands of the RPF and the aid agency, Help.'

He tries to make it sound as if this is good news, but Hannah cuts across him, demanding why neither organisation is prepared to play a mediating rule.

'Both have to observe international protocol.'

'Oh, stop the bullshit.'

Phillips tugs uneasily at the lapel of his jacket, wishing she would go away. He tries again. 'The Australian government perhaps feels that to interfere might only make matters worse.'

'Worse for whom?'

He lowers his eyes, looking and feeling wretched as he tries to rub an imaginary spot off his blue and cream striped tie.

Hannah stands over him. Her voice is clear and direct. 'You're too decent a man to tell lies; so you just don't tell all the truth.'

Waldo, when he hears her account of the visit, says tersely that Gerry Phillips' attitude reminds him of the case of other hostages, including the young Australian David Wilson who, with his two travelling companions, has just been kidnapped in Cambodia. Governments are prone to renege on their responsibility in such situations; they pass it to the United Nations, or to the country where the terrorism has occurred. They play diplomatic games with skill and finesse. They express compassion, always they express compassion, and even regret. But all the while that they talk, the shadow of execution lengthens, and sometimes hapless prisoners end up as corpses in foreign lands.

Waldo stops short. He wishes he hadn't embarked on the story. He reaches out.

Hannah springs away. 'Don't. Don't touch me.'

Joe Schwartz is about to call Los Angeles when Hannah barges into his office.

'Are you going to give the aid for Alice or aren't you?'

Joe frowns and pretends he hasn't heard. Hannah repeats her question.

Joe takes off his glasses and polishes them. 'We're waiting on advice from headquarters.'

'What sort of advice?'

'Policy advice.'

'Policy advice? For God's sake, Joe!'

Joe avoids her eyes, continues his polishing. 'It's a policy issue.'

'It's not a policy issue, it's Alice's life. Don't give me this crap.'

Joe sighs. 'Look, of course we want to see Alice free. But there's an issue about the safety of others. If we give in with Alice, what's to stop them kidnapping other aid workers, again and again? It's a really serious issue, Hannah, and I don't have the authority to make such decisions.' He laughs nervously.

She tries to will him to look at her, but he won't. His eyes are fixed on his fingers, which keep shifting pieces of paper on his desk.

A small group of aid workers have gathered, listening. Judy Morrison squeezes Hannah's hand. Two little red spots have appeared on Hannah's temples. Judy intervenes. 'Ask Theo. He's still in charge of the International Mission. He could make those decisions.'

Joe Schwartz shrugs and says that Theodore King is away in Los Angeles and won't be back for several days.


Hannah apologetically asks Waldo to join them for dinner, guessing that he finds this an ordeal. She is correct. Waldo is tired of eating potato stew and tired of the restrained *bonhomie*. He is also distressed by the sight of Hannah's gaunt face. His own pink face is sunburned and causing some pain, and he has a rising sense of panic. His eyes catch Joe's and he hastily looks down at his plastic spoon.

'Would you mind saying grace tonight, Waldo?'

Good God, not him. Waldo fills his mouth full of food and shakes his head as if this is his excuse. He hears the note of irritation in Joe's voice, sees the thin brows pulled together in a scowl.

For a moment it looks as if Joe will turn to Hannah and she is already prepared to refuse. Vehemently. Thank you, God. For what? Thank you, God, but where were you when babies were skewered, when women had their breasts lopped off and men were left to die with their penises stuffed in their mouths? Where were you when Alice was dragged away?

Joe purses his lips and says grace. Nicola smiles nervously.

They pray for Alice, and Hannah feels angry. God has a lot to answer for.

'You can't blame God for Alice,' says Waldo later. 'She wanted to see her father. Besides, if you keep going on these expeditions, why shouldn't Alice?'

'Go to hell.'

Hannah does not want to be meek and mild and in the grace of God. She wants to shriek and wail.

*'Sister Hannah, Sister Hannah, when were you saved?' they keep asking me, these young priests with their big black hats and coats, and long legs. Sometimes I think they can be little older than Alice. 'Sister, Sister, when were you saved?'*

*Ah, I wish someone would save me, make it all right for ever and ever amen. I sigh and look at these young boys with their shining eyes and beautiful smiles, and say sadly, 'Not yet, I'm afraid.'*

Hannah puts down her pen. She is writing by candlelight and her eyes are tired. Nicola brings her a mug of tea which she accepts gratefully. Writing a diary helps.

*I am losing my self, I sense it leaching away, a slow disintegration that I find frightening because I cannot remember where I have been or even where I am. Confused, fragmented, one thought flowing into another so that I seem to exist in a baffling fog. I wake up and wonder if I am imagining what has happened. Have I strayed into one of Waldo's scripts, and when I come to my senses will Alice be safely at home? I lie here, remembering when I was pregnant with Alice and I used to hold my belly and talk to her. I do it now. My baby, may you be safe, that's what I whisper over and over again. My baby Alice, may you be safe.*

# *fifteen*

Early afternoon, and Hannah and Waldo are waiting outside the United Nations building for the arrival of a delegation headed by Dr Giovanni Pizzetti, poet, scholar and international bureaucrat. Hannah dislikes him but she has decided to ask for his help. Anything is worth a try. Waldo is dubious – Hannah has a glint in her eye which disturbs him.

Several large cars bearing the blue and white pennants of the UN drive slowly up to the front entrance where a small crowd has gathered to welcome Pizzetti. He alights with dignity. His shiny black shoes are the first part of him to emerge. His legs and his plump body are elegantly suited in navy-blue silk. His thick black hair is smoothed back like a 1930s matinée idol. Hannah thinks he looks like a cockroach.

Pizzetti brushes himself down, adjusts his tie, which matches the blue of the UN flag, and strides into the building.

'Pompous idiot,' mutters Hannah, uncertain what strategy she should use to engage his sympathy. Probably motherhood and peace. Pizzetti busily cultivates a reputation as peacemaker by exalting the peacemaking qualities of women. No research shows that women are any more peaceable than men when they are in power, for the simple reason that few women have held power, but Hannah recalls how Pizzetti dealt with Margaret Thatcher's foray into the Falklands – by stating firmly that she waged war simply to obtain peace. Woman as peacemaker, woman as goddess, woman as the source of goodness and light, these are the measures of Pizzetti's urgings, while intelligent over-worked young women scurry around, responding to his every whim, handing him documents, reclaiming them, nursing his books of poetry, which are published by the UN in slim, hand-somely bound volumes and autographed in his flowing hand.

Hannah remembers that Pizzetti is particularly appreciative of first ladies and princesses, mainly because they are usually married to presidents and princes. And although he knows it is politically incorrect to introduce eminent women as 'the wives of', he finds it hard to desist. He once introduced Jane Fonda as the wife of Ted Turner.

Hannah had first met Pizzetti in Copenhagen at a global jamboree on world poverty, one of a series of mega-conferences marking the UN's fortieth anniversary. Thirteen thousand delegates from a hundred and eighty countries had one week to resolve the problems of the world's one billion poor.

'And did they?' Aunt D had asked when Hannah returned and was in the kitchen pulling clothes out of her travel bag, searching for the presents she had brought home – a blue and white striped jumper for Alice, a bag for Aunt D and aquavit for her father.

Hannah paused, holding some squashed chocolates which she had forgotten to declare.

'They signed a ninety-page declaration – non-binding of course – to tell us that poverty is a scourge, that resources are inadequate, that the debt burden of developing nations is appalling. And they offered a plan of action which guaranteed inaction.'

'Sounds like the barber's cat. All piss and wind,' said Aunt D, pouring tea from a cracked blue enamel teapot.

Hannah laughed. 'I was much more polite in my piece to camera. I called it an exercise in futility.'

Hannah remembers these words when she comes face to face with Pizzetti in Kigali and begins telling him about Alice. As she talks, his dark eyes rapidly lose focus and he steps to one side, murmuring, 'My deepest sympathies, Madam.'

Hannah blocks his path. Pizzetti mops his brow with a white linen handkerchief. 'Madam, what can I do?'

'You could intercede.'

He looks incredulous. 'No, that would not be desirable, nor indeed possible.'

Hannah flushes. 'Why? Why not send some soldiers to free her, you've got enough of them hanging around.'

She is oblivious to the small crowd that has gathered in delight at the prospect of a scene, but someone is skilfully extricating Pizzetti and, like the Cheshire cat, he is fast disappearing. When she tries to follow, the space is blocked by soldiers and more soldiers. Suddenly, someone grabs her arm and forces her into an ante-room. The door slams behind her and she is confronted by an angry Ezekiel.

'Hannah, are you a crazy woman? We need all the help we can get from the UN and you go insulting the man.'

'He's an impotent prick,' she says.

'Hannah,' says Waldo, who has just slipped into the room behind Ezekiel, 'you can't say that.'

'I just have.'

Ezekiel turns to Waldo. 'Take her and look after her, will you?'

Hannah has no intention of being looked after. She breaks free and runs into the crowd. Waldo finds her two hours later, sitting on a high-backed stool in the Tivoli bar behind a line-up of empty bottles.

She waves a beer bottle at Waldo. 'Here's to Dr Giovanni Pizzetti, limp and lousy lover.'

Waldo is fascinated. 'How do you know he's a lousy lover? Did you sleep with him?'

Hannah peers at Waldo. 'I'd sooner sleep with a hippopot-amus,' she says in dignified outrage. 'Wanna know how to tell if a man's a lousy lover?'

Waldo fears he is entering dangerous territory. He nods cautiously.

'You look at his bum, right!' Hannah giggles. 'You thought I'd say look at his dick, didn't you? Nope. His bum.'

Waldo tries to remember the backside of Giovanni Pizzetti, housed in its navy-blue silk. 'His looked pretty generous to me.'

'Got it in one!' shrieks Hannah, kicking her shoe in the air. Waldo catches it.

'Wanna hear an old African saying?'

Waldo groans. 'Go on.'

'Men with big bums have little dicks.'

'Why?'

'They don't get any exercise.'

'Why?'

'Because they have little dicks. Old African saying told to me by old African woman, hope to die.' She hiccups. 'Oh, forget it!'

Waldo wipes his face on a paper napkin he pocketed at the UN reception and some of the paper gets stuck on his chin. Hannah lurches forward, tries to pick the tissue off his chin, misses and falls to the floor. She looks up at him scathingly.

'You don't count. You gave your dick away for Lent. If you have a dick. Ever had a dick, Waldo?'

Later, Waldo creeps into the men's toilets and examines the shape and extent of his backside. He is peering over his shoulder when Joe Schwartz enters, gives him a quizzical look and hastily withdraws.

Hannah has a hangover and is contrite. Waldo has a hangover and is silent. Hannah is determined to visit the Kigali hospital and make one more round of enquiries about Alice. Waldo doesn't want to go to the hospital, he wants to rest.

Outside the main entrance, three men lurch up to them on crutches. One man is dressed in matted rags, eyes peering through hair which scrambles over his face; he is weaving and bending so close that Hannah can smell the beer on his breath. He has something precious to sell, a gold bar – are they interested in a gold bar? He wants to make an assignation, this old man.

'Me come from Zaire, Congo, I got gold, you need gold?' Carefully he unwraps a dirty cloth and shows not gold, but a packet of cigarettes. 'You meet me tonight, I give you more gold.'

They are moving on when they hear Australian voices. The group of military nurses Waldo met during the amputation are clustered at the front entrance.

'Bloody matches, they don't work back home, they bloody

well don't work here,' says a sergeant, his big pink hands struggling with a damp box of matches. He is already tired. Since yesterday, they have dealt with eleven road accidents and five people blown up by landmines.

Fabiani, the Italian surgeon with the heavy-lidded eyes, and the young Australian doctor, Michelle Roberts, come out for a short break. Fabiani lights a cigarette and nods hello to Waldo. 'Another fucking amputation. Kid of eleven. Mine blew off his foot.'

He inhales deeply, chucks away his newly lit cigarette and starts up another. 'Eight hundred people die every month, mostly children and I have to say, Sorry it hurts, sorry you don't have your hand, sorry you can't see, sorry, sorry.'

Waldo and Hannah both know that in between his field jobs, this man campaigns ceaselessly against landmines. He goes to New York to speak at the United Nations, attends disarmament conferences, pours the full force of his energy and anger into trying to achieve change.

Waldo thinks of his own inactivity and feels ashamed. To his astonishment, he hears himself asking Fabiani if he can watch the next amputation. He doesn't understand why the hell he has made this request; he had to leave at the start of the last one, but for some inexplicable reason he is determined to stick this one out. He takes leave of Hannah and follows Fabiani.

A small boy lies on the operating table, his large dark eyes wide open and frightened. The Swedish anaesthetist is stroking his forehead. The boy tries to sit up, his skin flushed, but a nurse calms him while the anaesthetist gives him the injection. He flops into unconsciousness. One of the child's legs is whole, the other is a stump of mangled flesh and bone.

This time, Waldo manages to hold out for about two

minutes, the duration of an average television grab. As chunks of the boy's leg are thrown into a big green garbage bag, Waldo is strangely reassured by the fact that they look like pieces of fillet steak, whereas the bone which shows through could well be a leg of lamb. He likes the idea of this association with four-legged animal life. But would lions or hyenas or polar bears or elephants leave such a carnage of cruelty? he wonders. How would he have coped if his own leg had been blown off when he was this kid's age? How did his father cope when he lost both legs?

Outside, the sky is a mean and dirty grey and Waldo's head aches. He tries to divert his mind to something spiritual, but as so often happens he is unsuccessful. He has searched for the meaning of life in places as diverse as Kilimanjaro, the Himalayas, a bombed-out church in Sarajevo during midnight mass, and a café on the Greek island of Halki, where the air smelt of lemon thyme and the fish were small and sweet and silvery. Just when he believes he has pinned down an answer it always slips through his fingers, like those silvery fish.

He tracks down Hannah to a ward full of amputees: men, women and children. The children lie in big beds, their faces white against the sheets, their great dark eyes staring at the ceiling or the walls. The boy who was just operated on is now conscious. He has been given painkillers, but his eyes are filled with tears.

Waldo shudders. 'Fucking hell.'

As he is leaving, he bumps into someone who is vaguely familiar – thin, pink and white, frail. Bath Shop Bruce, who goes scarlet with embarrassment when he sees Waldo.

'What on earth are you doing here?' Waldo asks.

'I come and talk to people,' stutters Bruce. 'Not really talk, because of the language,' and he gives a nervous laugh. 'Just hold their hands. I'm used to people being very ill and dying. AIDS, you know. It's something I can do quite well.'

Alice is frowning. General Mgumbo has a poisoned thumb and is waving it under her nose, demanding, 'Fix it.' The thumb is swollen, red and festering. She takes it in one hand and lances it with the other, releasing a large quantity of greenish-yellow pus before she disinfects and binds the wound. Her movements are quick and efficient. She uses a Red Cross kit which is on the general's table.

When she is done Mgumbo says, 'Thank you,' and waves a hand indicating that she should sit. She still has shackles on her legs but shuffles her way to a chair, where she perches awkwardly and a little fearfully. It is night-time and two bare electric lightbulbs throw off a crude yellow light. The hut is basic – a bed, two upright chairs, a desk and a photograph of three young girls wearing white blouses and navy-blue uniforms. Alice asks if these are his daughters. Mgumbo nods. He is busy examining the binding on his thumb, turning it this way and that.

'You have done well,' he says finally.

The silence between them is discomforting. He dismisses both his guards and her apprehension increases. She reaches down and jangles her irons. 'How about removing these?' she suggests hopefully.

General Mgumbo gives a laugh which sounds like a winded donkey. He opens a bottle of beer. 'I can open beer bottles with my bare hands, Mademoiselle, but not heavy chains.'

He pours her a glass of beer and seems eager to impress upon her that he is a civilised man, not given to wanton cruelty.

She wants to ask him, How could you do it? Slaughter your neighbours and friends, children who played with your children? But she is scared and keeps her silence.

Outside she can hear the wind blowing in the trees. She clears her throat, sits upright and says politely, 'I think if you don't mind I'd like to be taken back to my hut.'

Mgumbo looks up. Beads of white foam encrust his moustache. 'I knew your father,' he says suddenly. 'In Paris. We were students at the same time.'

'He was your friend?'

The general shakes his head. 'Acquaintance. Paris had many African students.' He looks at her questioningly. 'How old are you?'

Alice meets his gaze. 'Eighteen, I'm eighteen.'

'My eldest daughter is now seventeen.' He waves a hand at the photograph. 'She has grown since that picture was taken.'

'What's her name?'

He doesn't answer. Alice scuffs at the earth around her feet. 'Is she ... all right?' she ventures, knowing that fighting has killed people on both sides of the war.

'She is all right. As far as I know.'

'Where is she?'

He shrugs. 'I sent my family to France.'

After a few minutes' silence he claps his hands and one of the guards comes to take Alice away. He is rough with her and Mgumbo raises a cautionary hand. Just as she is leaving, Mgumbo calls out, 'Chantelle, my eldest daughter is called Chantelle.'

Alice feels as if Mgumbo wants something from her. Absolution? No, how can she give him that? She wasn't one of the victims of the massacre. Is it that he sees in her some small possibility of behaving decently? For him, did the killings get out of hand?

She has been given a work table and basic medications in one of the village huts adjoining the military compound. Each day soldiers and villagers come to her with their ailments. Sometimes she is led at gunpoint to a hut where a sick person is too ill to move. The villagers are friendly but communication is limited. They think because she is brown-skinned that she must be able to speak their language, and when she looks blankly at them or draws an outline of Australia in the dust, and sometimes a valiant attempt at a kangaroo, they break into laughter. She tries to find out the name of their village and its location, but is unable to understand their reply.

Keeping fit is an ongoing challenge. She exercises, within the limits of her chains. She plays hopscotch, even though she keeps falling over, and when she gets too tired for hopscotch she turns the markings on the ground into noughts and crosses. At night, when she lies curled up on a rush mat one of the village women has given her, she plays out imaginary scenarios of future family life. Sometimes she has Hannah, Waldo, Ezekiel and herself moving between Australia, England and Rwanda in various permutations. Other times she lives with Ezekiel, helping Rwanda recover. She is careful with this particular idea as she hasn't yet met Ezekiel and doesn't even know if she will like him.

The longer her captivity, the more she thinks about Hannah. When she was pregnant, did she ever contemplate having an abortion, and, if so, what made her change her mind? Does she miss her, Alice, when she is away, or does she just pretend? Alice is torn between admiration for Hannah's independence and resentment at her absences. So many questions, so many paradoxes, as she sits with her bare feet in the dirt, feeling increasingly perplexed, imagining how Hannah would answer her captors and how she would behave.

Alice has developed a routine. She had been in captivity for less than a week when she realised that this would be an essential element of her survival. Rhythms of life which bring their own harmony, no matter what the circumstances. Even those ordinary rituals at home in Sydney marked a sweet order in her life, something she treasured as a necessary contrast to the frenetic existence of her mother. Here, in the camp, she is woken at dawn, given tea and millet porridge, and then taken to the rudimentary clinic.

Then one day, her routine is suddenly broken. She gets no breakfast, nor is she taken to the clinic. When she asks why, the guard shrugs his shoulders. His orders are to take her to the general, who is talking heatedly with a small group of officers.

Mgumbo ignores her, so she squats on the floor to wait, but one of the officers yanks her to her feet and slaps her hard on the face. Her head jerks back, her eyes fill with tears. This man, Lazaro, was one of her initial kidnappers. He has always behaved aggressively towards her and now he stands so close that she can smell his breath and see the red streaks in his eyes. He hits her again and again until her ears are ringing.

'Stop!' she calls out. 'Stop, stop!'

She looks beseechingly at Mgumbo but his back is turned.

'Speak your African language,' Lazaro hisses.

'I can't,' she pleads. 'I only know a few words.' Blood is running down her face and she puts her hand to her nose. General Mgumbo unexpectedly passes her a handkerchief. She wipes her face. 'Why are you treating me like this? What have I done?'

He gives her a thin smile. 'This is not a tourist resort.'

Alice is defiant. She stands with her feet apart, her arms crossed. 'I was wondering why I didn't have breakfast in bed.'

Mgumbo says sternly, 'The deadline has passed. No prisoners have been exchanged. We have not received any aid.'

He walks up close to her and says in a whisper, 'Is it because they don't love you enough?' His breath smells of alcohol.

They are trying to undermine her confidence, Alice thinks. Somewhere she has read that this is how people's spirits are broken, how confessions are obtained. Pains shoot through her head and her nose is still bleeding. She remembers Hannah once saying, 'If you're in a tight spot, don't panic, think.'

Mgumbo clicks his fingers and calls for paper and pen. 'This is your last chance. Write that we are running out of patience, and you are running out of time. Write!'

So Alice writes, her fingers cramped against the black biro which only works if she presses hard on the pad.

Back in her hut she lies on the ground, trying to ease the pain in her head and jaw. For the first time her mind keeps returning to the possibility that soon she might be dead. She stretches out her hands and wriggles her fingers. She cannot imagine them unable to move. She listens to her breathing. In and out, in and out. She cannot imagine herself unable to breathe.

For some bizarre reason her mind wanders to the memory of a dead frog floating in the twin-tub washing machine in Broome, belly up in the dirty water, its skin boiled a rosy pink, its flaccid legs splayed apart in a way that seemed indecent. Distressed, Alice lifted the lid of the second tub, and couldn't help laughing. In the centre of the snowy white froth spun the vibrant green head of a live frog, its poppy eyes glistening as they whirled round and round. She turned off the machine and put her hand underneath the frog, which hopped out in one gallant leap and bounded away into the bush.

Alice is feeling a bit like that frog. She doesn't suppose they will boil her alive in a washing machine, but she wonders what else they might choose. Shooting? Hanging? Banging her on the head with a mattock? She shudders and wonders why Mgumbo's demands haven't been met. Don't Hannah and Waldo realise the seriousness of her situation? Or perhaps they have also been kidnapped and there is no one who can help? She stares miserably at the ground and churns the dirt with her foot.

In Broome, Waldo had told her a joke about two prisoners facing a firing squad. When a soldier went to blindfold them, one of the prisoners declared that he didn't want a blindfold. The other prisoner was alarmed: 'For goodness' sake, don't make trouble!'

Alice hugs her knees. Somehow or other she has to find strength and calm. She closes her eyes. She is on a headland at Roebuck Bay, watching a flock of birds gather on the sand, flap their wings and fly, wheeling their way in a great and splendid arc, angling in on the sun and taking their direction from the stars. They will give themselves to fierce winds and icy gales, they will trust in themselves and keep on flying until they reach their destination.

# sixteen

Hannah knows by the way Joe Schwartz keeps avoiding her that he is having difficulty getting head office to agree to the demand for aid. As for prisoners, Ezekiel has said he can't. She feels no one will take responsibility for their actions; everyone is blindly following orders, no matter what they are. She despairs, but Waldo says she must keep trying, they must both keep trying.

She harangues Joe, but he plays at trying to extricate a stone from his sandal. She kicks the ground, letting fly more stones, but still he doesn't look at her.

'Joe, you're a coward. You could disobey. You could send the aid. Be decent. Be brave.'

But Joe looks miserable and returns to his sandal and the stone.

She tries again. 'Would Help excommunicate you? Is that what this is about, Joe? Would you lose your promotion?'

'Certainly not,' says Joe stiffly, pulling out the offending stone with a look of self-justification. 'But these things aren't always easy.'

Rage swells within her, red and bold, springing from her impotence. She wants to pound his head with rocks, break his arms, destroy him limb by limb, slam shut her ears so she cannot hear him scream. Blood engorges her, the blood of Alice, the blood of innocence, until she is drowning in blood, unable to breathe, unable to hear that Joe is quietly speaking.

'I'm failing you. I'm sorry.'

She stands in silence, then walks away.


'She says you are a shit,' says Waldo, who is sitting in Ezekiel's office, feet spread trenchantly apart, determined to make one last attempt to get this wounded and isolated man to take action.

Ezekiel smiles ruefully. 'She's probably right.'

Waldo hesitates, not sure how best to proceed. The two men sit for a moment or two before Waldo tries again.

'Surely you could persuade your colleagues to make some kind of offer, some compromise? Maybe not twenty prisoners but ten?'

Ezekiel shakes his head. 'They won't.'

Waldo shifts ground. 'Do they know Alice is your daughter?'

'Some do. But most of them have lost their own families. They're not interested.'

Waldo leans forward. 'But *you* are. You have lost your sons and your wife. Don't lose Alice too.'

Ezekiel does not answer, but reorders the books on his desk, pushing them this way then that. Waldo picks up one of the books, curious, and reads the faded spine. It's a James Baldwin: *Fire Next Time*.

Ezekiel takes the book impatiently and puts it back on the pile. 'God almighty, Waldo, you overestimate my influence with the rest of my colleagues. I am stuck, man, stuck!'

Waldo gets to his feet and plonks his hat on the back of his head. 'Then you'd best get unstuck.'

Outside, it is Waldo's turn to feel despair. Time is running out. All pathways seem closed. And then, unexpectedly, he bumps into Hannah, who is walking in the opposite direction to him, on her way back from town. She grabs his arm excitedly.

'I was coming to look for you. Two men came up to me at the bar and said they were mercenaries. They could rescue Alice, they said.'

Waldo stoops to tie a shoelace. 'And pigs can fly.'

'Pigs might have to fly.'

'What do they want?'

'Money.'

'How much?'

'One hundred thousand US dollars.'

'No way.'

'For Christ's sake, Waldo, this may be our only chance.'

'It's quite likely they're phonies,' he says, trying to calm her down. He has always hated mercenaries. At least regular soldiers are supposed to have some code of conduct, but mercenaries live off the blood of others, kill for the highest bidder.

'Look, Hannah,' he says impatiently, 'how do we know they're not working for the government in Zaire and just stringing you along for a quick quid? There have been mercenaries around these parts for years. The White Legion and all that stuff.'

She frowns. 'Stop giving me a lesson on mercenaries. If they can work for the Zairean government there's no reason why they can't work for us.'

Waldo tries to propel her gently along the road but she shakes him free. They both know they are running out of time.

'I guess we meet them, then.' His voice is reluctant.

Waldo approaches Theodore King with diffidence. King's fundamentalism is difficult for Waldo to accept, and over the years his sentimentality has embarrassed him, but he clings to some vague belief that the man is basically kind.

Theodore King's star is on the wane. Territorial colonialism has given way to economic colonialism. Missionaries are out, market economists are in. But the old man still has some influence, particularly as long as he remains International President of Help.

He finds King outside his tent, sitting on a striped green camping stool. King has rolled up his trouser legs and is dipping one foot into about two inches of water at the bottom of a bucket.

'I have corns,' says the international president cheerfully. 'They come to us all eventually.' He peers at Waldo. 'I do not recommend old age. Avoid it at all costs.'

When Waldo tells him about the latest developments with Alice, King listens with tears in his eyes. 'Please God they do not kill the child. I would help, you know I would. In my day, we would have given whatever they asked. No question. But now, not many people listen to me.'

He shaves away at his yellowing corn and Waldo winces.

'I am resigning soon. This is my last tour. They let me do this one because of the years I have spent with the organisation, but after that I must leave. They found me out, you know.' He gives Waldo a sideways look. 'And it was a sin; yes, I knew it was a sin. But never children. I never touched children.'

Waldo watches King in silence for a while as the old man engrosses himself in his corn. When Waldo eventually gets up to go, King looks at him with a beatific smile. 'Leave it with me,' he says.

Like Hannah, Waldo reflects that everyone keeps saying, 'Leave it with me.'

He goes back to his hotel room, picking his way through his room-mates' mess – clothes strewn on the floor, a couple of copies of *Playboy*, apple cores, cigarette ends, battery packs. His own bags are neatly stowed under his iron hospital bed and he pulls one out, rummaging deep inside, eyes closed, fingers stretching until he secures what he seeks. A crumpled paperback, the cover torn, the pages dog-eared: a crossword book Alice had given him when he went to Somalia all those years earlier. He hasn't done any crosswords for a long while, but threw the book in at the last minute in case he needed some light relief. The thought of light relief is now a joke, but he needs something, anything, to take his mind off this terrible waiting. He sits on the side of the bed, screwing up his eyes in the poor light.

Three across, seven letters: the man allowed for a wreath.


Waldo and Hannah are to meet the two mercenaries at the back of the Tivoli bar. Waldo asks what they look like. Hannah has a memory of two large men, wearing maroon berets and carrying guns. One is dark and hairy, one is blond.

The men are as Hannah described, except that Waldo cannot check whether either of them is hairy, their shirts are buttoned to the neck. He feels vaguely cheated until he spots black hair on the back of one of the men's hands and fingers. The hands of the other are surprisingly small, white and delicate. Waldo imagines those hands making fine wire nooses.

The men introduce themselves as Eric and Milo, and claim they are members of an organisation known as Co-lateral Solutions. The blond man, Eric, strokes his moustache and carefully places a glossy brochure on the shaky table top.

Co-lateral Solutions offers management and policy advice, and training and equipment services for clandestine warfare, guerilla warfare, combat air patrol, armed warfare, basic and advanced battle handling. The company guarantees to succeed where the United Nations fails.

'We take sides, deploy overwhelming force and fire pre-emptively on any contractually designated enemy,' says Eric.

Waldo considers the phrase 'contractually designated enemy' and wonders aloud how he might turn his bank manager into one. Eric gives a thin smile. He explains that he and Milo are presently freelancing. He makes it sound as if they work for a suburban weekly newspaper.

'We are good friends,' he says, gesturing at Milo. Eric's accent sounds South African.

Milo nods his head emphatically. He drinks his beer in loud noisy gulps, not bothering to wipe the foam from his face. Eric drinks his beer in small silent sips. Milo's brown army boots are scruffy. Eric's are highly polished.

'We can free your daughter,' Eric is saying, but Waldo

demurs. He points out that they have no idea where Alice is being held.

'We can find out.' Eric puts his hands together so that his fingertips meet. He looks as if he is about to pray.

Milo lights up a cigarette. 'Fuck it.' This is the only thing he has said so far.

Eric gestures at his companion. 'He's not supposed to smoke. Had a heart attack. I told him living is more dangerous than dying.'

Milo blows out clouds of smoke and grins.

'How much do you want?' says Waldo. He is anxious to get to the point and anxious to finish his whisky, which tastes like fermented furniture polish.

'One hundred thousand US dollars.'

Waldo rises from the table, his face filled with disgust. Being a corporate soldier obviously pays – better than the poor old foot soldier in days gone by with his one shilling per day.

'One hundred thousand,' repeats Eric, his Adam's apple moving up and down in his white throat.

As they walk down the road away from the bar, Hannah notices that Waldo is rolling from side to side.

'It's that damned whisky. If you put a match to me, I'd explode.'

A vision suddenly flashes before Hannah of another kind of explosion. Supposing those mercenaries botched the job, what would happen to Alice then?

Back at Waldo's hotel they ring Sydney and Los Angeles to try to raise the money. Hannah's father says he can find it, although he is dubious about the plan and worried about the danger. Aunt D says emphatically that the men sound like rascals.

Hannah taps her foot up and down impatiently. 'It's a risk we have to take.'

When she hears a small sniffle on the other end of the line she realises her aunt is crying. 'Hold on,' she says swiftly, 'It'll be okay. The *I Ching* says we should be bold.'

'I didn't think you had the *I Ching*. Not with you,' says Aunt D, sounding immediately brighter.

'I haven't. But that's what it would say.'


Gerry Phillips moves a clean white sheet of blotting paper uneasily around his desk. His eyes are lowered as he tells Hannah that if she has anything to do with mercenaries, he believes the Australian government will withdraw its support.

'What support? All it has done is appease. None of you, including the UN, cares about Alice.'

Gerry Phillips blanches. 'Every avenue is being pursued.'

She stares at him, then is already out of the door when he calls her back. 'Hannah, I'm sorry,' he says awkwardly. He picks up a silver-framed photograph of a young girl. 'My own daughter, Phillippa. So I have some idea of how you must be feeling. We can only do the best we can.'

Hannah goes to lie under the eucalypt trees outside the Help buildings. This is her favourite retreat. She likes to look up at the canopy of forgiving grey-green leaves and trace imaginary hieroglyphics on the trunks. It helps distract attention from the fact that she aches as if she were hanging by her wrists over a precipice, waiting to fall.

Waldo massages her head and shoulders. 'Don't give up, Hannah.'

She doesn't answer. Once more, she is imagining Alice

being killed in every conceivable way. She sees her being shot, hanged, beheaded, thumped on the head with a hoe, raped, dismembered. Fear hides in Hannah's armpits, her toes, her clothes. Fear squeaks on the ground as she walks. It never leaves her. Terrible fear.

When Ezekiel invites Hannah to meet him at his living quarters at 6 o'clock that night, she wonders what he wants, what he will offer. Her mind races through a hundred different scenarios as she dresses. Ezekiel's apartment is not far from Help and she walks there, faster and faster, her heart pounding with anticipation. She is shown into a room which looks as if it has been hastily furnished, with a couple of cane couches and chairs, a television set, some books on a table in the corner, a standard lamp with a large yellowing shade. Ezekiel arrives ten minutes late, apologises, pours two beers from a fridge in the corner and raises his glass.

'*Salut* – to Alice's release.'

For a moment Hannah thinks he has news, but he says no, nothing further. He sits opposite her, leaning forward, and asks her to tell him about Alice. She is taken by surprise and fumbles in her field bag for her photographs. He says no, he will look at those later, he wants to hear Hannah's own words.

'What was she like as a baby?'

'She was a very long baby, with light brown skin, and she was perfect, with dark curly hair and amazing long eyelashes. I used to try and count them but I never got very far.'

He smiles. 'It is hard for me to imagine you as mother. I only knew you as lover.'

'She took your place.' Her voice was dry.

'And when you were pregnant, how was that?'

She lies back in the chair, her feet stretched out in front of her, her arms over her head. 'Difficult. I was frightened. And angry.'

'With me?'

'With you.'

'What about your father and your aunt – the one with the funny name?'

'Aunt D? Yes, well she wasn't too pleased with you. When Waldo came to see us, he gave Alice a silver bracelet and Aunt D said it was a pity he wasn't the father, at least we'd see him every now and then.'

He frowns, exasperated. 'I couldn't help it. How could I help it? If you'd been around when I rang Paris, our whole lives might have been different.'

For a brief moment, she thinks of Waldo in London and feels a twinge of guilt. Then she rejects it, strongly.

'You could have found my number in Australia. There's such a thing as directory enquiries.'

'Hannah, we were in hiding.'

She is about to expostulate when he lays a finger over her mouth. 'Hey woman, don't let's fight. Tell me more about Alice. I already know she's beautiful.' He speaks with the arrogance of a handsome man who expects his offspring to be equally perfect.

'Yes. Yes, she is beautiful.' Hannah looks at him, wondering if she should try to seduce him. She could, she is sure, they are both lonely and there is still a frisson of excitement between them, but she knows it would not change anything for Alice and it would be wrong for Hannah. So she holds back.

He takes her hand. 'Remember Paris?'

She doesn't want to be diverted. 'Ezekiel, you've said you can't act because your colleagues won't let you. But if it were left to you, what would you do? Would you authorise a prisoner exchange?'

She measures his silence.

'You shouldn't ask me that, it's not fair.'

'I am asking you.'

He meets her eyes. 'I will do everything I can to free Alice except release those murderers. Not after what they've done.' He waves his hands in a gesture of despair. 'God almighty, Hannah, every single day I see the bodies of my wife and sons. I reach out and touch Bertha's hair and my hands are covered in blood. I take the bodies of my sons, those poor dismembered bodies, I carry them to the morgue, I am in a daze and I am still in a daze. It is like a piece of my life has gone. I breathe in the suffering, the suffering of everyone, until it grows and fills the whole world. There is nowhere to hide.'

She moves across and holds him close, feeling a surge of unexpected tenderness. The sudden physical closeness surprises her, the familiarity of his body even after all these years. His skin smell. There is some strange sense of coming home, and for a moment she wonders if this is love. Then she realises she does not need to know the answer. Indeed, any answer would be impossible. It is enough that she has pulled up some kind of net from the past, and it belongs to them both. What has happened is so terrible she wants to bury all anger.

He takes a shuddering breath. 'Such a long time since Paris. So very long.'

# seventeen

The general has left for a few days, and Lazaro is in charge. He swaggers around Alice, watching while she works, a swab for this child's throat, disinfectant for a wound – is it a wound caused by fighting the Tutsis? It is still a wound, gaping to be healed, and all the while Lazaro pushing up against her, so that she can feel his body next to the thinness of her clothes. She tries not to feel afraid because she knows this will make his behaviour worse.

One morning Lazaro comes with a soldier who has scissors in his hand. He drags her outside and orders that her hair be cut. Out there in the open, with sand under her feet and the sun burning hot on her head. Her hair, her beautiful long brown curly hair.

'Why?' she shouts at him, her hands around her head, but the soldier pulls at her hair, hacks into it, slashing until her scalp is bare, and all the while she wonders, Where is Mgumbo, and what will Lazaro do next?

Her hair is coiled around her feet, blowing gently in the wind, her head is bruised and bleeding, and Lazaro, well satisfied, walks away.

The women from the village are silent. The children are silent. When Lazaro and the soldier are out of sight, Alice gathers up her hair and hugs it close, then walks back to her hut and spreads it about her feet. She feels her bare scalp with the palm of her hands, and mourns her loss.

The following day Lazaro comes again, this time with two soldiers. Her heart is thumping. She has read in medical textbooks about thumping hearts. She has even observed them. But not her heart, her young strong heart, thumping as if it wants to leap out of her body as she is dragged with her bruised and aching head into the centre of the village again.

The women wait. The children wait. Lazaro waits, his eyes flickering as her hands are bound behind her back, his breath sour on her face as he advances and punches her hard, on the face.

Her eyes are swollen and streaked with tears, one of her teeth is loose. She supposes that if she is about to die, a tooth is the smallest of her worries. She focuses on her toes, watching a small line of ants crawl over them, one, two, three, four, five toes, this little piggy went to market. She thinks of Hannah and longs to see her again, to have Hannah's courage, to spit in the faces of these men who have bullied and hurt her.

She raises her head. Lazaro is cradling something in his arms, pointing it at her. She shuts her eyes and draws in her breath.

Thirty seconds, one minute. Nothing. She hears the soldiers laugh and opens her eyes to the dark glassy lens of a video camera.

A soldier rips down her dress. Oh God, don't let them do

this to me, don't let them hurt me. Hannah, don't let them. Mummy, don't let them. Her breasts now bare, her nipples shrinking, her vagina shrinking, a wave of fear coursing through her body. It's not happening, tell me it's not happening. Her feet turned inwards, urine trickling down her thighs, now they are laughing and pushing her from one to the other, like a football they throw her and she falls to the ground and the stones graze her face and legs, and she is struggling to breathe as her face is pressed into the dirt, now they kick her, pull open her legs as she screams and screams, trying to keep them closed, she fights, she scratches, they are shoving something up inside her, something cold, a gun, a gun that kills is up her cunt which should give life.

She screams once more and is lost in an explosion of pain which seems to have no beginning and no end, but all the while she is desperate to stay conscious with her spirit intact, even though her body is being battered in this tidal wave of horror. Lazaro hauls her to her knees, undoes his trousers, yanks her head down into his crotch, and shoves his penis against her teeth. She gags and chokes. From some other place, outside her fear, she hears a gunshot. Followed by another. The soldiers pull away, straighten themselves. Alice collapses into the dirt. General Mgumbo is standing there, revolver in his hand, shouting at the soldiers in Rwandan. For some crazy reason she expects him to pick her up, but he doesn't even look at her and leaves her bleeding in the dust.

Later, when it is dark, the village women whose families she has nursed creep over and bathe her face, give her water to drink and carry her back to her hut.

Hannah has dragged Waldo back to Zaire to tackle Colonel Dondo once more. Joe Schwartz is against it and warns that Dondo is dangerous. Waldo is against it and says that Dondo is bigger than he and certainly dangerous. Hannah knows they are both right, but refuses to listen. She is convinced Dondo knows more than he reveals.

The colonel receives them sitting in a vast cane chair on the terrace of his residence. This time there is no chocolate cake, no Bach, and the little red train is nowhere in sight. A small table by Dondo's side bears a silver tray, a soda siphon and a large bottle of Gordon's gin. He drinks from a tall glass filled with ice-cubes, which he sucks with a loud noise. A servant stops Hannah and Waldo on the terrace steps, so that they are standing some distance away from the colonel and lower down. The heat is intense and Waldo fans himself with his hat. When Hannah mentions Alice, Dondo rolls the ice round in his mouth before spitting it on the ground. It bounces down the steps and settles by Hannah's foot.

'Is my daughter in Zaire?' Hannah demands.

Dondo slaps his huge hands on his knees and says sulkily, 'I have nothing more to say.'

'But –'

'Do not imagine you can wave the magic fly whisk and wham-bam, your daughter reappears.' He rises to his feet with some difficulty, picks up a Stetson hat and a riding crop and waves their dismissal. The interview, which has lasted barely two minutes, is terminated.

Waldo and Hannah have just reached the foot of the steps when Dondo calls after them. He is leaning against a marble pillar, his enormous belly spilling down over white riding breeches.

'If you want to save your daughter you had better hurry. You have twenty-four hours.'

Hannah turns and rushes back up the steps. 'Why only twenty-four hours?'

Colonel Dondo cracks his riding crop and she drops to the ground. 'You are no longer welcome,' he shouts. 'Go!'

A livid mark has appeared on Hannah's cheek. Waldo takes her arm and pulls her to her feet. They head for the jeep, scrambling frantically. George has the engine running and both doors open. Hannah throws herself into the back seat and turns to see Dondo standing at the top of the steps, holding his riding crop as if it were a rifle and shaking with laughter.


Where do you go when you don't know where to go? They drive in silence until they have left the huge entrance gates well behind and are on the main road heading towards Goma. George is the first to speak.

'Alice is in Bukavu.' He says it with the quiet assurance of one who does not doubt he is correct.

For a moment no one responds. 'But . . . but how do you know?' splutters Hannah.

George pulls the jeep to the side of the road and turns to face Hannah. 'I used to know one of Dondo's guards, when he lived in Uganda. There are Hutu soldiers and military all over Zaire, and the guard is frequently used as a messenger. He knows all about Alice.' He pulls out a map and shows it to Hannah and Waldo. 'Look, Bukavu is at the other end of Lake Kivu to Goma, and just west of the Rwandan border.

Hannah feels strangely numbed by the news, hardly daring to believe it might be true. They decide to head straight back to the Goma camp and discuss the situation with Joe Schwartz, who, they know, is there for the day. As the jeep bounces up the rock, they pass a row of corpses, each neatly rolled and tied in brown sacking. A woman's thin, brown hand bearing a wedding ring has fallen out of one bundle. Further up the hill, more corpses are being loaded onto a burial truck. Nearer the tents, a group of women and men are gathered together on the side of a hill and for some inexplicable reason are singing and dancing.

'It's Sunday,' says George. 'They are praising the Lord.'

Hannah, in the front passenger seat, opens the window a fraction and suddenly shouts at George to stop, pulling the steering wheel to the left. She has seen a bundle lying abandoned on the roadside in front of them. When she clambers out, she finds a newborn baby, a wee creature covered in blood and in ash from the volcano. She scoops the baby in her arms, and Waldo hauls her back into the jeep.

'This isn't a time to be rescuing babies!' he admonishes.

'Here,' and she takes the baby, which is making small mewling noises, out of its rags and wraps it in a large headscarf she keeps in her bag. Such minute fists, and bright eyes peering out of a wizened little face. The fact that this is new life in the middle of such a catastrophe is in itself important, but for Hannah there is also the memory of holding Alice in her arms, of feeling a fierce protectiveness that astonishes her. She puts out her finger and the infant grasps it.

Further on they drive through crowds which become more and more unruly. People are pushing and jostling, hammering on the windows of the jeep.

Waldo remembers and is alarmed. 'God, we have Ugandan number plates. Last time we masked them, this time we forgot.'

'It is very dangerous,' gabbles George. 'The Ugandan army helped train the Patriotic Front. These soldiers do not like the Ugandans.'

Hannah holds the baby tightly with one hand and grips George's shoulder with the other. 'Hurry! Accelerate. Don't stall.'

Sweat is running off George's face.

'And don't run over anyone,' says Waldo, closing his eyes every time a fist or a face appears at the window.

But the jeep can no longer move. Soldiers are banging machetes on the sides, loud noises ring in Hannah's ears, the jeep is rocking back and forth as Waldo grips the seat behind her, his pale face even paler.

'Get out,' urges George. 'They are telling us to get out.'

Waldo blanches. 'Certainly not. Keep driving, George.'

A small army of men is blocking the way. A machete blade crashes on the window nearest Hannah, sharp steel glinting, shattered glass tumbling. George's arm is cut, blood is gushing forth, a hand thrusts through the window, pulls open the door, yanks Hannah out, still clutching the baby, the precious baby. The soldiers' faces are near her face, their bodies press into her body, someone is pulling at her hair, kicking her legs, shaking her.

'We are your friends,' shouts Waldo to the mob.

'You are our enemies,' says a soldier, his grimy hands and nails digging into Hannah's arm.

' "Onward Christian soldiers," ' Waldo and George sing in loud cracked voices, ' "marching as to war,/with the cross of Jesus, going on before." '

The soldiers are confused. They let go of Hannah. 'Friends,' says one soldier suddenly. 'Friends in Jesus.' He grins as he clasps Waldo's hand and pumps it up and down.

'No friends. Enemies,' says the man who had pulled Hannah out of the jeep.

'With the cross of Jesus, going on before,' booms Waldo again, sweeping his hand grandly in the air as they climb back into the jeep. George puts it in gear and eases forward. The soldiers wave their rifles and machetes and part to let them through. As soon as they are clear, George slams his foot on the accelerator. Hannah rocks the child.

No one speaks until they are safely inside the camp at the top of the hill. Hannah's fingernails have dug so deeply into the palms of her hands that they are bleeding. She makes George drive with her to the camp hospital and all the while she holds the baby close, occasionally peering at the chewed-off umbilical cord. When Alice was born, she had somehow or other imagined it would look different. A neat grey silken thread perhaps, or a scarlet ribbon, but not that pulsating fibrous bloody bundle which in some earlier civilisations would have been kept and buried as a magical link with the new soul. Hannah is the link for this new baby. She wants it to live.


The video is fuzzy but the young woman on the screen is unmistakably Alice, even though her hair has been hacked very short and looks like a purple bruise covering the top of her head. She lies naked on the dusty ground, her feet in leg irons, blood running down the inside of her thighs. Her eyes are open, fluttering. Her left hand moves.

'Oh no, oh no, oh no,' sobs Hannah, her voice little more than a whisper. 'What have they done? My girl, my only girl, how could they, oh no,' and she wants to lean into the picture, lift Alice gently off the ground, cradle her in her arms, and make it better for ever and ever amen.

But she cannot. So she has Ezekiel rerun the video, his face grim, and when they get to the part where Alice moves, Hannah says, 'See, she is alive, thank God she is alive.'

Waldo jumps up and switches off the video. His hands are shaking. She is alive, he thinks, but for how long?

Before they leave Ezekiel's office, Hannah calls the hospital to see if the baby's body lies amongst all the other bodies waiting to be burned. It isn't there.

No, says the doctor, the baby lives.

# eighteen

Late afternoon, and Waldo slumps on a rock above the camp at Goma, staring at the bubbling misery below. A bleary sun begins to dip over the horizon, and he panics because the day is ending. The video of Alice's bleeding body has horrified him to such an extent that he cannot sleep, cannot rest; he feels desperation in everything he says or does.

Every hour increases Alice's danger. Even though they have raised the money for the mercenaries, Waldo remains dubious about them. He has attempted to check them out but with little success. Both men have indeed worked for Co-lateral Solutions, both are now without work, but he has been unable to discover much else about them.

He has poured over maps with Eric and Milo, tracking the route they might take, straight across country from Kigali, crossing the border near Cyangugu and reaching Bukavu before dawn. The men have even managed to discover the hut where Alice is being held, and to get a rough layout of the village and the military compound. When Waldo asks, Eric says modestly, eyes downturned, that they have ways of finding out.

Tomorrow is D-Day. Eric and Milo have been told to arrive at Bukavu just after dawn. They will be accompanied by a small group of soldiers, will take the village by surprise and rescue Alice. In the desperation of diminishing time, Ezekiel has managed to convince his colleagues to agree to back up the raid with helicopter cover, leaving from Gitarama, well within the Rwandan border. Alice will be airlifted to safety, while Waldo and Ezekiel will be with Hannah in Gitarama, waiting.

That's the plan, but Waldo is growing increasingly uneasy. Milo and Eric were due to arrive at Goma several hours ago and haven't turned up. They have half the money already. Unless they arrive soon ... But Waldo cannot finish the thought, and is filled with dread.

He looks up when he hears the sound of feet clambering over the rockface, and recognises Theodore King, panting and fanning himself with a hat similar to Waldo's.

'I came to wish you God's blessings on your journey.'

Waldo is startled. 'How did you know about my journey?'

'Divination.'

Waldo does not hold with divination, but in view of his uncertain future he wouldn't mind a tot of absolution.

Theodore sits down on the rock beside Waldo. He is still breathing heavily and his face is flushed and mottled. 'There are rumours everywhere, my boy, that you're going in with a brace of machine-guns, that you've offered the Zaire military a part in your next Hollywood movie, that Hannah is doing a swap for Alice, and so it goes. Oh, and rumours about what's-his-name, the Minister for Communications, being Alice's father. True? Ezekiel 13: "beware of false prophets".'

'True,' says Waldo in a matter-of-fact voice.

Theodore King pulls a hipflask from his pocket and waves it at Waldo. 'Brandy?'

Waldo takes a swig, and hands back the flask. The old man peers at him. 'I'm a secret drinker. D'you know that? Guess not. Wouldn't be secret if you did. Hah! Grace knew. Grace knew everything.' He stares ahead of him. 'Grace died.'

Waldo remembers that Grace was Theodore's wife. 'I'm sorry,' he says.

'She had a stroke. It should have been me who passed over. But no, the Lord chose to punish me by letting me live.' He hands Waldo the brandy flask again and waves his hat in an extravagant sweep. 'Simple, isn't it?'

'What is?'

'Everything!' King pauses and scratches his head. 'At the bottom of everything is . . .'

'A treacle well?' says Waldo helpfully.

'Love!' Theodore beams triumphantly. 'Love is all that matters.'

'A touch of food wouldn't go amiss every now and then,' says Waldo, patting his pockets to see if any more barley sugars remain.

'Son, people starve because there is no love. Maybe God is to blame?' He leans heavily on Waldo, using him like a book end.

'Things must be bad, you poor sod, if you're blaming God,' says Waldo, pushing Theodore into an upright position.

The old man sneezes and wipes his nose. 'Say your prayers, keep to the golden path, praise ye the Lord, the Lord's name be praised.' He sits in a morose silence for a while before exclaiming, 'I tried. I tried, Waldo. But now look at me.'

Waldo regards him with affectionate concern. 'You look just fine.'

'You think so? I'm okay?'

Waldo sees a vulnerable, drunken old man, with his underpants showing above his trousers, his belly a gentle paunch, veins showing in his ankles, and rheumy eyes. 'Okay. Yes, you're very okay.' He waves his hand at the turmoil in front of them, the darkening sky filled with choking fumes, smoke from a thousand fires, the wail of humans sick and dying.

'Look at it,' he says in wonder. ' "Ever-living Fire, in measures being kindled and in measures going out." '

The old man peers at him. 'That's not from the Bible.'

'Heraclitus.'

Theodore takes another swig of brandy. ' "Be sober and hope to the end": 1 Peter.' He slumps again on Waldo. 'Unless you believe in the Kingdom come, how can you bear this horror, Waldo, this horror that never ends?'

Waldo doesn't answer for a moment. He is feeling his backside. In the heat of the day, it is damp from leaning against the rock. 'Can't say I do believe in the Kingdom come, Theo, life's enough for me.'

They sit in silence for a while and then, unexpectedly, Theodore King opens his mouth wide and begins singing. Robustly, fervently, drunkenly, his teeth – capped to perfection – glinting in the moonlight. ' "God moves in mysterious ways, his wonders to perform. He plants his footsteps in the sea and rides upon the storm . . ." '

'Okay, have it be God if you want,' says Waldo, moving his toes, which are going to sleep.

Theodore gazes hard at Waldo, wagging his head. 'You're a good guy, Waldo, I like you, always have. Even if you're a heathen. Did you sing hymns when you were a kid?'

Did he sing hymns? Yes, he did. From a hymnal which his mother insisted he took to church every Sunday, even though there were hymnals already laid out on the pews. Once, he tried to press a flower inside its pages, a marigold which made the paper turn orange. His mother had slapped him and said he had stained the songs of God.

'You love her?' Theodore asks suddenly.

Waldo knows he doesn't mean his mother. 'Hannah? Yes, I love her.'

'And Alice?'

Waldo nods. He looks around him. The sun has disappeared, leaving a big sky devoid of stars. He likes the darkness. It has no borders.

Theodore is singing again. ' "Amazing grace, how sweet the sound,/that saved a wretch like me./I once was lost, but now am found,/was blind, but now I see." ' He burps. 'I wish I did see.'

'One question I must ask you,' says Waldo. 'None of my business, but what the hell. That time in Ethiopia, all those years ago, why a health club and a Turkish bath, for God's sake? Why weren't you more discreet?'

'It was the steam. I swear to you, Waldo, I went there in innocence, but the steam always opens the pores of my longing. And oh, those beautiful golden young men. Grace never understood.'

'I wouldn't think she would.'

'Do you think I'm sinful?'

'No,' says Waldo simply.

Theodore waves a large arm in the air and plonks it round Waldo's shoulders. 'I'm coming with you, Waldo. I am coming to rescue Alice.'

Waldo looks at him with sudden interest. In the absence of Milo and Eric, maybe this is the only remaining solution. He, Waldo, must rescue Alice. But not with Theodore, who is now slumped like a tea cosy in a saucer of rock, head nodding, mouth wide open. Safe in the arms of Jesus. Equally, Waldo can't leave him here all night, out on the rock. He prods him to his feet and drives him down the hill, weaving in and out of the crowds, the old man wide awake again, singing loudly and lustily.

Back at the Goma camp, the others are already asleep. Waldo spreads a sleeping bag on one of the long cane benches and helps Theo bed down for the night. They have been comrades in war and peace over many years and must look after each other, no matter what. As Waldo pulls off Theo's cowboy boots, he is making up his mind, pulling his thoughts together in a new plan of action, however ragged. There is still no sign of Eric and Milo. He has no option but to go himself. He realises this could be a suicide mission, and a pointless one at that, because how can he, one man, take on an army? But he has some vague idea, rapidly taking shape in his mind, of offering himself as a hostage in exchange for Alice. Or of engaging in diversionary tactics while Ezekiel's men embark on a helicopter rescue raid – like the Israelis at Entebbe airport.

He takes the jeep he used for driving to Goma, and heads for Gitarama, the point in Rwanda between Kigali and Goma, where he has arranged to meet Ezekiel and Hannah. He will have to cross the border some way up from Goma, at a place where there are no frontier guards, and he hopes to God he isn't ambushed, and that Rwandan soldiers don't take pot-shots at him. The countryside is still swarming with military.

The cloud has lifted and the night is suddenly filled with stars, so when Waldo reaches Gitarama he can see the soldiers quite clearly. Ezekiel comes out of the shadows, a revolver in his belt. Hannah is close behind. Ezekiel's leather jacket is crackling as he moves, and Waldo rather wishes he had a leather jacket, it would make him feel more heroic. He outlines his plans.

Eric and Milo had reported that guards around the military compound and the village were few in number. Mgumbo must be feeling there is little immediate chance of RPF soldiers coming back into Zaire – not yet, at any rate, while all the focus is on Rwanda. Waldo realises he is talking like a film script, the plot unfolding easily and convincingly. Ezekiel listens without comment and this encourages Waldo, but Hannah's silence is surprising. Every now and then she prowls a few paces.

When Waldo says, 'Eric and Milo have done a bunk, so I'm going to try,' he hears the firmness of his voice. Ezekiel remains silent. Hannah looks at him in disbelief.

'You'll be killed! It's crazy.'

'No crazier than doing nothing.'

'And Alice? She might be killed too,' says Ezekiel gently.

'If we do nothing, she certainly will be. Time's up. It's our only chance.' Waldo hesitates, draws a quick deep breath of the cold night air. 'Look,' he begins, 'I have no children, no one in my life except you, Hannah, and Alice; you're my family. I want to go.'

He thinks back to the days when the three of them worked together, days when Ezekiel was full of hope for the future of his country, when Waldo was still learning and exploring new ideas, when Hannah was little more than a child, blazing with idealism. Their lives were fluid then, their pathways unknown. He can see this next bit of his own pathway quite clearly, but he doesn't want to know how it will end.

'Somehow or other, I'll make them listen to me,' he says. Ezekiel shakes his head. 'I'm going too.'

'*That* would be crazy. No, I'll have the helicopters for back-up, and let's arrange an estimated time of arrival.'

Hannah comes over to Waldo and hugs him. She doesn't say don't go, and for a moment he feels more than just scared. Perhaps he hoped that someone would say don't go?

He climbs back into the jeep, puts his foot on the accelerator, hears the throb of the engine and calls out as he drives away. 'While they're rescuing Alice you might consider asking them to rescue me. I'll be the one in the Panama hat, shit-scared!'


Just out of Kibingo, Waldo stops to recheck his passport, his medical kit and his supply of barley sugar, before he sets off in the direction of Bukavu. Once, he is held up by soldiers and dragged out of the driver's seat to be searched.

The nearer he gets, the greater his fear, but the clearer he is about his actions. All his life he has retreated from confronting deep personal choices – because at some level these retreats never compromised the core of his being. It is this part of him which now demands he help Alice. He is trenchant about this, blind to all the enormous difficulties he will face. All he knows is that those buggers aren't going to kill his Alice, he will prevent them. At the same time, he has a sneaking hope that at the last minute something might save him. Eric and Milo might miraculously appear; Ezekiel could arrange the rescue before he, Waldo, arrives; Alice could escape and wander towards him on the Bukavu road. He doesn't want to die. He feels sick at the thought of pain.

He sniffs the air, rubs his chin. Should have shaved before he left. He wonders if he should be rehearsing the words he will use, but he cannot form them in his mind. He isn't sure if anyone will speak English or French, and he feels that whatever he offers will sound histrionic and improbable.

'I have come to offer myself as hostage.'

'*Je suis ici parce que* . . .' What's the French for hostage?

And why would they want him, Waldo nobody, when they have the daughter of a government minister?

Could he perhaps fling a few Hollywood names around? '*Je suis un ami de* Steven Spielberg . . . Marlon Brando – no, too old but possibly politically correct. Elvis Presley – he's dead. Mel Gibson. Michael Jackson. Cool it, Waldo, you're losing your mind.

He looks across to the passenger seat where, propped up so that one end is sticking out of the partly opened window, is a broom handle, on the end of which he has tied a large white sheet. He pinched the broom from the Goma house and hopes the soldiers will know this is a flag of peace. By now he can see Bukavu ahead of him, a cluster of buildings and trees etched against the sky.

Suddenly, a salvo of machine-gun bullets whizzes by his ear and he stamps his foot on the accelerator, his stomach lurching. It is too late to go back. He spins the wheel left and right, left and right, hoping he isn't going round in circles. The area is heavily mined, he knows that; oh well, he just has to trust to his own good luck. More bullets, and now deep fear, sweat pouring off his face. He forces himself to focus on Alice, her vulnerability, the terror she must be facing as he bears down on the accelerator with all the weight of his love.

He tries to sing 'When The Saints Go Marching In'. His

voice is cracked, his mouth is dry, but now something interesting is happening. After another volley of gunfire he begins to enjoy himself. He is suddenly beyond caring. He is Hector and Lysander, Superman and Batman. His white sheet flaps crazily overhead.

Then another round of gunfire and the steering wheel spins out of control. The car veers dangerously to one side, the bonnet starts spouting water, or is it petrol? Time to bale out, Waldo thinks, time to bale out. He clambers out of the jeep, his heart pounding, and holding his broom-flag aloft he walks as steadily and firmly as he can towards the gunfire. Miraculously, it stops. He feels more scared at this moment than he has ever been in his life. The silence is awesome: only the sound of his feet crackling on a few twigs, scuffling the dry earth.


Alice is lying on the floor of the hut, arms flung backwards like a baby. She is still bruised and this is the first night since her assault that she has managed to sleep. She wakens suddenly to hear machine-guns and loud shouting, followed by silence. She stumbles outside, sees the soldiers running and shooting, sees Waldo – my God, Waldo! Hears him shouting at them not to shoot.

The silence which follows lasts only a few seconds but seems like an eternity. Waldo is alone in the open, clutching a broomstick and a white bed sheet. Utter stillness. Then a huge explosion, as if the world has been set on fire, as if everything is melting into flames. Helicopters swooping through the sky, gunfire, shells, tracer bullets whipping across the ground, soldiers running, Alice blown backwards with a roaring in her ears. Waldo – oh God, where is Waldo in the midst of this chaos of fire and flesh and steel and flying earth? Her eyes seeing Waldo crumple and fall. And then before she can scream or run, a helicopter flying low over her head, hands grabbing her, buckling something round her, lifting her.

Lifting her high into the pale dawn sky.

Hannah is on the airstrip where the helicopters have just landed. She is holding her daughter's bruised and battered face in her hands, the two of them weeping uncontrollably, and then Hannah spinning into disbelief as she hears Alice screaming, 'Waldo is dead! Waldo's dead!'

Ezekiel appears behind her, grim-faced, and doesn't say anything for a moment. 'They killed him,' he says at last.

Hannah hears a howl rise within her, doubling her up in pain, blotting out the noise of the helicopters. The wind almost knocks her off her feet and Ezekiel reaches out an arm to steady her. The three of them stand huddled together in the middle of the field, holding tightly to one another. This is their first union, Hannah realises, and she tastes the bitterness in her mouth.

# nineteen

Joe Schwartz has brought Waldo's body back to Kigali in one of the food trucks that run between Rwanda and Zaire. Waldo would have liked being part of a food run, thinks Hannah, as she stands next to his body in the hospital.

There are no signs of gunshot wounds. Waldo is covered by a pale green sheet, his eyes are closed, his face white and his expression somewhat startled, as if his last thought had been, Good God, so it's finally happening. This is it.

This is it – that's how she and Waldo had often talked about their dying moments. This is it, thinks Hannah, and I wasn't there to help you.

She touches his eyes in wonderment, noticing again the whiteness of his lashes. Moves her fingers across his chin and feels the new growth of red grizzled beard. So strange that hair goes on growing after death. When she bends to kiss him, his skin is cold and stiff. Where is he, she wonders, where has he gone? Because gone he has – there is nothing remotely connected with the generous living warmth of Waldo in the body that lies before her, not his wisdom, not his humour, not his soul. She hesitates to use the word soul but can think of no other, because she cannot conceive that his spirit was annihilated when his body ceased to breathe. Waldo would be impatient, she knows that – he always rejected any idea of the great kingdom in the sky.

For a few moments she forgets that Alice is standing behind her, knuckles pressed to her mouth, eyes wide open and filled with tears. Hannah steps to one side, but when Alice bends over to touch Waldo and to kiss him, she breaks down sobbing, 'It's all my fault.'

Ezekiel, behind them, puts his hand on Alice's shoulder. 'You didn't kill Waldo, Alice. The soldiers did.'


At the funeral service in the grounds of a blackened church near the centre of Kigali, the rain buckets down relentlessly. A crowd of mourners gathers under a motley collection of umbrellas. A hastily erected canopy of green canvas is supposed to keep the site dry but mud is sliding down the sides of the grave. Hannah's hair is soaked through as she struggles with Waldo's old collapsible black umbrella.

Ezekiel has arrived on his own, but Hannah notices two armed soldiers standing by the gate. He pushes his way through the crowd to stand between her and Alice. Hannah dashes the rain away from her face and tries to look for familiar faces in the crowd. Daniel Keneally is wearing a collar and tie instead of his bandanna, and Beverley Prettyfoot has hidden herself under a rose-pink scarf. George has turned up the collar of his jacket to protect him from the rain. He holds a single white rose.

In front of them, under the green canopy which protects the grave, is a shiny pine coffin covered in flowers. Such a small-looking coffin for such a large and generous man.

A group of musicians launch with joyous fervour into 'Nearer My God To Thee'. They play triangles and tambourines, and a large woman in a brilliant floral dress thumps away on an organ inside the bombed-out shell of the church. Children with solemn faces try to keep the musicians dry with a collection of umbrellas and cardboard boxes, but they are very small and have to stand on tiptoe.

Oh Waldo, Hannah thinks. The problem with the death of someone you love is that they're not there to laugh with you and make the sadness bearable. You were such a good man, such a loyal and loving friend.

Theodore King clears his throat, and for a moment Hannah is afraid that he will start preaching to the multitudes. She couldn't bear this. But the old man holds his hat over his chest and his voice wavers when he says that morality does not have to be grandiose, and that Waldo had lived with modesty, kindness and, at the end, great bravery.

The pallbearers – four soldiers – begin lowering Waldo's body into the ground, releasing the ropes lashed around the coffin. The coffin wobbles, and for a second it looks as if Waldo will land upside down. Hannah draws in her breath. The pallbearers heave backwards on the ropes, and the coffin safely reaches the bottom of the grave.

Hannah looks down and she knows that her loss is huge. Such strange journeys they made together, through such momentous times. She bends and takes a handful of earth, throws it on the coffin. Alice and Ezekiel do the same. Red mud stains Hannah's palms and her fingers. She wipes them on her skirt.

Up at the church a cluster of journalists waits for them, with cameras and flashlights, recorders, all the tools of her trade. Hannah leaves Ezekiel to cope with them and she and Alice slip away to be on their own. They find a bench beneath a frangipani tree, which spills its creamy white blossoms on the ground. Some of the flowers are sodden and trampled, new young ones still hold to the stubby branches of the tree. The rain has ceased now, and Alice takes off her raincoat and spreads it on the wooden seat.

Hannah is very tired. She feels as if winds have carried her a great distance, one that has neither beginning nor end. She looks at Alice but her daughter is silent, her shoulders hunched, her body taut, one foot kicking at the ground, churning up the mud.

'Why, oh why?' Alice's voice is low and hard to hear.

'Waldo? He wanted to. For him, it was right.'

'He was like my father.'

'He was.'

'Ezekiel isn't like my father.'

'No.' Hannah is silent. 'But he could be a friend.'

'He could,' Alice says tentatively, and burrows even more deeply into the mud, so that it oozes up over her sandals and between her toes. She shifts the weight of her body, a move that turns her towards her mother.

Hannah looks at her daughter, at the bruised thinness of her face, at her long skinny legs stretched out in front of her, and at the moment when their eyes meet, she reaches out a hand. Alice takes it, cups her own hand inside Hannah's and rests it on Hannah's lap.

# acknowledgements

*Lines in the Sand* was written with the assistance of a fellowship at Varuna Writers' Centre and the generous support of Peter Bishop, Director of Varuna. My warm thanks also to those long-suffering friends and family who helped and encouraged me in their different ways, including Georgia Blain, Drusilla Modjeska, Rosie Scott, Allison Southern, Lynne Spender, Susannah Spittle, Ruth Little, Julie Simpson and Bruce Sims. Sioned Fay dared me to take up the challenge of this work, and Susan McPhee kept me on track from earliest times with her humour and insight.

Much of the background for this book comes from films I made in Africa and South-East Asia and I want to thank all those who worked with me on these assignments, giving their friend-ship and generous support, in particular Philip Hunt, Warwick Olsen, Greg Low, Ossie Emery, Steve Levitt and Don Connolly.

Jill Hickson and Fiona Inglis have been the best of agents. At Penguin, I thank Julie Gibbs for making publication such a pleas-urable experience, designer Marina Messiha, and Meredith Rose for giving such intelligent and patient attention to every aspect of editing.

Alex de Waal, co-director of African Rights in London, challenged my thinking and I drew on his writings, particularly the publication *Rwanda: Death, Despair and Defiance* (1994). Médecins Sans Frontières staff – particularly Susie Low – and their publications have also been invaluable. Adrian Boyle, assistant warden at Broome Bird Observatory, was helpful and informative.

Grateful acknowledgement is due to Curtis Brown, on behalf of Sir Wilfred Thesiger (copyright © Wilfred Thesiger), for permission to reproduce the extract from *Arabian Sands* (first published by Longmans, Green, 1959) on page 143. The extract on page 97 from Henry Reed's poem 'Lessons of the War' is taken from *The New Oxford Book of English Verse*, published by Oxford University Press, 1972.

# THEA ASTLEY

## *Drylands*

In her flat above Drylands' newsagency, Janet Deakin is writing a book for the world's last reader. Little has changed here in fifty years, except for the coming of cable TV. Loneliness is almost a religion, and still everyone knows your business.

But the town is being outmanoeuvred by drought and begins to empty, pouring itself out like water into sand. Small minds shrink even smaller in the vastness of the land. One man is forced out by council rates and bigotry; another sells his property, risking the lot to build his dream. And all of them are shadowed by violence of some sort – these people whose only victory over the town is in leaving it.

*DRYLANDS is a wake-up call for millennial Australia … Astley's brilliance rests not only in her distinctive prose style but her willingness and courage to make social statements, to assemble portraits of pain as a bridge to compassion.*

THE BULLETIN

## Chandani Lokugé

### *If the Moon Smiled*

As a young woman in Sri Lanka, Manthri marvels at the promise of life and yearns for a future of fulfilled dreams. Years on, she finds herself in a loveless marriage, in a foreign land, and estranged from her two Australian children. Torn between an idyllic past to which she cannot return and a present that breaks her heart, she never loses touch with those dreams, nor abandons her passionate enchantment with life.

*If the Moon Smiled* is a stirring and lyrical novel, a poignant tale about the powerful bonds that shape a woman's life.